CW01508939

THE DISCIPLES

ALSO BY GOPAL MUKERJEE

THE ARMAGEDDON MANDALA

THE DISCIPLES

A NOVEL FOR THE APOCALYPSE

GOPAL MUKERJEE

Revenge Ink

British Library Cataloguing in Publication Data
A catalogue record for this book is available from the British Library

Revenge Ink
Unit 13 Newby Road, Hazel Grove, Stockport Cheshire, SK7 5DA, UK

www.revengeink.com

ISBN 978-0-9565119-5-9

Typeset in Paris by Patrick Lederfain

Printed in the EU by Pulsio Ltd.

For G, in gratitude and obeisance

This is Revelation and Prophecy of what I can pick up without FM on my 1920 crystal set with antennae of jissom... Gentle reader we see God through our assholes in the flash bulb of orgasm... Through these orifices transmute your body... The way OUT is the way IN...

William Burroughs, *Naked Lunch*

PART ONE

ANOINTING

It starts the same way this time. I'm on the couch lotus-posed, pecker blue steel, pores wisping fulgent smoke when the dildo lights up.

Tweet, it goes. Tweeeet.

Dig them shaft-veins squirming purple, glanhead glowing crimson.

Tweeet.

And I'm thinking of dungeon screams. Drills shattering blue dentoids. Hammers splintering bare skulls.

Tweeet.

Beyond the sound the voice. Beyond the voice the eyes. Beyond the eyes the abyss.

TweeEEEEEET!!?

I reach. Grab the dildo. Press TALK.

"Yeah."

He says nothing at first. Just hum in a toneless croon that raise my hackles. He hit a low note, soar, pause abrupt.

"Bitch." His voice. Trotjohn.

I grin. "Slut."

"You ready asshole?"

I distend my nares. Smack my lips. "Ready as a blade baby. Hard clarity. Throb throb."

He chortles. "You gon' have to hold oane to that boner sweetheart. We start at seven."

"Seven?"

"Seven oane the cold coon clit. Seven oane the napalm nipple."

"That's a whole HOUR from now."

He whistles. "Dang. Bitch can count."

"But I'm ready NOW. Like, PRIMED."

He snorts. "The pox oane THAT mocha boy. We start at seven. Meister's orders."

"Meister? Shit. He didn't say WHEN."

"No, I'M saying. Seven. Seven dark. You know us and the dark. We've had it goin' so long, hot and heavy..."

I toss the dildo and sit back, teeth grit. My lashes flutter, an image flashing stark: torn lizard on shattered glass, blue guts on a mosaic of red.

"HATE!" I yell, "HAAAAAATE!"

The room reverberate, echoes in wild skitter.

Minutes pass in slow piss-drip, my thoughts adrift. I stir at last, blink. Late afternoon light, the day's gloaming.

My gaze wanders, frames the room. Shithouse inventory: blotched walls, rancid curtains, jizz-stained couch, SAT-tube hunched dead in the corner. Threadbare carpet strewn with crusts, rinds, bashed swill cans, fuckmags, dry douche bags, rubbers limp from solitary use –

I bare my teeth, applauding silent. This dunghole I pay to live in. To die in. With my rent-cred gone negative, Jimmy Rotgut due at noon tomorrow. Rent boss come to collect, gut slung low over a gatorskin belt, lipless mouth working in imitation of speech. And me going: *yeah, da, oui, got your CUT right here massah boss...* my sickle slicing hot and clean, gut-gash vomiting entrails –

I reach, grab my headset, slap it on and press PLAY. Brrroooom: grindcore slashervox, Lem from *Angstführer* screaming in on a distortion wave going:

Snake eyes death dream second sight,
Blood rain storm fire dark arctic light –

The sound builds in steady throb: massive, unrelenting. *Here it come*, I whisper, *here it come*. And it does. Something tears loose and blazes up from the root of my brainstem, fanged mouth in a soundless howl and I'm laughing...

***

I'm on this rocky shore knock-kneed, tongue out, boner in hand thinking it's a dream. Got to be. This kinda crap I've never seen awake. Like giants fucking in a hot marsh, cyclops doing a cooze colossus in a sea of boiling shit. Under a rust sky. Dog style. The scene vivid as hell, me wondering is this live or is it spandex. I can hear the moans, slap of daubed flesh, rat-headed gulls keening.

I want it to go on forever but it don't. Never does when you really want it to. Suddenly this black-robe Jap midget float down from way above, deus ex machina, arms raised high, grinning lunatic and going: *Eeyo. Eeyo kensho. Eeyo kending. Eeding kendong. Eeding dong...* DING!

Starting awake sweatcold, my headset hissing static. I'm hunched over but my pecker's still doing the old führer salute, straining up from the rictus of my lap.

DING! the doorbell, DONG!

I unfold my legs and rise wincing. Zip up DING! make for the door in slow hobble DONG! no rush DING! reach and turn the knob DONG! yank it open DING! no surprise DONG! his name gristled under the cusp of my eye-teeth DING! our Bull Run sachem and enforcer: Trotjohn.

***

It's dim out on the landing. Smoke dim. Just a sick glow off the overhead, not enough to spot a blackhead on an albino's butt. Tough on the eyes, sure, but I can see him well enough. No way I couldn't. Trotjohn clear even in tenebris, and looking good. Sharp always with the threads, John, a sartorial paragon, but he's outdone himself this time, this night of their Lord.

Wearing jackboots, I mean riding boots, black leather. And jodhpur pants maybe grey, I can't tell. And a longsleeve turtleneck, black. His beard trimmed black, his hair drawn in a braid, blueblack. At his ears bright steel, double-ringed. And on his chest the shine: death's head medallion burnished gold –

"You plan oane keepin' m'sweet ass out here all night?"

Cold. His eyes black ice.

I smile. "Was bettin' on it. But come in anyway."

He brush past me coming in: whiff of soap, cologne, crotch powder, armpit gel –

"Well shit TJ," I go, "you smell like a slammerbitch fresh from a steamroom lave. What you tryin' to do: pimp down the warden?"

He pause in half-profile. Chuckle. His laughter low and even, flashing tooth-white in the gloom. An easy sound, no threat, like *har har*, another good one. But it's just me, you dig. He'll take it from me. I call him a slammerbitch, a crackslut, a peckerfairy, he'll come on with a cackle, ask for more even. But he's iced people for less. Much less. I mean iced 'em cold –

"Say now son. You feel like gettin' some light oane in here?"

John bedarked, in vague silhouette.

"Nope," I go shoving the door shut, "not really. Us and the dark, remember?"

"Sheeat."

I snicker, step over to the gooseneck. Click: the beam hitting a pair of fuckmags below.

"Mmmyeah," John, "Lash and Cumtwats. Heard about those."

"Uh-huh. Came in last week, avant-garde smut, courtesy Fatman. Trust that fuckin' hump-mountain to – "

But he's not listening, Trotjohn. Him looking around with kind of a grin/grimace going:

"Hoo-DAMN! This ol' place look worse'n usual boy. Smell worse too. I'm thinkin' dead biker's asshole."

I snort. "Well I wouldn't know. I done never bung-sniffed a biker, dead or otherwise."

"You HAVEN'T?" John mock-incredulous, "hell, ain't nothin' to it. All you do, you dig up one them bad boys, strip'm down, stick your nose up where the sun don't shine and IN-HALE! – "

Which sets me off, like:

"WaaHAHH! Hell, I'd sooner tongue-wrap a gator at high noon than sniff a dead biker at dusk – "

John with a snort going: "Sheeat. No surprise there. I'd sooner rim one them mudpit grizzlies, hell, I'd sooner dong-lap a bone-sick icebear than just about any other critter – "

***

We're seated on the lounger, me and John. Him at one end, feet up, face shaded against the light. Myself cross-legged at the other end, watching him, thinking how much he resemble one them loan shark screen devils come to collect. Past his shoulder, the view out the window: lights strewn across the valley like fallen stars, freeways worming out to the hills. These hills hazed far distant, peaks ranged like dinosaur teeth under a charred moon –

"Well sheeat. Guess it's that time o' year again."

I nod. "That time again."

John lick a forefinger, touch his beard.

"Don't know about you, but I figure it's gettin' weirder each time."

"And more intense."

"Intense is right. Fuckin' third degree. I figure pretty soon it'll be OUR asses oane the line. Like, the ultimate sacrifice."

"You figure right. That's how Benny went out. Ultimate sacrifice for the Meister."

John blinks. "Benny?"

"Yeah. Benny Santeria, a Bull Run sachem and enforcer from the old days. Went out flaming in a neo-Fauvist death orgy last Friday night. Way up on a floodlit helipad, *Sacher Masoch Tower Nine*. His kowtows and pussy drones slit open his belly with a Southern Baptist sacrificial knife, garroted him with his own guts, set him ablaze with a blue sapphire torch and slung him out into the night with a jerrybuilt trebuchet. Howled his rawhide ballsack off right through but it's how he wanted to go, his tribute to the Meister, got to come up with something better when it's my turn."

John stare. Blink. "Heard THAT."

"Course it won't be death per se, not death *qua* death. More like transcendence, the hot holy summit. Or the abyss if you prefer. The *ganz andere, mysterium tremendum*."

"Mister Ganz WHO?"

I shake my head. "Transmogrification is what. Flesh consubstantiate. The Lord's own Spook gusting out your ass..."

"I ain't plannin' oane dyin' any time soon," John frowning, "not even for the Meister."

I smile. "Me neither. There's time yet."

"You goddamn right there is. And speakin' of dyin', you make sure Jimmy Rotgut's comin' in t'morrah?"

I snort. "Didn't have to. My rent cred's nixed down to

dungtown. He'll come sniffin' for his green, noon tomorrow, sure as shit on a hog's tookus."

He nod, but he's not quite listening anymore John. He's got that faraway look I know well, the one he get when his thoughts pulse and snarl around some malformed totem of blood and murder. He stare through me a moment. Then he blink, surge up off the lounger and stride over to the window where he stand pent and rigid, going mumble grumble, words I can just about hear:

"Zzeebothommrr. Hrrmbmfuckin riot unnbeloff. Harf! Try sheehmmmhell – "

And on, his fists bunched, words misting on the pane. No telling how long he remain there: maybe a minute, five minutes, a quantum eon, no way to tell. I can feel it drift, time, like mist in a dying man's dream, myself on the lounger crosslegged, volition suspended, pulse near flatline. A *zazen* zombie me, till my breath catch and an image blip on in my head, a one-eyed swamp cuckoo going: *Yocknapatawphaw yockock! Yocknapatawpoo yockock!* –

I sigh deep. Stir. "John" I go, "now John."

He curse, Trotjohn. Turn. And start away from the window. Him in rapid approach, kicking crud from his path: food crusts, cartons, laxative gelcaps laced with gunpowder, a sugardaddy buttgun, a Special Issue pornzine flying open: double page gloss of Silicone Pam goosing a shackled cleric –

"Yeah work it," he goes stomping past, on up to the front door where he pause, turn:

"Hey fuckwit. You gon' make me wait in here all night?"

Myself up in a flash going: "Hoo! Watch out now, WATCH out, y'all break it up, make way for the boss enforcer, the master sachem, big dawg, bull moose, swingin' dick Trot-John – "

***

He steps out first, John. Him first, myself after, pulling the door shut with the lock on. The old three bear goldi-lock. Not that I'm afraid someone come burgle the place or some such, no. Stuff in there isn't worth a hamster's turd on a hot plate. Just that I don't want anyone, a neighbor, some fuckin freelance samaritan cleaning the place up while I'm gone. Like disinfect the kitchen, sanitize the crapper or some such. Wherefore I slam-lock the door, kiss the peephole and turn –

To find John at the stairhead looking down. Trotjohn graven in profile, like one them Greco-Roman sculpts you see piss-stained in city urinals. *What's he planning to do*, I wonder. *Drop a spitball? Conjure a corpse? Rouse demons from chthonic sleep?* –

"Did I mention," I go, snapping my fingers, "did I by any chance mention how SHARP you look this night of their Lord, how PREPOSSESSING, how IMBUED so to speak and as it were, with a sort of BESTIAL PULCHRITUDE – "

"No," he goes turning, "no you didn't. But I do remember sayin' YOU look like SHEEAT. As usual. Like a fuckin' road turd beggin' to get squashed..."

He cock his head, paint on a smirk:

"Y'all check him out now: dirty hightops, shredded baggies, T-shirt the size of a fuckin' tent, bandanna look like an asswipe and smell worse – "

"WHOA!" I go, my hands rising, "WHOA now. Easy on the SPLEEN there SON. You know it's like some of us don't have rich plantation-house grandads coughing up antebellum blood money for psycho grandsons on a boontown kill-rut. And besides, this here bandanna's no dishrag. It's avant-garde. Damnation chic. Scum-chakra demon baroque. Hellvision on pure cotton. Double weave darkness visible – "

John in high mirth breaking into a hillbilly jig going:

"HOO! When the kid get goin' he do by GAWD get goin' HOO! – "

"And speakin' of GOING," I interject, "we best get our numbnuts on a roll NOW, or else – "

John still a-cackle, turning, starting downstairs at a fast clip, boots thudding old wood and myself slapping the balustrade in reproof going:

"WHOA now hoss. A little DECORUM if you please sirrah. We got to set the MOOD, go about it MINDful – "

John to my surprise, pausing in midstep. Composing himself. And moving on penitent, head bowed, myself following solemn, watching my hightops by turns draw me down.

***

It's deeper in the hallway, the gloom. One bulb at the far end in yellow nimbus, another halfway down we move towards, doors on either side like faces in a morgue. Walking mindful John and I, our steps muffled by floor-shag, odours wafting up in greeting. Stale smoke, curdled pain, meat sweat: these effluvia through which we move silent, heads bowed, myself hawk-eyed watching my feet move, them like muzzled snouts I keep an eye on lest they run amok, one darting this way, the other that, myself split down the middle, nuts floor-crushed.

They've got a life of their own my footsnouts, no telling what they're liable to pull, when. Like this one time I came awake and found them locked in embrace, coupling sole to sole, heels bumping. Ever see a pair of feet get laid? I did, that night. My own feet fucking while I slept, foul impertinence -

I pull up sudden, John having stopped short ahead.

"What?" I go, "What is it."

John turn to the door on his left, his scowl etched in profile. "Check it out."

I step up squinting, see what he sees: a heart-shaped cutout in the door, a couple feet under the peephole. This cutout sealed on the inside with a plate sheathed in red velvet.

"New neighbor," I murmur, "fat old dude named Dave Satrap. One of them face-painted bung bitches. Knock on the plate three times and see what happens."

John cock an eyebrow. "You want me to KNOCK?"

I grin. "Three times. Right on the plate."

John curse under his breath, bend, thump the plate three times. There's a pause. Then a faint yelp on the inside, feet shuffling. The plate slides out of view, a pair of buttocks filling the breach. Pale, flabby buttocks, the flesh pinched and quivering.

"Do me quick boys," yips a voice on the inside, "do me NOW. I can't hold out much longer."

John gives me a look, his mouth twisting in a snarl. His left foot draws back and flashes up, the boot-tip plunging in gibbous rump-flesh. The buttocks vanish with a loud squawk, the velvet plate sliding into place: John stepping away with a cackle, myself in tow, livid invective in our wake.

Moments pass, John and I marching in lockstep, silent and ceremonial down the passage. We're ten feet from the end when he falter, stop short.

"Shitbejeezus," I mutter, "what is it this time."

But he doesn't have to answer. I can hear it well enough: a rhythmic creak, someone getting fucked against the door at right. On the inside. I can see the door give with each thrust, the knob blurring concussive, a girl-voice gasping: *no Dad... please... stop... no...*

John turn with a grin, brows raised quizzical, eyes bright with murder. Me shaking my head going:

"Not now John, we got to get on. The Bull Run first. We can play on the way in."

He stare, his face bone-hard, eyes in luminous pinpoint. Just ahead, the door still catching hell, girl-voice gasping.

"Play oane the way in?" John in a near whisper.

I nod. "On the way in."

He blink once. Twice. Then he turn abrupt and march on, myself with palms joined penitent, starting after.

***

The old parking lot shows pretty well vacant this evening of their Lord. Long gone with their rides, all the cuntlaps and poonjocks, having driven out to nocturnal pleasure. Just an old station wagon I see at the far end, with a muddy pickup out by the dump. These appearing clear at that distance because of the light, the lot being goodly illuminate this evening I'm talking about. He keep it dim most nights, Rotgut. Cheap and dim, but not this time. All the yellow globe lamps on sick and fierce now for some reason, go figure. He's a whimsical fucker, Rotgut, no telling what he do when. Like the time he heated the splash pool to boiling and tossed in a sackful of used dentures. Or the time he dressed up in a clown suit and trundled old man Grable around naked in a wheelbarrow -

"Pretty ain't it. Ay?"

I pause. Hop up three steps. John at left, arms akimbo.

"Sure," I go, "pretty. Too much light, though. I kinda like it darker, plenty chiaroscuro, dense wash of demon baroque – "

John turns with a scowl. "I meant the CAR, fuckturd."

I blink. Blink once more. "Well I'll be shot and shanked up m'shithole in Shiloh – "

Wondering how I could've missed it: John's car sleeked beside my Pukemobile not far ahead. His brand new Durerro convertible gleam-black, top down, with gold hubs, red flank lightning, grey death's head plated on the hood –

"Well?" John, "whaddya think."

I smack my lips. Shake my head. "Cold, baby, stone cold. Steel-mean vicious killer bitch of a car. Street-war snatch-magnet boner machine in excelsis. Kickass death's head to match."

John grunt. Step off the sidewalk. "Skeeter's design, the death's head."

I nod, moving. "Uh-huh. Look like his work sure enough."

We approach, the death's head looming with each step. Myself digging that loom full on, eyes wide shut. A Skeeter original, no question. Grey skull with bleeding eyes, crumbling teeth, busted sinciput puking black bugs, green snot gouting from a nostril, bullet bursting out the right cheek –

"No prizes," goes John with a snicker, "for guessin' which car we take."

I hawk. Spit out the side of my mouth. "The pox on prizes. The fuckin' bubonic plague on prizes. My Pukemobile been good to me these many years. Polly Pukemobile hath served me well – "

"Uh-huh," John a-grin, "like a bag lady with bone-ache, gutgas and a steamin rotcrotch – "

"Yeah well, you oughtta know. All them hags poppin' your wad for a slug of Dickel, a jolt of Night Train – "

"HAR!" John thumping my shoulder, "well you know whut they say: try everything once, and keep right oane tryin'."

I nod. "True enough, but that don't explain who you got stashed there in the back seat."

"Huh?" John, "whut – "

Breaking off as he catch sight of her: little dirt blonde in the back seat of the Durerro, tank top and cutoffs, sucking her thumb.

He doesn't quicken, John. Doesn't break stride. Just saunter up, lean over and –

"Ass out, bitch," he goes real casual, "out now."

The blonde raise her head. Flutter her lashes.

"Ass out," John repeats, "you heard me."

The blonde smiles coy. Pulls her thumb out with a long sucking sound.

"Yeah," John "Uh-huh – "

Her thumb travelling wet down her chin, her neck, circling her breasts in figures eight, tracing runes on her bare midriff –

"Don't you?" she croon, "don't you guys wanna take me out for a riiide?"

I cough. Slap my crotch. "Down. Down boy."

John cackle. "Real ORIGINAL there hon', but it's like I got this little rule: no backseat boogie with bitches over sixteen. Or under seventy. I like my meat blood rare or charred black, one or other, dig?"

The blonde blink. Work her lips into a pout.

"But I'm only fif-TEEN. I really am. You can ask... anyone."

John bare his teeth. "Fifteen you say? Well now. We'll just have to SEE about THAT – "

Bending as he speak Trotjohn, fingers spread, his hand on her belly circling once, twice, then sliding down the front of her cutoffs, his fingers under faded denim annelid, probing –

"Mmm…" her droop-eyed, "that feels so... ow!" – wincing "Stop! You're hurting – "

He straighten, John, sniff a snatch-wet finger like one them vineyard trannies sniffing wine:

"We-ell now," he goes "you don't smell like fifteen to me a-TALL. More like seventeen, maybe even eighteen. I'm talkin' baaaad vintage – "

The blonde snort, roll her eyes. "Oh puh-LEEZ. Enough already. Why don't we just cut the – "

He reach down, John, grab a handful of girlie hair and pull. Not hard you dig, just firm, her not resisting, not making a sound, just coming off the seat with a grimace, out over the side –

Which is when I see what a fine piece she is, all warm and ripe, now as in the beginning, when she knelt in dishabille before her Lord, Him going: *partake thou of my celestial succulence* –

Feeling a twinge, me, as I eyeball her, shades of the old ache, like in them bygone days, Pater Jed ripping candy out of my hand going: *dump that shit little boy, I got something better for you right here* –

Except this time it's not ol' shrivel-dick in charge, it's the Meister, whose diktat I can't think to stain with zaftig trash quim, though I'm sore tempted, as I'll wager John is: him up close, running a finger over her mouth, her cheek, the line of her jaw, down her neck, circling a breast –

"Some other time, slut," he husk, wheeling around sudden and vaulting into the driver's seat yelling:

"ASS IN MOCHA BOY! ASS IN – "

Myself galvanized, trotting around and vaulting in likewise, John pumping the pedal fast, faster, gasping in rhythm, howling orgasmic as he fire the engine, VVRRROOOOM!, the car squealing back in an arc, surging forward past the blonde, myself with arm outstretched trying to cop a feel, VRROOOOM!, foiled again: out.

***

"We don't need the freeway," I tell him, "be crowded as hell this time of evening. I know a shorter route, much shorter out thataway – "

But he's not listening, John, him going: "This kinda car need the freeway, and the freeway sure as HALE need this kinda car – "

Which in his lexicon mean but one thing: smoke tarmac at two hundred, the old glitterbug speedking routine at Mach Two, maximum overdrive, except that it's Friday midsummer this year of their Lord, the freeway glutted this hour with tech-drones breezing downtown, and boon country cretins in for a weekend spill –

"No way you get past eighty," I go, "much less one HUNDRED eighty – "

But it's no use. He's got his mind made up, Trotjohn. Made up good. Because it's not just the speed, it's the chaos he dig, hustling the freeway, weaving in and out, missing 'em by microns, all the honks, screams, curses, bullets in his wake and collisions if he gets lucky: metal thud, crunch, splintering glass (sweet music) –

Which in truth is how it turns out, almost. Trotjohn rampant in his new Durerro with me strapped beside, shotgunned through a forty-minute deathgame, him cutting all twelve lanes in crazed sigmoid, teeth bared, going: "YYAAAARRRHHH! – "

Myself grinning in silent rictus with a near-death hardon thinking: *this is it. Where it end. Even before it have a chance to begin. Here on freeway blacktop. In a widening gyre of flame and steel. With Churchtown outspread below, a million lights. And the hills beyond brooding out to an unplumbed dark –*

But it doesn't end, thank spit. We make it through miraculous, out past the city limit on a raging death high, Trotjohn in a frenzy, humping the wheel, jerking the shift, scrambling atop the backrest whoop and holler (me steering with one hand, pushing the pedal with leg outstretched), a passel of pole bunnies cutting ahead with a bare-tit cheer –

On to where the sign read: South Zone 1st Exit, which we mean to take and do, John screeching a wide curve off the main drag, down a pocked and corrugate ramp into the saddest, crummiest hood this side of the Appalachian, little slum-pile you can spot under a crudded bulb on a nightsoiled preacher's map, halfway between Mason's armpit and Dixon's asshole.

***

A busted streetlight drift past. A second busted streetlight. A third.

John shift down with a curse, click on the brights. "Cain't imagine why he planted his freckled ass in THIS hood," he goes, "not like he cain't afford better."

I turn with a frown. "You can't imagine. YOU. John the shit-eatin' slumspice king. The mudfolk marquis. The bag lady boogie prince. The gangbang ghetto ghoul – "

"Fuck-a-rooney," John, "the pox oane that-a-rooney. Let me clue you in oane how it is-a-rooney. Whiteboy can go slummin' all he want, but he got to have a clean pad to drag his ass back to after he done messin' with the spooks – "

He turn, grinning wolfish: "Course that's not somethin' jungleboy JB know much about. Ay?"

I inhale deep, shake my head. "Nope. Not really. Not with Massah John fuckin' Bwana keepin' the peace with gun and bullwhip, aiming his dog-clap schlong at the slave seraglio – "

"HAR!" John slapping the dash, "Man I luv it. Spark his wick a touch and zooooom the kid's up and GONE – "

The car shake with a thud-crunch: pothole strike. John thumping the wheel hard, going: "FUCK! FFUUUCKHHH! – "

Myself grabbing his shoulder going: "Easy there, shagdawg. We don't want the Pigs on our tail, messin' up the script – "

He slap my hand off and lean in, his mug all twisted.

"Pigs? PIGS? MAN, DIDN'T I TELL YA? DIDN'T I JUST. FINISH. TELLIN' YA?"

The car now at a crawl, slow drift through ghetto gloom. John gone Cujo, his face an inch from mine.

"WHAT," I bawl pressing my nose to his, "FINISH TELLING ME WHAT."

"THE PIGS!" John starting to chuckle, "NO PIGS IN TOWN TONIGHT! NO PIGS!"

"Say WHAT?"

He straighten, still chuckling, the car in slow cruise.

"You heard me," he goes, "no Pigs in Churchtown tonight. Not a cotton-pissin' one."

"Fuck you. You're shittin' me."

John shake his head. "I shit you not, bitch dawg. No Pigs in Churchtown tonight. They up in Delroy County every last fuckin' one of em. Fightin' a jailbeak is what. Bigtime. Organized. New Klan boys, Terre Blanche Militia, Bubba Brownshirts, Coonkill Clems, Gomer Gestapo. Buncha redneck hardasses tryin' to bust out, takin' oane shitkick razorheads down from Bragg. Razorheads don't need no help, but Churchtown's finest hauled ass and pitched in anyhow, our very own split-hoof hawgs playin' backup – "

He break off cackling, me giving him a long look, trying to figure if it's real. *Do he speak true,* I wonder, *or do he prevaricate, spilling some old kill-strut jive. HUH?*

"You wouldn't be puttin' me on," I go, "playin nookie with my noodle now, would ya?"

He grin, rousting his crotch one-handed.

"You best believe I'm NOT. Pigs got a major shitstorm oane their hands. Them out there now, helpin' to stomp it dead."

I blink, my pulse quickening. "Don't recall catchin' this shit on the webvine – "

"You won't hear jack, till it's over and done. Not you, not anyone. Not till the suits get done mashin' it to fake birdshit and packin' it in plastic – "

He turn, still grinning: "Sound too good to be true, don't it?"

I exhale slow, my thoughts candent. "Too good is right. So where'd you come by this dope anyhow."

"Poondawg," John tapping the pedal, "Poondawg got a kid brother just joined the heat. Fuckin' rookie Pig. Mah man on the INside, you dig."

I nod, look up. The sky soot black. Touch of yellow cloud swag. No moon.

"Fine," I go "last question. If the Pigs be gone, who we got keepin' the peace? Coddling the rich? Shepherding the donut? Drubbing the dreck-folk? Skull-fucking the – "

"RESERVES, jellyBEAN!" John slamming the dash, "Buncha boozegut wannabes they fish out the shithole when the big boys go a-huntin'. Nothin' to worry about. Nothin' we cain't handle. Hawg ass possum smoke, harf harf – "

I turn away, slap my tingling nuts, put out a baboon shriek. Then I sit back, letting it sink in. The beauty of it. Pig exodus. Pigzodus. Them leaving like it was ordained. Making way for US, we few, we happy few in obeisance to our Meister, *Buford Aloyius Howell, Lord Baron of Pain* –

"Man," I go shaking my head, smacking my left tit, "man oh man oh man – "

My thoughts starting to incandesce, catch fire: "This here meatchunk of scuttlebutt be ALL RIGHT now son. Stone cold FINE. I mean like, SAVAGE. Like, I will be purely GODDAMNED. Like, pecker-whipped in a boondock gatormarsh. Cockadoodled in a bear-pit under a poison moon. Strapped to a bullmoose in a bionic bloodrut. Lashed to a – "

"YAAARH!" John, snagging a pothole, "YYYAAAARRHH! – "

Myself segueing into laughter, head thrown back, bawling mimetic with teeth bared, my dawg tongue on the flap "YAARRARRHARRRH! – "

And on, this two-man ghetto blood-howl echoing out to the skydark.

***

Driscoll it's called, the street we're on. Driscoll narrow and cragged, occasional seep of yellow light. Far above, the moon sickened to a possibility, no help at all vision-wise, not that there's much to see. Just tenement blocks the colour of gangrene, junk-pile weed lots, little stucco box-houses with crumbling porches. Not a blip or vital sign save this corpulent tabby I spot over a stormdrain, tail erect, green eye shining. And this old dude motionless under a porch bulb, his face a wreathed mask, Trotjohn with a whoop going:

"Wee-eell if it ain't Uncle Remus gone quiet after Brer Fox stole the Tar Baby and sold it for a MILLION."

And farther down, a soul sistah tending her clothesline, John going: "Aunt Jemimah NO SMILE. That syrup bottle they used her for empty in her own house – "

And "YAAARRRHHH!" the car quake and shake bunging potholes, "YAAAAARRH! – "

Myself in high mirth, digging the rubble and ordure piled around, the gutted houses, the road slushy on account of busted hydrants, or maybe one them freak rain spells, these weird rainshowers we been having of late, like bursts of firewater that burn and peel skin, leave oily puddles you see winking in the dark (points of red like insect eyes), little grease pools that waft a hell reek like some sourgut geezer farting brimstone –

Thump: John's fist on my shoulder. "That it up there, BITCH?"

I curse, turn. A four-way ahead, yellow lights on flash.

"Yayup. That's the one."

"Left?"

"Left is right."

"Sheeat."

John speed up approaching the four way, screech left in a wide arc –

"Dig it," he goes pointing, "Snotnose Susie makin' her rounds."

I laugh. Snotnose Sue on wino walkabout, clogs and canvas partlet, berating phone booths, scolding hyrants in guttural monologue –

"YOU TELL 'em SUE!" bawl John swinging past, the old tramp croaking a reply I can't catch.

"Whut'd she say?" John grinning.

"Not sure. Somethin' about spit-roasting your nuts, feeding 'em to idiot orphans in a squatter highrise. Not a bad idea. Plenty nutmeat to go around."

John cackle, shift gear: the car surging up Sloane. A good driving track, Sloane: broad, smooth (nothin' like a smooth broad on a hot night), no potholes, streetlights in good order glowing.

"Not a bad track," I go, "gremlin?"

John snort. "Sheeat. Wouldn't piss oane it oane a bad bladder night."

"Bet you would. With a stolen dick."

John cackle, start whistling. Getting cheery by the look of him. Trotjohn drumming on the wheel, kneading his meat. And whistling. Not your average stroll-in-the-boonies-with-your-fly-open kind of whistle, no. Not even the old ticks-on-my-honey-dick-they-gonna-suck-me-dry whistle. No such luck. More like this eerie ultrasonic microtone he learned from Monk, a lip-squeal meant to shatter etheric walls and trans-dim barriers, pave the way for polymorph demons hungering to get in –

"How much longer now slick," he ask yawning, "how much more to Waldron's."

I bite the inside of my cheek, rip out an eyelash.

"Ow. Not too long. Nearabout ten minutes as the crow shits, give or take a turd – "

John nodding vigorous, still whistling.

We're halfway up Sloane now: the street silent, neighborhood dark. Domiciles shuttered or boarded up, playcourts empty, hip-broken phone poles keeled over. No one in sight save a pair of hobos crouched over an oil fire in the lee of a dumptruck. And ahead, a gnarled mandarin in a *Liquor&Kimchee* store massaging a feline, trenchcoat wino outside, pissing in the icebox, a trajectory in green –

John cackle, point. "See that big ol' warehouse yander? Past the *Lick'n'Kim*?"

"Uh-huh."

"You ever been in there?"

I frown. "What the hell for."

John suck spit, shake his head. "Clueless little coon ain't ya. That there's the bitchinest hoedown hotspot in the whole fuckin' county. Or used to be. Haven't been there in a while. *Ja Love Jungle House* they called it. Wingdings wild enough to blow your nuts out. Like the one I was at back when. Helluva night. Kid Afrika workin' the beat hot and heavy, dishin' hump-juice and boogie sweat, *boompapa-whap boompapa-whap*, ballbust and belly-thump, the crowd all wig, howl and mojo, till the Pigs showed, buncha roid-jacked donut-fuckers swarmin' all over, flash'n'wail, homeboyz up against the wall chainganged, down on carhoods gettin' the billyclub goosebump, Pig-in-Chief goin': *haw haw! Don't get your hopes up now people, ain't no handy little eyecam catchin' this*, and me greasin' outta there in a hurry, ass in a sling – "

"You missed it," I go pointing, "there."

"Huh? John, "Wha?"

"The turn. You missed the turn."

The car slows, John turning slit-eyed: murder on ice.

"Woulda HELPED if you'd'a wagged your PECKER-LICKIN' TONGUE a little sooner ya little – "

I hold up my hand, palm out. "Peace. Friar forebear. No need to turn back or reverse in haste. All you got to do is cut across this here lot you see on your right – "

John with a curse wrenching the wheel, the car veering over a strip of grass, over the kerb, to land bouncing in the lot –

Myself clapping appreciative going: "Awwright. Sharp move there kid. Just like in the old days. Right around here, remember?"

John clicking on the brights, punching my shoulder going: "Don't remind me. Don't even BEGIN remindin' me – "

SALTUS.

***

It's dark in the lot. No light save that coming off the car, the Durerro's brights funnelling out a path with John cruising easy, keeping an eye out for potholes. Never could abide potholes John, though he don't mind speedbreakers and roadbumps, specially if they're alive. Like he'll go out of his way to squelch a critter (muskrat, coon, possum), or better yet, some sorry lush passed out on a sidestreet (dig that skull-thud, rib-crunch), but potholes he cannot and will not in any wise countenance, much less craters, wadis, kloofs, cwms or crevasses. *Be hell drivin' on the moon*, he like to say, *fuckin' craters all over, Aiken Drumm lyin' naked all putz and bunghole* –

Hence his caution negotiating this here scape, this expanse that used to be the Old Mall parking lot till it got shut down, the abandoned Mall building still intact there at left, bulked desolate. Makes me a trifle sad to look at it, like nostalgic, thinking how it was in the bygone. Grey afternoons spent in this very lot playing *Find or Bleed* among the cars (thousands of 'em phalanxed beneath a dead sky), us scuttling around war-masked, daggers in hand, slicing the stray calf, ankle, toe. Or just wandering adrift, conjuring distant arcologies of glass and steel, blood and depthless torment. Or often as not, lounging in hebetude, sweating languid in John's car or Monk's, doors half-open, the juke twanging hotwheels honkytonk, following nubiles with lidded eyes and half-hards, thinking: *mmmbaby slash and drill* –

"Fuckin bejeebers," John sitting up, "SHEEAT."

"Huh?" me "wha?"

But I don't have to ask. I see 'em come on, the lights. Pigflash red and blue, highbeams white –

"Pigmobile," I go disbelieving, "fuck-in' Pig Mo Bile – "

John slamming the dash: "Fuck. FFUCKH! – "

I shut my eyes. Open them. Shut them again. Open. But it doesn't help. There it is still, Pig cruiser approaching flash and wail –

"The bag!" I croak grabbing John's shoulder, "fucker's gonna find the goodybag – "

John slapping off my hand and shoving me back:

"SHUT up. SHUT your fuckin' piehole and RELAX. Bag's in the trunk. No WAY he's gon' get his hands oane it – "

Sitting easy now John, suddenly calm. Shifting down to third. Second. Myself hunched, hands on crotch.

"That's right," John "you keep a choke hold oane them nuts, you be fine."

"Mmnng!" me tightening my grip, "mnNNGH! – "

The cars slow in approach: the Durerro easing to a stop, the cruiser halting twenty feet ahead. Both motionless, brights on, no sound save the moan of wind across the lot.

"What," I begin "what do we – "

"LIGHTS OFF!" Pig voice crackling loud over the amp, "TURN YOUR LIGHTS OFF NOW!"

John reach, click off the lights. Smiling. This strange little grin on his mug I don't much like the look of –

"AWRIGHT! NOW I WANT BOTH Y'ALL OUT THE CAR, REAL SLOW, OUT TO THE FRONT, YOUR HANDS ON THE HOOD, FEET WIDE APART WHERE I CAN SEE YEW. AND NO SMART MOVES NOW PEOPLE, OR I'M GON' HAVE TO PUT DOWN SOME SERIOUS PAIN OANE Y'ALL TONITE."

Pause. Me and John exchanging glances, knowing it isn't for real: the tone of voice, the words so hokey –

"Lone reserve," mutter John squinting into the light, "some boogerhead they hoicked out of old boyscout sewage – "

"I SAID OUT NOW!" Pigvoice boom and crackle –

John and I moving simultaneous, out the car and around to the front, Pigvoice going: "HOOD! HANDS ON THE HOOD! – "

John turning and standing spraddle-legged, myself following suit, our backs to the light, heads bowed, the hood warm under our palms.

Silence. Cruiser-lights pulsing.

"He's got a name," goes John tapping the plated death's head on his car hood, "dja know that?"

I cough up a loogie, swallow. "Name?"

"Peter. Peter Priapus the Boner-Monkey."

I snicker. "Peter Priapus. What you lookin' at Pete."

"Ain't lookin' at much now," John "but he will be soon enough."

I blink, looking askance. Trotjohn still with that smile, his face shadowed –

"John," I go "you're not. You're not gonna – "

"Did ah say," clink, boot-thud, "did ah say yew boys could have yourselves a CON-VER-SATION?"

Pigvoice right behind, cheesy without the amp. Me wondering how I didn't hear the fucker walk up –

John cough, look over his shoulder. "Well now daddy-o, you didn't say we COULDN'T now, did ya?"

Pause. Light-flicker and windmoan.

"Well well," the Pig, "what we got here's a CLEVER boy. Coupla REAL clever boys doin' the ghetto round. Lone Ranger and nigger-Tonto fixin' to get themselves a big bite o' down-home sickle cell coonmeat – "

The smell of him hitting me as he speak: gut-rot halitosis, tang of rancid sweat –

"Or maybe a whole HUNKA coonmeat, hawr hawr! – "

Him stepping up, bootscuff and keychime, "but they ain't gettin any toNIGHT, no-sirrEE. What they ARE gon' get is – "

I don't feel it clear at first. Just the bare impact, Pigboot going whump! on my ass. Whump! a second time. And then the pain slow in its wake –

"THAT's just for starters," Pig taking a step, "plenty more where THAT came from. PLENTY more – "

Whump! Pigboot on buttflesh, not mine this time but John's, the boot I see out the corner of my eye, John shaken by the force of it, but the smile on his face unchanged –

Whump! twice. WHUMP! thrice, real hard the third time, John arching under the impact –

"THAT," the Pig stepping away, "THAT's for talkin' when you've not been told."

Pause. John silent. Myself rigid, head bowed.

"Well awwright," the Pig "so what ah'm gon' do now, what daddy gon' do now is frisk y'all real good. Make sure there ain't nothin' nasty stuck up where the sun don't shine, hawr hawr. And THEN yew boys gon' help me roust up this pretty little car slow and savage. Break out that ghetto stash where ah can SEE it, hawr hawr – "

Myself with teeth grit thinking *yayup, that's Pig laughter all right, no question, though not quite authentic. Not haw! haw! the way real Pigboys laugh, but more a wannabe Pig laugh, the kind a swag gut reserve put out tail up on a rumble –*

"Yew first niggerboy," Pigboots moving, "ah bet yew gon' LUV this – "

His hands on my haunches patting, squeezing, working their way up, down the front to my crotch, squeeze, down my legs and back up, probing the old rump-rift, fingers worming up where crud dries and critters die –

"Nothin' up there maaan," I go grimacing, "been empty for years."

"Ain't empty NOW," the Pig, "got yourself a shitload o' knuckle-sausage, hawr hawr – "

Me thinking: *it's never gonna come out of there, that fist, size of a slop-gorged hoghead, never ever come out –*

But it does, thank jizz. Eons later. The Pig straightening with a chuckle, stepping up behind John going:

"Your little spic boyfriend's clean, hotshot, but I'll wager you're – "

He doesn't finish the sentence, the Pig. Or maybe he does and I don't hear, my vision nightmared in slow strobe watching it unfold –

Trotjohn pulling back his sleeve, fingers in parallel extension – his wristblade shafting out with a click, bright steel – him moving, turning in a dancer's pirouette, teeth bared, his death's head medallion rising golden – his hand arching around palm up, whipping clean under the Pig's chin – the Pig's eyes going wide with dull wonder, gore blooming at his throat like wisdom – him staggering back, night-stick clattering to the ground – dropping to his knees, hands at his throat – slashed Pig moribund, keeling in slow collapse –

"Timber," John stepping away, "tim-fuckin-ber."

Pause. Myself against the hood, staring. John with sullied blade, arms hanging loose. Cruiser light on his face blue-red, his aura flaring kirlian. His führer-blaze coruscant, his mein kampf shine –

"John," I murmur, hands in slow ascent, "Johnny Angel. Johnny Handsome. Johnny Mnemonic. Johnny Baptist. Diddle dumpling, my son John – "

"Cut the crap," John with a scowl, "dig the shit-stack. DIG him."

I blink, turn my gaze full upon the Pig. Him on his back, legs folded under: twitch, rasp, gurgle –

"HUH?" John stepping up, "WHUT'D YOU SAY? SPEAK UP NOW PIGGLY WIGGLY! SPEAK UP! – "

But he don't, the Pig. Can't. Just gloop and gurgle, hands falling away from his throat, his wound incruent –

"Well," John, "if THAT'S how it's gonna BE – "

He make like a punter John, draw back his left foot and Thwud! boot slamming hard into the Pig's ribs, Thwud! again in the ribs, Thwud! yet again in the very same ribs –

Myself with a laugh going: "Easy there, friar. The felled hawg will not speak. The slain porker will not give utterance – "

"THAT," John glaring down, "THAT's for NOT talkin' when you're TOLD."

Pause. Pig gape-mouthed, gloop and rasp.

I chuckle, walk around. John and I squared off across the Pig supine, the wound now in full spate, gore pooling around his head like a halo.

"Pretty ain't it," John "ay?"

I nod. "Goya ghetto baroque."

"Huh?"

"If ain't baroque, best to fix it."

John snort. "Ain't no one gon' fix HIM."

"Nope. All the Pig's horses and all the Pig's men."

"Sheeat."

I smile. "Bubble."

"Huh?"

"Down there. His mouth."

"Whoa," John bending, "yeah."

We watch: a blood bubble growing on the Pig's lips, small at first, then large, larger still –

"Goddamn," John "wish I could blow 'em that big."

I chuckle, thinking of Waldron. The time he scarfed down soap and guzzled glycerine, him farting long iridescent bubble-trains out to the clinic –

"It's free," John, "on the loose."

I nod. "Free at last, thank gawd a-mighty, free at last."

We watch: the bubble unstuck now and rising. The Pig's last breath in this monad compassed, spit-blood death-capsule floating up and hanging lucent, my eyes on its surface mirrored, and in my mirrored eyes the bubble mirrored, and in the mirrored bubble my eyes again mirrored –

Eye and bubble alternating thus in mirrored regression to the end, to the beginning, our Meister's Notion between these ensconced, like a diamond whose Form in awe I behold, till the bubble burst with a pop, or a plop, or mayhap a pflop, or even a flopf –

"Sheeat," John dismayed, "it's gone."

I sigh, shake my head rueful. "Gone indeed, gone gone to the other shore gone – "

John curse. Step up.

"Do that AGAIN," he demand, booting the Pig, "spit up another bubble. Spit! SPIT! – "

Myself slapping my nuts, shaking loose my tongue going:

"Friar, ixnay. Cease prithee and desist, for the Pig is no more, having lanced his mortal boil and relinquished his inner moiety, which in the demotic mean: HE BE STONE FUCKIN' DEAD – "

John desisting then and stepping back, myself posed vulpine, tongue coiled, eyes on the Pig gone flatline, his flesh starting to run cold in intimation of adipocere: this scene limned stark in cruiser-light, there in the enveloping dark.

***

"So what we do," I go breaking the silence, "I figure what we do is, we stick the fucker back in the Pigmobile, turn off the lights and leave. Get the hell out, not that hell have a movable locus, being omnipresent – "

John nodding vigorous going: "Uh-huh. Yayup. Yaah. Sure – "

That strange grin back now on his kisser, the sort of grin a meatcage display baboon wear when he get done savaging his rival, thinking: *mmm, them purple-ass mamas all mine –*

"What," I go frowning, "what's so dang funny."

John's grin broaden. Him shuffling in place like a decorticate boxer loosening up for a rigged deathmatch, going:

"Well sheeat, har har. Well I'll tell ya. You know I've har! you know I've cockadoodled some strange critteroos in my time. Some OFFBEAT varmints I've hosed, yassuh. Like that ol' seein' eye dawg gone blind, yassuh. And that bigass freak possum from up hill country, yassuh. And that punkinhead feral kid with shit for brains, yassuh. And that dry-gash gorgon up at Fran's Country Graveyard (you stab 'em, we stash 'em, I screw 'em), yassuh. And that little lemon-skull midget with wood-chips for teeth, yassuh. And that bull dyke with the glass eye and club foot, yassuh. And that ricket-legged ol' geezer with three bitch-tits and a two-foot tail yassuh. All these and more, PLENTY more I've humped and hashed over the years, skewered and porked every which way, but I ain't NEVER, listen up now, never but NEVER fucked a dead Pig reserve in the neck after dark in a shopmall lot – "

He break off cackling, John, myself in anguish, eyes closed, going:

"No, no, no, no, no, NO! – "

Hoping against hope, hoping with and for hope that he won't, yet knowing in the pit of my loins that he will –

"HEY!"

I start, eyes open. John a-snarl. Glaring.

"CUT the fuckin' pussy-bitch drama and help me move the Pig up to the cruiser NOW. WHORE."

I blink, shaking my head convulsive. "No. NO. We got to get a move on, we GOT to – "

"You're not HEARING me Jay BEE. Whut I SAID was, GRAB that cold fuckin' HAWG and help me DRAG him over to his CAR. DIG?"

I dig. Hear him clear and dig. But I don't move right off, no. I wait, looking him in the eye. Looking at him look me in the eye looking him in the eye. Us like oldtime bigscreen gunslingers facing off at a dirt street showdown –

But it don't last long, sad to say. Doesn't. I fold in a hurry, exhale hopeless going:

"Fine. Just get it over with quick, ya sick little shit."

John nod, flash me a grin. "You got it. They don't call me Johnny Quick-Jizz for nothin'."

I glare at him a moment, temples throbbing. Then I curse, bend, grab the Pig's left wrist. John with a chuckle grabbing the other wrist going: "Heave OANE now SON. Hoick up them grapenuts and HEAVE."

I heave. Dig my heels in and heave, bones creaking, joints

squealing. He's a heavy mother the Pig, heavier dead than not, uglier dead than not, his head lolling, wound agape like a clown mouth on the bleed –

"Whoof!" me, "heavy little porker you got yourself here. Pretty too."

"You know it," John towing one-handed, "I wouldn't fuck just any ol' fresh-killed hawg."

I curse, throw him a look. No, not throw, more like lob, toss, shoot him a glance. Trotjohn still with that grin, moving effortless, not even breathing hard, like a kid pulling his gramp's baccy-chaw, beef-champ, rust-metal dentures on a string –

"You don't need ME for this," I huff, "doin' fine by yourself."

"Sheeat," him snickering, "you gettin' winded awready, TONTO?"

"Well, mmph! I'm not exactly oof! the corpse-haulin mmp! boar-hawg buggerin', pork-poundin', ham-humpin', sausage-slammin' type – "

John all har har reaching out, knuckling my skull going:

"You can hand me that hernia now, hon."

We're eight feet from the Pigmobile (give or take ten) when I quit, drop my load. "That's IT. That is fuckin' IT – "

John still har har, not missing a beat, dragging the Pig on one-handed to the flashing cruiser, hefting him up against the fender and stepping back with a clap going:

"How's he look, ay? How's m'Pig look. Ya think he souped up enough for a cut o' hot rawhide, a goodly piece o' farm grown schlong-meat?"

I chuckle, rub my aching wrists:

"Look primed enough. That there slit lubed up with pure Bama Pig-blood. Just the angle I figure you got to get right."

"Angle," John with a frown "whut angle."

"Angle of inclination. Your boner point up twenty degrees

from the horizontal, a hundred and ten from the nether vertical."

John snort. "He's awright. I know when a Pig's stacked high enough to hump."

I shrug. "Ish yo' thang."

"Goddamn right."

I mutter, turn, start walking.

"YO!"

I pause, turn. "The answer's NO."

John chuckle, spit on his palm. "Dontcha wanna stay and watch, hey? Maybe get some leftovers?"

I look away, moving. "Just get it over with quick."

I hear him cackle, call out once more, but I don't look back, not till seconds later: glimpse of John unsheathed, spit-shining his dong –

I walk on, reach the Durerro, stand there with arms folded, ass on the hood. My gaze turned down in refusal, not wanting to watch, to dignify his rut, the horrors of Trotjohn at play, scenes past I well recall –

"Don't," I tell myself, "don't watch. Do not. Dune aught. Due knot – "

But it don't help. Does not. It's too strong, the pull. Like when you're at cliff's edge and can't help but jump. Or when you're holding a gun to your misshapen skull and can't help but shoot –

Myself turning slow, eyes wide, the scene oozing into focus: Trotjohn with pants pooled around his ankles humping hard, his bare ass a pale moon between two highbeam suns.

"He's doing it," I whisper in a language I don't understand, "he's actually, truly, doing it – "

And he is, sure enough, no trick. No demimonde shadow-satellite smut-hologram. Trotjohn in full view playing Pigfuck necrophile, the corpse-head canted sideways, mouth agape, dead eyes skewed sightless...

Don't know how long I watch, agonized. A while, a long while before I see it: the FORM. My gaze sweeping the lot, the Old Mall there in silhouette and far in the distance food signs up like brands held to the sky's underbelly, of which one I see rising bifurcate, golden, like some mythic bird caught in midflight, its tail aimed at the ass below, John's bare ass far down on the nether vertical, a moon between two suns, these to my geometer's eye linked in a triangle: gold-bird, sun-brights, butt-moon —

Beholding which, I smile. Nay, laugh. Nay, laugh and smile both (no mean feat), my thoughts flaring in grunge-head satori *qua* Euclid, my legs crossing right over left, hands rising to play an invisible lute, your daddy posed like blue Krishna alone in the grove at midnight, all them luscious cowgirls at home asleep, in red love-dreams yearning...

***

Can't say how long it lasts. A minute, eight minutes, who knows. I'm not too good with time, specially trance time. Eons, maybe kalpas before I hear his voice, Trotjohn going:

"Whee-eeeEEEE!"

Which mean he have come, spurted chowder, worked a homuncular jailbreak, the sound he make gouting nad-aspic over bag ladies dead on winter sidewalks —

"Wheeee-eeeEEEEE! — "

His very own ballbust, cojone-crunch, jizz-shriek, like Bwana Tarzan with his bull-ape victory cry, post jungle-hump, myself coming to with a start (not less starting to come), John ahead turning, his schlong rutilant:

"MMMmmmYEEOW! Now THAT'S what I call a GASH!"

And with voice raised: "YO JB! YOU GOT SOMETHIN' I CAN WIPE OFF OANE?"

I blink, frown. "IS THAT 'WIPE' WITH A 'P' AS IN 'PSYCHODROME' OR 'WIFE' WITH AN 'F' AS IN 'FOOFARAW'?"

Pause. John's brow seeming to darken, his dong still up in führer-salute:

"WIPE, YA LITTLE RATSHIT! WIPE! AS IN GET THE BLOOD-SLIME OFF DOC PECKERWANG!"

I sigh, start forward at a trot. Moving with an easy lope, moi, a sort of tardigrade sprint, strolling, if not ambling up, going:

"You ask for a sudarium where a loofah mitt would suffice. Why not wipe off on his hair, sirrah, or his earlobes, his chin bristle, his rump – "

"Say WHUT?" John aghast, "wipe m'holy hotrod off'n this PIG?"

Pause. Scowl. "I don't see why NOT. You done THROAT-fucked the critter not a minute back."

John cough, suppressing a chuckle. With bent head studying his gore-daubed saber:

"We-ell now that's DIFFERENT, see. That there was a VIRGINAL wound. Your papa boldly thrustin' where no schlong have thrust before – "

He break off, look up brightening: "Say now. How bout that there headcloth you're wearin'. Ay?"

I blink. "My bandanna. YOU want MY bandanna. My HELL-realm HEADcloth."

John nod, eyebrows raised. "Yeah! Put it to good use. Dry off m'dingaling. Ain't doin' much good on that freak head o'yourn anyhow – "

Which get me laughing, it really do. Just the idea of it. Myself by the violate Pig all cachinnate going:

"WaaaHAHHH! Wipe off on my bandanna, mmph! That sure be rich, waaHHAAAAH! – "

But it's just me, I quickly notice. Just your mocha daddy laughing. John mirthless as a neutered owl staring baleful, which, like, kills my giggles in a hurry. Myself falling silent, not *falling* exactly, more like collapsing, John and I facing off once more: grungehead lawman versus testosterone outlaw, slit-eyed and purse-lipped, hands poised above absent holsters.

"Hand it over turtle-dick," drawl John in bogus movie Texan "toss it on over fore I scalp it off ye."

I don't move. Don't speak. My thoughts on the run: *bandanna. Printcloth. Damnation chic. My saltsweat. With Pigblood. And Johnny jizz. Yes. A fine mix, yes. Scum corpus hellmelange, yesss –*

"Well shit," I go yanking off my tarbus, "if bandanna Johnny want, bandanna Johnny get. For His is the conundrum, the buzz and the blarney, forever and ever, ay-fuckin'-men – "

I scrunch the cloth into a ball. Kiss it. Toss it over.

"You be gentle with her now."

"Gentle as a tooth-pickin' meat-drill," he goes, catching it one-handed.

I watch him a moment, squint-eyed, lips twitching. Then I look away, my hair tumbling sweatcold down my nape, my left eye shut wide, shooting optic probes out to the northern dark: that starry synod I haven't seen in years and likely never will –

"I'm through," John over my shoulder, "you can have your tampon back now hon."

I turn with hand raised. Catch the clothball. Press it to my nose.

"Mmmmyeah. Smell like one them old time, rot-crotch, nad-gangrene longjohns you saw on old seadogs nurturing scurvy. Sweat, blood and jizz in sweet fungus salmagundi – "

"HAR!" John pulling up his jodhpurs, "baby you KNOW you want it."

I shake loose the bandanna. Stretch it end to end. Flip it over my head. Work the ends into a knot, back of my skull. Doesn't feel too good I'll admit, the dampness on my pate, but it make sense at some meta-noetic level. In realms other than our own. IT being of the essence. Of the Meister's Notion IT –

"How's this look?" I ask yanking the tails of my bandanna.

"Like a pecker-sheath," John "used prophylact on a dung-dipped hashbrown dickhead – "

Turning as he speak, surveying with arms akimbo his bloody handiwork: slash-fucked Pig on the fender.

"Well gee," he goes soft-voiced, "he's dead. He's really dead."

I cock an eyebrow. Whistle. "Damn. You noticed."

"Dead," he echo, "stone fuckin' dead – "

His voice trailing off, him like a kid who stepped on a bug he didn't really want to kill, just dismember and preserve wingless in a plate-glass solarium –

"Well it's like this TJ," I go, hand on his shoulder, "what happened was: we were drivin' across this here lot, just two good ol' boys, never meanin' no harm, when this here Pig flashed up, stopped us, put us up against the hood, booted us, frisked and goosed me, wanted to frisk you and search the car, but you didn't let him. You slashed the fucker cold and he fell, his prana energy goin' nuts, shooting up unsublimate, piercing his smoke-meat chakras to the top of his pithecanthropoid skull and out, through the astral umbilicus (dark tunnel with a light at the end, kinda like lookin' up a headless giraffe at high noon) into a radiant celestium. Heaven, that is. Groovy incense, harp and dulcimer, big-dug houris in hyaloid muslin, buck-naked apsaras around a rainbow font, Pig all jizz and drool going: *DANG! If this ain't paradise I don't know whut is*, which is when you kicked in, humping the gash in his larynx, humpety-hump-hump and vrrooom! Pig out and down, back through the tunnel, scum-chakra freeway dropping south – "

I pause, my eyes, nose, prepuce gone moist, Trotjohn wonderstruck going: "Hot-DAMN! I did all THAT?"

Myself in high-pitched tremolo going: "Bet your hotbeef boner you did, good friar John, and the pox on the first sumbitch that say otherwise. You did all that and more, sent the Pig down where he belong: in chains, manacles white hot, his butt coal toast, torment interminable, sorrow without end, in the brimstone depths of Old Nick's kiln – "

***

We don't bother moving him, the Pig. Don't bother dressing him in camisole, garter, high-heel (snout farded red) and driving him off a cliff the way they do in old screen flicks. Don't bother, knowing we'll be over and done with, the Run complete and the Notion full manifest, the Meister placated before the Pigs get around to figuring things, if they ever do. We leave him as is, cheek on fender, deader than ever before or since, the scene unchanged except for the lights. We do turn off the cruiser's beams and roof-lights, or rather, John does, knowing how, having seen the insides of Pigmobiles aplenty. He turn 'em off dead, but not before taking a piss, a long leisurely leak in the Pig's ear, his hair, his violate wound, draining the old hosepipe before cutting the lights and walking back, pocketbeam in hand, a white point afloat in the expanse –

Back in the Durerro and vrrroooom, off once more, highbeams beating back the dark, myself with lids aflutter thinking: *nothing's changed. Everything the same as before. The Old Mall bulked there at left. The golden bird poised high above. With John driving speechless, myself without speech. All the same except there's one less Pig in the world. One bogus Pig too dead to flash up, block our way, give us the full cavity shakedown. For which I'm glad and grateful. Or rather, conscious of gladness and gratitude, yet fearful somewhat of recurrence. Like what if the same shit happen again a minute from now? WHAT IF? Be a real drag doing it over, slashing another Pig, leaving him with a crawfulla jizz. I mean shit like that can get old real quick –*

But my worries prove groundless, thank spit. We drive on unmolested, without further incident, on till the lights come into view: yellow lights lining an empty street –

"Left," I go, "left on Brooke and down a mile – "

John with a grunt cutting a leftward swathe, the car bruising up over the sidewalk and down into the street, boom-thud, myself with a yelp going:

"Fella, you gonna mess up this car in a hurry, drivin' like that. The car and my glazed numbnuts, both."

John shifting gear with a curse going: "You keep bitchin' thataways, I'll mess your NUTS up, runnin' 'em OVER."

The car surge, night wind roaring. Me with a knuckle pushed into my right eye looking around in, uh, surprise? Yeah, surprise. Seeing trees, actual live dendrites either side, the road flat, smooth, hard (the way some them idiot Teutons like their gash-meat), the lights and sidewalks in good repair.

"Well hell," I go mashing together my thumbs, "old Brooke ain't half bad. Not near as bad as I thought. Or thought I'd think."

John going: "That's cuz you don't think bad enough, not near – "

Or some such, in sort of a growl, real grumpy. His temper befouled, Trotjohn, not whistling in invocation of a demon blitzkrieg, no longer yakking. Him gone purse-lipped post slash'n'jizz (*post coitum animal triste*), which, like, puts a damper on my own dawg tongue, rendering me speechless. Myself in silence listening to the wind, the occasional sputter of gutgas (my very own, all spice and balsam) and the hiss of tyres on wet tarmac, it having rained around here like I said, the air still damp, redolent of flophouse farts, bootleg beershits, or effluvia more corrosively mephitic –

The car now slicing up Brooke with nothing or no one to cheer our way, no bystanders caged or chained, no carousing cyprians waving severed heads, no scrofulous dotards juggling prosthetics, not a mammal in sight, dead or otherwise, save this old codger I see on a sidewalk bench gnawing on his walking stick, his mange-wrought terrier nearby crapping on a discarded shoe, or is it the dog gnawing and the codger dejecting, I can't quite recall –

Perhaps a mile (give or take six) before John slow, the road ending ahead at a gate: ivied brick columns topped with bronze lions couchant, an arched sign above that reads: PLANTATION SOUTH.

"This where he live?" John, flashing me a scowl.

I nod. "Yayup. This, verily."

John mutter, tap the brakes and drive on through, the road narrowing considerable past the gate, winding around domiciles with stucco fronts, dumpsters the size of home-grown pachyderms, little plots of turf unfenced, streetlamps in gloomy nimbus –

"Which one the fucker live at?" John starting to cuss under his breath, his odourless, deep-freeze, killer breath –

"Block D," I go, "block D, eleven."

Pause. John hitting the brakes, turning slow, murderous:

"D? We PASSED that TWICE ALREADY, ya jive WHORE. Whut'd you do, have your TONGUE up your ASS again?"

I shake my head, smile rueful. "No, but I did have m'dick in m'hand. And a right tricky dick it is too. Require constant vigilance: a pump-fist proctor, a spit-palm chaperone. But not to worry, there it be, Block Dee, lousy with virginity – "

And it is, sure enough. Block D, right ahead. Waldron's little two-seat, six-cylinder Fuggo parked there in profile.

"That's his car awright," goes John approaching, "he better be up and ready. And I mean READY."

"Oh, not to worry," I go reassuring, "ready he'll surely be. Never a slouch in such matters, Wald. Gore-spunk country matters. Always on for a high-power hell-rut by fiat, by leave of Lord Meister Howell (take not his name in vain, Cain) – "

But he's not listening, John. Never does when it's not unimportant. Him steering into an empty slot, killing the engine and vaulting out, myself more staid, draping myself over the windscreen, slithering down the hood to land headfirst on the sidewalk –

"Whoa," John's voice in the gloom, "check out this bigass dent."

I rise, tasting blood. Dust myself off. Walk around limping.

"Look like an accident," he goes, indicating a crater in Wald's cardoor, "or maybe he gave it a mean head-butt for the luv of fun."

I shake my head. "Accident it was. Happened last week. He was cruisin' along whistlin' Dixie, when all of a sudden this old bat came barreling out a sidestreet on a two-wheeler, smashed straight into the flank where you see it. Didn't hurt Wald any, he was all right, but the bat busted in headfirst through the window (scud geriatric), Wald winding up with a scalp-rug on his mug, glass eyeball in his ear, dentures clacking in his lap – "

"HARF!" John, "bat! Crash! Bazoom! Voomf! Bloom! Pow! Whoop! Scud! Clackety clack! Ka-thwoom! – "

And so forth, but I'm not listening. For once, him waxing

motor-mouthed and me not listening. Or rather, half-listening. Or rather, half-listening with one ear and half with the other –

"Bartlett," I go, looking across, "Bartlett."

John pause in mid-babble: "Wha? Who?"

"Bartlett's car over yander. Damned if it isn't."

"Well sheee-it," John peering, "shee-yat."

I move: walking around Wald's car, John in tow. Ten paces on to the vehicle I've spotted, a rusted hulk big as a boat.

"The right reverend T. Carter Bartlett," I go stepping up, "his hot holy ghostmobile."

John brush past, stop by the rear fender.

"Dig it," him pointing, "dig."

I dig. The sticker on the trunk large and lurid: a mutant *agnus dei*, billy goat nailed to an invert cross at the heart of a flaming pentagram, haloed goat-angel with hooved stigmata and locust wings, vaginal third eye spuming gold dust in the shape of a grail.

"New logo," I go, thumb in navel, "Church of Ancients."

John hawk. Spit. "Uh-huh. Old one wasn't too bad, but this'n here kicks. And I mean KICKS."

I turn. Give him a deep look.

"You realize what this means."

John frown. Nod. "Mean Wald followed him here. Followed Cart Bart."

I smile. "Bingo. So there be a method to his madness."

John shrug. "Guess the Wald's smarter'n I thought."

I shake my head vigorous. "Nope. Not really. Just that he got this idiot savant thing goin' – "

John make a retching sound. Move.

"Yeah well. I'm gon go fetch the little turd. You can stay here'n suck oane that tailpipe – "

"Nein," me starting after, "I komm fetch Wald. He of the Meister's *quintessence*, the rotten kumquat of his *mantic Eye* – "

We march over damp grass. Up the walkway to a covered porch, John with both elbows pushing through into a foyer, or is it a faux-ear, I can't tell. Doors either side, a stairway ahead leading up. Real gloomy, just a couple yellow bulbs the colour of cheese torched by pathic mice.

"Lousy little shack," goes John starting forward, "wormshit, puke, piss, gangrene – "

Hitting the stairs at a run, myself in hot pursuit (*hot! warm! lukewarm! luke!*) breathing through my one chosen nostril and through pores marked NNZLK! in blood red by the Sapphireville dermal elite, as also through my crudded fontanelle forced open after the Eighth Diablo Mudslide -

In short, trying not to breathe at all (*NYET! NYET!*) given the smell, the reek in the foyer and on the staircase, a subtle alimentary pestilence, whiff of the unsealed crypt, the disinterred putrefact, John stopping short all of a sudden, his elbow ramming my brow (*welcome pain: let there be a wound, lawd, a bruise fulminant, a seething prurit*) –

"Stink," he goes sniffing the air, "fuckin' reek."

"Yayup," me, "it's – "

Whack: John back-handing my mouth as he jettisons a spitball, the gobbet flaring in green dolor, pulsing amoebal in descent, fine acid spray stinging my cheek –

"Yow," me rubbing my lip, "demon water. Duct-juice desecrate."

"Huh?" John, "say what?"

"What."

John curse. Turn. Cover the last four steps in a single bound, his legs stretched near horizontal, myself with a wince thinking: *groin. Groyne. GRAWIN'* –

"You need a special invite, bitch?"

John at the stairhead scowling.

"J'arrive chérie," I squeak, hobbling up knock-kneed, "j'arrive."

He let me brush past, John, then turn slit-eyed.

"Which one's he at. Ay?"

I pause on tiptoe. Look around. The second floor landing a small carpeted square, a hallway directly ahead. In the corner at left, a pail: metal alloy bucket brimming with chipped toenails, crushed eggshells dyed blue and red. The sight of which puts me in mind of cromagnons, fearful prehominids embracing trees -

"That his door?" John pointing.

I nod. "Yayup. Second from the left."

John move up. Start chuckling. "Check this out, har har."

I step up. Smile. Smile and cackle both (no mean feat), digging the stuff pasted on Wald's door. Dongs, twats, tits, nuts, bungholes in rampant cutup. With Superman presiding. Superman with missile-schlong gone ballistic, a glanhead nuke aimed at the doorknob, this here knob shaped like a pair of moose-nads or hogbollocks (take your pick), the peephole above molded to resemble a thrombosed annule, a hemorrhoidal asshole of purely Saxon origin (vide: the weekly disburthening, black bullets ringing white porcelain) –

"Wald been stealing ideas from the Fatman," I go, "from the Fatman filch ideas he – "

But he's not listening, Trotjohn (don't know why I bother). Him with back turned going: "Dig it. House Bartlett. Dig."

I turn. Exhale with a long whistle. The door across marked with a sticker, same as the one on the car outside: mutant *agnus dei* with locust wing, gold dust grail –

"T. Carter Bartlett," I go, my voice in echo "H.Q., Church of Ancients – "

John raise a hand, cock his head. Raise a cock, head his hand.

"What," I go, "what gives."

"Voice," John, "I hear a voice."

"Sure you do. You hear me. Vox mein in displacement ventriloquale."

John scowl. Jerk a thumb. "Behind Wald's door, whore."

I blink. Step sideways. Press an ear to Wald's door. "Uh-huh. Sound like Wald humming. Or reciting – "

John grab my arm. Yank me aside. Stick his ear to the door (clink of earring on cheap wood).

"Fucker's right behind," John with a frown, "mumbling."

I yelp. Thrust a pinkie up my right nostril.

"Mumbling what?"

"Sound like: *eat up and bask yucann quinn.*"

I slap my left tit. Knuckle my sternum.

"Wrong. What he's saying is: speak up and ask if you can come in."

John straighten with a snarl.

"Oh WAALD!" he go singsong and dulcet, "open up NOW Wald, or I'm gon' have to bust in and rip your tonsils out the wrong EEEND."

Pause. Muffled giggle. Then a click and bolt-thud: the door opening some, a face showing in the breach. A round cherub face, flaxen hair cut in bangs, wide eyes, button nose, dimple cheeks. Smiling.

"Wald ya little putz," John, "you best – "

"YIP!" the face, "yeeEEEP! – "

And gone, the door ajar.

John mutter profane, boot the door open, step in. Myself after, elbowing the door shut.

I don't spot the kid right off (my vision awash in blue) so I work my eyes some finger-wise (scrape, gouge and crush) to where I can see him. Directly ahead. Wald at attention, big grin, middle of the room. A blue chandelier quaking above as from a

Richter pulse: tink-tinkle, tinkle-tink, blue shadows flitting about like wraiths. No not flitting, more like skittering, gambolling.

John smack his lips. Make a hooting sound.

"Wald. Ya little putz."

Wald grab his crotch. Giggle. "Little putz. Heh heh."

I inhale through a vacant pore, look around. Not much to see. Wald's living room featureless, bare almost. Just a workstation in a corner by the window, big screen, a console horse-shoed around a swivel stool. The screen-saver showing a cartoon cumshot pink and green: shark-head priapus jizzing a dollar-sign mushroom cloud.

I chuckle, digging the image. Recalling the time we hit Wald's old West Zone pad, John and I busting in to find him naked, near dead. Wald curled foetal, frothing drool, just the whites of his eyes, a noose tight around his neck, a Korova milk bottle up his ass, a shit-caked gerbil gone belly-up beside. The kid's torso slashed bloody, his purple mug turned to the old web-screen pulsing livid: some kinda war-snuff collage in rapid flicker, rogue razorheads on night detail, a kill-fuck desert rampage, flash-stills of sandnigger slaughterporn –

"JayBEEEEP! Heh heh."

I blink. Turn. Wald with hands way up, Laughing Buddha pose. Him all dressed and ready to roll, wearing a bowtie this night. A black four-leaf bowtie on a pale short-sleeve shirt, a pair of belted schoolboy shorts with Orphan Annie buckle, a pair of laced shit-kicker boots steel-muzzled. Freaky gestalt all in all, but cool, kinda like killer clown meets slasher catamite –

John mutter. Stroll up. Pat Wald's cheek.

"We were delayed some, Wald. And I do mean de-LAYed. Pig came in the way, so I had to kill him. And fuck him."

"Hockkh!" Wald letting his arms drop, "HAWKKHHH! mmbrf! – "

I move. Away from the door and across to the window, John and Wald now in profile, facing each other. John a head taller, Wald by the same head shorter. Both with eyes wide, lips in heavy pout.

I curse, shake my head. *No surprise. Commence palp-meld. Same shit, different –*

"Plum," goes John raising his right hand, fingers spread.

"Plum," Wald raising his left hand, fingers spread.

"Goo," John raising his left hand, fingers spread.

"Goo," Wald raising his right hand, fingers spread.

"PLUMBY!" John pushing forward, "PLUMBY!"

"PLUMBY!" Wald pushing forward, "PLUMBY! – "

Their voices in echo, arms in partial extension: John's left hand and Wald's right, Wald's left hand and John's right, palp-joined, eight pairs of fingertips kissing, plus thumbtips, John and Wald merged thus in holy palp-meld, jowls a-tremble.

Silence. Quietus in blue dream. Myself by the window playing witness. Breathing diaphragmatic. Neurons in concert spinning the lunar ferriswheel. Air moving bold, silken in my valorized nostril –

"Move," I whisper, "twitch, shudder, locomote – "

Wanting it to end, *moi*, wanting to violate their repose (if not their stasis), corporal force vectors in zero sum –

But they don't move, John-cum-Wald. Do not. Them palped rigid in breathless meld.

I put out a throttled bark. Turn to look out the window (Wald's window being the kind you can look out of). A dim and drear prospect. Streetlights glowing feeble, trees beyond like a line of black surf. The freeway far distant, carlights in slow drift –

I turn con-fenestral, with new hope. *Terminus?* Nay. The fuckers aren't done yet. John-Wald with palps wedded still in nuptial simulacrum –

I wince, feeling pain. Nether pain. *Pylorus? Caecum? Duodenum?* No. Bladder. The old juice-bag gone sloshful, threatening a piss-burst.

I start across, thinking *crapper, crapper.* Past the palpsters to a narrow passage where I pause, grope for the switch: click. More blue light. Wald got a thing for blue light, no question.

I step into the passage, moving past the kitchen (glimpse of eggs wasted with a hammer, a pile of ingrown toenails, cabbageheads weeping green tears on a mosaic of spam and ketchup, bitter tears for NNGLKFF! the vanished bucolium, for DRRLK! the lost spinach kingdom), on to the door at right (gleam of porcelain), myself putting a knuckle-grip on peewee, sliding in with a grimace, unzip, unsheath and aaaaaahhhh: hot bladder-juice through my unstanched flume –

I frown, hearing a loud splatter. *Rain on blood-stiff bodybag?* No. Seat-cover. *Shoulda raised it first thing. Too late now. Let it flow, let it flow, let it flow –*

I sigh, feeling muscles relax, bones yield and snap. My eyes droop, thoughts oozing languid. *Man got to piss standing up now Clem. Or lying down. On a corpse. In a prison courtyard. With severed limbs etherized on a table. Man got to piss erect, prone or both, but not sitting, by gawd. The hell with sitting, that pantywaist pussy crouch. Strictly for swish boys and kiddie girls, candyasses in soprano. FUCK THE URETHRAL MEAN –*

A minute pass. Two minutes. The torrent slowing to a trickle, drip, stop. *Consummatum est. Old German Kant's last words: it is finished –*

I flap the old fanion. Furl. Move to the door (squelch of piss-wet sneakers). Stepping in the passage I pause, head cocked. A voice. From the right. Behind the bedroom door. "Weewummmum. Weemummee." *Some kinda vesper mantra? Vox coronach?*

I turn. Head right on eager feet. The voice waxes as I approach, sounding in my left nostril, in the caried heart of my one true molar. At the bedroom door I pause. Grasp the knob sans touche. Turn it bothways simultaneous. Push.

"Tweedledum," comes the voice loud and clear, "Tweedledee. Tweedledum. Tweedledee – "

I step in blinking. Can't make out much at first, just a form shadowed. But then my eyes adjust and I SEE. An old geezer in the corner naked, blindfolded, his legs manacled to the wall. Not quite naked. Geezer got jumper cables clamped to his tits, a gold leaf over his crotch. His brow shining silver-blue, phosphorecent lips on the move going: "Tweedledum. Tweedledee. Tweedledum. Tweedledee – "

I look away, my gaze drawn to the light. Light at the room's centre: an azygous eye-lamp hung low, scrutinizing a sliced frog on the floor. A dissected frog belly up on a square of red plush, barbwire coiled around. At the frog's head, a pink cartoon clock ticking. At its feet, a dollar bill nailed to a clapboard crucifix.

The frog isn't dead, not by a long shot. It live and breathe, ashen lungbags laboring in sync with the geezer's mantra: "Tweedledum (inbreath). Tweedledee (outbreath). Tweedledum (inbreath). Tweedledee (outbreath) – "

And on, unseamed batrach and tit-pinched geezer in agonized syzygy –

"SHITWIENER!" John's voice up the passage "YO SHITWIENER!"

I curse. Turn. Step out. Back through the pasageway to the front: John and Wald unpalped there under the chandelier, staring.

"What were you doin' in there," John, "shakin' your shagpole?"

"Yeh," Wald, "shagpole. Heh heh."

I give John a look. "Somethin' you oughtta see back there. In the bedroom. Artwork *qua* Wald."

"Fartwork," Wald, "heh heh."

John walk up with a scowl. Shove me aside. Step into the passage.

"KEEP PUSHIN', ROSCOE!" I yell over my shoulder, "THAT'S ROSCOE WITH AN 'R' AS IN 'R' FATHER BITCH ART IN HEAVEN'!"

"Bitch art," Wald, "heh heh."

I take a deep breath. Turn smiling. "Wild shit back there Wald. Geezer's a bit paunchy, the frog a trifle misshapen, but it works."

"Urk!" Wald tugging at his lower lip, "urk!"

I stick a pinkie up my right nostril. Cork out a crust.

"Where'd you find the geezer Wald. Where find the geezer you?"

Wald hold up a fist. Open his mouth wide. Work the fist in.

"Yowch," me, "that must hurt. Lucky you."

"Nngn!" Wald, fist in mouth, "nnglln!"

I move aside, hearing footsteps.

"Big deal," John striding out the passage, "sag-tit asswipe mumblin' over slit kermit. If THAT'S art I'm a fuckin' rat's ass monkey's uncle."

Pause. Lapdingus lacuna. Wald pulling his fist out his mouth, eyes brimming.

"You hurt the Wald's feelings there friar," I go, "that's 'hurt' with a 'k' as in 'granfaloon'."

John make a choking sound. Turn incredulous.

"FEELINGS? Sheeat, the little putz ain't got feelins to HURT – DO YA?!!"

The Wald cringe. Grab a handful of crotch.

"Bumble," he goes, "big butt beebee bumble bullwinkle booboo beef bubble bum."

John flash me a grin. "See whut I mean?"

I pucker my lips. Pinch an earlobe.

"Speaking of mean: Monk's gonna turn nasty mean, we don't get there in a hurry."

John scowl. Turn. Start for the door. "We out. Out NOW."

I chuckle. Give Wald a look. "Wald son. You ready to leave now, Wald son?"

The Wald shuts fast his eyes. Tightens his crotch-grip.

"Blllllb," he goes, "bllllllbmmmm."

"Fuckim," John at the door, "he'll come around. Or he won't."

I move: sideways on crab legs, head twitching.

"Hither Puck. Quick now, Puck. Let's get the fuck out now, Puck – "

But it's no use. He don't move a muscle, Wald. Him posed stiff as bronze, hands on crotch –

"Carpe scrotum," I go pausing at the door, "carpe scro-tum-ta-tum-tum-tums – "

I clap twice. Slap my nuts hard. And step out wincing.

***

We wait out in the hallway, John and I. On either side of Wald's door, backs to the wall, arms folded, like dugless castrates guarding a quadruped harem. A while before I break the silence, no not break, more like part the curtains of silence with furtive paws, going:

"Can't wait around much longer now, friar. Cannot."

My voice in echo-cho-o.

John shrug. Scratch his beard (scrape of rust blade on bare bone).

"Don't sweat it, depp'ty dawg. He be out presently."

I shake my head. "Hope springs sempiternal. Same pitiful urinal."

A pause ensue. Seconds like jellied boli passing.

"Huh?" John all of a sudden, "whut in HALE?"

I straighten, raise a hand. "Hold now. Hold."

Music fills the hallway. Strange music. Notes waxing eldritch, in dissonant caterwaul.

"Say WHUT?" John straightening, "WHO?"

I lean back and sink, feet in slow slide, rump kissing the floor in slow pratfall. My head tilted freakish, thinking: *music of Erich Zann. Charnel house cello. Abattoir blood-fiddle. Hillbillies in wolf-howl circle-jerk –*

"Bartlett," goes John, voice rising, "fuckIN' CART BART."

I cough. Start to speak. Pause. Light shows under the door across. Bartlett's door: a sliver of red.

"VESPER SERVICE!" I yell over the note-swell, "BLOOD AND OUNS, BART PLAYING A THEREMIN WITH SKEWERED PALMS."

John push himself off the wall, fists bunched. "I'M GON' GO HAVE A LOOKSEE. HAND HIM A WANG-SLAP NUTCRUSH – "

"HOLD!" I go leaping up, "HOLD ON NOW FRIAR. WE GOT TO GO BY THE – "

I break off, a door opening behind. The Wald stepping out with a smile, a broad smile: twenty-five incisors, sixteen canines, eight rot-pulp premolars, no molars, one tricusp lycanthropic wisdom.

"Ooohhhh," Wald barely audible, "ooohhh, heh heh."

Cheerful enough, by the look of him. Wald's tears gone dry, brine tracks on his cheeks blue-green, salt streaked out to moon dark and terror of northern ice weeping the torn child –

"YOU TOOK YOUR TIME!" I bellow, "THE TIME IT TOOK."

The Wald turn in profile. Stick out his butt.

"YEEEEH!" he explain, "YEEEEEHHH – "

Silence. The music dying all of a sudden, notes in diminuendo fading to a whisper. Tinnitus.

"Well that's done," John "about fuckin' – "

Thud. Boom-thud. A scream half-human. Then a scurrying sound, like some part-time quadruped in a rush and THUD-WUMP: sound of unwashed bodies in collapse –

"Here it come brothers," I go "here it come – "

And it does. The Lovesong of T. Carter Bartlett: Thwack! Followed by a cry. Thwack! A screech. Thwack! A scream –

"Goddamn," John, "ol' Bartlett be layin' into his bitch somethin' nasty – "

Thwack! comes the sound from behind the door, Thwack! Thwack! Thwack! the blows sustained, rhythmic, the shrieks rising in pitch and volume, Thwack! Thwack! Thwack! –

John moving his hands in sync, like one them candyapple poofs conducting the philharmonic –

On and on, Bartlett working up an open palm catechism, me wondering when it's gonna end, *when Lawd, when?* seem like it never will but it does, the thwacks ceasing abrupt, the shrieks persisting yet a while, then yielding to sob and wail, sob-sob wail, sob-sob wail –

"Fucker didn't do it," I go, "did not it, the fucker do."

John turns with a frown. "Do what."

"Victory cry. Victory cry of bull ape. Like Bwana Tarzan put out after he done workin' a jungle shitkick – "

"YeeeEEP!"

I turn. To see Wald posed on the landing with foot raised, hands up in mudra: Lord of the Dance, idiot-savant version.

John curse. Step into the landing. Cosh Wald's skull with a loose fist. Wald toppling downstairs with a squawk, John in pursuit.

I remain in place a moment, listening. Then I step away, moving in sync with sob and wail. Sobsob wail, sobsob wail: Two quick steps plus one, two quick steps plus one, my head bowed, fists pressed to my temples, hop-hop jump, hop-hop jump: my sneakerdogs syncopate, drawing me down.

***

I figure he'll take the freeway John, but he don't. Doesn't. He cuts past the thruway instead, on into the interior: South Zone in yellow gloom. Cruising easy Trotjohn, keeping an eye out for potholes, houses drifting past ramshackle, detritus playlots vacant. In silence, my own dawg tongue well furled, John tight-lipped steering with one hand, one finger, one hangnail, his auxiliary automotive dactyl, Wald in back face down, butt steepled up. Street signs drift past fluorescent, the car turning every which way, myself at length yielding to doubt, going:

"Hope you know where we're at friar, because I sure as hell don't."

John snort. "Fuckin' A. Better believe I do."

I nod. "Groovy. Belief as existential choice. Having to believe. Pascal's Wager. The predilection of a grunge-warrior – "

The car slow. Turn. Cruise on a few yards. Turn again. A sign drifts past in green shimmer: EVANS. The road ahead straight and narrow, John hitting the pedal with a grunt and vrrroom the car gathering speed, brights on the burn.

"Yeeaaayaywoe," goes John singing tuneless, "yeeeaaayayy – "

I yelp. Lean forward squinting. "What's that now. Ahead."

"Awww nothin'," John avuncular, "just m'big ol' dick in mirage."

"Nyet," me "this here's bigger – "

"HOLY SHITBEJEEZUS!" John sitting up, "ROAD LUSH!"

"Ulm?" Wald looming "ULM?"

John stare a moment, the car slowing. Then he bare his teeth and floor the pedal.

"YAAAAH!" John, "YYAAAAARRRHH! – "

The car surge, highbeams flaring. Wald on his feet, hands gripping the headrests going: "YeeEEP! YeeeEEEEP! – "

The car judders, night wind gone banshee, the target now limned brilliant, growing: figure of a man in gape-mouthed sprawl, skidrow stumblebum comatose on damp blacktop, blood clotted dark at his nose, puke on his chin –

"Awww shit," I go, my feet against the dash, "shit. Shit. Shiiiiiit – "

The target close now, closer still –

"YAAAAAAAAAAAAAARRR! – "

Thump-thud-crunch: the car floundering an instant, then bursting free, John with head thrown back venting a victory howl, the Wald lapsing back in a mega-decibel rave going:

"WHUMP! BUMP! THE TRIUMPH! BETIMES WE SEDUCT AT THOR'S SEDERUNT! IN MEMORIAM, THE POOR SOT FIREWATER DEFAMED! WHO IN DESPAIR BLEW CHYME UPON HIS SUBCOSTAL NETHERHEAD! BOILING BOLUS THAT WE DO IN ALL APTNESS APPERCEIVE! TILL EFTSOONS IT SUFFER ITS COMEUPPANCE VIA MEPHISTO, WHO GENUFLECTING DID EXPECTORATE, AND RUMP UP, THUNDER IN FLATULE! OR WAS IT SIRES A DEMON'S FLUX IN FIERY ARC SEEN OVER GLEN AND DALE, REEKING MEPHITIC IN PURSUIT OF REALMS SUPERLUNAR (IF NOT SIDEREAL) WHERE THE COSMIC TADPOLE DID WEEP AND PINE HAVING CROSSED THE MYSTIC BOURNE WHILE YET FAILING TO BREACH HEAVEN MAMA'S ZONA

PELLUCIDA? WE AWAIT THE ANSWER ERUCTANT! MARKING TIME BY HANK HOGBOLLOCK'S ATOMIC CLOCK! AND PETE PROSTATE'S NEUTRON GROIN-WATCH! AND BOB BROKEDICK'S GAMMA DUNG-CROCK! NOT TO MENTION CHOCO POOPLE RUMPLE! AND KOOOPIPIPIPI DIMPLE! AND MMMBRRRAPAPAPAPAFRRAAP! – "

And on, Wald, on and on, in idiot-savant mode bawling logorrheal, words arcane and livid like the ones above more or less, not quite the same, no, but of cognate ilk, on till John stop the car, leap back and choke him shut, Wald yielding with a twelve-second thunderfart, spitting blue foam as he convulse white-eyed, deathly silence as John rise, return to his seat and start up the car.

"Hope you didn't kill him there friar," I go moments later, car on the move, "sure hope ya didn't."

John with a snort going: "Sheeat, he'd've plumb died if I'd'a killed him. Fucker ain't dead, just choked shut is all."

I dig a fingernail out of my palm. Nod.

"Well, all right then. So let it be. For thusly and suchly do we abide by the Meister's ukase, the little edict that say: NO CRITTER SHALL FAIL OR FALTER, NO VARMINT MUTATE OR ALTER, NO SCHLONG PISS BLOOD OR WATER, OR OTHERWISE DIE: BEFORE ITS TIME."

***

The roads get better as we go along. Roads and houses both. Neighborhoods cleaner, newer, brighter –

"Hoplite parTEEE!" I go slapping my thigh, "entering West Zone!"

"Sheeat," John sticking a claw in his crotch, "kid's a fuckin' genius."

Letterboxes drift past: designer boxes bonneted with wildflowers. And white picket fences sharpened to knife-point (bits of impaled slum-flesh still aquiver). And lawns of genetically enhanced sumac, levelled with gator-bone scythes. And oil of olay swimpools silver-blue, distant glimpse of albinos on deck-chairs sipping highballs –

"Low pigment neighborhood," I go twitching, "like, below ONE on the Melanin Index."

"Uh-huh," John, "high on the DAWG Index though. Hear 'em bark."

I nod. "I hear 'em. Nigger-killin' pitbulls. Spic-chomp dobermans. Gobble-gook German Shepherds."

John cackle. "Your kinda hood, boy. Mocha Mowgli feel right at home."

I grin. "About as much as a choirboy playin' chickenhead for his Churchpaw."

"HARF!" John, "yowp."

The road rise, bank leftward. Trees now on either side, hills showing ahead in silhouette: flank of a sleeping saurian.

"Ten minutes to Monk's," John announce, "ten and counting."

I frown. "Ten? Shit. You shoulda taken the highway."

John flash me a scowl. "Highway my ass. This here's a shortcut."

"Yeah right. Shortcut to the shithouse. Someone hit the flush – "

I blink. Turn. He's up again, Wald. Propped on an elbow, grinning.

"Ass," he croaks, "shit. Flush. Heh heh."

A trifle woozy, Wald, but good to go.

"The Wald officially sentient," I announce, "awake and up for business."

John glance back with a smirk. "How dat throat o' yours little boy."

"Deep throat," Wald, "heh heh."

The road dip and crest, beams hitting a signboard ahead: SUNSET COVE. Past it a lone road cutting out to the hills.

I clap. Raise a fist. "Yea verily. I'se knows wheres we's are's nows."

"Bitch get smarter everyday," John forking left onto the road.

"Bitch day," Wald, "heh heh."

John shift gear, hit the pedal. Vrroom. The car in smooth surge glomming the strip.

I sit back with a sigh, night wind in cold shear. Cobbled driveways zip past, lights in fleeting shimmer. Glimpse of croquet lawns, pools large enough for mastodons. Sinanthropoid mahouts on guard, gaily bedecked crones sipping absinthe under adobe parasols. *Ethel dear, can you spell GNU?* –

I shut my eyes: windroar dark. My thoughts collapsing to a pixel, then exploding soundless: nova.

The car slows spasmodic, banks right. Crunch of tyres on gravel: stop.

I exhale with a shudder, open my eyes. Monk's driveway looms: the hacienda ahead in full colour. At right, the front yard lined with spotlights: astroturf, fake origami flowerbeds in fulgent overkill.

I don't see him at first. But then he appears in sudden relief: Monk posed in the middle of the yard, standing with arms raised, head cocked in bogus crucifixion.

"Sheeat," John, "whut in HALE?"

I chuckle. "Some kinda protest. Us being late and all."

"Protesticle," Wald, "heh heh."

We sit and watch. Monk motionless in fiery raiment: wine-red moccasins, saffron singlet, ochre capuche. Monk martyred at the crossbeam nexus, eyelenses agleam, beard flaming gold.

"Well suck m'dick and scream," goes John vaulting out, "let's go get 'im."

I grunt. Vault out likewise. Wald in turn making the attempt but collapsing aground, John in high mirth going: "HARF! Haaa-HARF! – "

I start across, moving rapid. John in tow, Wald hobbling after.

"Monk," I go sidling up, "ooooOOP! BRRrrMM! Monk?"

No response. Monk speechless, rigored illuminate.

John step up with a scowl. "Muthafucka, whut you up to?"

Nothing. Monk in durance vile, eyes cancelled by lens-shine.

"Well sheeat," John, "dig it."

"Huh?" me, "wha?"

"Blood. Fucker's bleeding."

I frown. "Bleed, you say?"

John reach. Slap my skull. "His HANDS, bee-YATCH. You fuckin' BLIND now?"

I blink. And see. Monk a-bleed sure enough. Middle of his left palm. And his right. Sacral wounds in slow drip.

"Well damn," I go, "I didn't even notice."

John snort. "You wouldn't notice a big screen dick pissin' MILK."

I chuckle. "Or a zoom-lens asshole shittin' buckwheat."

"HARF!" John, "yowp."

"Bigshit pissmilk buckhole zoomdick," Wald over my shoulder, "heh heh."

I cough, clear my throat. "That REAL blood he's leakin'?"

John curse. "Ain't yo' pappy's TAMPON juice."

I nod sage. "Uh-huh. Shoulda known. Monk's do-it-yourself Stigmata Kit. From Acme."

John crack a knuckle. Two knuckles.

"Monk," he go, "Monk son, listen up. You don't start movin' in a hurry, I'm gon' whup you bloody. Bloodier'n you are now – "

I hold up a hand palm out, like Marlow on the Nellie:

"Ixnay. No whupping this night. This be a sacrificial offering, you see. Blood and ouns. Flesh transfigured by the Meister's Notion. Transmogrified. Transubstantiate. Other alchemical verbs starting with 't'."

"Blood-ass flesh-whup," Wald, "heh heh."

I turn. Wald on tippy toe, hashing his nuts. Big grin.

"Any ideas Wald?" I ask.

The Wald nod vigorous. Then he squeeze past me and John. Stand at attention facing Monk.

"Sheeat," John, "this oughtta be good for somethin'."

The Wald scrunch up his mug, put out a seal-yawp. Then he proceed to tap Monk's lenses with a forefinger. And stick a pinkie up his nose. And stroke his beard. And pinch his upper lip. And scratch his throat. And head-butt his sternum. And slap his celibate crotch.

A pause ensue, but not for long. The Wald reach up, pull in Monk's arms by the sleeves and lick the blood off each palm: first the left, then the right.

"And I thought I'd seen it all," John.

"YeeEEEEP!" Wald hopping aside, "heh heh."

I swallow an air bubble. Burp through my teeth. "Monk? How NOW Monk?"

Monk stir. Drop his arms. His capuche falls back, hair spilling gold.

"Monk," I go, "brm! ZooOOOPF! Monk?"

Monk turn some, his eyes coming into view: arctic winter. Freezing mist.

"You bastards took your time," he pronounce.

John make a whinnying sound. "WE took our time. WE."

Monk run three fingers through his beard. Purse his lips.

"Ah, Trotjohn. Brother John Trotville in the flesh."

John thrust up a hand, thumb and forefinger spanned rigid.

"Bitch, I'm THIS close to rippin' your face off with my TEETH. Dig?"

Monk blink. "Oh quite. Touch of choler. Hint of spleen. Sturm in the heart of drang, Mars being ascendant."

John turn slit-eyed. "Bitch be talkin' funny."

I snicker. "As always."

"Funny bitch," Wald kneading his erectile, "heh heh."

Monk sigh. Turn. Start walking. "Please to follow, idiot children. Follow, please."

Myself clicking my heels, putting out a yelp and starting after, John with a curse falling in behind, Wald waddling up last. Us four, we four crossing the yard single file by your leave now, debauched lecteur, Monk's robes before me undulant, light catching in its folds like fire: him like some old time bhikku discalced, in weary retreat from all the world's burning.

***

We troop out across the yard, up the driveway and around the flank of the house. Darker there, me wondering: *where to? where?* The old Rust'n'Wreck I hope. Monk's little rust garden out back: twisted machine innards on tamped sawdust and mashed dung, ringed with phallic cast-iron menhirs –

"Say now, Monk," I go, "you plan to have us do this on the old Rust'n'Wreck?"

"No," Monk, not turning, "inside. New room I think you'll like."

He lead us halfway up the side of the house, then stop abrupt.

"Here," he goes, "enter here."

"Sheeat," John stepping around, "you mean bust oane through the wall?"

Monk cough. Clear his throat. "*Primum mobile ego autem.*"

"Huh?" John, "say wha?"

"*Primum mobile,*" Monk once more, "*ego autem.*"

Pause. John muttering bilious, me going: "Monk kid, wha – "

"*PRIMUM MOBILE EGO AUTEM!*"

Monk's shriek in echo-cho-o. A moment's silence. Then a hum: the wall moving. A section of it rising like an eyelid: yellow light within.

"Concealed garage door," offers Monk, "voice operated."

"Well I will be hawg humped and hung out to dry," John, "sheeee-it."

"Dry hump," Wald, "hung like a hawg. Heh heh."

Monk sniff. Step forward. Duck in. John moving after, with Wald in tow, your sweetgum sugardaddy easing in last.

"Dang," John looking around, "this here's one bigass garage."

I nod, blinking. "Big is right. Big enough for a barge."

"Big enough for a coupla eighteen-wheelers, is what."

"Uh-huh. Plus a *Gutenjahre* blimp."

"Bigass blimp," Wald, "heh heh."

I glance around in rapid scan. Stuff scattered, hung all over in random bricolage. Appalachian critter-kill devices. Catechistic torture implements. Stucco Iron Maiden with gator teeth for spikes. The Satanic Commandments etched in blood on a wall plaque (*Thou Shalt Kill, Thou Shalt Commit Adultery...* and on). In one corner a crude waxwork, depicting the Death by Water. Beside it an embalmed Norwegian, harpooned face up on a hobby horse. No vehicles in evidence, far as I can tell, save perhaps those camouflaged by Monk's customized cloaking device –

"Where's the old ping pong table now Monk," I ask, "hey?"

"GONE baby!" John bent bowlegged, gouging an anal prurit, "LONG gone. Ol' Ping fucked and killed Pong, burned part of him and ate the rest. Dang cannibal Chy-nee."

Pause. Monk staring.

"Ugly mama," goes Wald all of a sudden, "ugly."

"Huh?" John straightening, "whut now?"

The Wald point. Giggle. "Ugly mama."

I turn, following his finger, his crushed thumb. Out to semidarkness, far end of the garage. A figure seated there in vague outline. Beneath a ragged baldachin.

"Well now cap'n," I go, "sensors indicate life form. Question is: WHO?"

Monk cough. "No one of interest. Just grandma."

"Grandmaw?" John with a head-jerk, "GRANDMAW?"

Monk turn, give John a look. Clinical. An entomologist studying a rare insect.

"We must proceed," he goes, "with haste."

John smirk. Dig out his pocket flash. Click.

"Gwammaw," he husks moving, "gwammy gwammaw – "

"Wrong way," Monk, "WRONG way – "

John marching on, undeterred.

I watch a moment, hesitant. Then I shrug, start after. "Wait up now hon'. Wait for MEEE – "

Wald skipping up, going "Mama. Ugly. Heh heh."

We approach rapid, John mutter and groan, beam wavering. Close. Closer. Stop. Monk's wizened grandmater now in full view, enthroned ahead. In a wheelchair. Under a ragged burlap baldachin fixed to a post. Old dowager motionless, in semblance of some hoary icon –

"Gwammy," sighs John, "gwammammammy – "

His beam on the move, mapping the crone. Dwelling worshipful on the snow hair tussocked. On the parchment brow. The nested eyes. The hooked beak. The fluted cheeks. The hirsute chin (pink wart in full sprout). The wasted frame swaddled black, gnarled claws resting parallel –

"Awww mama," John's voice cracking, "aw FREAKY mama!"

Echo. Silence in yellow gloom. Freaky mama unmoved.

"No heat there TJ," I go, "she don't look alive to me."

John make a choking sound. "Awww MAAAN! Don't SAY that! don't – "

"Oh she's alive all right. No fear."

I turn: Monk at ease, five paces off.

"Didn't hear you come up," I go.

"Didn't hear you not hearing me come up," Monk.

"She be in deep mortis," me.

"Alive and well," Monk.

"She don't move," me.

"Strapped and bound," Monk.

I frown. Turn. The old bat's strapped down all right. Gyved tight to her chair, tighter than Murphy to his.

"She speak not," I go.

"Gagged," Monk.

John's beam move. Zero in on the beldam's kisser.

"Something stuck in her maw," I go.

"Shaved pine cone," Monk, "a pacifier."

"PACifier," John with a snort, "ain't she pacified enough?"

"Negative," Monk, "she poses a threat. Will bite testicles off through clothing."

John put out a yelp of delight. Tilt his head indulgent. "Awww, mah honey. Mah MEAN little VICIOUS HONEY."

"Testicle honey bite," Wald, "heh heh."

I click my tongue. Suck spit. "She look like one them ol' prayer wheel Tye-betans. Schlongdong Rin-po-chay."

"Har!" John, "HARF!"

"Schlong wheel," Wald, "heh heh."

Monk sniff. "Most amusing, yes. However, I suggest we leave her be and proceed. Time being of the essence."

I nod. "Being and time, in-der-welt-sein, hot essence up my cold spine – "

John move up sudden. Train the beam full on the bat's mug. "No," Monk, "don't."

John move up another step and pause: his foot propped on the rim of the crone's chair wheel.

"I ain't gon' HURT her any, Monk boy. Just PLAY with her some. Dig?"

"Play," Monk, "PLAY."

John cackle. And begin playing. With his free hand tickling her chin. Diddling her dewlap. Zinging her wart. Worming her nares. With cartographic zeal tracing the veins on her brow. With puckered lips blowing in her ear. With quivering tongue-tip circling her sye-sockets. With kitten paws cuffing the chalk skull, mussing her clumped hair. Through it all, the old lass silent. Unmoved.

"Aww honey," sighs John straightening, "if I didn't KNOW better, I'd think I wudn't turnin' you OANE!"

Monk cough. Take a step. "You're pushing it there, old son. You are. Pushing it."

John turn, grinning fiendish: beam flaring out red from under his chin.

"Awww, he's jealous. Monkboy's JEALOUS. But we ain't gon' let him do it, NOOOO we're not. We ain't gon' let him shit up our SHINdig now, ARE we – "

Looking away John and bending, mouth in obscene moue. Up close, his lips an inch from her glutted maw, myself thinking: *here we go, here it come, him corking out the pinecone, invading the edentule –*

But it don't happen, no. Him drawing back at the last instant, straightening with a snarl going: "No free show for CANDYasses. Pussywhips PAY to watch Trotjohn get DOWN."

Pause. Creak of skullplate. Squish of guts in tumult.

"Well that's all right then," Monk, his voice even, "we may without further ado proceed."

"Seed," Wald, "candy puss. Heh heh."

John cackle, click off his flash. "ProCEED you say? Well sheeat. Why didn'tcha SAY so beFORE."

***

We quarter across the garage single file, Monk in lead. Past the Death by Water, the gator Maiden, some techno-corp Boss Hog hung crotch-up in tropical effigy (dig them pineapple nads, parrot-beak dong), on to the door in the far corner, Monk pushing through with an elbow and both feet, hand raised in a mudra of benediction.

Through into a vestibule: a windowless chamber yielding to a passageway. This here chamber alight: a flamingo lamp in one corner, pink feathers aglow. The walls wainscoted, the floor carpeted matte black and *Louis Quinze* green. Images on one wall, Monk's forebears framed in daguerrotype: paleface farts in top hat, monocle and cravat. Triumphant white hunters skinning dead Bengals. Bearded tycoons signing deeds for plantation and diamond mine, darkies in mute assembly. Stern clerics on the *Mission Civilisatrice*, shouldering their end of the Burden –

"Dig it," John with a nod, "bigass bowl."

"Ass dig," Wald, "heh heh."

I turn. A large emerald pot shows in the corner, handles shaped like ears.

"Art nouveau scatologue?" I ask, pointing.

"No," Monk, "chamber pot."

"Huh?" John, "chamber?"

I chuckle. "The kind them old timers used to shit in. About once every month."

"Shit chamber," Wald, "heh heh."

I move, heading towards the pot. The air ripen as I approach: intimations of raw dung. I pinch my nose shut, step up, peep over the rim. I figure it be empty, but no. An ink-black floccule sit at the bottom. A floccule sentient, quivering.

I draw back with a curse. Beat a hasty retreat.

"Somethin' in there, brothers. Live and stinkin'."

"Harf!" John, "sheeat."

"Indeed," Monk, "possibly a turdlet. Lone turdlet in bitter divorce from its fellows."

I frown. "You mean it's still in USE?"

Monk nod rueful. "Use, yes. The Pater's weekly dejection."

"Pater?" John brightening, "your old man's CROCKPOT?"

"Yeeh!" Wald breaking into a jig, "YEEH!"

Monk stare. Shake his head. "*Monstres gais*. The apes of god are mirthful."

I raise a hand solemn. "Cease and desist now, fellas. The Monk is not amused. We offend his pride. This here pot be much more than a receptacle for geezer guano, pater poop, daddy dung. It be a FAMILY HEIRLOOM. Monk's folks been shittin' in it for generations. What we got here's an ARCHIVE, a storehouse of FECAL GENEALOGY. Turds going back to Plymouth Rock, and farther still: a long line of sun-blackened floaters concatenate, touching the shores of the Old World – "

John stomping the floor: "HARF! HARF! – "

Wald doing the frog hop: "YEEH! – "

Monk looking on disdainful.

I let it work a moment. Then I raise a foot, clap twice:

"Enough. Vamanos now compadres, we best move on in a hurry."

"Wise counsel," Monk starting into the passage, "onward lest through decerebrate dalliance we engender a new dunciad – "

Moving once more: us four, we four, single file as always with Monk up front, Wald in caboose yelping rhythmic, myself with head bowed watching my footsnouts in binary concert draw me on.

***

It's sort of a maze we find ourselves in: the passageway turning at strange angles, walls panelled in gauntlet. Us moving single file by choice and custom, eyes downcast, buttocks rallying in support of damp recti. Pucker-lip bulbs drifting above, the carpet green-black –

"Huh?" I go, "what now?"

John curse. "LAByrinth I said. This here's a fuckin' LAByrinth. Where you takin' us, Monk bitch. Ay?"

"The LIGHT," intones Monk, "at tunnel's ENNND. Is your OWNNN. Immortal SOULLLLLLLL – "

"Sheeat. I'm gon' tunnel up your mortal ASShole, we don't get out in a hurry."

"Eagerly anticipated," Monk.

The corridor take a sharp right. An arabesque left. Broaden into an alcove.

"WHOA!" John stopping short, "whoa HO! – "

Myself fetching up with a gasp, Wald bumping my rump: "HeeEEP!"

Monk walk on a few steps. Stop. Turn.

"It's only a door," he goes weary, "just a door."

I stare. "Door HELL. More like a GATEWAY to the sultan's drag queen BOUDOIR."

"You exaggerate," Monk, "egg."

I don't respond. Can't. I'm too busy taking it in: this huge trefoil arch door at right. A door built in sections big enough to screen mammoths fleeing the intergalactic quasar police, churning pachyderm angel dust off the crab nebula (answer: MU!). But it's not just a door (no such luck). It's also a mural. A four-panel mural painted lurid with an atrophied limb (in thought, a midget artist trapezed in harness, his high-domed skull dripping brain-fluid through a trephinate wound as he spit, sneeze and vomit colours on bare wood) –

"Aww MAN!" John starting to cackle, "get a LOAD of this groovy sheeat. Get a LOAD!"

I get. With eyes wide, nares flared, nads in spasm. This doorfront tableau, pathic easel-geek's rendition of a brimstone saturnale. At left, misshapen corybants gorging, bleeding, hurling, defecating, fucking, amid decapitate corpses spouting gore-wine, distended recti gouting shit-syrup, priaps pissing bladder-sherbet. At right, corpulent slatterns drooling vulvate by firelight, lycanthropic trolls wolfing viscera, boarhead satyrs swinging hammer-schlongs, jizzing yellow gleet to the skies.

Seconds pass. Minutes. Us looking on wordless, sucking gristle through stained teeth. At length, John with a sigh, going:

"Hot-DAMN! Now THAT'S a picture you can take home to MAMA."

"Got THAT right," I go wiping spit off my chin, "a scene of mmMBRRRR! A scene of barbarous and ithyphallic splendor."

"YeeEEP!" Wald on the hop, "mmMRRHAP!"

John cackle. Turn. "What's behind the door now Monk. Ay?"

Monk look away, caressing his beard. "My pater's boudoir. His hallowed sanctum. Think not to enter, ye of negligible worth. Perish the thought at inception."

"The pox oane THAT," John, "your old man in? Whore?"

Monk look down, studying his palm. "I am not privy. Sad to say."

John curse. Step up. Press his ear to the door. His head now framed in crural chevron, i.e. compassed by a slattern's painted thigh-spread.

"Sound like a fuckin' HAWG farm in there."

I sidle up, press ear to wood. Bark of robot voice. Hog squeal.

"Pater in his virtual porcine barnyard," offers Monk, "not unusual."

John snicker. "Sure sound like it. Papa bangin' a hawg hip-deep in slop."

"Nope," me, "more like: pronging a prize sow, face down in offal, cybernetic hoghead presiding."

"Pigface prong," Wald, "heh heh."

Monk turn, in ochre waft receding.

"WHOA now!" John, "hold up there Jack. HO! – "

We move on. Through the maze in step, humming soft and toneless. The passage zigging some, zagging some more, then straightening sudden.

"Well shit," I go, looking past Monk's shoulder, "this here's a dead end. A *cul de sac*. A sack of friggin' culos."

Monk sniff. Keep walking. "Faith alone shall dispel the cloud of unknowing."

"Not with Savonarola in lead," me, "Quasimodo bringing up the rear."

"Up," Wald, "rear. Heh heh."

Monk march on resolute, us in tow. The floor-shag ahead patterned convolute, stretching out to Mandelbrot's fractal kingdom.

Ten feet from corridor's end, John curse, step out of line.

"Hell with THIS. Fucker gon' walk through the wall, leave us holdin' his dick."

"Dickwalk," Wald hopping aside, "hellfuck. Heh heh."

Monk slow, scrape to a stop. Him now three feet from the end, head bowed, fists clenched.

"What next, genius?" John, "dead-end clusterfuck?"

Monk cough. Clear his throat. "Barracuda lumbago."

"Huh?" John, "Barry who?"

"BARRACUDA LUMBAGO!" Monk, arms lancing up in vertical thrust.

"Yeeow!" me grimacing, "ouch."

"Tear the fucker's beard off," John.

A hum fill the air, hum shading to a whine. Ahead, a wall panel rising off the floor like a portcullis: sound of water, shimmer blue.

"Follow," commands Monk, ducking through.

I don't move. Myself spraggle-legged, thumbs rigid, dread like a sick crab on the floor of my skull.

"Get a move oane, beeyatch," John, giving me a shove.

I stagger forward, stumble through. John in right after, dragging Wald.

"Lo and behold," Monk, "The Lotus Chamber."

I gasp, my eyes going wide.

"Goddamn papa SHIT-Moses," John, "DANG!"

Wald on his knees whimpering.

"Observe and appreciate," Monk, "but please to avoid paroxysm and apoplexy."

I squeeze my eyes shut. Count to the square root of two. Open. Still there, the vista. An enormous igloo with a low dome, blue bead lights inset by the thousand. Some stuff far across I can't quite see, forms in vague aperçu, but I'm not looking. It's the object in the middle I can't get my eyes off. The fountain. A blue-white lotus fountain, luminous: the lotus moulded in white marble, a blue font rising high, branching in groovy watersound, light reflected in spectral shimmer.

I watch silent awhile. Watch and listen. Then I feel it: words forming glutinous in my throat, squeezing past my uvula, blooming on my mongrel tongue.

"Blue spit foam," I go, "blue spit foam jizz Xanadu dream.

Serpent tattoo kundalini Queequeg whalespout sperm geyser Coleridge ambergris."

Monk sniff. "Bon mots galore. His *sprachgefühl*."

"Cain't be real," John, voice gone small, "cain't be."

Wald still in a crouch, whimpering.

"It's real all right," Monk, "real as the polyp that went pop."

I shake my head. Exhale slow and long.

"It's the sheer scope of it that bewilders, brother Monk. That gasts the old flabber. I mean this here's one BIGASS igloo. Big enough for pork-fed amazons. For scrimmaging neanderthals."

Monk cock an eyebrow. "Indeed. Their shouts resound."

"And weep the hungry stones," me.

"Plaudits for the pundit," Monk.

The Wald gibber, John, with a harrumph, going:

"Yeah well. Fine. Question is: what next."

Monk turn, lenses washing blue.

"I'll tell you what next: we doff our vestments, encircle the Lotus in ritual sederunt, invoke the Meister's Notion to preface our imminent Bull Run."

John scowl. "You keep talkin' like that bitch, I'm gon' get NASTY."

Monk stare. "Quite. Decorticate neanderthal sees red."

John take a step, brow darkening: "I'm gon' RED your – "

"What he MEAN, friar," I go placating, "what the Monk MEAN is: we got to strip down, sit around that there Lotus, trip out on the Notion and rack our gonads for the Run."

John stand still a moment, glaring. Then he snort, shake his head. "Well shit a brick and squeal. I shoulda known."

"Brick-shit trip-out," Wald still on all fours, "heh heh."

John look down, stick a boot in Wald's rump.

"Ass up, doughboy. We's got to get NAKKED."

The Wald raise his forepaws, brightening.

"Nakked? Noodie nakked?"

"That's right," me, "prick in the breeze, butt blowin' after."

Monk cough. Raise his arms overhead.

"KATZ!" he bark, kicking off his moccasins, "KAAATZ! – "

His robe dropping like a veil, like a narcoleptic eyelid, like a virgin's camisole. Monk standing raw-boned, in blue albus.

"GodDAMN!" John, "bitch been practicin'."

Monk lower his arms. Turn. "You next, sachem."

John curse, start to strip, Wald with a gurgle following suit.

I hiccup, my lashes in rapid flutter. Scenes quake across my mind's eye, old time jungle scenes. Dealated birds with fused beaks shitting yellow. Blind wildebeest discovering a new continent. Snoutless aardwolves pissing on dead springboks –

I turn, images dissolving in font-water sibilance. Done? Yayup. Their accoutrements arrayed neat on the floor. Monk's capuched singlet and rawsilk moccasins, his fishnet brassiere, his g-string sans 'g'. John's jodhpurs and turtleneck, his enamel groin cup, his scented bullet-proof socks, his boots, his wrist-blade, his death's head medallion.

I study the wrist-blade a moment: broad velcro straps, ivory casing with steel-tip at one end. Designed and assembled in Angkor by lobotomized chindits still fighting imperial nips in a slave-labor time warp, courtesy *Dupont*. Wald's shirt and shorts folded beside, along with his split-crotch bubble-plastic diapers, his shitkicker thugboots, his gunk-wet rectal beads, his bowtie perched atop like a moth on guard.

I nod satisfied, look up smiling. John, Monk, Wald, buck-naked, heading for the Lotus. Monk ascetic, skeletal. John muscled, lupine. Wald cherubic, adipose. In that order, respectively: ecto, meso, endo morphed in blue lambence, three ghouls culled from hadal depths –

"HEY!"

I start. Stop. Start. John looking back in anger.

"YOU DONE GREASIN' YOUR GOOSENECK MOCHABOY?"

His words in tunnel echo watersound.

"ALARUMS!" I yell, "T-5 TO SLUMGULLION! – "

Clapping a palm to my cheek (cheek-by-jowl), with eager hands starting to undress.

***

They're seated and ready when I get there wind-girt, sky-clad, swinging-dick. Monk, John, Wald, ass down on black zafu cushions placed equidistant around the Lotus. Wald slouched hemorrhoidal *comme d'habitude*, John and Monk ramrod in perfect lotus: no surprise. Monk having been an ace yogi in his time (bubblegum league). John, no yogi, just a sweet-stretch natural, limber as a jellybone chimp, pull poses you wouldn't believe. Like that time at his ranch-house, Riotfest Roguefuck, John on the floor, legs stretched way back, head between his knees, blowing himself in closed circuit yelling: *I AIN'T SHARIN' MAH MEAT WITH NOBODY –*

"Huh?" me, "what now?"

"Your seat, prithee sirrah," Monk pointing.

I nod, step sideways, lower croupe to zafu. Then proceed to fold my legs in *Siddhasana*, the Posture of Attainment. How? As follows: 1. Press left heel to perineum (that mossy region spanning nad and bunghole). 2. Place right heel over left, pecker sandwiched between. 3. Place hands on knees palm up, fingers in mudra. This here Posture to be avoided by the novice on pain of pecker-death, nad-atrophy and a long stint as guardsman to the sultan's seraglio –

"YES?"

I blink. Look up. Monk gimlet-eyed, staring.

"All set," I go, nodding with both heads, "that's 'set' with an 's' as in 'hernia'."

John curse. "Someone yank his nuts off."

"Nut set," Wald, "heh heh."

I look around, expectant. Our four-man lotus sederunt now in full effect. Monk and I facing off on the ordinate, John and Wald on the abscissa, the Lotus dead-centre, coordinate origin.

"Monk," I go, tongue on the flap, "Monk?"

No response. Monk gone rigid, eyes glassy, visage bisected by the stem of the font.

"MMMBRRAAP!" I go, working a Daruma Zen Shout.

Monk blink. Tweak his nose. And begin: through parted lips a chant, his voice reedy, adenoidal.

I listen. First with one eye, then the other. Wondering: *what language that? Can't make it out. Mayhap not a human tongue at all. Perhaps Enochian, language of the archangels. Monk know Enochian, having learnt it via subtle transmission through Pranic ether, through layered morphogenetic fields vibrating at the Sheldrake peristaltic constant across the Great Vajra-Shakti Sambhogakaya Spectrum —*

Pause. Monk gone silent, hand raised. A pause pregnant if not explicitly gravid, me thinking: *smeg patooty, now what?*

"Brofth!" barks Monk sans preamble, "ding brob shun sput glick harf drub kepf schwing TRRooOOK! Shaka nslem yotz. GOLEM?"

I blink thrice. Draw a cured hangnail across my brow: blood welling sweet along that dermal line (an't please the Most High).

"Drub!" Monk, "kopf! ZZooOOMP?"

I look down. Nod. Yes indeedy. There it be, sure enough. Beside my right knee: a black varnished bowl, shape of a brine-stiff yarmulke. In it a pair of pills blue and red, pills I recognize by way of back-brain atavism: Blue Soma, Redburn.

"BrrOOF!" exhorts Monk, "Tremp! Grock! Schlum! HabRAPH!"

"Huh?" me, "say again?"

"BrrOOF!" Monk with a scowl, "habRAPH!"

I sigh acquiescent. Reach with my right hand. Forcep the red pill. Place it prayerful on my flayed, gunk-battened tongue.

Fzzz, goes the pill dissolving, fzzzz.

I savor the feel, recalling the old days: us naked on the compost heap at Trotjohn's, popping glitterpills, bliss-buttons, alpha hallucines, smash swedenborgs, fakir mushrooms, silver shamans, brujo bon bons –

I wince. Sharp pain, top of my skull. Redburn kicking in: CRACK. Sound like a snapping twig, my head coming apart in blood-red globules, thoughts like firebirds around an eclipsed sun. I scream, riding the crest of a gravity wave, shooting lepto quarks off a cyclotron sling –

"FLUMPFDAT!" Monk's voice booming, "HUNDRAPHAT!"

I gasp, come to panting. Lactating. *Whelp? Yes and no.* My vision now tinctured red. The Lotus, the font shining pink and violet.

I laugh aloud, a strange sound: plaint of a querulous mule. *Redburn fuck up them vocal chords, like fartwarm helium –*

"You guys look weird" I go, my voice distant, in metallic echo.

No response. Monk, John, Wald gone Reticulan: panoptic eyes, vestigial noses, absent ears, slit mouths, chins shaped like nipples. Monk seated impassive. John with a twisted grin. Wald rocking back and forth, a simpering neonate.

I shut my left eye, focus with my right. *Micro-vision. Fine droplets wafting off the font. See the pores on Monk's brow (hundred and eight and counting). His nosehairs sad and nameless (eighty nine give or take, mostly give). The long starched filaments of his eyelashes (fucker shoulda been a girl). The adamantine crud-nuggets lodged in his canthi (twenty three at last count) –*

I turn wide-eyed. Smile. I can see them now. The objects off at the far end. A low table shaped like a Mobius Strip. Three snake-head recliners with forked seats, fanged armrests. A pair of bookshelves rising in double helix, tomes slotted in, some titles I recognize:

Demon Love: A Primer. Papal Incubus. The Coprophage Cookbook. 120 Days of Sodom. Snowdrops from a Curate's Garden. Apocalypsis Revelata. And others. Texts wayward and arcane, arward and waycane. Me with a lump in my throat, my crotch thinking: *ah brother Monk, thou critter of selcouth enthusiasms, passions recherché, outré, mantaray –*

"HEEG!"

I start.

"HEEG!"

I turn, nod. Monk working a Tibetan Pho-Wa, bellowing at just the right pitch, three second intervals.

"HEEG! HEEG! – "

I wince, feeling the pressure build. Hate's purest distillate in my skull coalescing.

"HEEG! HEEG! HEEG! – "

I groan, grit my teeth. Wald at right with fists bunched, shuddering in fantod. At left John rigid in durance vile –

"HEEG!" Monk pitiless, "HEEG! – "

I moan aloud, cranial pressure now in mega-unit pascal.

"HEEG! HEEG! HEEG! – "

Ow. Yow. Something got to give. Now. Gib. Daw. Mac. Shit. Whip. Smut –

I shriek open-mouthed, my pate giving way. A shift in ossature, my fontanelle in bloom: HATE spouting bloody from the crown of my skull, the crown of John's skull, Monk's skull, Wald's skull, four identical arcs rising, merging high above the font, a dark blood-ball coalesced there, raining ichor, Lotus petals writhing, smoking (reek of coal-tar and cooked flesh) –

"HOOM!" Monk switching seed-mantras, "HOOM! HOOM! – "

I sigh. Shut my eyes.

"HOOM! HOOM! – "

Coolness. Skull facets creaking into place. My fontanelle sealed, Hate discharged in sacrifice.

"HOOMMMM! – "

Silence. Monk's seed mantra in echo. My lids now rising in slow dance, pupils farting trapped optic wind. Status? The redness gone, but my comrades unchanged. Them still Reticulan, orbs unblinking.

"You bastards still look like shit," I croak, "fuckin' bighead scuttlebugs."

John cock his head, laugh: strange sound. Equine amphibian whinnying in a submerged tanker. Horsehead walrus announcing a blubberfuck –

"Brothers!" cries Monk, his voice aquake, "Brrmf! Bhrath! Pffutt! Snippletrip! Hnngaackh! Hrrotlarph! Tropdwickdwick! MUTTON?"

I frown. Shake my head. *Nope. Don't think so. Not yet. Not just yet –*

"HRRAFTH!" Monk, "MMRABRAFTH! SMMYEEBL! SNIPPLETRIP! TROPDWICKDWICK! – "

I sigh. Grasp the blue pill with chicken finger and ape thumb. Open wide. Stash the pill under my slug tongue. *Fizzzzz? Nope. Of course not. Blue Soma don't fizz. It deliquesce noiseless into the bloodstream, seeping blue mist. Can't even feel it kick –*

I blink. Look down. Yayup. Doc Peckerwang gone to a blue

87

throb. In full salute. *Sieg heil to you too, putz. Look what Santa brought ya. Too big for THAT stocking* –

Hhssshhh. I frown, look up. A blue wave in approach. Tidal. Close. Closer. Whhoooshhh*: mama take me DOWN* –

I shut my eyes. Inhale deep. Open. Blue everywhere, deep blue. Like being underwater, way down, minus the high pressure skull crush, the bliss of drowning, depth charge mangling your nuts –

I blink. Vibration somewhere. A thrum. Stethoscoped wombsound drawing near –

BOOM. I recoil, a thunderclap sounding overhead: white foam, blue bubbles. And a squid. A giant squid showing above in a morass of testicles. No, tentacles. And beside the squid, a whale: a white cetacean with clouded eye, no mouth. Squid and whale poised face-to-face, unmoving.

They float there in timeless suspension, squid and whale, Monk's voice rising again in chant. Some kind of neo-pagan Norse paean by the sound of it: gore, booze and jizz in the mead halls of Valhalla, Odin clubbing a pachyderm with heavy glan beef –

"UMLAUT!" shrieks Monk sudden, "ÜBER UMLAAUT! – "

The whale lunging in response, slamming headlong into the squid's belly, the squid flinching but holding its own, tentacles closing around the whalehead like labia, the two thrashing now in mergence, their motions clouded by ambergris and squid ink –

"DURRBARRR!" roars Monk, "VOON DURRBARRRR! – "

Us yielding convulsive: Monk, John, Wald and moi, toppling back simultaneous, continence relinquished, our jizz-spurts up like signal flares in vesper twilight, four blazing sperm-comets rising and uniting brilliant above the Lotus to form a pearl, a spunk-pearl going nova, then fading gradual in descent, us on our backs watching it fall, Blue Soma deserting us now in waves, myself with head turned, watching my comrades revert: Reticulan to Retihuman to homiculan to human to demon: three mutants demorphed, repristinate.

Silence. Tumult in echo. Us motionless, supine.

"Well?" I go, breaking the silence, "WELL?"

No response. Monk, John, Wald, belly-up, unmoving.

I curse, struggle upright, my head still abuzz.

"You putz-heads gonna lay there all night?"

John mutter. Turn on his side. Push himself up.

"Bitch don't ever quit bitchin'."

"Yeh!" Wald, working a heel into his crotch, "night bitch."

Monk sitting up silent, lenses agleam. Before us, the Lotus auto-fulgent as before, font in soft hiss.

"Some ride," goes John using words, speaking his language with wolf tongue.

"Cum ride," Wald on his back, boner trapped between his heels, "heh heh."

Monk nods grave, beard in hand. "Oneiric delirium tremens in excelsis, yes. Mysterium tremendum et fascinans, yes. Mens sana in corpore sano, yes – "

Or some such, I'm not sure. I'm no longer listening. Myself with eyes half-shut, watching some freaky shit go down: my nether *ursprung* quaking at Richter Nine, with the Notion on my brow coruscant, chakra wheels sparking down the length of my spine helixed blue-red, a scene groovier than the Borealis or Elmo's fartfire, your wisdom daddy a-grin thinking: *with a view like this, with a fulgurant spinning chakrarama like this who needs the sun, the moon, the stars, stripes, Agent Orange or even Spanish Fly, on the Fourth of friggin July –*

***

PART TWO

HOMAGE

We take the same way out. Back through the maze, panelled corridors angled weird. Monk fore, myself aft, John and Wald between. Us marching as before, switching modes at my command. "HAARRKH!": marching pigeon-toe, feet pointing in. "HULPF!": on duckfeet, toes pointing out. "HAARRKH!", ten steps pigeon-toe, "HULPF!", ten steps duckfeet, alternating in rhythmic progression as is our wont, our penance and predilection. With my thoughts drifting regressive in slow time, conjuring the slagheaps and scumbogs of *auld lang*.

Recalling the walkathons we used to pull back in the old days, weeping the ozymandian dream tears of fallen heresiarchs. Like that time at John's ranch, late fall in eighteenth brumaire, year Three-BRrrRRP!, us four in stately procession at dusk around roadkill scraped off warm tarmac, this bust-gut possum we'd squeezed into a carboy half-full of Schlock Creek moonshine, us circling it watchful at constant radius, naked, with soup cans strapped to our flayed skulls, our nostrils plugged with neap mud, nipples pegged, Monk swinging a crockpot censer and droning excerpts from the Reichstag Necronomicon, four devout and tormented acolytes marching ten step pigeon-toe, ten step duckfoot, plus three marsupial hops and a pirouette with controlled shriek, this pattern repeated ceaseless through the night, through the small hours, the big hours, the biggest hour, till at last the bells tolled in announcement of Our Lady's

Trillionth Equinoctal Malediction, us tumbling aground at the sound of it, in unison bursting shit and jizz, poison bile on our tongues aflame, then as now, now as then –

Except this time we don't fall, burst or burn (no such luck), us marching steady through the maze with Monk in lead, past his pater's door/mural (hogfarm pixel-rut still sounding within), on through the slop-pot vestibule into the garage, past the suit balls-up in effigy, and the old pine-crone in her chair gyved silent, Trotjohn blowing her a kiss and breaking into a run, Wald in pursuit squawk and giggle, under the garage door, "WHOOOO!": out.

***

"You bastards certainly took your time," goes Monk squinting, "thought I'd have to wait forever, bleeding in stigma."

We're out in Monk's driveway again, the yard still bright, John getting the car started, Wald seated beside.

"Regrettably, yes," I go, "but we were detained. Pigflash in the Old Mall lot. Most unexpected."

"Pig?" Monk, "Pig stopped you?"

I nod. "Fuckin' reserve flash up gung ho, try a full cavity shakedown, so John slash him dead and throat-fuck the cadaver. You know how it goes."

Monk's mouth twitch: shadow of a smile. "Yes, quite. The old Slash and Jizz routine. Second time this month."

I blink. "Second?"

"Second, yes. Some bumpkin crossed our enforcer at the *Boarhog* last week, an altercation of some sort. This very bumpkin found dead an hour later, one eye gouged out, socketful of crotch custard. Pigs came sniffing, but our man had an alibi. Always does."

I grin. "Uh-huh. Like: *me and m'boys were at the Luau the*

WHOLE TIME officer. You know, the ol' South Pacific Circle Jerk. Just ASK 'em, they'll tell ya."

Monk sniff. "Something of the sort, yes."

"Yayup. Man got to have a hobby."

"Quite. And speaking of hobbies: Churchtown promises to be Pig-free this weekend, I hear."

I stare. "Well, lick m'peener and howl. You KNEW?"

Monk frown, studying his fingernails. "Would appear so, yes. High-placed sources, you understand. Friends of the pater."

"Well, damn."

"Damn indeed. But who told YOU, if I may be so bold."

"Who? Well, Poondog. Poondog's kid brother turned rookie Pig tell John, who tell me."

"Ah," Monk, "an open secret."

I shrug. "Yeah well, gotta admit, I'm kinda – "

"FUCKERS!" John revving the engine, "FUCKERS, IN THE CAR NOW, OR FOREVER HOLD YOUR MEAT!"

We move. Me and Monk up the driveway striding.

"Say now Monk, son," I go, "you gonna leave all them yard lights on?"

Monk nod, quickening. "Lights stay on all night. The pater likes to toddle out in the wee hours, piss on all that fengshui foliage, ejaculate in the gazebo, disburthen in the toolshed – "

Myself with a cackle trotting around the side and vaulting into the backseat, Monk more casual, sliding in opposite, the car now in full rev screeching back in a tight arc, VRROOOM! out into the night.

***

"EASY NOW SON!" I yell, "EASY – "

But he's not listening, Trotjohn. Him hunched with the pedal floored, highbeams in full flare routing the dark. In back, Monk and I wind-lashed, angry foliage hissing past in gauntlet.

"Dispaced libido," goes Monk leaning in, "sheet-metal *lingam* seeks chrome *yoni*, pube wires meshing – "

A figure flashes past in momentary spotlight: glimpse of a chalk butt, blue headgear, strip of red, disc bronze –

John slamming the brakes with a shout going: "Papa, SHIT oane ME. Who in HALE w'DAT?"

"Ow," me, rising from a jack-knife lurch, "yow – "

Monk straightening with a scowl going: "That's old man Switzer on walkabout. DON'T slow down."

"Swit WHO?" John, the car now at a crawl.

Monk sigh. Shake his head. "Old man Switzer taking his nightly constitutional. Blue bonnet, red g-string, bronze escutcheon strapped to his back. Plus a harness for his sixteen-inch syntheplast strudel, a chamois leather fob for his hypertrophic gonads, a graphite heel for his thalidomide foot – "

"HAR!" John, "HAHARF!"

"HeeEEsh!" Wald, shaking beside, "heeEEsh!"

I look over my shoulder: shadow receding.

"Knew it," I go, "knew I'd seen him somewhere. That dibbled aitchbone, that opal rump. Old *Kiss'n'Kill* Switzer, nine wives in as many years. Killed and ate 'em all, different cookbook each time. Married Number ten last month, a rail-thin *haute couture* anorex. Can't see her make much of a meal, so maybe he just boil her down for catwalk consomme and throw them spare ribs to the hounds – "

John with head thrown back: "HAR! HAR!", Wald slap, gibber and screech, Monk nodding sage with the car speeding up, slowing at lane's end, sharp left and vrrroom, dust cloud and tire squeal, due west.

***

"Yo TJ," I go leaning forward, "where you takin' us. Rubblesville?"

John mutter. Lean right. Stick an elbow in my face.

I yelp. Sit back with a curse. "Fucker can't tell my nose from his elbow."

"Nose-fuck," Wald, "heh heh."

I savor the throb, looking around brine-eyed. Rubblesville it is all right, this half-built burb we're driving through. The road unpaved, winding, butchered trees either side, detritus hillocks. Dozers in silhouette, roadcones, demarcation barrels, pits ribboned off –

"If I'd wanted construction," I go, "if I'd wanted fuckin' construction, I'd've brought my fuckin' helmet."

John snort. "You don't HAVE a helmet to fuck with, DWEEB. You ain't CIRCUMCISED."

"Ah," Monk, "too-shay."

"Dweeb helmet circum-fuck," Wald, "heh heh."

John tap the brakes, veer around a gravel heap. Then he speed up, wheels churning.

"You want to be careful now, friar," I go, "this here's a beast-rig drag track."

"Thanks DAD," John, "when I want your fuckin' adVICE I'll – "

A shape looms, John with a yawp wrenching the wheel. Too late. Daboom: glimpse of a barrel in flight, thud, rumble, John out of his seat frothing murder, myself delirious watching the barrel roll, envisioning a painted hippo wrapped in seaweed on a black marble Afro-Jap soul-sushi bartop –

Pause. The car at a dead halt, John with face shadowed, turning.

"You MADE that happen didn't ya. Ay?"

I bare my teeth. "Yeah, right. YOU'RE the one driving but I'm the one who made it happen."

John fix me with a kill-gaze. Then he curse, vault out the car, walk around front.

"You can't walk out on me now hon," I call out, "not after everything we've been through."

"Walk on me hon," Wald, "heh heh."

John stalk back around, jump in. "Lucky for YOU, it ain't much. Just a little dent."

I click my tongue. "Awww, too bad. I figured we could qualify for the big-rig Monster Smash. Come on right after *Mons Pubis* bangs *Mons Veneris* under redneck Klieg lights – "

VrrRROOM: the car coming to with a rev, and on, John driving slow now and watchful. More half-built burbs, roads unpaved, myself droop-eyed thinking nothing –

The car kicks, catching traction. I look up, see lights ahead. "That the beltway up there?"

"Ain't yo' papa's whore-pit," John.

"Beltway it is," Monk, "yes."

"And you know what THAT mean," John.

I frown. "No. What."

"DEATHsound baby, DEATHSOUND."

I smack my brow, open palm. "SHIT yeah! Where is it."

"Under mah butt," John, "where else."

"Where else indeed," Monk.

"DEATH!" Wald, "DEATH-butt. Heh heh."

I bend. Reach under the driver's seat. Draw out the box. This here box shaped like a shamrock with discs slotted around. Thrash-sound John blare, going supersonic on freeways in Churchtown and out, a selection of the best speed, death, grind, krush, scag, wig, skank, buzz and skum depositions of our time.

"Whut we got," John slapping the wheel, "whut we GOT."

I prise off the boxcover. Begin sorting.

"Demongutz," I call out, "Speedkill. Sugarnuke. Snotburn. Hammerhog. Whorebroth. Snatch Salvation. Blood Sausage. Brother Moloch. Angstführer – "

"YEAH!" John, "führer! Bring on the FÜHRER!"

"HeeEEEP!" Wald, "FYOOHRER!"

I snicker. Pinch out the disc. "Führer it IS."

I hold the disc up a moment, studying the cover. Not enough light to slap a schlong by, but I can see it well enough. *Angstführer: Auto-da-fe.* Covergloss showing an Inquisitor in drag torching the feet of a blonde Huguenot, spooling up her entrails on a windlass. Below, a calligraphed verse, apocalyptic prosody by Lem:

Stark and Hellbound I drew my last Frozen Breath.
Nearing the Chasm
the Final Burning Spasm
of Heavy Metal Death.

I chuckle, hand John the disc. "Let 'er rip."

"Rip!" Wald, "rrrRRRIP!"

The sound strikes as we loop off the ramp onto the beltway, Lem screaming in on a riff hot enough to scorch flesh, riding drum-thunder, going:

We are the Hounds of Hell
New Pain, New Fire
Spawn of the Beast
Blood Hate, Blood Desire
No Hearth, no Home
We're Berserkers on the Roam
Hellions Riding High
Hear our War Cry:
Burn. Fuck. Smash. Kill.
Burn. Fuck. Smash. Kill –

And on, the car in deathsound overdrive, us with hands raised in demon mudra, teeth bared, high-road rivet-heads working the headbang, fighting the windblast, the beltway before us miraged aflame under the lights, under a sky with no moon.

***

"SLOW!" I yell, grabbing his shoulder, "SLOW DOWN!"

He look up wild-eyed, John, face clotted in rearview. *Whut. The. Fuck?* His lips forming the words, voice smithereened by deathsound.

"WE'RE ALMOST THERE!" I yell pointing, "ALMOST THERE!"

John stare a moment, eyes mirrored black. Then he cut the music and swing right, the car quartering under the exit sign out to the ramp, honks sounding in our wake.

"SUCK M'RAWBONE TURKEYNECK!" John bawl, flipping 'em the bird, the car hitting the ramp fast, screeching precarious around the bight, your daddy holding on with teeth set (Lem's parting shriek in echo), thinking: *here it come. Here it COME. My right ear give way, sluice hot gunk –*

But it don't happen, thank schmuck. Doesn't. My ear holds, John slowing, looping off the ramp onto Hillview.

Silence. Engine hum and tinnitus. The car cruising uphill.

"Hot-DAMN!" I go, slumping, "now I know what MARS feels like."

Pause. John scowling in rearview. "MARS?"

I smile benign. "The planet Mars. The way it swing around the sun. Like a friggin' slingshot."

John shake his head. "Man, if I wudn't drivin' I'd stop the car and slap you upside to tarnation."

I nod. "That makes sense. Somewhere."

John curse, switch gear: the car with a cough, surging.

"No rush sweetheart," I go, "it's only the first trimester."

John mutter. Tap the brakes. "Guess I oughtta give her a breather. She been sweatin' hard for daddy."

"Hard daddy," Wald, "heh heh."

A Volkswaffen zooms past, going downhill. I follow it with both ears, one eye, a snot-free nose. Not much action on Hillview this night. Vehicles heading down in random smatter. A few rigs grinding up, tankers mostly. And carriers. Roadwar landrovers. Armor-plated riot-busters. High-suspension silo-smashers. Tripod boulder-stompers. Godzilla.

The road curve some, lights appearing at left: the A9 service station outspread, rigs stupored under the awning.

"Behold," Monk, "how like centipedes, those rigs."

"Nope," me, "millipedes. Killer millipedes on rollerskates."

"Not quite," Monk, "Divinity school students turned killer millipedes, skating through an *arrondissement* of ill repute."

I smack the side of my nose. Nod double-jointed.

"*Touché, maître.* Question: how do you tell a centipede from a millipede? Answer: you don't. They know the difference."

"Mirth ensues," Monk.

John slap the dash, speed up, loop around a carrier. "Fuckin' trucks."

I harrumph. Click my dawg tongue. "Me and mah good ol' boys been fuckin' trucks lawng as I kin remember. Whut yew do, yew start with'm TAIL pipes and work yer way up. Then yew sit back'n watch yer pecker drop like burned cream cheese."

"Ah," Monk, "quite."

"Pecker-cheese," Wald, "heh heh."

John mirthless, steering.

The road bank left. Right. Left again. Hillview starting to wind a fair bit, vegetation thickening either side. Above, the sky clouded dark, hint of a tremulous moon –

Plop. I flinch. Plop. Plop-plop. Plop.

"Tut tut," I go, "looks like rain. Tut tut, looks like rain."

Monk stick out a hand, palm up. "True, Pooh."

"Raise high the roof Seymour," I go, "HAI!"

A whine sounds behind my head: car roof rising. I lean back, watch it slide into place, the windows in turn rising to meet it.

"Sealed adiabatic," I go, my voice unnaturally loud.

"Immured," Monk, "entombed."

John whip around sudden, face mottled. "You guys SHUT the fuck UP. You're gettin' me riled."

"As we forgive them," Monk, "that rile against us."

"Off track," I go pointing, "goin' off TRACK – "

John turn with a curse, the car skidding back on track.

Silence falls. Like a snowflake under an alpine moon. No sound save the engine in low hum, patter of drops on the roof, swish of wipers.

I lean back with eyes closed, tongue coiled, working a Bhutanese MBRRP! Dikdik Eggbeater mantra.

A vehicle dopplers past, rainswept. John cuss after it, his words parsing lurid. Hypnos amnion, dreamwater chlorophyll. My mind sentient silk. And then I hear them: *Skrrk! Bwa bwa skrrk!* Sounds drifting in on waves of prana ether through the Bodhi Vajra Prism. Or mayhap the Kalachakra Siddhayogi Prism. Distant trucker-voices in radio dialogue:

Skkrk! Jimbob to Billybob, Jimbob to Billybob, over. Skkrk! hey there Jimbob, whut you got, over. Skrrk! got hawg scent down Blyville Junction 94, freeway fuzz on the gun, over. Skrrk! copy that'n Jimbob, blueboy with boner Blyville 94. How 'bout we do us a beer in Memphis, over. Skrrk! you betcha. Throw in a T-bone and taters, blonde wig, garter and high heel, shave 'em pubes, tape down that wiener, we got us a deal, over. Skrrk! Ok that'n Jimbob. Add a fish-oil tampon, one them hashbrown dildos to go, no extra charge. Billybob out –

***

R.E.M. again, flash-dreaming in hypnagogue. Myself a monitor lizard dying under an eggpile, vast arrays of beakless hens looking on, eyes glinting homicidal under a neon sky. *Help,* I croak in lizard glot, *help*. Kathump, kathump: Farmer Brown walks in headless, naked on stilts, his sixteen nipples in pink floral cluster, a painted gekko suffocating in his rot-crotch. *Help!* I go, *help!* His belly-button twitch in response and burst, a hog-snout pushing through. *Grrrrunttt –*

"Huh?" me, "wha?" Monk's voice in echo.

I groan. Crank up my lids. Monk up close, lips moving. "Asleep on the job. Yes?"

I sit up, sucking drool. "Nope. Visioneering is what. And besides, we're not in rut yet."

Monk straighten. "*Visioneering.* That's a new one."

I rub my eyes, look around blinking. Hillview gone narrow, pine cover dense, either side. Ahead, a traffic light going red, vehicles starting across. Mason.

The car slow, come to a stop, the sign above, gleaming.

"Mason," goes John over his shoulder, "ay?"

I nod. "Son of May."

"Your old man still live on Mason?"

I nod. "Same old place."

"Still workin' Mission Mars?"

I jab my cheek with a fingernail. Smack my lips.

"Yayup. Egghead emeritus, last I heard. Got some greenhorn geeks shovelling his shit, sucking him off for a stint with the heavies."

"Harf!" John, "I'll bet."

A flatbed growls up at left, stereo humming. Mute strains of retro country: Bocephus fretting his gold-string *guit*-tar.

"YEAH!" John pounding the dash, "Hank Jr., YEAH!"

The light turn green, John quick on the take, crushing the pedal. Vrroom: tire screech.

"Easy now son," I go, "you know it get tricky ahead."

John snort. "Not tricky enough for Tricky Dick."

"Dick trick," Wald, "heh heh."

The car gather speed, approaching a curve. I figure John'll slow some on the centrifuge, but he don't. Him tearing around the bight full throttle, tyres in schweinkampf squeal, myself with a grimace thinking *here it come, here it come* –

And it does. Sh-thoomf: crud sparging hot from my right ear, blotching the pane: shape of a kitten paw.

I curse. Wipe off with my sleeve. "Real ORIGINAL there, friar. You oughtta be in screen vision. One them crash-porn adrenaline flicks."

"Damn right," John, "here instead, chauffeuring a buncha live turd assholes."

"Apology accepted," Monk.

"Turdhole show," Wald, "heh heh."

The road straighten, rise. At right the hillside falling away soundless, Churchtown appearing below. Lights in the valley, a million lights speckled horizonward. Signs lancing up bright and violent, the sky fevered in vague aureole.

"Pretty," I go pointing, "hey?"

Monk sniff. "Pretty as a bruise, a rash, a lesion, a furuncle, a cicatrice."

John cackle. "Bitch got a way with words."

"Word bitch," Wald, "heh heh."

The road level, turn in a wide curve. Lights appear on the hillside, lights of domicile. Rich-folk homes, the richest this side of perdition, old money and new. Wisp-haired dotards drooling antebellum, decrepit scions of old plantation south. DAR hags croaking Manifest Destiny, fending off hottentots with bejeweled claw. John Birch millionaires muttering cabal, brooding in a shoreless haze of conspiracy. Blue chip bosses in green heat, cutting deals at poolside. And not least, cliques of master-race rocketboys yammering in Übermensch, mapping deep space lebensraum, plotting an interplanetary anschluss –

I start. John pounding the dash: "GO! GO! GO! – "

I frown, sit up. "What now?"

"The light," Monk weary, "he aims for the light."

I lean forward squinting. Traffic light green ahead. Way ahead.

"Awww shit," I go, "no way."

"Way," Monk, "way indeed."

"John," I go, "GOOD brother JOHN."

John hunched, the car gathering speed.

I lunge out of my seat, grab his shoulder.

"GodDAMMIT John, you're NOT gonna MAKE it, it's too damn FAR, you're not – "

But he's not listening, Trotjohn. Him hellbent, roaring up the stretch, "YAARH! YAARH!", urging on his steed, the needle at 110 and climbing, the car now fifty yards from the light, forty, thirty, the light going yellow, "YAAARRH!", myself frozen, the light going red, Wald with skull on the dash thumping rhythmic, ten yards, five, vehicles ahead in silhouette starting across, "YAAAAAARRRRHHH!" and me thinking: *this. is not. how I meant. it to end...* John's voice now risen to a keen, limned faces turning aghast, a bright sliver of silence, then an eruption: carhonk, tire-squeal, steel-thud, headlights flared for a blinding instant and through, John with a long wolf-howl slicing free into the night.

***

Silence and car hum. No rain-sound, the cloudburst having ceased. Just the hiss of canned air, damp tyres sibilant on packed earth.

"Ffuckshhmmrrm," I go, tooth-gnashed, mouth gone dry.

"Huh?" John, glancing up, "whut now?"

"Ffukhshhmmrrm."

John chuckle, smirking in rearview. "Whatsa matter toots. Your panties change colour?"

I convulse in sudden heat, slam his headrest.

"NOT funny, what you pulled back there. You almost bollixed the Run. Keep pissin' around like that, I swear I'll abdicate and rat you out to the Meister."

John reach back with a cackle, fingers nipping crabclaw.

"Gimme that tongue o'yourn, punk bitch. Hand me that pretty little throat."

I weave, slap aside his claw. "I MEAN it. You pull that deathgame shit again, I walk. And talk."

"Awwwww, come oane now," John in mock chagrin, "baby you GOT to know I'm oane yo' SIDE."

"Shitgame death baby," Wald straightening, "heh heh."

"Ah," Monk, "sluggard roused from accidie by butcher talk."

I shake my head, sit back. We're off Hillview now, heading into the woods. Trees dark on either side, Dirt Road fluming pale ahead.

A moment pass, wordless, the car cruising. Then John mutter indistinct, shift gear and floor the pedal.

"Easy on the speed old son," offer Monk, "you know this track's wound tighter than a snake in a sahib's – "

"Asshole," finish John, "and yo' daddy know this stretch better'n you know his broke dick. Dig?"

"Dick stretch," Wald, "snake hole. Heh heh."

The road constrict sudden, winding sigmoid. John

wrenching right and left, speed barely diminished, myself with hands on ears trying to wax querulous, but failing abortive, my tongue having cleaved to my palate as did Jehozaphat's when he beheld the rites of Sodom, him speechless on club foot, shitting black salt in awe of the Lord's looming fundament –

Dirt Road bank left, hit a final hairpin, straighten expansive. John with a yelp, slotting into overdrive, the Durerro blitzing the track, woods on either side a dark blur.

"EEEeEEP!" Wald quaking, "yeEEP!"

I blink, lean forward squinting. "That a fogbank up there?"

John reach with a curse, smack my brow open palm.

"You let daddy handle the road now."

I subside, cuss-words massing behind the ramparts of my teeth. My vision clears, the car plunging soundless into the fogbank.

"Yeeeh!" John, "HAWWW!"

"Possible head-on with pornhogs up from Bluto's," announce Monk, "or with woodland creatures on the hunt."

John snort, balling sightless through fog.

"No varmints big enough to knock ME off. Not in THIS neck."

"No?" me, "think again monsignor. Think bigass albino possum."

"Ahhh yes," Monk, "hypertrophic marsupials with diminished pigment. John knows about those. He's shagged a couple, what?"

"You know it," John, "got m'nuts scratched off damn near."

"True," Monk, "it's on film."

I nod reminiscent. "I've seen it. *Critterfuck Special* on *Nat Geo Netwave*."

"Special indeed," Monk, "an absolute must-see. John hunched coital over a bloodless opossum. A large one."

"Large as a ham-fed pitbull," me.

"Possum claw rending nuciferous sac," Monk, "testicles unhoused. All six of them."

"Six," me, "SIX?"

"Forsooth," Monk, "he's thrice the man you are. Or I am."

"Got THAT right", John.

I frown, the fog ahead brightening. Dull roar.

"Whoa!" me, "WHOA! – "

John with a throttled shout torquing the wheel, the car off track scraping treebark, a bigwheel pickup blaring past, snout agleam.

"FUCKHH!" John, churning back on track, "muth-a-FUUUCKH!"

I cackle, gasping. "You blinked, papadawg. YOU BLINKED."

John shaking his head, the car gathering speed.

"Nah. Judgement call. Cain't play chicken with wheels three times bigger'n yours. Got to have a level playin' field."

"Quite," Monk, "ceteris paribus."

"Uh-huh," John, "critter-piss cherry-puss."

"Chicken cherry," Wald chortling, "play puss. Heh heh – "

We clear the fogbank silent and sudden, Dirt Road stark once more. John with a grunt hitting overdrive, vrroom: brain-drag to occiput.

I wince. "Jee-zus. We gonna have us a mess of roadkill tonight."

"The more the better, baby," John, "possum stew for sundee vittles."

"Not just possum," I go, "Artie."

"Huh?" John, "WHO?"

"Artie Mangus, boon country cretin, rogue punkinhead, feral minstrel. Now, Meister's famulus."

Monk nod. "Ah Mangus, yes. Arthur, the idiot bard of the Appalachian."

"The very same," me, "he's with the Meister now, so we don't want to run him over. Artie got a thing for hillside roads. Like to sit on 'em and hump the Muse."

"Harf!" John, not slowing, "yowp."

"Road hump," Wald, "heh heh."

Monk cough. "Been a while since I saw him last. Arthur Mangus."

I shrug. "Caught him at the Grotto once, Idiot-Savant Night."

"Huh?" John, "idiot who?"

"Idiot-Savant Night. This little hootenanny Billy have every year. Booze and vittles on the house for hillbilly rainmen, slingblade simpletons from Monroe County. Choice of dishwater draft, pasteurized battery acid, rancid tapioca swill. Plus a shitload of finger-chow. Rocksalt pretzels, dried catfish scales, hogbollock dim sum, bugmash beluga, caseated kidney dip, creamed cerumen, bonemeal crackers, pustule twists, tooth-plaque tacos, ground-glass gumbo, caramelized cat-crap – "

"HAARF!" John, "ha-HAARF!"

"ULF!" Wald, "mmph!"

"Disjecta," Monk, "worstword ho."

I nod. "Pap and pabulum on the house and a show after. Entertainment courtesy ISA, *Idiot-Savants of Appalachia*. Fuckers put up a good one last time around, the Grotto bursting with trashville culottes, ragass bumpkins from all over. Billy'd jerrybuilt a stage by the bar, rigged spotlights, festooned the joint with polished rodent snouts, soiled loin-straps, baked-dung dildos, nightglow titty-cups, pecker-sheaths stuffed with slop. First up, an acromegalic boon hulk in treebark bloomers doing an Algonquin moose jig. Plenty applause, the rabble clapping chapped hands, tossing sweaty caps. Smog-dense halitosis, had to tear open my doublet to keep from choking.

Next up, a Queen Albion lookalike, shrieking doggerel and slicing a hoghead with a chainsaw – "

I lick my lips, my thoughts in candent recollect.

"Then a murmur rising to a chant, the ruck in unison going: 'R.T.! R.T.!'. Artie Mangus they were calling for, him and his odes to granite, huckleberry, grits, crablice, shoe soles, hashbrowns, dentures, crotch fungus, gum disease, chitlins, ruptured eardrums, cold sores, gas-gangrene – "

"MMHAARF!" John, "yowp."

"Nohow on," Monk.

"Grit gangrene," Wald, "heh heh."

"Plebs goin 'R.T.! R.T.! R.T.!', dissolving into applause as he shuffled onstage. Mangus in pegged brogans and velvet overalls, his hair tousled, jaw slack, eyes crudded, a drool-thread trembling chin to chest (his one-string Aeolian Harp). Fucker looked like he'd come awake from a six month Rip Van, him standing with lips fastened to the amp head, a mutilated kiddie doll stuck in his left armpit. Quiet a moment, the polloi hushed. Then Artie with a twitch and grunt starting in on his magnum dopus, *Ode on an Orange*, delivered in a halting mumble: *it's right there. I can see it. the orange. blue and green. the fruit I see. and pluck. and squeeze. feeling the juice run. run juicy run. juicy run run. run juice to mama. juice run to mama. watch her eat. and drink and eat. with two lips and three teeth. and drip-dripping tongue. drippy drip smack slurp. schlup slurpy drip droop...*"

I break off mist-eyed, following Artie down imbecile freeways, his words in echo sparged through foaming spittle, verbigeration to logorrhea. John up front thumping the wheel, "HAARF! WAHHAARF!", Wald with knees up, head forced between, Monk with beard forked, the two ends stuck in his mouth going:

"Holy holy holy holy, holy Allen in mortis, holy howling Allen in excelsis – "

The car a highbeam arrow piercing the cerements of dead rock over this benighted hillside.

***

"Nngh! nnggrrnf! nngyarrf! – "

John chuckle. "Wald gettin' antsy."

I sit up. Peep around the headrest. Wald curled foetal, chewing on his knee.

I reach, pat his shoulder. "Almost there, Wald. Coupla miles more or less. Bluto's comin' up in a hurry, not to – "

"NNGYAAARRFFF! – "

Wald up in maddawg jaw-snap, teeth missing my fingers by an inch, John with a howl going: "FEEDIN' TIME FOR CUJO, BRROWFF! BRROWFF! – "

I spit out an oath, retreat in blood-dimmed animus. Wald thrashing in his seat yelp and gurgle, John still "BROWFF! BROWFF! – "

Monk turn, beard wagging. "Satori, yes? Sudden enlightenment at fanged bite site of rabies?"

I scowl. "Satori my ass. More like – "

I break off: Wald's face pale over the headrest, demon cherub with a child's smile. "PEEKaboo! Heh heh – "

I rear up, slam the headrest. His face vanish with a squawk.

"THAT'll teach ya. Fuckin' fatass freak."

John cackle, glance up in rearview. "Say now Jabe, we past the ol' Warehouse yet?"

I glare. "I get my fuckin' fingers bit off damn near, and he wanna know – "

"There," Monk, "no sooner invoked than manifest."

I turn: foliage thinning at left. Glimpse of a lightless scape, a structure bulked vague in the distance.

John grunt. "Think anyone's in there playin'?"

III

"Very likely," Monk giving me a look, "yes?"

I don't answer. Myself slumped taciturn, thoughts wafting moondust. Recalling old Warehouse encounters, scenes bygone. The sign by the entrance that read: HIDE SHIT. HILLSIDE SHOPPING CENTER is what it mean to say, some letters missing. A mall half-built for neighborhoods never built, big as an airplane hangar, freaks convoking inside day and night. Dixie Dervishes, Rinzai Rockers, Tits'n'Ass Tantrics, Doowop Druids, Wangslash Wiccans, Satan's Samaritans, Daughters of Baal, Churchtown Chthonics. Not to mention the Boonside Thrillkillers, John's step'n'fetch minions. That time I walked in and saw 'em jock-strapped, holding dwarf scimitars, faces masked by kendo visors. John with visor raised, diddling his meat going: 'SAMURAI CIRCLE JERK! ROOM FOR ONE MORE!'. And the time I hid out, watching nymphs naked under the skylight, them around a makeshift altar, a grizzled priestess presiding black-smocked, chalice in one hand, dagger in the other. Her catching sight of me yelling 'CASTRATE!', myself out clutching my three-piece *bijouterie*, nymphs in hot pursuit. Shoulda stopped and faced 'em. Not everyday you get savaged by a troupe of well-stacked vestals. And that time I strolled in, saw guys in gold loincloths writhing on the floor like salted slugs, their groove guru in fez and djellaba thumping a tabor. *Feel free to join in,* he say, *m'boys here warmin' up their power spots.* And that rain-wet afternoon I saw figures misted blue, dervishes spinning with arms outstretched, perfumed incense, smoke from a *narghile* dream. And that dusk time I wandered in to the smell: blood over by the window, buzz of feasting flies, runes chalked around a slaughtered infant, twilight breathing evil –

The car slow. Slow some more. John slotting back twice, the tyres catching licks of tarmac.

"You want to go dead slow now son," I offer, "that there's a mean dawgleg ahead."

John shift down once more, scowl up in rearview.

"You lookin' to get HIT again, ho?"

"Slow ho," Wald, "heh heh."

A dwarf pine shows ahead at the bend: roots exposed, bark shorn and brindled.

"An accident by the look of it," Monk, "loss of motor control."

I exhale fart-lipped. "Loss is right. Some whore'n'hound idjit come tearin' up, don't slow for the turn, go screeee WHAM! out the window into the woods, skimming the treetops like it's a bird, it's a plane, no, it's Bubbaman – "

John cackle. Ease around the dogleg. Slot up a notch.

"Well awwright," I go, "four, three, two – "

"ONE!" yelp the Wald, fists up, the car cruising into a clearing.

"Well sheeat," John tapping the brakes, "hawgs ever'where."

I frown. The clearing near full: cars, pickups, four-by-fours, high-grip hogs. Beyond, Bluto's in silhouette, eaves shadowed, screendoor demon-bright. The old sign up over the porch, red wire neon: BLUTO'S BBQ.

I point. "Just drive on around, park over yander."

John grunt, tap the pedal: the car working a loop around the clearing.

"Fuckers come in droves," he goes, "ay?"

I shake my head. "Nope. No fuckers here. No down-home, salt-of-the-earth, corn-fed fuckers at Bluto's, nawsuh. Just jizz-freaks, putz-pounders, dummy-humps."

"HARF!" John, "yowp."

"Porcine offspring of Trimalchio and Elagabulus," Monk.

"Putz hump dummy jizz," Wald, "heh heh."

The car slow to a crawl near clearing's end, pull in between a cedar and a pickup.

"Well," Trotjohn killing the engine, "go do yo' thang. We'll be waitin'."

"Homage on our behalf," Monk, "needless to say."

"Yo' THANG," Wald, "heh heh."

I sigh. Push open the door. Climb out.

"Say now Jabe," John turning, "that there sign, BLUTO'S BBQ. How come a porn-hole get a name like yat?"

I frown. "You KNOW how come. I've only told you a couple MILLION times."

John grin, teeth checkered pale. "Be a good little honey bitch and tell me AGEEAN."

I fix him with a scowl. "Somethin' to do with polarities and opposites. God, Spirit, Popeye, Spinach vs. the Devil, Flesh, Bluto, BBQ. Fatman prefer the latter, hence Bluto's BBQ."

John crack open his door. Spit. "Yeah, whatever. Like I really GIVE a shit."

I curse, slam my door shut. "Hope you guys're fuckin' DEAD by the time I get back."

Mirth all around as I start walking.

***

I feel it as I walk: grass dew-damp brushing my ankles, the back of my shirt sweatcold. Past pickups gone mute, cars still hot from the ride, crepitant. Across the lot and up to the porch, the screendoor opening as I draw near: a bearded prole stepping out, package in hand.

"Mmmyeah," he goes reaching, "mmhmmm – "

"Skunkfuck," I go, slapping his hand off my crotch, him weaseling past with a snicker.

I stand on the porch a moment, cursing. Then I step up, boot

114

open the door. Wham: light white-hot in my eyes, my lids snapping shut. Fire, black motes in crimson sky. Blood horizon, vision apocalypse –

"You cain't stand the heat, get out the kitchen. Huff huff."

I cork up a lid. Both lids. A face swim into view: long cords of rat-hair, bug eyes boiled colourless.

"Jack," I go, "Bama Jack on nightshift."

"Bet your sweet ass. Workin' it good. Huff huff."

I blink, look around squinting. Good-size crowd by the look of it. Schlong lords, nad barons, pussy prelates from Churchtown and around. Hump-juice burnouts in for a prescription pornshot, smut-junkies for a hit of snatch serum. Cooze crackers hard on the beaver trail, stalking the aisles stiff-pricked, scanning captive poon-prey –

"Workin' it gooOOOD. Huff huff."

I turn, trying not to inhale. "Fatman in?"

Bama Jack chortle: a char-lung croak. "Bitch got no place else to go."

"Heard that," I go, stepping away.

"Say," Bama Jack, "you wanna tell me what it's about?"

I hold up a finger. "Just goin' to meet the Man."

Chortle. "Better you than me, toots."

I walk on. Down aisle one with bowed head and measured tread, this pornhole penitent walking a gauntlet of skinflicks, fuckmags, muff-hair toupées, foreskin bracelets, edible rubbers, spunk tapers, hog-snout strap-ons (and best for last) death's head vibrator dildos set to max, chip inserts beeping *God Bless America*.

At aisle's end I veer, the smell now rising acrid: lust like burnt tar, hate like rancid milk. Ten steps on and stop: door. *Employees Only*, lettered black on red. I smile, recalling Fatman's design plans:

We're gonna bust down the back wall and stick in a giant double door: a shock-pink bilabial with red clitoral knobs, purple pube fuzz. Freudian rococo on acid, baby. With a new entrance to match: a phallic façade with urethral vestibule and scrotal foyer. That way we balance front and back like Yang Yin, Yab Yum, Shiva Shakti, contraria sunt complementa sub specie pornographis –

My hand on the knob I push, step in. Semidarkness and stale air, a narrow passage walled white, bead lights strung down its length like animal eyes. I pull the door shut and move, surefooted. Bead bulbs drift past: first one, then another and another. In thought an endless runway, lights winking out to a vanished horizon. Far distant, a dragon tongue unfurled, fluorescent nailheads framing an uvular doorway –

I frown. Pestilence. Storage door ajar at left, glint of polished metal. Fatman's backup chamber pot, his damascened dung bowl. *danger. hold breath now. pull on gas mask. it be toxic death when the Fatman crap. like beep, beep, sound alarm. quarantine area. fartcloud up, raining ichor. avians drop out of the sky, livestock keel over stricken. crops wilt, harvests fail. citizens wander scorch-lunged wielding scythe, adze, shear, mattock. pig-nazi robots keep order with bazooka and road-drill, lameduck Prez pounding First Hard-on for world in entropic collapse, zymotic decay, heat death –*

"Owwww!"

I pause, grimacing. Collision: the crate in the corner, my left ankle on raw wood: pain.

I nurse my ankle a moment, cuss-words in livid crackle. Then I straighten, turn. Directly ahead a door ajar, wedge of yellow light: Fatman's lair.

I take a deep breath. Limp up five steps. Ease in. Transition to Tartarus: dungeon gloom ripe, feculent. My vision shading light and dark, an oil slick spreading –

"Whaddya want."

I squeeze shut my eyes. Open them. The Form clear now in outline: chalk flesh hillocked. Fatman by lamplight. On his waterbed, reading.

"Whaddya want!"

The Boss in repose, gut slung askance like a wayward moon, eyelenses agleam above its planetary swell. Myself in awe thinking: *all praise the cloistered leviathan, praise all the cyclopean eremite. blessed they who dare compass his girth, and adoring, worship their lipid lord, their adipose avalanche, their cellulite colossus –*

"I SAID, WHADDYA WANT!"

I cringe. Fatman's troglodyte bark.

"Homage," I go, "greetings from our Meister, Buford Aloysius Howell, *Lord Baron of Pain*. Homage and greeting."

The lenses rise. Turn in azimuth. "Shit. More dumb cartoon shit. Same old same old. Still, gotta hand it to him. A real sick fuck, Howell. Sicker than I'd ever want to be."

I nod. Take a backward step –

"HEY!"

Pause, sphincters clenched.

"Where do you think you're goin'. Hah?"

I sigh. Unclench. "Nowhere. Just a little trip. Nothin' to worry about. I'll be in Monday."

A crease appear on Fatman's brow: thin blue line.

"A TRIP, you say?"

"Yayup."

The lenses flash. "Shit. You ain't takin' no TRIP."

I frown. "Goddamned if I'm not."

The Fatman stir, flesh in slow quake. "Slam your scrawny ass if you ARE."

I bare my teeth. "Whup your boulder butt if I'm not."

"Shit. Purée your pecker if you are."

"Dice your nuts, I'm not."

"Diesel fuel enema, you are."

"Crowbar colonic, I'm not."

"Hot cactus cornhole, you are."

"Blowtorch buggerhump, I'm not."

Pause. Counting two, three, four and hear it at five: sound like a death rattle. Fatman laughing.

I watch: his bulk gone seismic, laughter waxing catarrhal, waning to a rumble, wheeze, silence. The behemoth motionless once more, painted in chiaroscuro.

"Be in to work Monday," I go, "not to worry."

The Fatman's lip curl. "Well shit. Piss off if you have to."

I nod, my gaze on his pate: glabrous expanse shaded against the light. His eyes grey flints under a cromagnon brow. That look of infant concentration. Or idiocy. No, not idiocy. Fatman's no idiot. Worse: he's a philosopher. Or used to be. Taught it way back when, some preppy boys' school up north. The Lickspittle Lyceum. Or was it The Addleshit Academy. Fatman a gadfly, buzzing his ephebes, working his brand of hands-on hip-to-ass dialectics. Twilight edifications in urinals, locker rooms, broom closets –

"HEY!"

I wince. "What. WHAT."

The Fatman's hand rise, a sheet held between thumb and forefinger. Scrawl of black ink. "Know what this is?"

I frown. "No. And I don't – "

"This new book I'm writing. *The Gonadology.*"

"The WHAT?"

Chuckle. "*The Gonadology: Ending the Dialectic of the Sphincters.*"

I snort. "That's the title?"

"YEAH!" Fatman faux-enthused, "the TITLE!"

I sputter fart-lipped. "Great. Now I can rest – "

"This bit," he goes, frowning over the sheet, "this bit you got to hear – "

"No. NO. I got to get – "

"Hence it is to be hoped," intones the Fatman, voice waxing grandiloquent, "it is fervently, even devoutly to be wished that those in the know, I mean those of us who comprise the *cognoscenti*, the intelligentsia, the *haut monde*, will post-haste come to see the need, the need, I say, for a new approach, a shift in paradigm, a radical revaluation of our weltanschauung and the lebenswelt that grounds it, the zeitgeist that nourishes it, a vision that unites opposites, resolves antinomies, curbs the proliferate dualisms of Occidental Reason, that shatters the integument, crumbles the carapace of a superannuated metaphysics, a *theoria cum praxis* (to wit) that ends the Dialectic of the Sphincters (buccal and rectal orifices no longer at odds but harmoniously conjoined), that overcomes the Gigantomachia of the Genitals (prick and puss, urethra and uterus no longer at war, but annexed in repose), a new *ursprungsphilosophie* (in sum) that sees Plato meeting poontang, Aristotle ass; Scotus finding scrotum, Aquinas quim; Descartes doing dick, Spinoza spunk; Schopenhauer touching schlong, Kant cunt; Nietzsche slapping nad, Fichte fesse; Bradley stroking beaver, Santayana snatch; Wittgenstein courting wang, Maine de Biran muff; Gasset sniffing gash, Russell rump... and on, till the line bends to a circle, till our sterile and hypostatic demesne implodes with a bang, and post-coital whimper – "

Pause. Fatman looking up with a grin: glimpse of filed ferret teeth.

I nod. "Impressive to lay the yeast, uh, to say the least. A propaedeutic. A prolegomenon to any future prophylactic. The pornosophe speaks. He alone who strives to put the sin back in ratiocination, jizm in the syllogism – "

"Hah," Fatman, "Good. But there's more. Listen up – "

And on. Same shit different page. Crap I've heard before, ad nauseum. I let his voice fade, with wall eye scanning his lair. Fatman's brimstone bethel, his cloacal catafalque. A kitchenette in the corner, plates crudded in the sink. A window with shades drawn (hillside vistas never seen). A telescope on tripod, glass eye scrutinizing the floor. And books. Books everywhere, crammed in drawers and closets, piled high on the floor. Philosophers mostly: dead eidetic fantasists in memoriam. Some alchemists old and new: Fatman a wannabe warlock straddling the philosopher's stone, turn his nuts to gold –

"– thus Pornography is to Philosophy what Matter is to Idea, Content to Form, Flesh to Spirit – "

I turn, scanning the wall at left. It plastered end to end with brush and charcoal sketches: nightmare panorama. Like Bacon and Klimt in a dream-racked demonarium. Outsize shapes blazed in torment, steel-ravaged flesh in bizarre geometry –

"HEY!"

My breath catch. His Fat-manticore yawp.

"You're not LISTENING."

His eyes on me: bits of burning flint.

I shake my head. "I WAS listening, daddy-o. Just that – "

"NnNNRRHrr," Fatman in snotted upbraid, "NnnnRhhh – "

I sigh. Jerk a thumb at the wall. "Checking out your sketches is what. Wild shit."

Fatman blink, grin spreading. "Sketches you say?"

I nod. "Say."

The Fatman's hand drop, fumble and rise: a square sheet-board held to the light.

"Check this out. One I finished yesterday."

I step up, lean close. Another brush and charcoal sketch. Demented caricature of a suit in trouble: some blue chip techno-corp hog with exploding guts, a chain mail fist ramming through. Above, steel talons ripping off the head, eyeballs starting from their sockets, mouth spraying shattered teeth. Below, the hips arched in violent thrust, toes curled, ridged ratpecker pulsing in incipient orgasm.

I exhale puff-cheeked. Straighten. "Let me guess. You've been watching *Disneyville* on *Netwave*."

The Fatman giggle. "Right the first time."

"And the last," me taking a backward step, "I got to get – "

"HEY!"

I wince. "Awww MAAN, what the FUCK?"

The Fatman grin. "You worked out there today, didn't ya? Afternoon shift?"

"Fuckin' A."

His grin widen. "DEBRIEF, brown boy, de-BRIEF. How'd it go. Do tell."

I shake my head. "Can't do it. What I don't have much of is time – "

"Fuck all THAT. Debrief or DIE."

I sigh. Hard words from the Fatman. Hard, but no real threat in them. Fatman couldn't threaten a fly to save his ass. Or save his threatened ass flying –

"Ok Bossman," I go, "you got a minute. Shoot."

The Fatman purse his lips and smile. Like a kid in a candy store, knife in hand, clerk slumped over the counter bleeding.

"Bartlett," he go, "Reverend Bartlett show?"

I nod. "As always. Sharp at noon. Green shades this time. Plenty makeup. Mutant insect scuttling around, loin-bulge the size of Matterhorn. Skankville preacher out to bridge Heaven and Hell, Son and Satan, Sylph and Salamander, Tits and Ass – "

"HAARKH!" Fatman, "HAARRKH!" Ferret teeth in silverpoint.

"Uh-huh. We got a little date with him later tonight."

"Don't tell me," Fatman, "don't HAAKH! tell – "

"I won't."

He pause, gurgling. "Who else."

I smile. "The nipple-ring biker twins Sodom and Gonorrhea. Up in aisle six doin' the Hell's Angel hump."

"HAARKH! No kidding."

"Nope."

"So what'd you do."

I shrug. "Nothing. Just told 'em we deal in cause, not effect. Stimulus, not response. As in: buy it here, work it elsewhere."

"Shit yeah! And?"

"They bought it, went elsewhere."

"Damn."

"Uh-huh."

"Who else."

I cough. "The Jerk and Run Kid. As usual."

"HAKH! So what happened."

"The usual. Kid caught sight of me, bolted in mid-spurt."

"HAAHAARRKH! Got to get him to give us a demo sometime."

"Uh-huh. Swingin' dick situationist putz-whack."

"HAARKH!"

"Yayup."

"What else."

"Not much. Coupla cute phone calls. Cuter than usual."

The Fatman's eyes gleam. "Yeah?"

"Some guy yelling: *THAR'S A PARAKEET UP MAH ASS GON' DIE IF YOU DON'T MAKE ME CUHM!'*

"HAARKH!" Fatman, "HAARRKH!"

"And this other one like ring-ring: Hello, Bluto's. *Hullo, um, I've, like, got a, um, request? A request. Yeah, um, could you, like, hold the phone to your pussy?* Say WHAT? *Um, I said could you –* I HEARD what you SAID, FUCKwit, do I sound like a BITCH to you? *Um sure, dad always did.*"

"HAARKH! HAAARKH! HAHAAAARRKH! – "

Fatman on his back, heaving. From his gape mouth, a dull bronchial roar.

I move, thinking *now or never*. A foot from the door I pause, glance over my shoulder. Fatman like a stricken walrus, waterbed undulant. I glom the scene an instant, palms joined. Then I mutter prayerful, bow sideways and step out into darkness.

***

I pass through bead-light gloom, pause at corridor's end, push open the door and wham: light in my mug like a flaming hull. I hold still a moment, grimacing. Then I step out into the store and move, head bowed. Up aisle one following my own sweat trail, past the dildos beeping a ditty *(Yankee Doodle went to town, riding hot and horny, stuck two Flintstones up his butt and called 'em Fred and Barney)*, past 3D interactive skinflicks, mobile hologram fuckmags, christmas pornophernalia. A face appear at aisle's end, hazing again into view:

"Bet you worked him good. Huff huff."

"You know it," I go brushing past, Bama Jack chortling in my wake. On to the screen door, left foot punt: out.

I break stride on the porch. Break stride, break wind and pause, breathing deep. Ahead, the lot full as before, glint of quiet steel. And beyond, the woods dark, distant corona of city light.

I shut my eyes, vanished thoughts in echo. Darkness. Then an image in slow bloom: boy crouched on a gilded mirror, man with sodden loins laughing. Through the glass darkly a voice in song, the words strange, gravid with absent meaning:

Slipstream hogpike slammer peekaboo
Dickweed dog-schlong stroke a kangaroo
Don't keep diddling that drool-slick cockatoo
Or you'll end up spewing your sticky foghorn stew –

I flinch: something against my leg. I look down, shake my head. Little Boy, Fatman's fat cat, a chocolate-point Siamese. Gazing up, eyes sheened in rondure.

"Little Boy," I go, "Little Boy, you prickless wonder."

Mrreeowww.

"Little Boy, ya fat castrate."

Mrreeeowwww.

I sink to my haunches, begin scratching his chin. His lids droop.

"Jubilate Agno," I whisper, "Smart's cat Jeoffry."

Little Boy flop on his side, purring. I rub his forepaws, comb his fatted flank. The purring deepens, pleasure detonating silent down his length, out to his tail.

For this, his truest delight, the truest he's ever known.
For he is of the neuter, a eunuch.
For he quickens not to the throb of seasonal lust.
And rends not his rivals in feral rut.
Nor unseams them neck to netherhole in mad pursuit of pussy.
Wherefore this joy I unstintingly offer him: scratch, comb and tickle.
Rub, knead and tweak till he fall overcome and stiffen –

I rise. Bow. And on tiptoe leave him, cat to catatone. Myself silent down the porch steps, a shadow moving nameless across the lot.

***

They emerge as I approach: John, Monk, Wald, out the car stiff-legged, muttering.

"Bitch took his time," John, slamming his door.

I step up, hands on crotch. "Time, yeah, but only in a manner of speaking. Vis-à-vis the unity of pure apperception. Sic passim."

"With green tigers sleeping furiously," Monk.

"Green sick," Wald, "heh heh."

John peel back his lips. Spit bare-fanged.

"Shoulda killed all three of 'em. Back when."

I hold out my hand. "Your pocket beam please, sirrah. No time to waste."

John pull out his pocket beam, toss it over.

"Knock yourself out."

I catch it left-handed, click it on.

"Walkies now children. Walkies."

They fall in behind. John first, Monk next, Wald keestered, sputtering gutsmoke. Single file out the lot, across the road and into the woods, my footsnouts crunching dead leaves, bumping pine cones, the beam in my hand a luminous sabre, foliage closing in susurrant. Voiceless we, in descent, words mysteriously stanched in gravitas.

A rustle sounds overhead and I start, beam raking foliage. Glimpse of red featherwing: gone. A cardinal by the look of it, bird out of season. Must've lost its way. Separated from its fellows. He-bird or she-bird? Hard to tell. Doth it mount aflutter or crouch demure? Can't say. Just a cardinal in the dark. As in: Ode to a Cardinal, by Steak the palsied poet:

My wind breaks,
And a deadly pungence assails my sense,

As though of moonshine I had drunk,
Or troubled a foraging Dixie skunk,
That threatened with redolence,
Of its poison posterior incense,
With etiolate aphasia,
And too early senescence –

"Where you takin' us jungleboy, fuckin' Solomon's Mines?"

I pause. Turn. John's scowl spotlit.

"You're startin' to ride me haggard now, fella," I go, "cut the bwana jive and follow quiescent. We're almost there."

John mutter, plant a boot in my rump and shove. I stumble, shout out an oath, proceed cursing. John all hoot and cackle, Wald in echo.

The gradient levels off ten paces down, us coming out the woods onto a clearing: a paved terrace walled off in a semi-circle. I flash the beam around, catch it: a battered sign that read: LOUT PIT, some letters missing. LOOKOUT POINT is what it mean to say.

"Git a move oane, bitch dawg," goes John thumping my shoulder.

"The erle king speaks," Monk, "voice of thunder."

"Thunder bitch," Wald, "heh heh."

I curse. Click off the beam. Walk over to the wall and stand with foot propped, night breeze whining.

John saunter up a moment later, pause beside.

"Some view," he goes, "ay?"

I nod, gazing. Beyond the wall the hillside in collapse, Churchtown showing below in fulgent expanse. Lights aswirl, foodsigns spiked livid.

"City's shaped like a heart," goes Monk at left, "an animal heart."

"More like a spangled asshole to me," John.

"Heart-shaped asshole," Wald, "heh heh."

I chuckle, feeling it: the city's fibrillate pulse, blood heat rising. The rabble ranged abroad in obligatory disport, ravening. All but a few who remain indoors, or beyond city limits: Fatman diddling his dialectic, peddling pecker-thrills. Duquesne under his yak-fur cape, abject before an altar-portrait of Crowley. The Thrillkillers ringed around an eviscerate possum, jizzing incarnadine. Skeeter in his tat parlor drilling a razorhead, misting gore and ink. Gilmer at the State Park boomeranging squirrels, or in his shack glomming snuff. Artie Mangus excruciate in the Meister's shadow, or in delirium, mumbling odes to Koch spit. Jimmy Rotgut on his backroom bidet, laving his haemorrhoids with warm stoat bile. Pater Jed at home playing Martian sugardaddy, tits soused with goatmilk. Reverend Bartlett in the throes of prophecy, pounding his gook slave to kingdom cum. Rick the Scavenger discoursing mantic, mana of the transcendent or insane on diseased lips. Billy Hyuck'n'Dang at the Grotto dishing his swill, watching fratyobs rage in drunken fleshmeld. But above all, our Lord Meister Howell in his fastness *causa sui*, stoking the fires of abyssal torment –

I straighten in slow exhale. Turn.

"Time now brothers. Meld time."

"Huh?" John, "say what?"

"Meld," I go, "remember?"

John grunt. "Sheeat. Let's get to it."

Monk turn, beard in hand. "Meld, yes. Not to forget."

"PooOOP!" Wald, pulling a two-hand nad grab, "heh heh."

I stick the beam in my pocket. Walk to the middle of the terrace. Stand spraddle-legged, arms loose. John, Monk, Wald, approaching a moment later, standing likewise.

"You guys ready?" I ask, limbs twitching.

"Sheeat," John.

"MmBRRP!" Wald.

"Fire at will," Monk.

I cough, inhale deep and let fly.

"STRIKE!" I shriek, throwing my arms up and out, fingers splayed.

"STRIKE!" they echo, arms up likewise.

Silence. Us spraddle-legged in a circle, arms raised, fingertips joined.

"Many many MOOOONS," I go, nares twitching, "MOOON."

"Many many MOOOONS," they echo, "MOOON."

"Multifarious moons of DRUMMM," I go, lashes fluttering.

"Multifarious moons of DRUMMM."

I shut my eyes, feeling my palps tingle. *Here it come*, I think, *here it come*. And it does.

A tremor pass through my body, arm to arm, rippling around the circle. I open my eyes slow and see it: a pencil of blue light emerging from my brow. From John's brow. Monk's brow. Wald's brow. *Lowenbrau*. Four smoke-blue brow pencils lengthening, meeting at a point above our heads. At this nexus a Form showing in miniature: the Meister's Notion as diadem.

"See it," I go, "oooh."

"Dig it," John, "aaaah."

"Grock it," Monk, "mmmm."

"Hung," Wald, "heh heh."

Seconds pass. On bloody stilts. Us posed motionless, browbeams porrect. Silence till I move my lips, sonant.

"It have Form," I go, "determinate structure."

"Determinate?" Monk, "I think not. To determine is to negate. To negate is to limit. But the Meister's Notion be without limit. It subsumes and transcends... to formlessness."

I frown. "Form, brothers, FORM. Etched boundaries. N to the power googolplex, N being the dimensional constant at any given micro-instant – "

"KAAAATZ!" shriek Monk, wild-eyed, "KAAAATZ!"

A shudder pass around the circle, browbeams retracting annelid. The Notion bereft, going nova, falling like a child's rainbow tear.

"Well shit," I go, dropping my arms, "that's – "

John reach with a curse, grab Monk's beard.

"WHUT'D YOU DO THAT FOR, WHORE! WHUT THE FUCK YOU DO THAT FOR."

Pause. Monk chin up, frozen.

"SPEAK UP, COOZEPONE!" John tugging, "SPEAK UP!"

Monk move: his right hand sliding up his left sleeve. Sliding back out. Metal gleam.

"Now, hatchetman," he goes pointing, "let go please, or spew brain rearwise."

John stare, beard still in hand. "That a snubnose?"

Monk seem to smile. "Quite. *Beretta Nouveau*, model NX$-11. Fresh off the market. Nine bullets. Small but potent."

"Beretta ay? Didn't spot it on ya."

"No," Monk, "well concealed. In my armpit. Subdermal cavity. Sort of a gun graft. I'm going to count to three."

"Gun graft," John, "GUN graft?"

"One."

"Sheeat."

"Two."

John let go with a curse, wheel around.

"Bitch ain't worth it," he mutter, moving.

I watch him stalk up to the edge of the clearing, vanish into the woods. Then I turn, speak in query:

"Dang, boy. You'd've killed him for THAT?"

Monk smile, tooth-white: a weird sight.

"Braindeath," he go, tucking away his piece, "the beard being sacrosanct."

"Beard," me, "SACRO?"

Monk don't answer. Him nursing his beard two-handed, going:

"Wee little one. Wee wee little one – "

I spit. Shake my head.

"See y'all at the car," I go, starting back up, "holy see."

"See yes," Monk, "weeeeee – "

Wald still posed with arms on high, going:

"Bitch. Beard. Death. Brain. Little One. Heh heh. Heh heh. Heh heh – "

***

Trees float past. No, not trees. Brains. Bicameral brains sparking and quivering in a red plenum. Somewhere a radio crooner going:

Ooh starry night baby winken blinken love,
Whip leather slash ooh fit me like a glove –

I turn, hearing laughter: Trotjohn naked on a surfboard, a starved infant hung between his thighs. *Harf harf,* John, *harf harf –*

Oooh my white hot magma,
Oooh your funky yellow smegma –

The infant stir, start to fatten. It rise tumid, cheeks in purple swell. John laugh, grab a passing brain two-handed. The infant's mouth stretch to reveal bright piranha teeth. *Get a load of THIS*, goes John, the infant plunging head-first in cortical cleavage. I scream, come awake, John's laughter in echo.

Silence, engine hum. Trotjohn at left, hunched. Ahead, Dirt Road in highbeam span, foliage on either side glowering.

"Where we at," I mumble, "hey?"

John give me a look. "End of the road baby. You been down a while. Bad trip, by the sound of it."

I grunt, flick crud off an eyelash. "Bad trip is right. You and your little crotch-ghoul fucking an adult brain."

"HARF!" John, "figures."

I look over my shoulder. Monk in back, cross-legged, Wald slumped beside.

Monk raise a hand in weary benison.

"In sleep as it is in waking. Give us this day our daily brainfuck."

"Crotch-trip ghoul-fuck," Wald, "heh heh."

John curse, wrench the wheel: Dirt Road gone sigmoid.

I sit back, branches clawing the roof. "Comrades John and Monk. Did y'all kiss and make up, hey?"

"Damn right," John, "bitch copped a feel, caught some tongue action."

"And more, after these messages," Monk.

The car skid around the last curve, hit the stretch out. Vrroom: trees blurring dark on either side, a spot of green shimmering in aperçu. Roadsign.

"Slow down;" I go hand raised, "Hillview comin' up – "

But he don't slow, John. Him tearing past the roadsign and slicing left at the last instant, my right ear giving with a pop, gunk warm on my shoulder as the car screech in a tight, blazing arc.

"YEEEE-HAWWWWW!" John, his head canted centripetal, Wald yipping catarrhine, myself waxing profane as I flick ear-mush off my shoulder, the Durerro back on Hillview, balling in descent.

"You needs must ease up now old son," enjoin Monk, "traffic lights ahead in serial plethora."

John curse under his breath, barreling heedless. The road curves, a light drifting into view ahead: red orb in nighted suspension.

"Here we go," I announce, "fucker's gonna run red again, tragedy repeated as farce."

The light loom, turn green as the car zip under.

"One down, bitches," John, "eight more to go."

"You got lucky," me, "won't hold till the next one."

But it does hold, his luck, the second light going green as he smoke under, the third and fourth following suit.

"Either the fucker's charmed," I declare, "or else them lights be linked across the morphogenetic field via the Sheldrake Constant. Or mayhap it be some kind of electromag synergy, or photon beam resonance, or some kinda phlogistic neoplasm in vibrant harmony – "

Whack: his right hand lashing out, knuckles smacking my jaw, me recoiling with a yelp, my head thumping windowglass.

"You best clam up in a hurry now, ho," he advise, "had just about enough of o' your lip."

"Charmed fucklip," Wald, "heh heh."

I lean back, hand on jaw, cursing sub-audible.

"Whut was that now?" John, turning threatful.

"Oh, nothing. Just a prediction."

"A prediction."

"That's right. You're gonna have your nuts ripped off in your sleep one of these days."

"Haarf!" John, "yowp."

"Rip your pre-dick-tion," Wald, "heh heh."

Silence ensue for a minute. John hunched grim over the wheel, steering with chin and lip. Nothing to slow us this time, not even hotrod harvesters. Us zooming in descent, trees on either side cringing, bluffs rearing back astonished.

Churchtown appear halfway down, the hillside dropping at left. Night city in silent disquiet, dreaming bloodsport and orgasm. In thought a daedal knife tracing lines on pale belly-skin. Jaguar teeth embedded in a milkwhite thigh. Gore-snout pitbulls at the throat of a chained bear. Starved lions crunching the skulls of the faithful. Ship's captain keel-hauling the flayed seaman. Marquis in coloured muslin dismembering the lashed soubrette. These and others in the clouded iris of night's eye death-blind –

"Harf," John, tapping the brakes, "check 'em out."

I blink. "What now?"

"Up there, bitch dawg."

I frown. A vehicle ahead cruising downhill.

"Who," I go, "who dat in – "

John put out a whoop, surge up behind the vehicle in seconds flat. John now at the tailgate sniffing fender-rump. Inches ahead, a black van with an emblem on back: grey death's head with busted sinciput, bleeding eyes, pincer teeth. Thrillkillers.

John honk, cut left. The van driver turn as we draw level: a face like bashed fatback, shaved piltdown skull, pig eyes narrow with hate. Poondog. Beside him Peckertrash half in profile: hook-beaked, cachectic.

John reach, hit a button. My window slide halfway down: windroar.

"YOU BOYS BEST BE OANE TIME!" he yell, "OR IT'S YOUR ASS!"

Poondog nod brief, look away. Peckertrash holding up a twisted claw.

My window slides shut, the Durerro cutting ahead. On past Mason, the light above still green. Hillview heading straight down now, pine cover thickening either side.

The road level out moments later, curving some. Lights appear at right: the A9 service station, eighteen-wheelers being lubed, gassed, pumped, drained. Attendants in chimp suits riding spokeless unicycles, juggling dipsticks, lugnuts, live jumper cables, dead batteries pouring smoke.

"Poondog," I go, "how come Poondog and Peckertrash back there?"

John tap the brakes, suck spit.

"Fuckers drivin' in from Ardville. Aladdin's funeral up in Ardville. Wudn't much left to bury. Thrillboys ate most of him."

I chuckle, remembering. Old Aladdin. Trapezoid skull, prosthetic antlers, dripping moose tongue. Kinda quiet for a Thrillkiller, had a thing for fat mamas. Infant *idée fixe*. Liked to play diaper dummy. Aladdin in his vaginal crib, bonnet and loinwrap, gettin' whaled with a plastic popsicle, three hundred pound dominatrix doing the needful. Dead now, more's the pity. Aladdin roaring downhill on his hog, take a wrong turn and sail off into the night. Real mess when we found him: all brain, gut and twisted limb, Trotjohn going: *it's awright, kid saved us some trouble. This way he be easier to cook and eat –*

"The sickness," intone Monk, "how he rose from the sickness."

I turn. The Wald up and grinning, mouth gone soggy.

"Spit'n'swallow," he husk, "heh heh – "

John curse, glaring in rearview. "Boy, you mess up my car with your nad gunk, I'm gon' pull your tongue out your ass and nail it to a tree."

The Wald don't answer. Him back at work, deep-throating his confection.

"It's your fault, Teej," I go, "you been too easy on him. Rulebook say: don't feed the monkey."

John speed up, mutter and growl, the car hitting the exit loop at a mean clip.

"Slow," I quaver, "go slowww daddy-ooo – "

But he don't. The car in full keen, brain drag in g-force centrifuge, my left ear giving with a tinnital squeak, mush gouting warm on my left shoulder.

"Fuckin' dong-chomp," I go wiping off with the tail of my bandanna, John with a hoot merging on the beltway.

I sit back, run a hand down my mug. Not much to see on this stretch. Just rigs in rapid approach, streaking past in redshift. I shut my eyes, retinal trace lights blurring in jagged streamers. My thoughts drift, images flickering in REM. Somewhere on a pudendal dreamscape, a three-foot homunculus bursts out of my pecker, shrieking in faux deutsche. With my bunghole gaped annunciate, bawling in counterpoint going: *Kill 'em all, bionic surf Nazis kill, kill, kill…*

***

It's dark when my eyes open. Not dark per se, not dark *qua* dark, just darker than before. Ahead, a straight stretch: Route 54 heading east. At left, open land, lights in the distance. At right a nighted expanse out to the hills, the TV tower winking red.

I sit up, press my cheek to the window. Skydark, no moon. Quiet inside the car and out, just the hiss of vented air and a soft snore: Wald in back, spent. Beside him, Monk wide awake but in stasis, lotus-posed with head bowed, chin tucked in the hollow of his throat. Stoking the old Kundalini fire, Monk, transmuting curdled jizm into prana energy. Subtle ganglionic fission, keep them chakras spinning. What he do when he's deadly bored. Like if there's nothing else, why not deliquesce your own dram. A hip gnostic celibate, Monk, has been long as I've known him. Spill his seed only in ritual, usually a triple cum-squirt over a flaming mandala fed with dry flops and clarified butter. You put Monk in a moving car, he'll do one of two things: sublimate nad-elixir OR crack a beat-riddler koan.

Fine. Man's got to have a hobby. Like Garbage Gary who fed his kin down a disposal unit. Me, I write mind-poems when there's nothing else. Gedanken verse on the windows of my skull. Like I did in the old days, back when. Dead time alone in the house when the minutes bled, the hours weeping clockless. In that azoic fastness invoking the Muse, naked before a gilded mirror dreaming cornhole quatrains, shithouse shlokas, spunk-sonnets, hamfist haiku. Two in particular that I recall well:

Hiawatha Hyuck'n'Dang

Sock'n'slam, we'll drain our dram
Raise good boys guts fulla spam
Hyuck'n'Dang! Slap dick 'n' wang!
Blow hog's meat Alabam!

Catkill

You got a filthy cat
Ugly as sin
You let him out
Look what he drug in
No don't tell me
Yes I will
You got to see
It's some kinda kill:
Got bloody fingers bloody toes

Bloody ears a bloody nose
Bloody eyeballs on a stick
A bloody little peewee prick:
Bitch, didn't I tell yew to quit sucklin' the critter?

These and others flowering in thought like marsh loti under a diseased moon –

"Har har," John, "har har."

I turn. "What now Mojimbo."

"Up ahead," John jerking his chin, "Smiley's."

I squint. Lights up ahead by the roadside. Scooter Rambo's body shop. Beside it, Smiley's Beverages.

"You never did tell," John with a snicker, "never did tell why you quit workin' Smiley's."

I frown. "I didn't quit. I was shitcanned."

"Yeah yeah, but how COME."

"CUM!" Wald rearing up, "CUUUUM – "

"Down WHORE," John whipping a backhand, Wald retreating with a jagged hawg-squeal.

I shake my head. "Not like you haven't heard the story before."

"Not like I cain't hear it AGAIN," John, "not like I cain't BEAT it outta ya, if I DON'T."

I snort. "Yeah well. Old Smiley. Haven't seen him in a while. Demented old putz, three dickheads short of a pecker. Recall the first time I laid eyes on him. Bulb nose, beady eyes, pinhead pupils: sanpaku. *You don't look like you're from around here,* he go. *I'm not,* I go, *my old man bought me off a Dutch nun, Island Maurice, stuck me in a puppy hamper, smuggled me into good ol' down-home Churchtown. Well awright,* he goes, *I've had pickaninnies workin' for me before.* Uptight old hump, Smiley, didn't pay much, kept a bloodshot eye on me all hours. But an easy stint, easy pelf, nightshift off the freeway. Sell swill, stick bills in the till. Drum-gut truckers, killer razorheads, baccy-champin' good ol' boys glomming six-pax, tall colds, boiled eggs pickled in boarpiss. Nubiles sashaying in moist-lipped, me trading grog for tit-gropes. Plus some lush geezers limping in regular. Like old Philo Sumter, boontown sadsack shuffling in past sundown for a hit of hillbilly moonshine. Philo slack-jawed, lamenting his dishwater sperm, his fused vertebrae, his scirrhotted liver, his caseated kidney, his atrophied nads, his cataract eyes, his suppurate septum, his boiling buboes, his fissured bunghole, his filarial foot, his besnotted lungs, his rot gut, his calcified joints, his wasted gums – "

"HAARF!" John, "HAHAARF!"

"Slacknad bungshine," Wald, "heh heh."

Monk silent but with head cocked, hearkening.

"Healthy little turd, Philo. Not around anymore, sad to say. They found him dead a couple years back, half-eaten by a guard dog he tried to fuck. Had a thing for dogs, Philo did. He'd humped a few poodles in his time, coupla chihoos, but that wasn't enough. He wanted the big boys: Doberman, German fuckin' Shepherd, Mastiff, Rottweiler, Great Dane, maybe even a ham-fed Pitbull. Just one of Smiley's people, kind that came in every night. Guess I'd still be farming the joint if it hadn't happened. If Smiley hadn't walked in one night and found me ass down on a beerkeg mashing my mongoose. Just about wigged him shitless, that did. Him all foam-lipped, nystagmic going: *Whut the HALE? Whut the HALE?* Myself in mid-spasm going*: whoa now, easy there slim, don't hit the deep end with your shoes on, we were just passin' the time is all, me and little man onan, just sittin' here angling my aardvaark, knuckling my noodle. Corking my codpiece, belting my bugle. Icing my igloo, diddling my dickiebird. Jerking my jimweed, hashing my hamburg. Mangling* *my meatball, slapping my sauerkraut. Pounding my piddlestick, flapping my funspout. Trashing my tupperware, rousting my rattler. Violating my varmint, whacking my wiener. Quashing Queequeg, ogling Opie. Goosing Garfunkel, educating Eddie –* "

John convulsed, thumping the windscreen: "HARRH! HAHAARRH!"

Wald with feet up kicking the roof, "HEESH! HEHEESH!'

Monk stroking his beard speculative, blinking rapid.

Minutes pass in caesura, my thoughts inchoate. The car silent once more, slicing through open land bedarked, Route 54 East. I'm sinking, my eyes touching the silken hem of sleep when lights appear: yellow, blue and red blurred on the gauze of my lashes.

"Skeeterman," goes John drumming the wheel, "here we come."

"Yeh!" Wald, "SkeeEEET! Heh heh."

We blitz past a truck, a couple cars. They don't look like they're moving. I glance at the console: speed needle touching two hundred. A shade under destruct velocity.

"Slow down now friar," I go, "Wheeden Creek coming up."

John mutter, cover his eyes. "Bitch think I'm blind."

The road rise some, the car hitting the bridge with a clamor. Glimpse of creekwater below: dark, winking red. Looks alive somehow, like it want my sweet ass. No surprise. Time was, you could make your water and drink it too. Now you quaff the stuff, your tongue burn, your eyes go lachrymose, your teeth come loose. Then your gut bloat with sewergas, your bunghole shoot fire, your kidney hit your nutsack, your prick shrivel like a crushed raisin. Stuff I'd pay to see.

The road curve past the bridge, the lights showing clear. EZ Stop Gas/Grocery. Mika Jack's Diner. And beyond, a sign in blue and red: SKEETER'S TATTOO.

John slot down, cruise past the gas station. Past the diner. Skeeter's parlor accrue ahead in silhouette: beaverboard shack with a low stoop, not much to look at. Kinda place you'd drive past thinking: *just another trash tat joint.* But it isn't, Skeeter's being special. Man's an artist, is what. A gin-you-wine skinstain virtuoso. A genius, Skeeter. And a lunatic. Some days you see him in his cassock, mooning drivers, jiggling his beergut, pissing on mailboxes. Kinda like Diogenes the Cynic. Or Cryogenics the Dick. Or one them beat zen filth wisdom types, only beater and filthier. Other days you see him fast-walking backwards, eyes wide, arms outstretched yelling: "BLUE TIT SMACKDOWN! EGGSHELL! EGGSHELL?" Harmless dreck for the most part, except for the time he burst into Mayor Bob's office tossing boiled jellybeans yelling: "KILTFREAK BUTTERBALL! BEANMUSH FLOOSIE! APE! APE! APE!" Got cuffed for that'n sure enough. Skeeter's done plenty time in the cooler. Various minor offences. Pigs used to put the rumble on him back then, not anymore. Best that way. Stick him in the brig, he end up decorating the interior with a cellmate's turd –

Knock knock. Knock knock.

I blink. Turn. Trotjohn outside rapping the window, Monk and Wald beside. The car parked, lightless. I shake my head, push, climb out.

"Bitch holdin' out for a special invite," goes John, stepping aside.

"Yeh," Wald, "special bitch. Heh heh."

I curse, slam the door shut. "With you guys, a man can't hold out for anything. Not even his own dick."

"Hold dick out," Wald, "heh heh."

John spit, turn, start walking, Monk and Wald after. Myself following reflexive, my muzzled sneakersnouts gone kinetic.

Skeeter's lot isn't paved, I notice. Used to be, but isn't now.

Flat hard earth strewn with rubbish: bottles, cartons, discarded footwear, rubbers half-eaten, rusted tattoo drills, a craphole plunger, shredded tyres, decapitate girlie dolls, plastic porn icons impaled with kebab skewers. I kick the stuff aside to make way. I kick a painted femur drilled with holes, kick it a long way off saying: "I refute it THUS."

Skeeter's Parlor look empty this night. No sound that I can hear. *Or mayhap he be working on someone real QUIET like?* I fondly ask. No, can't be. Skeeter's a noisy hump. Plus the Durerro's the only car in the lot.

I look over at Mikajack's. Busy night by the look of it. The lot full of cars, pickups. Through the pane, a glimpse of hog-jowled mugs feeding. Tonight's Special: gatorbrain goulash with pickled kudzu. Dessert: a choice of glazed cedarbark, honeyed compost, xanthum gum sucree –

"YO SKEETERMAN!" goes John, booting open the door, "WHERE YOU AT, FUCKBONE."

Pause. Then a squawk within. Not Skeeter.

I jog up to the stoop. Step in after John, Monk, Wald. Silence. And light. Lamps on near the couch. Near the wash stand. Near the papal fuckdoll, the hardwood pillory, the nylon noose. *But Skeeter? Whither Skeet?*

"Harf," goes John, "fuckin' eedjit."

I turn. Smile. There in the corner at left. Skeeter on a deckchair facing a miniscreen SAT tube. Him with feet drawn up, cassock pulled back over his knees, heels propped on the rim. No skivvies in sight. Not a stitch. His schlong in full evidence, praise lawd. And his nuts. These showing in bold relief as they must. Conspicuous as a corpse in a kinderpen.

Skeeter's wang look the same as ever and always: like a woodland varmint asleep. Or hibernating. Or stupored in deep melancholia (*why so pale and wan, fond pecker?*). His nuts hang low over the rim of the deckchair. Low enough to sweep the yard with, walking on his knees. Or scuttling on all fours, naked at high noon. Skeeter's toads swag pendulous on account of their size, each one big as a north Georgia kumquat, each one pink, glabrous, unwrinkled. And identical: them nestled side by side, plumb even. Not one below the other, as you'd expect. Skeeter don't have a Papa Nad and a Baby Nad. He have two heavy-ass, dead-ringer dinosaur eggs. A twin pair of hypertrophic grandaddy horse-bollocks.

Moments pass. Myself by the door digging Skeeter's meat, John's words echoing in recollect: *Skeeter's an ace friggin' lust-meister, a sperm king with cast iron cojones. He blow his wad the 13th of every month, past sundown. You can hear it miles around: sound like a bazooka goin' off in a vat of lard. Usually kill the bull-steer he been fuckin' –*

"Skeeterman," goes John, "yo Skeeterman."

Silence. Skeeter motionless, eyes glazed, colours aswirl on his brow. From the SAT tube a squawk, canned laughter.

I step away from the door, walk around to the deckchair.

"Skeeter. Man Skeeter."

No response. Skeeter glomming his glass teat, cataleptic. I turn to look. A funshow on: *Nat G Special.* A pack of wild dogs closing in on some pith helmet schlub, a Saxon Island dweeb on Big Shikar. The dweeb have a rifle, but he isn't using. Just hopping in place going: *awwwk! awwwkh!* Piss rills down his bare leg, canned voices titter –

HawwWWKH!

The canned audience roar, dweeb going under. Now the dogs ravening at his crotch, his throat: one hackled cur making off with a clutch of entrail, another pissing on pith. The audience in tumult, the scene a roil of gore-fang and blood-snout. Buzzards swoop down, wings husking. Lions approach flat-eared, baleful. Leopards cough, change spots. Wildebeest low, drop dung. Elephants test the air, trunks raised. Monkeys leap and chitter. Nature alive for the sponsors, the wilds stoked by design –

The scene switch: end Funshow bathos. The host appear, weeping with mirth. *Well folks,* he gasp, *that was the short happy life of Francis Hamburger. Next up, a shipping tycoon poops on the poop deck, then jumps overboard to feed the sharks in situ –*

Click. The scene fade, collapse to a point, Trotjohn stepping up with a scowl:

"Cain't suck oane that there tube when you got guests, Skeeterman. CAIN'T."

Pause. Skeeter unmoved, unblinking. *Is he dead,* I wonder, *rigor mortis with nuts in the breeze, pecker aimed at death's dream kingdom?*

John move up a step. Reach with his right foot. Nudge Skeeter's ballsack with the tip of his boot. The gonads shake ponderous, like apples in a giftsock, like the dugs of a bull elk in rut.

Skeeter stir, sigh, look up blinking.

"Johnboy," he grate, "John Trotville in the flesh."

John shake his head. "Sheeat."

Skeeter smile, lips oozing apart. I wince. Fucker's teeth haven't gotten any prettier. Them worse than ever: discoloured, lanuginous, like they've been boiled in sulphur, beeswax, verdigris. *Best not get too close. His basilisk breath can kill –*

"Johnboy," goes Skeeter, "yah. Ha ha."

I exhale in increments, staring. His teeth gone worse, yes, but his mug unchanged. Cropped mule-hair pulled back from a high spalled brow. Dead blue eyes, honed beak. Withered sulcate cheeks, cleft chin. Like Manson meet Rasputin in a backwater gulag.

I reach. Touch his shoulder. "Man Skeeter. Hey."

Skeeter look up grinning. "Kid JB, yah. JB in the flesh."

"Fleshtube," Wald by the door, "heh heh."

Skeeter lean over the hem of his cassock. Spit on his dick.

"Baby Wald, yah. And the Monk. And Trotjohn. And kid JB. Four rapscallions, scallywags, spalpeens. Cold dawgs in from the courtyard – "

He grin all around, Skeeter, eyeballs on the roll.

John move back a step, lip curling. "Man, that ain't a mouth. That be a fuckin' sewer."

"Sewer man mouthfuck," Wald, "heh heh."

Skeeter raise his brows, break into hoarse laughter.

"Ho ho, yaah. Ho ho. Nasty now, NASTY."

John curse. "This ain't a social visit, dig? Looksee's what we're here for. Quick little looksee. We don't have all fuckin' night."

Skeeter nod, grinning. "Natch. Didn't think you did. Boys up to some nasty business this night. Scuttlin' for Buford Howell, yah?"

John's face tighten, eyes lightless. "Who the fuck told YOU."

Skeeter chuckle. "Shee-it. Thar's no night or day I know of you boys ain't out trippin' with the Devil."

I cough. "Skeeterman. Before I forget: greetings from our Meister. Homage and greeting, Buford Aloysius Howell, *Lord Baron of Pain.*"

Skeeter cackle. "Shee-it. That time of year agin."

I nod. "Just a little looksee. Our talisman."

Skeeter scratch his head, set down his feet.

"Your wish, my reprimand."

I figure he start right off Skeeter, but he don't. He pull a little stretching routine first: bone creak and tendon twang, fartbursts to round off.

"All set," he go shuddering, "on with the show."

John step aside, hand over nose. "Fuckin' hell hole death gas. Gut fulla tokay bootleg, roadkill ringworm."

Skeeter cackle, walking. "This way, girls."

I start after, unbreathing, John, Monk, Wald, falling in behind. He quarter across, Skeeter, myself tagging at a healthy distance. I watch him walk, digging his peculiar gait. Not as odd as Watt's, but close enough. Like he's dragging something with his right foot. Something heavy, like a float of rodents in forced embrace, copulating without purpose. Skeeter move with an elaborate chaingang shuffle, knees bent, buttocks cleaved haemorrhoidal. Put me in mind of a syphilitic leprechaun, a wingshorn buzzard, a consumptive coyote with the soul of a primate.

Skeeter make it across in hobbling saltigrade, out to the far corner where he do his tattooing. This here corner sectioned off with an assortment of objects that evoke folly, liminal torment, the ineradicable pallor of living death.

I dig the objects with both eyes, mark them well. Them thrawn and fetid in arcane dispose: a rusted pannikin, an outsize plastoid nipple, a taxidermal stoat, a stained crapseat bitten off at one end, a jar of moribund termites, a turquoise *ouch* glued to the back of a dead gekko, a decaying ox-tongue pasted to a pink conch shell, a mound of sewage topped with a white Stetson, a cowheart wrapped in green diaphane, a child's appendix in a bowl of yellow vomit. All these placed equidistant in an arc subtending the angle of his work corner.

Skeeter's *atelier* thus form a wedge one-fourth the area of a hypothetical circle sixteen feet in diameter, give or take a yard. Upon this wedge stand the instruments of his trade. *What instruments?* you ask tearful, *what?* These: 1. A small but functioning guillotine. 2. A four-hole pillory (three for head and hands, the fourth for engorged dick). 3. A barstool with a noose suspended above. 4. A wolf-trap with serrated edges. 5. A large ivory-grip tattoo drill.

Skeeter use these instruments in conjunction when he work. You want a Skeeter tattoo, you got to stick your head in his guillotine first. Then stand in pillory. Then jam your foot in his wolftrap. Then sit on his barstool with the noose tight around your neck. In that order. Guillotine, pillory, wolftrap and noose in steady rotation while he work on you, moving in circuit till he get done. IF he get done. Good chance he never will, given the high risk of decapitation, excruciate maiming or barstool garrote. The price you pay for great art.

He's a tachist, Skeeter. A tachistic action tattooist. He stalk you as you make the rounds, jabbing and swiping, a dot here, a slash there. He dance as he work, a strange ataxial jig. Only, you can't see the dance if you're getting tattooed. Why? Because you're blindfolded, that's why. Skeeter blindfold his clients with a ragged talith he bought off a hebe boltgun operator in a Dixie slaughterhouse.

Skeeter used the talith on me once. And on Trotjohn. On Monk. On Wald. We all got Skeeter tattoos, having been deemed worthy. John with fluorescent death's heads in his armpits and on his perineum (that mossy, fertile region between nad and bunghole). Monk with runes, glyphs, mandalas on the insides of his eyelids, on his gums, under his clove-scented tongue. Wald with little gator snouts, hyena dicks and killer borg roaches on his scalp, halfway up his nose, around his dodecahedral glanhead, on the grooves of his moth-eaten nutsack, between his toes. Me with a pair of nipples on my rump, one on each butt-mound. Why? Not sure. Figured I needed tits on my ass if not vice versa ipso facto –

Click. I blink. Lights on overhead: a pair of spotlights trained on the barstool. Skeeter sidling up, a-grin. Grabbing the stool.

Hopping on with a grunt.

"Whooo!" Wald, "jumpa horsy!"

Skeeter chortle around the side of his head, off his nape. Him now on the barstool facing away, John and I by the guillotine, Monk and Wald by the pillory.

"Awright now Skeeter," goes John, "we're waitin'."

Skeeter mumble. Bow his head. Extend his right foot, toes pointing. I see what they're pointing at: the wolftrap set five feet off (as the slug crawls), steel maw open wide.

"Doggie," goes Skeeter quavering, "here doggie. Here now doggie."

John turn with a frown. "Whut the – "

"Doggie!" Skeeter, voice rising, "here now doggie! Pappy callin' now. Come to pappy – "

Grrk! the sound. Grrnk! –

"Doggie! Here now doggie! – "

Grrk! the wolftrap shifting spasmodic, grrnk! in incremental approach, grrnk! closer and grrrnnk! closer still –

"Woo doggie. Woop! doggie. Ch-ch-ch-poop! HOOP! doggie. Mmm-p-p-p-rrOOO – "

The trap surge off the floor, clamp shut over Skeeter's right foot. Skeeter flinch. Then he throw back his head and put out a howl. Not a howl per se, more like a threnodic wail, a baboon shriek looped through porcine cords: sound he make fucking bulls knackered off the yokel rodeo.

On it goes, him swivelling thrice full circle, mouth gaped wider than Bacon's screaming pope. Skeeter venting a lungful, myself in awe thinking: *dang, just like the 13th of the month, him out by the slaughterhouse humping croup hip deep in dung under a dead moon –*

Stop. Silence and echo. Skeeter with head bowed, flesh in deep tremor. The wolftrap clamped tight over his foot, gore in slow drip pooling dark on the floor. This pool shaped like a raccoon paw, a crushed clover, an infant's hand.

"Goddamn," goes John, "fucker puttin' on a – "

Skeeter moan. Reach up with both hands. Pull the noose down over his head. Draw it tight around his neck.

"Looksee!" he croak, "lookh! ook-seeh! – "

I move: forward around the barstool to the corner where I pause, turn. Skeeter now full frontal: some view. His mug mottled, writhing. His cassock bunched around his waist, fingernails gouged deep in thigh meat. His dong quaking at half-mast, nads in erethistic tumult.

"Llrrook-sheeh!" Skeeter, "oorrk-heeh!"

I nod, walk back around to the guillotine. John wink as I approach. "Ever bang a wolf in a tattoo parlor?"

"He look ready," I go ignoring the question, "like a batrachian mutant fallen prey to a Gaullist chef."

John bare his teeth. "Let the fuckin' games begin."

I grunt. Turn. "Go to it Skeeterman," I command, "GO TO!"

Silence. Skeeter unmoved, time like a bolus in alimentary arrest.

"Skeeter!" bark John, "you heard the man. GO TO!"

Nothing. Skeeter on his stool graven. On his grave stooled. Blood from his foot going drip, drip, drip –

"Godammit Skeet," I go, "you – "

I break off with a frown, turn disbelieving: the Wald having erupted, sans preamble, into song. Him gape-mouthed with eyes wide, hands clasped, throat-apple on the bob. Wald playing *chanteur* castrate, chub-world diva *con cojones*.

John snarl. Take a step. "Fuck THIS shit. I'm gon' rip – "

"Hold," I go hand raised, "hold prithee. Sirrah."

John curse, hold. Wald coming on like a wigged out choirboy, the way a choirboy sound after his church paw get done juicing his confection. Wald's voice rising and falling in weird portamento, trilling in split-level concord. Him gone polyphonic, sounds issuing from every orifice.

I shut my eyes, hackles rising. Such a fey and eldritch nocturne I've never heard before, nawsuh. Put me in mind of the Hymns to Nyarlathotep, chants from the Cthulhu Doxology. I feel my pubes crawl, my pit-tufts horripilate. Soon my pineal gland take up the vibe, sparking visions. I see Obeah women placating Mojo, or is it Shango, I can't tell. Death-realm dakinis smashing heavy metal yantras with Fortean Tesla weapons. Mad chiliasts announcing Armageddon with fart-blown signal flares. Demented highlanders skewering livestock in dry-sperm kilts. Others I can't at this juncture invent, much less recall.

The aria waxes brief, ends abrupt. The parlor in echo, silence falling from a great height. I hold still, fists clenched. Then I slap my left tit, cork up my lids. There: Wald still with mouth agape, hands clasped, eyes brimming.

I blink, catching movement. Skeeter's hands now in ascent, cassock slipping off his shoulders, spotlights illuminating the stain beneath. The tattoo on his back showing stark, nape to rump, flank to flank: our looksee.

"Dig it," goes John hush-toned, "DIG it."

I dig. With twelve fingers, three spatular toes. Skeeter's dorsal derm-print. A samurai warrior kneeling on a tatami mat, blade plunged deep in his side. Across his belly a crimson clown-smile, blood-gash vomiting entrails. Below, his schlong shafting up engorged, spitting jizz. High above, clouds in lurid roil, lotuses in bloom, buddhas in zen groove, wrathful deities at war, dragons clashing furious. On the warrior's visage, rapture and torment mingled equal: the look you see on razorheads cornholing sandniggers, the one the Meister wear, shagging his nettled thornbush. Between drawn brows the warrior's Third Eye blaze coruscant, beaming light to a blackhole sun. A kensho cumshot *qua* seppuku. Enlightenment via disembowelment orgasm.

We look on in silence. Not silence per se. Wald on the nod, gurgling. John under his breath, exclaiming. Monk in an endorphin fog, sighing. Myself with teeth grit, muttering.

"Decay of the angel," declare Monk at length, "we approve wholehearted."

"Yowp," John nodding, "damn right."

Wald wide-eyed, whimpering.

"Was't a god who drilled those hues," Monk, "or was't a mortal hand?"

"Mortal," I husk, "old school nip named Saikaku. A floating-world type turned tattooman for the yakuza. Skeet stinted with Saikaku on Hokkai Island a few years, zone yakuza. The only gaijin steer-hump ever to get up close to them bad boys."

"Ah," Monk, "quite."

"Sheeat."

I exhale. Bend. Dig an elbow in my loins. Straighten grimacing. "A great piece forsooth, brothers, no question. But it only make me yearn for more. For Skeeter's own work, scenes drilled on pink, freckled flesh. Stuff Norm Rock's evil twin might've spawned if he hadn't been strangled at birth – "

I break off and turn quizzical, John having grabbed my shoulder.

"Zip it," Trotjohn, "or your nuts are critterfood."

I nod, tonsils twitching.

John turn, start away. "We out. Now."

"Out indeed," Monk starting after, Wald in a daze following. I watch them march to the front door. Then I turn, eyes moist. Skeeter on his perch motionless. On the floor the bloodpool growing, shaped now like a bear paw in a groper's mitt.

"Skeeter," I go, "Skeeterman."

No response. Skeeter graven voiceless in tattoo heaven.

I shrug, start away crabwise, quartering across. At the door I pause, thinking *light, light?* There: a panel behind the door, toggle-switch erect. I reach, slap it down: darkness in soundless jaw-snap.

"Gracias Skeeterman," I go, "plenty gracias."

Skeeter don't answer, didn't think he would.

I chuckle, turn, step out onto the stoop.

"See you in Erebus, Skeet," I go pulling the door shut, "that's 'Erebus' with an 'H', an 'E' and two 'L's."

Silence. Shadow-image of Skeeter noosed and clamped, in slow bleed, enisled there in the dark.

***

A sign appear ahead, grow large, zip past, green letters fluorescent: CHURCHTOWN CITY LIMIT.

"Out," I go clapping twice, "we out."

John snort. "Kid's a fuckin' genius."

I smile, suddenly enthused. Wanting this instant to get up on the roof and declaim, hold forth. Maybe even sing a scherzo, a Swiss Guard anthem, shout out a bawdy and scabrous philippic –

"I wouldn't, if I wuz you."

I frown, turn. Trotjohn in profile, jaw set.

"What," I go, "wouldn't what."

"Whatever it is you thinkin' of doin'."

I shake my head. "Man's a fuckin' mind-reader."

"Mindfuck," Wald, "heh heh."

I curse, sit back, shut my eyes, my thoughts in wild scatter.

Them like strobed minutiae dancing Brownian. Geodesic paramanus rising on fountains of light. Fulgent microbes playing musical chairs –

I open my left eye. My right. Route 54: a black ribbon spooling beneath. Open land either side, the hills far south, brooding. The moon somewhat in evidence now, face of a wan child at a fogged window.

I sit up, belch through my teeth, glance at the console. Speed: ultra-fast, escape velocity verging on auto-destruct. Only, it doesn't feel like it. Feels like we're frozen in place, watching this giant cyclorama, the scene blurred only at the edges, in canthus-vision.

The road rise, crest. Lights appear way off at left, lights of domicile. Ranch-houses off Espontaneo, North Zone, John's ranch-house among them. Not John's per se, more like his grandad's, not that it matters. The old codger don't live there anymore: him out in Alzheimersville crooning toneless, his mind gone under snowdrifts of amnesia.

We visited him once, John and I. This estate for gelt-battened dotards: high ivied walls, a wrought-iron gate. On grassy knolls, wheel-chaired fossils drooling. Grandpa under a greenback parasol cocking an occluded eye, going: *you're Mildred's boy ain't ya?* John spitting baccy juice, going: *nah. Mildred's the slut you knocked up in the gazebo, got her that no-neck cretin runs around oane all fours eatin' cowpats.*

Good thing the old turd's not around. Have himself a seizure if he saw the shit goin' down at his ranch. John's wangslap wingdings, hooter hoedowns, hawg-hump hootenannies, riotfest roguefucks, fartknocker fiestas, bikerbitch bacchanales, cockwhip cookouts, lapdingus luaus, smut saturnales, slimepit circlejerks. At Trotjohn's, the party never end, not till the Bunko Squad look out the precinct window and see jizzburst auroras, come wailing in on a rumble –

"Har har," John, "funtime."

I blink. "Wha?"

"Fun fun fun on the autobahn."

I straighten, see it: a vehicle ahead, lone pickup.

"Here vee komm," John in borg movie deutsch, "vee komm – "

Crushing the pedal as he speak, us whooshing up behind the pickup, brights aflash. Glimpse of mud-stained red, bumper sticker, flag.

"YAAAH!" John honking and flashing, "YAAAHARRRHH!"

Wald in back, squalling mimetic.

The pickup holds course a moment, then cuts right. John on the ball, veering pursuant, sniffing up anilingal.

"It's RUTTIN' time bitch. I'm oane yo' ASS."

"RUT!" Wald, rearing up between the headrests, "RUT! RUT!– "

"DOWN dawg," John, lashing whip-knuckle, Wald recoiling with a gander-croak.

I laugh, glance back. Monk posed hieratic, hands on crotch. Around his head, boredom in smoky aureole.

The pickup slow a mite, then surge, John raving in pursuit. I catch the bumper sticker: GUNS DON'T KILL, I DO. Above, a Confed flag half across the rear window.

"You're pissin' off a good ol' boy," I go, "he'll run us off the road, find me alive, gunfuck my glottis. Then he'll ram that barrel up my sweet ass and blow off my crown. Chances are, he's got more than just a gun. Chances are, he's got himself one them big–dick, heavy-metal, have-load-will-shoot bazookas you can mail order off the Killer Kooks, the Hot Holy Hessians, the Cyber Centurions, the Funkill Fascists, the Jarhead Jingos, the Hellspawn Hoplites, the Nuthouse Nazis, the Sickle Cell Stormtroopers, the Rumblin' Razorbacks, the Cracker Cossacks – "

Movement. Something in the hold of the pickup, a shadow rising. Doghead in outline: a pitbull.

"HotDANG!" John honking, "hotdang diggity DAWG!"

The pitbull snarl, snout caught in Confed cross-stripes.

"YEAH!" John thumping the wheel, "YEAH! – "

The pickup jerk, cut left. John not missing a beat, veering likewise.

"He means to kill us," pronounce Monk thoughtful, "the hatchetman means to kill us. With car steel and canine."

"YEH!" Wald bouncing in his seat, "YEH!"

John cackle, start tapping out a Morse message on the carhorn. Bip beep bip-bip beep bip beep-beep. Translation: *yo' mama was a pitbull bitch.*

"It's barking," I go, "rrhuff! rrhwuff! rhuff! – "

The dog with forepaws on the backboard, fangs bared, jaws working spasmodic.

"WHARRF!" John barking in repart, "WHARFF! WHARRF! – "

"This just in," Monk, "the canine means to jump. Soon."

John snort. "Yeah, RIGHT. If that critter's a jumper, I'm a goddamn – "

I don't hear the rest. Wald's howl drown it out. Glimpse of the dog in flight, it's head looming, fangs slaverous. Then a loud thud, the impact jarring the screen, dogflesh blotched huge for an instant, gone. John cutting out with a yawp and bursting past the pickup, myself turning to cop a look: a painted face stuck out, hair windblown: a good ol' GAL. Bubba with boobies, Goober with gash, mouth twisted in a cuss-scream, read them sweet lips: "YEW SHEEAT MUTHER FUCKIN' – "

John with head thrown back, putting out a jungle roar, the car forward in warp-overdrive, myself jerking side to side laughing lunatic, Wald in back thrash-limbed going:

"WOOF! BOOM! BULLDOG! BIGHEAD! BUCKO! YEEHAT! TURBO! BUBO! INTROIBO! LICKSPIT! AGENBITE! INWIT! – "

And on, drivel-mouthed, the Durerro in full throttle trashing Newton, porking Einstein, redshifting down the drag, Route 54 slashed black and endless under a jaundiced moon.

***

The car slows, approaching a truss bridge. Slow some more. A tanker dopplers past, going west and I scowl after it, cursing. Fuckin' animal. Juiced up speed freak on the lam, farting cheese dust –

The car switch notes hitting the bridge: hollow clamor. Dappled view of water beneath, its surface gleamblack, points of light winking: *that ain't water, Clem. That be a hymeneal membrane stretched over a chasm. A chasm depthless, strange orbs on the blink. Any moment a hydra-head burst up through the surface, disc mouth gaped ravenous –*

John curse under his breath. "Water smell like HELL, boy. Like a fuckin' crab-loused crotchpit. Rotpecker jockstrap someone took a DUMP oane."

"Rot crotch pecker-dump," Wald, "heh heh."

The road broaden past the bridge, trees appearing in random scatter. Trees and more trees, vegetation thickening.

"Last stretch to Foofaraw," John announce, "belt up or puke up."

"Raw puke," Wald, "heh heh."

The car seethe, trees blurring, a sound either side like enfilading fire. *This here's what a tachyon feel like. At this rate we'll hit our Bull Run terminus yesterday –*

A glow appear at road's end, brightening. The lights of Foofaraw, Foofer lights. A signboard glimmers past, too quick to read. Mo matter. I know what it say: Welcome to Foofaraw. Est. 1901. Pop. 300. Three hundred, my ass. Foofaraw don't have three hundred at the best of times. A hundred at most. Little shithole Podunk is what. Route 54 piss stop.

John slows past the sign, shifts down. Slow some more, shift down. Slow again, shift down. Decelerating in stages John, jerky and abrupt, braindrag to sinciput each time he tap the brakes, blood and brine squirting fine out my pupils, displaced rhinal air farting out my valorized nostril.

The Plaza appear a half mile ahead. Foofer Plaza all closed up for the night. We cruise on past the Plaza, past trailers hitched in an unpaved lot, a sign that reads Foofaraw City Limit. The road start to wind some, past the sign, trees clustering in gauntlet. *We back in the woods Ethel. The deep dark woods where they live, Ethel. Them squat bearded woodsmen hung like bears, Ethel –*

John hawk, spit on his palm, wipe off on his beard. His earrings glint, his medallion shine like it's been polished with owl feathers off a lime twig, with a cannibal's second skin –

"Watcha lookin' at bitch. Ay?"

I shrug. "Nothing. Just wondering if the Duke be in."

John snort. "He BETTER be in. Tear him a new one, he isn't."

"Fundamental rupture foretold," Monk, "accolades."

"New bitch rupture," Wald, "heh heh."

The road bank left, straighten. A light show ahead, smokeblue. Light I know. *Casa Duquesne.*

The light grow in approach: a large smoke-blue eyeball accruing gradual. An eyeball with a black iris, red pupil. John slows drawing near, but not by much. Look like he mean to drive on, but no: he wrench the wheel at the last instant, screeching past the eyeball into a driveway. I dig the ball in passing: it about the size of a Brobdingnagian tumor, a Cyclopean testicle, a teen Reticulan skull. A glass orb mounted on a post with a misshapen plaque nailed beneath: *Madame Duquesne*.

John churn up the gravel driveway, skid to a halt.

"Tear him a new one," he repeat, killing the engine, "tear him, if he don't have our shit ready."

I grunt, push open my door, climb out: night breeze sweatcold at my back. Casa Duquesne mute at left, windows lightless. I stand by the car, scanning. Mot much to see. Two storeys, a gambrel roof, busted shutters. Above, a circus windvane with pointer shaped like a donkey schlong.

"Haul ass jungleboy," John brushing past, Monk and Wald in caboose.

I watch them a moment, thoughtful. Then I slap my nuts with both hands, fall in behind. I look for lights as I walk, lights inside. Can't see any. Just a faint glow ahead, off the porch. Elsewhere, Casa Duquesne in tenebris, gloom insinuate in its breathless demesne. The house a sliver in dark's forepaw, a boneshard in the teeth of night.

A second eyeball shows by the porch, same as the one in the driveway. Blue orb on a post, a plaque nailed beneath: *Madame Duquesne*. 'Madame' being his actual name, not a designation. The Duke's first name, the tag his mama stuck him with on the whelp.

"Porch look bigger," goes John climbing the steps, "ay?"

I pause, take a good look. Bigger, yes. Much bigger. Not like it used to be. Used to be small, this here porch. Beaucoup small. But not any more. Now it's large, large enough for a riddim fest, a lysergic love-in, a honkytonk hoedown.

"Fucker had it bigged up bigtime," John, scowling around.

I nod. "Enlarged yes, like his prostate. But he had help. Critters and varmints helped him. Weremoles and werehawgs from the sere wilds of Yazoo."

John curse, moving. Us following indian fashion, as is our wont. I stumble as I walk, limbs flailing in expressionist parody. There's dreck strewn all over the porch, objects ancient and spectral: an eviscerate beanbag, a slashed nerf ball, a regurgitate hockey puck, a bogus sandcastle made of desiccate milk solids, a glaucous snapshot of a Ruskie lit-scribe and nymph-hound turned butterfly-killer.

John walk up to the front door, give it a boot. The door fly open on dragon wings, breathing fire. That's how it is and ever be with John. He never open doors regular like other people. He kick 'em open, punch 'em, knee 'em. I saw him hump open an oakwood door once. Cartwheel through a screendoor. Torpedo through a plex glass door. Got a thing about doors, Trotjohn. And windows. I figure it goes back to his kiddie days: his old man chaining him in the closet. Shutting him in the coffin. Strapping him to the livewire rack, down in the basement. Not that papa didn't care, he sure did. Just tough love is all. Just another hard-workin', church-humpin' patrician. Too bad he ain't around to see his boy all growed up. Fucker bought the farm on a cold night some years back, cornholed to kingdom cum by a gang of deranged Jansenists on a PCP binge –

"Duke," goes John stepping in, "Duke?"

No response. The front room empty, a crudded bulb screwed into the ceiling. Yellow light in dusty nimbus.

"Duke's living room," goes Monk stepping in, "lovely."

John snort. "If you call whut he does a livin'."

I step in, pull the door shut. I'm always pulling doors shut every chance I get. Doors and windows both. Can't stand to leave 'em open, for some reason. Maybe a deep-seated need for *Closure*, a repudiation of *Incompleteness*. *Uncertainty* a nematode, *Nothingness* a helminth at the heart of *Being*.

"Dig the wallpaper," goes John, "harf."

I dig. The pattern. Kind of a fractal dog-cubist action collage. Brecciate penrose tiles in barbarous profusion –

"Key," goes Monk high-pitched, "spirit key."

I turn, following the direction of his liver-spotted six-digit forefinger. There: a fluted tapir rib hung from a peg by the front door. Duke's spirit key. A key to realms non-different from our own, worlds identical to ours in every respect.

"Screw the key," John, "it's Duketime."

"Duketime puketime," Wald, "heh heh."

We start across: boot-thud and floor-creak. Heading for the door in the corner, a white door with black lettering. The letters a *mélange* of Nadsat and gutter Gnostick: the Duke's bethel and sanctum.

John walk up, cuss under his breath, headbutt the door. I hear the latch snap, door swinging open.

"Bungdawg," he go stepping in, "papa bungdawg."

Silence. Myself sidling in last, pulling the door shut. Cough, muttered oath, myself squinting around. Dim inside as usual, dim being really dim. No matter. The Duke recommend himself well enough to our debauched senses. Him perched on a five-rung stepladder dressed like a prelate, like an old time boss bishop. The Duke in alb, stole, tunicle, dalmatic, chasuble, maniple, pallium, amice, miter, lappet. Only thing missing is the crozier. Man don't have his stick. He have a thurible instead, a censer in his right hand swinging between his knees like a dowser's pendulum. Smoke aspire from the cup of the thurible, fragrant smoke. Whiff of curried gator-tail on a bed of pork rinds pickled in *Tsingtao*.

Monk cough, gulp. "Duke," he go, "Duke?"

Duquesne's mouth open, glutinous. Close once more. No sound. I notice they're red, his lips, his mug painted garish: rouged cheeks, chalk brow, eyeshadow, bogus lashes, lipstick. Face of a bloated doll.

"Sheeat," John, "fucker look like one them mangatoons."

I raise my left leg, spit on the kneecap.

"He IS a mangatoon. We all are. Nightmare toons."

Monk clap. "Duke. Do you hearken, Duke."

No response. The Duke with eyes downcast, censer swinging.

John take a step. "I'm gon' ice the little putz – "

"De-SIST friar!" I yelp, grabbing his arm, "killing him won't help. Bad protocol. Displease the Meister withal. Allow me, prithee, sirrah."

John slap down my hand, turn scowling.

"You got a minute. Then I'm a-gon' chow down oane his rumplestilt. And yours."

I nod. "Done. Will need your pocket beam though."

John curse, fish out the beam. "Knock yourself out and fuckin' DIE."

I catch the beam right-handed, click it on, flash it around. Not much to see. The room bare, save for the altar at right. Duke's altar and reliquary: a large packing crate draped with damascened silk, topped with sacerdotal miscellanea. And above, a giant portrait of Al Crowley heralding a golden dawn –

"Forty seconds and counting," John, " thirty-nine – "

I sigh. "Zugzwang. Zug-fuckin'-zwang – "

"Eighteen and counting – "

I yank the beam away from the altar, train it on Duke's mug.

"Homage and greeting Duke," I go, voice rising in stringendo, "greetings from our Meister, Buford Aloysius Howell, *Lord Baron of Pain*. His greetings, our homage. We come to you reverent, Madame, much like them three wise men and old time orients bearing gifts, only, there's four of us, we ain't wise, we're not even men, and the only gifts we bear (and bare), are our own foreshorn dongs, our very own heaven-sent (and scented), demon-approved cuts of slap-sausage.

Nevertheless on bent knee we beseech, supplicate, humbly ask for what we came here to get: four names, Madame, the names of four eidolon spirit guides of the female persuasion as agreed upon at that watershed time under moon's turning – "

I pause, my words reverberate. Myself on bent knee, beam in focus.

The Duke don't move at first, don't make a sound. But with time's unplumbed passage, on the receding crest of duration, beneath the cusp of zeit as the finite horizon of sein, he blink heavy-lidded. And smile.

"Plopff," he go, holding out his left hand, "plopfoppopll-oplopll-pff-lop-lopffl-pss – "

I turn down the beam, see it. His fist closed over something: a strip of paper.

I rise, reach, extract the strip soundless and ginger, hold it up to torchlight. There: pencilled bold and succinct, our eidolon spirit names:

TROTJOHN – STINGER
MONK – FINESSE
WALDRON – OBLONGATA
JB – NOODLEBEAR

"Do we have 'em," John, sotto voce, "what we need."
I turn, toss him the torch, hand him the strip.
"We do. Peruse at will."
John scan the strip frowning. Grunt.
"Stinger," he goes, handing Monk the strip, "mah baby."
Monk nod. "Finesse. Yes."
"Oblongata," Wald peeping, "oooh! Heh heh."
I kneel once more, make a trilling sound. Myself with feet arched, knuckles joined over my head in gratitude and

contrition, in remorse for putative venality, alleged turpitude, for crimes yet to be committed *mens rea* by the light of a dying sun. Abject and beholden, me, having acquired what we came for: four female eidolon spirit guides, one for each swinging dick. Stinger for John. Finesse for Monk. Oblongata for Wald. Noodlebear for myself. Courtesy, Madame Duquesne.

That's pretty much what he do, Duke. Procure eidolon spirit guides for clients embarked on journeys arduous, missions impossible. Man's a Geistmeister of eminence, no question. Got a real handle on the deathrealm, Duke. The old Sidpa Bardo like his own backyard times four. Not that he'll work for just anyone, no. Pretty persnickety, Duke. I mean about his clients. You can't just walk in and score a spirit guide for the asking. You got to make the grade first, by way of an interrogation. The Duke asking questions, you answering *Yes* or *No*. Questions like:

* *Do you feel that the summum bonum derives from wood as opposed to clay?*
  * *Does the primordial leek precede the defeated wombat on OUR ethnobiological time scale?*
  * *Will the Overlords of Crash Sex and Cold Mutton impose their diktat on the subalterns of EL?*
* *Is 'Mecca Bullwhip Parthenon' an appropriate liturgical incantation for the mute denizens of Leng?*

And so forth. Questions recondite and arcane, the answers requiring formal lucubrations that last –

"EST?"

I start. Duquesne.

"What," I go rising, "what now?"

"CONSUMMATUM EST?" shriek the Duke spitting froth, "CON-SUM-AT-TUM EST!!!?"

I blink. Double blink. The Duke before me transformed: his eyes like saucers, nares flared, painted jowls aquiver. The moo-bells tacked to his lard chin going tink tinkle, his thurible swinging wild.

"Duke," I begin, "what – "

"HAHHAARRF!" roars John pointing, "BLADDERJUICE!"

I look down, curse. Piss dripping off the stepladder, pooling pale on the floor. As always and yet again: urethral failure *qua* Duke.

John put out a whoop, smack Wald upside the head, leap high, land on all fours barking.

"RRHWUFF! RRHWAFF! I'M GON' LAP IT UP! RRRHWAFAFF! WUFF! SLURP! WHAFF-SLURP! – "

I moan purse-lipped. Take a jagged breath. Bow deep. And with a howl lunge forward, planting a foot deep in the Duke's gut. The Duke gasp, keel back shrieking, myself in rebound yanking open the door, two-second foot-rev, a prolonged moose-bellow – and out.

***

"Fucker went nuts," goes John steering one-handed, "came at me with a rusted poker. Had to put him down, over and out."

Monk sniff. "Not a poker, really. An old Nantucket harpoon. He was Ahab, you, Dick."

"Dick poke," Wald, "heh heh."

John turn, flash me a grin. "You shouldna drop-kicked him the way you did. Meister not gon' like that. Me, I just wanted to play with him some."

I frown. "Play hell, you were gonna lap up his dong drip."

John cackle, punch my shoulder. "Got THAT right."

"Hell drip dong lap," Wald, "heh heh."

"He chased us out," add Monk, "very angry indeed. So perhaps he's withdrawn our spirit guides."

I shake my head. "Wrong. We still got 'em. Right here, on the dash."

"Huh?" John, "wha?"

Monk and Wald sit up, lean over peering.

"Yes indeed," Monk, "four liliputian sprites. I see them. Or perhaps I don't."

I reach, wiggle Monk's beard. "You GOT to see 'em fella. They're right THERE. Four little thumbelinas playing hopscotch, heads aflame."

Wald make a sputtering sound. Sit back with a giggle.

"No," Monk retreating, "nothing at all, I'm afraid."

John raise a hand, slam it down on the dash.

"NOTHIN' is RIGHT. You boys sit easy now and shut the fuck up or I'm gon' stop the car, strip y'all down and play Mengele with your pecker-nuggets."

I turn, eyebrow cocked. "Nuggets?"

John mutter, grab the wheel with both hands.

"Track's a real sumbitch, boy."

I groan, cover my ears. Route 54 now in anfractual groove, the road coiling like a gut in a granny knot. The car hurtling this way and that, singing the g-force blues, trees either side in leafy gyrus. I keep my ears covered till my shoulders start to hurt. Then I drop my hands and start weaving side to side like a bear at bay. This to offset the sinusoid.

"Had kind of an epiphany back there," I go, "back at Duke's. A vision, right before I kicked him. Like satori in floodlit freeze frame. All of a sudden the Duke was Billy Bunter, Monk was Harry Wharton, the Wald was Bob Cherry, you were Johnny Bull, and me Hari Jamset Ram Singh a.k.a. Inky."

John curse, reaming a tight curve. "You're doin' it again. Shittin' out the wrong end again."

"As does the Owl of Minerva," Monk, "who flies only at night."

"Cherry," Wald, "shittin' bull-gut. Heh heh."

A minute pass in silence, the car pitching and yawing. Then John relax with a grunt, us bursting out the woods. The road now a straight sweep through open land, the sky featureless, no moon. Darkness either side, raven-winged.

The road rise a quarter mile and hit a crest, a sign showing ahead. Green signboard once pristine, now gnarled in durance: *Dinglevale City Limit.*

"Switch on them Kliegs," I go, "spotlight on, crooner John."

Trotjohn cackle, belch reverberate and segue into a croon tune, some old hillbilly doggerel fed on rickets, hookworm and moonshine.

My sweetheart live in Dinglevale
No longer hearty and hale
She look like a whale
She's goin' stale
Got to put her up for sale.

My sweetheart's down in Dinglevale
She been lookin' kinda pale
She move like a snail
Leave a sticky trail
Gotta get me a new piece'a tail.

My sweetheart's dead in Dinglevale
I'm down here stewin' in jail
I plucked her like a quail
Cooked her in ale
Gotta spring my ass on bail —

The sign zip past, battered. Look like it's been used to torque out nose crud, scrape off tooth gunk: the legend obscured beyond recognition.

I sit up, vision on scan. No lights anywhere. Just vague contours by moonlight: shacks, patches of pokeweed, sumac, dead cotton. Ahead at left a barnyard and a bodyshop. Way off at right, the abattoir in dark outline.

"Fuckin' lovely," I go shaking my head, "as always."

John grunt, tap the brakes, the road narrowing into the main drag. Darkened lots and storefronts, bare stoops, food signs lightless. Same crap, different wrap.

"Smells lovely too," goes Monk, "as always."

John snuffle, turn, spit on my thigh.

"Got THAT right. Fuckin' Dingle stench."

"Dingle fuck," Wald, "heh heh."

I study the spitwad a moment: poison froth flaring green. Then I pinch up the affected area, wipe off under the dash.

"It's that slaughterhouse," I go, "hasn't been in use a while, but the smell linger. Blood, shit, torment: sweet mélange. Place got shut down a couple years back when the livestock wigged out nasty. Moo plague *Kreut-Jacobs* style, bovines sick as shit: tottering, drooling, blowing cud. Turns out it was a buncha good ol' boys doin' the cattle-hump, Clems workin' the cowfuck somethin' fierce. I mean sure, we got Skeeter poleaxing rodeo bulls with his redwood schlong, but it's just once a month, plus religious holidays. Dingle droogs were out slamming croupe eight nights a week and then some: a picket to keep that heifer in place, a stepladder to get up high enough to hump, duct tape to keep the old swish tail quiescent. It was startin' to get outta hand, half the town thronging for kine cornholes past midnight. That's when the plague hit sudden and fulminant, townsfolk goin' on a bumpkin rampage, don't know if y'all recall. Them fucking, killing, eating everything in sight: kinda like a west Texas steakpit on a bad night. Most folks were dead when Disease Control finally showed, the mayor in his backyard still alive, dry-humping a corpse, chowing down on innards – "

I pause breathless, John awestruck going:

"Well hotDAMN. That's some story. Got to get the Fatman to stock THAT clip, boy."

I smile. "He's got it already. *Dinglevale Danse Macabre*."

"Bump hump," Wald in belated echo, "dead dick. Heh heh."

Monk sniff. "To explain is not to absolve. The reek remains."

I turn. Monk posed ramrod, eyes bright.

"It ain't just the slaughterhouse," I go, "it's also roadkill. Used to be, Dinglevale was the roadkill capital of the south, this here strip too gored up to drive on. Suicide alley for critters and varmints. I should know. I skidded on a mess of coongut once, hit that kerb yander. Another time this hawghead flew in from nowhere, landed on the hood of my ride. Still show up in my dreams sometimes, that hawghead, floating over a pile of taterskins on a de Chirico mindscape, cussing in oldworld Transvaal Afrikaans – "

The car shake, tyres going squelch. John curse, turn quizzical. "Critter?"

I shake my head, squinting in sideview.

"Nope. Looked like a grown man's leg to me. Talipes."

Monk make a strangled sound. "Reek's gotten worse."

I nod, pinch my nose shut, blow hard: snot recoiling soundless into my larynx.

"Worse, yes, but not to fret. We're almost out. I'd say five minutes to the town limit, give or take an hour."

"Oh quite," Monk nasal, "merci blow croupe."

I watch: the road starting to curve, the slaughterhouse again in view, still distant. John shift in his seat, give me a look.

"You ever been out to that there slaughterhouse?"

"Can't say I have. You?"

John snuffle, hawk, spit on my knee: protoplasm in green fizz, wipe off as before.

"Better believe it," he go, "I been everyplace at least once, everyplace that's anyplace. Slaughterhouse wudn't my idea though, it was Skeeter's. Man wanted to pork one them young bulls before it got the axe. Thirteenth of the month I guess it was, drove him out there, parked halfway up the pike, jumped the fence, started walkin'. Skeeter with a three-leg milkin' stool and a picket, me with my flashbeam leadin' the way. Didn't need the light though, moon was out good that night. We saw 'em soon enough: beef on the hoof, eyes a-shine, tails high, shittin' flops. Shit'n'death is what it smelled like, not that it bothered Skeeter any. Him suckin' a big lungful goin': *mmm, now THAT's what LUUUV smell like. Go to it, punk bitch,* I said, *ain't got all night.* Him movin' off chuck-chuckle goin': *now THAT'n there got a REAL PURTY HAUNCH.* I'se just kinda standin' there flashin' my beam around and boom, I see the fucker square and cold: mah man Rick. Rick the Scavenger huggin' the underside of a moo-cow, suckin' oane a tit. Rick clung tooth and claw, cowpiss and flopmush drippin' off his hair. I seen some weird sheeat in my time boy, but this here took the bootleg and chitlins both. Rick gummed to the gut of a mama cow like some kinda milk-bone jungle monkey. I kept m'beam oane the fucker, glommin' the scene hot'n'hungry, no tellin' how long afore he moved, Rick turnin' white-eyed, cow-tit floppin' out his mouth. *Milk,* he croak, *do a body good –* "

The car shake, squish and thud, myself turning to look.

"Two skunks," I announce, "albino. Dead."

"Fuck 'em," John, "nothin' I could do."

"Smell can't get any worse," Monk.

I sit back, click my tongue. "If it CAN get worse, it WILL."

"Albino skunk-fuck," Wald, "heh heh."

"Yayup," I sigh, "this here's a strange town awright, no telling what you see when. Best to drive straight through, don't stop for nothin', not even a whizz. I did it once, back at that dead trailerpark you saw a mile back, stopped there one night to drain the old piss pouch. I figured no one live there so what the hell. Drove in, aimed my carbeams at a rusted trailer, walked up, unzipped and whoosh, hosing down my own shadow on a dead double-wide. Finished an hour later, finger-licked the last drop, zipped up, started for the car, stop. A sound at left, creak and slam, creak and slam: the trailer door opening and shutting in the wind. Shoulda taken off then but I didn't, thank putz. I walked around up the steps, pushed past the door. It was dim inside but not dim enough to hide him: a headless dude naked, back to the wall, ass on floor, legs spread wide. A chainsaw rammed halfway down his neck, his flayed skull pushed up between his thighs, his arms hacked off and laid out in a line between his feet. Myself glomming the scene thinking: *man coulda found a better way to kill himself.* I blinked at last, spotted the wall caption just above: I'M WITH STUPID in block bloodscrawl, an arrow pointing down. I'd've stayed a while soaking it in, but the smell got to me: blood, piss, shit, rot, puke and pain in extremis, a potent cocktail, myself staggering out hand over mouth, holding back hot chyme – "

"Out!" Monk clapping twice, "out and GONE."

I turn frowning "Say what?"

"We just passed the town limit, not a moment too soon."

Monk slumped low in back, fingers locked.

I look up: glimpse of a sign receding.

"Well great. Ten minutes to Billy's."

Monk smile tight-lipped. "But for you, we'd be lost in a temporal void."

"Butt void tempura," Wald, "heh heh."

I chuckle, turn away. Ahead, the road curving wide, trees copsed either side. Above, a moon-cusp gouging cloud-cover.

"So it IS a ghost town then," goes Monk, "no residents at all?"

I turn. "You mean Dinglevale?"

"None other."

I draw up my left leg, tendons squishing.

"Not really a ghost town, no. Folks still live there, stoop cretins mostly, hickville hottentots. Some of John's boys in residence, Thrillkillers. Peckertrash for instance. Ol' Peckertrash live in Dinglevale with his dead mama frozen in a dolphin tank. Him and his idiot brother Humpty. His mama lived in that dolphin tank years before she croaked. She was a halophile, stayed under water most of the time. Salt water. She'd grown a pair of gill flaps looked like deckled kudzu leaves, shared her tank with a striped moray eel, a dun-coloured coelocanth and a pair of gold-mane seahorses. All dead now, preserved frozen. Or so I hear, never have seen them critters myself. But I HAVE seen Humpty. WE have, me and John. Right Teej?"

John cackle. "You know it. Ever hear that story, Monk?"

Monk sigh. "No, but do tell. If you must."

I grin, wink. "Death by anecdote, baby. The rambling raconteur speaks. The peripatetic palaverer. Give ear or perish."

Monk sniff. "Quite."

I shift in my seat, prop an elbow on the dash, spit-lube my kisser and begin:

"Last Fall is when it happened. Me and John were out hunting Peckertrash, can't recall why. John owed him a kick in the nuts, a corkscrew nipple-twist or some such. We had the convertible, John at the wheel. Not this one, this here's new. It was the one he had then, the wine-red blacktop Fandango, a mean bone-crushing beast. So we leave Churchtown on the zoom, John in high dudgeon, hit Dinglevale in overdrive and realize neither of us know where he live. Shee-it. Whither Peckertrash, that's the million yen question. Incidentally, we got three other Thrillkill boys livin' in Dinglevale: Slutmush, Bitch-Tit and Cap'n Gangrene, a triad of pathic rawhide cunt-cannibals, god bless 'em. So there we were, drivin' around wondering: *où? Pecker? TRASH?* Didn't think we'd ever find him, not in this eon, but Abaddon was on our side that night, yassuh, and Beelzebub gracious, John turning into a sidestreet he thought he recognized. *This here's it,* he went, *where the fucker live.* The street went up a half mile, then hit a dead end, just one streetlight there, all gloomy and lonesome, us parking under and climbing out. No domiciles in sight, just high grass and trees, John striding off purposeful, myself following him into the bush, cuss-mouthed. *Whut you bitchin' about jungleboy* he goes, *this oughtta feel like home,* us ploughing through waist-high hawser grass, a friggin' jungle trek. Only thing missing was the guide in khaki and pith, black skulls erupting on white skin, witch-doctor curse, *Lukundoo.* Tough going for sure, but we hit a clearing soon enough, a beat-up shack showing moonlit, with a front yard cragged and tussocked, bashed autoparts strewn about. *Villa Peckertrash,* I went, *yes?* John nodding in confirmation. *No lights, no one home,* I said, *let's vamoose. The pox oane THAT,* goes John, *fucker's home awright. I can smell that bung-stain, hear them crotch-crabs scuttlin'.* Fair do, I go, *proceed as planned.* We cut across the yard, stopped ten feet from the porch. Still no light, no sound within. I started to say something but the friar cut me off. *PECKERTRAAAASH!* he bawled, voice bullhorned through cupped palms, *PECKERTRAAASH!* Silence and echo, the shack bedarked, no signs of life. *PECKERTRAAAASH!* John once more, *ASS OUT NOW, PECKERTRASH! OUT! OUT!* Myself wincing with teeth grit. *No one in, friar,* I went, *best head out and look elsewhere,* John brushing me off with a curse, hitting it once more: *OH PECKERTRAAASH! I'M GON' COUNT TO THREE NOW, PECKER HONEY, AND BEJEEZUS HELP YOU IF YOU'RE NOT –*

Skrrk! it went, Skrrk! Not too loud. Skrrk! like a tooth scraping volcanic rock. Then a click: light. Porchlight coming on ahead, yellow bulb hung bare over a seated figure. *No,* goes John, *no way. Si,* I go, *YES way. It's Massah Macroceph, Cranius Maximus, Punkinhead Prime. It is: the taterhead to end all taterheads.* We stood and watched. John in kind of a spasm going: *pure, man that's pure, stone fuckin' PURE.* And it was, sort of. Pure. The sight of him: alpha-freak with misshapen boulder head, straw hair eaten out in clumps, no neck, no ears, no chin worth the name, the nose like a ripe boil, purple mouth ringed like a baboon's asshole, the left eye big as a crystal ball, iris a-swirl (idiot divination in technicolour), the right eye absent, socket puckered shut. That monster skull propped on a flesh-mound in grey overalls, hands stuck out like balloon mitts, rooster legs a-dangle. Some sight. Stuff you can't pay to see – "

"Monster ball-pucker," Wald, slapping his crotch, "heh heh."

I nod. "Damn right. So there we stood, gorgonized, the porch ogre motionless, squid eye blinkless. Just his chair on the rock going Skrrk! Skrrk! Part of me wanted to howl, blow chunks, run around pissing. Only, I didn't know which part. The taterhead was all I could see, the wind all I could hear. That, and the creak of Humpty's rocker: Skrrk! Skrrk! But then I heard something else: Trotjohn low-voiced, sniggering. *What,* I whispered, *what. The bucket,* he went, *the b-HARF! the bucket.* I blinked then. And saw. A rusted pail by the rocking chair, a piss-tube snaking up and around to Humpty's crotch, his prick showing there through a flap: pale slug catheterized. Which is about when I let go, laughing open-mouthed, John's voice rising to a cachinnate shriek and Skrrk-rrk! Skrrk-rrk! Humpty's chair rocking fast now, faster still, his squid eye on the blink, blinkablink, blinkablink, curdled jowls aquiver, left hand reaching across, back and up, glimpse of a shotgun barrel, blinkablink, right hand on the rise, blinkablink, dented brow sweating murder. *Huh?* I went, *what? Run,* goes John smiling beatific, *run NOW.* And BOOM the gun going off wild, us whirling simultaneous, off at full sprint, buckshot whining overhead. I'm not much of a runner, specially on my own legs, but boy you shoulda seen me go: a coyote out of a chickencoop, farmer Humpty with gun up, blasting. A miracle we didn't trip up, that being a bad stretch to run on. Course we didn't get off stone free. I felt it out in the bush: hot sting on my earlobe, buckshot bite. Didn't hurt all that much, nothin' serious, but it got me screechin' like I had a toggle up my tookus, a girder through my groin. Mocha daddy don't handle pain too well except when he's enjoying it, you dig. John didn't catch buckshot, but got his keester shredded anyway, all that mean hawser grass ripping in transit. The shooting stopped soon enough, but we kept running: through the bush to the road, into the car, vroom and out. Didn't quite end there though. John kept up the hunt, found Peckertrash out in the sticks humping a syntheplast dummy, kicked the living shit out of him, pants down – "

I pause anhelate, John cackling. Monk with arms folded, studying a point on the roof. Wald slumped with knees up, going:

"Shred ass. Hump stick. Heh heh – "

I shake my head, turn and sit back, rubbing fatigue from my eyes. Sleep congealed dense, epicanthic, with Dinglevale well behind now, Route 54 grooved ahead through open land, the moon obscured by damp cumulus. Myself in sudden dolor thinking: *no light anywhere, light nought and nowhere –*

But there is. Light. The car's highbeams on, our path a-glow. And our eidolon spirit guides still on the dash with heads aflame, bouncing on a sea-green ectoplasmic trampoline shaped like a grown man's kidney, each bounce sounding a lotus bloom of sitar notes rising, scattering like fulgent pollen with my own thoughts unhoused, streaming behind like a comet's tail, a mane of fireflies.

***

An eighteen-wheeler roar up in approach, thunder past going west: windshock.

"Well fuck you too," goes John, steadying the wheel.

"Indeed," Monk, "quid pro coito."

The Wald chortle. "Fuck pro ho. Heh heh."

I grunt, sit up. The road now curving left, a shape coming into view at right. A large yurt. Ziggurat. Bigass stupa. Pyramid.

"Junkhill," I announce, "five minutes to Billy's."

John clear his throat, turn to the dashboard:

"No," I go, "NO – "

Too late. Spit lancing out from between his incisors, knocking Noodlebear off the kidney trampoline.

"Precision strike,' goes Monk, "smart phlegm-bomb. No collateral damage."

I give John a glare: optic death ray. "That was MY spirit guide you spat at, WHORE."

John snicker. "Sheeat."

I watch Noodlebear rise, get back on the trampoline. Her comrades bounceless waiting, their skull flames gone smoky, lambent.

"It's all right, girls," I murmur, "y'all are still the best, burn brighter than the rest."

The eidolons look up uncomprehending, their skullsmoke

174

shaped in a blue question mark. I click my tongue rueful: *if only I could speak Enochian, language of the archangels –*

"Looks different somehow," goes Monk, "bigger, more rounded at the top."

"Huh?" me, "what?"

"The junkhill," Monk, "that one there and none other."

I turn to look. Closer now, the heap, near abreast at right. An enormous junk cairn towering a half-mile off.

"Don't look any different to me," I go, "same as ever."

"Same is right," John, "I ain't never seen that ol' junkhill change ever. No salvage trucks goin' in or comin' out, no cranes, crushers, dozers, no lights, no junkyard dawgs, nothin'."

"Succinctly put," Monk, "kudos."

"It's immutable," I go, "like Mt. Sumeru. It cannot be muted."

"Flawed, but pithy and epigrammatic," Monk, "accolades."

John harrumph, grinning. "I get all nos-TALgic lookin' at that there junkheap, boy. M'dick used to be about that size, back when. Same height, narrower at the base. Chicks dug it bigtime, specially some them southside bag tramps. I'd lay back, they'd climb atop. Then I'd take the good lawd's name in vain and blow m'wad, them shootin' off like champagne corks – "

"Waaah!" me, "wahhaaahh! – "

Wald gibbering.

"Yes quite," Monk pensive, "I do recall reading about it on Netzone. Something like: *Youth Erects Robo-Priapic Sperm Cannon.*"

"HAARF!" John, "yowp."

"Waahah!" me.

Wald slobbering.

The junkhill drifts past, the road still on a leftward curve. Patches of vegetation appear in intimation of thicker foliage.

"Tell ya though," I go quashing my mirth, "that there junkhill's no laughing matter. Billy say it's a power spot. All kinda weird energies in confluence. I'm inclined to agree. Somethin' freaky about that heap, for sure. Give me the jeebes just to look at it. I mean it's more than just a pile of mech parts, car innards, trashed appliances, superannuate service borgs. It's like some old druidic burial tell. An elemental with its own machine manitou. That friggin' heap be ALIVE, brothers. I mean sentient in some rudimentary and preternatural sense, rudi and preter notwithstanding. It's got eyes is what, that there hill have eyes. It APPERCEIVE by means of a cyclopean and numinous orb that sparkle at its summit like a girandole, like the Northern Lights refracted through a giant speculum. I've seen that orb brothers, seen it via chakra-vision, by leave of the fifth Dhyani Buddha as invoked by His Transcendent Bogusness, Tuesday Lobsang. I've watched that heap watching me, watched it watching me watch it watching me. That's no ordinary junkhill, nawsuh. It's TRANSMONTAINE with two 't's as in 'titmouse' and 'titular'. And get this: that heap ain't packed solid, no. It's got tunnels running through, up, down, across. It be a warren, is what. A maze. Rick says so. Rick the Scavenger. Rick live in that there junkhill. He dwell and wander there, driven by a volition greater than his own. But he's not the only one. There's also the little people. Little folks living in the hill. I mean LITTLE people much like our own spirit guides you don't see frolicking there on the dash (great to have y'all on board Stinger, Finesse, Oblongata, Noodlebear). Different RACES of little people in there, says Rick. A whole BUNCHA races, but only six that matter, the six Rick told me about – "

"You're doin' it again," warn John, "goin' flap-tongue, shittin' out your piehole – "

"Six different races of little people housed in the fastness of that junkhill," I continue, unreined and logorrheal, "I got the

176

list right here, brothers, hearken and give ear. First, a race of bonsai Vikings nine inches tall on average, Vikings with horned helmets, ratskin cloaks, plastercast cuirasses with disposable groin cups, definitely humanoid, except they got one large nostril instead of two, and a couple wedge-shaped thumbs on each hand, instead of one. They group-fuck in makeshift saunas, feed on other little people and commit ritual suicide in droves. Second, a race of elastic unipod rhombus-heads who bounce around with arms pinwheeling at high speed, further details available on pain of death. Third, a race of slick-pate, one-eyed spermatozoids who slime around in clusters of three, known to be religiously inclined, possibly rogue Jansenists with a flair for voluntary torment accompanied by happy laughter. Fourth, a race of two-toed marsupials with face-pouches, sabre-teeth and nipples tapered like arrowheads. Known to feed on rust flakes and scorched syntheplast. A temperate race, reflective to a fault, except during Lent, when they succumb to orgiastic blood-letting. Fifth, a race of doghead homunculi with peckers for tongues and vice versa, further details available on pain of a slow-burn *auto da fe*. Sixth and not least, a race of tiny slushpool mermaids with strawberry heads, seal flippers and porpoise tails. A race now facing extinction. Considered a seasonal delicacy by bonsai Vikings grown weary of celebratory cannibalism and vapor chamber bloodbaths – "

"You don't fuckin' stop NOW," John, "I'm gon' yank that dawg tongue out your rumphole and – "

"These and other races I don't care to think of, much less list," I churn on, ferverish, "that there junkheap TEEMS with life is what I'm trying to say. Numberless entities, praise lawd, a little universe in and for itself. Which raise a pertinent and necessary question: do this universe have a presiding DEITY? Do the junkhill have its own junk god, a deus detritum? Do it possess an entelechy, a telos towards which it strive, if not aspire? Rick says there is. He say there's a hollow at the centre of that hill, an ovoid atrium that house the arch-monadic deity, a critter by the name of Zebtharkus, a.k.a. Zebtharkus the Drone. Rick hasn't actually SEEN the Zeb, but he's dreamed of him, beheld him in a series of oneiric encounters (onei-Rick, you dig). This critter Zebtharkus is part manta ray, part dung beetle, part gila monster: awesome to look at, though lacking in pulchritude. All the heapsters know about him, know he's lawd and massah. They know he communicate with his minions via dream projection, know he issue orders, resolve disputes, grant boons. HE SEES ALL by way of hypnopompic remote viewing. Nothing escape his scrutiny, even though he's asleep. The Zeb's been asleep a long long time, but he's coming awake, says Rick, Zebtharkus the Drone being roused from the sleep of ages by gunshots. That's right: gunshots. There's this platoon of razorheads show up at the heap every weekend to relive the old killin' days. They come in full battle gear, armed with tacks, pins, corkscrews, levers, wrenches and general issue automatics smuggled back from Nam, the Eighteenth Sequel. They ride up on camouflaged tandem bikes, enter the junkheap through a portal sodomized out of a crush of car chassis, and begin patrolling the junk maze, moving single file on full alert, machine parts beetling either side. Then one of 'em puts out a howl and the platoon go nuts, Search and Destroy, shooting straight up, sideways at the slopes, rending and slashing leather, buggering test dummies. Never seen 'em in situ myself, but Rick has. He was strolling around the maze one time, turned a corner and saw this razorhead rib-fucking a syntheplast display doll. Fatass war hawg bangin' away, torchbeam wrapped in red cellophane. Red Light Special: gookville trash-mannequin catching ofay hump hell (me luv you long time). Rick watched him a while, porker sweat and grunt. Then he amble up, tap his shoulder and go: *my turn, fella, you been workin' them ribs long nuff,* the porker freezing in mid-thrust, turning wild-eyed and bolting with a shriek, gunshots in echo – "

I pause, clenched and breathless, bracing for a blow. But the blow don't come. John seemingly numbed by my word-deluge, Wald in back retching, Monk silent.

"They shoulda choked you dead in the crib," goes John at length, "saved us a whole lotta pain."

"Me most of all", I go nodding.

"Dead hole," Wald, "choke pain. Heh heh."

John mutter, tap the brakes, shift down. The car slows, trees clustered thick now at left. At right, open land sweeping out to the hills.

"Billy's," I go, "Billy's at last."

Monk exhale with a long whistle. "The Grotto at last, the Grotto at last, thank gawd a-mighty, it's the Grotto at last."

The car surge sudden and bank left, tyres squealing. I put out a yelp, gunk bursting hot from my right ear, blotching the pane.

"Ow," I go, "hurt that time."

John curse, the car churning into the Grotto lot. Not really a lot, just this patch of bare earth bitten out of the woods.

"You blow ear-mush again," growl John, "you gon' have to lick it off."

"Not if the Wald gets to it first," Monk.

"Blow," Wald, "lick. Heh heh."

The Gateway drifts past at left, Grotto Gateway fringing the woods. Not much to look at. Just a pair of forked columns with a crossbar laid atop in architrave: Billy's dolmen. A red dragon lantern hang from the crossbar, a signboard nailed above: BILLY'S GROTTO.

"Behold the Gateway," I go, "ah."

"The Way and its Power," Monk, "mmm."

"Fuckin' dipsheeats," John.

"Powerfuck," Wald, "heh heh."

John cruise the length of the lot, tyres sibilant. Then he cut a tight loop at the far end and park.

"Bitches out," he goes, killing the engine.

"Bitch gate," Wald, "heh heh."

I shake my head, exhale through a clogged nostril.

"Can't believe we made it this far, boy. We shoulda been dead many times over."

"Indeed," Monk, "once is not enough."

John curse, shove open his door, duck out. We curse mimetic, duck out likewise. Impossible to remain inside curseless.

"Nobody in yet," goes John, surveying the lot, "that Billy's truck out by the Gate?"

I nod. "Yayup. Grotto hawgs don't come gruntin' in till midnight."

We stand by the car a moment, speechless. Night wind traverse the lot, dust in brief eddy, foliage susurrant. I shudder, my head sweatcold. Over the Gateway the dragon lantern dance, red shadows flitting –

"HEY!"

I blink. Trotjohn halfway across the lot, Monk and Wald beside. I wave, step up to the car, press my face to a pane. No sign of our eidolons. Not on the dash, not anywhere.

I turn, break into a run. Not a run per se, more an unsightly lope, legs in gangled saltigrade. A rig thunder past at left, heading east, dust billowing in its wake. I inhale gape-mouthed: a fine dry blunge of exhaust and powdered earth. I look up: the moon a pale blotch on a dirty mantle –

A mote flares somewhere in my skull, goes nova. I see my face spanned immense, stretched out to the horizon. The foliage my hair, the clearing my brow, the road a blindfold, the land beyond shaping my nose and mouth, the hills stubbling my chin –

The flare dies, vision fading. I shamble up, huff and pant.

"About fuckin' time," John, "pussy."

I bend over panting, hands on knees.

"Sun salute. Almost forgot."

"Yeah," John, "beeyatch."

Sun salute: this little ritual we work, before heading into the Grotto. Usually nearabout midnight with the sun at its strongest. As here, now.

I straighten, clasping a stitch in my side.

"Yow. You fuckers ready?"

Silence. My comrades lined abreast, facing the Gateway. The dragon lantern in slow turn, shadows bleeding across the lot.

I limp up, stand in line. Now us four, shoulder to shoulder, eyes raised to the Gateway. Silence and windmoan.

"Whut you waitin' for slut," John, "the second friggin' comin'?"

"Slut come," Wald, "heh heh."

I inhale deep, clear my throat.

"At dusk," I go, voice quavering, "at dusk the cock announce dawn. At midnight, the bright sun."

"Bright cock," Wald, "heh heh."

"BEGIN!" I yawp, "BIG!"

We move in unison, enacting our orison. Arms straight up, bend, touch toe, fall forward, swing dip, stand, repeat procedure. We repeat thrice: three complete sun salutes there in the Grotto lot, facing the dolmen. The ritual demand silence, but we don't comply. John with lips pursed, whistling for demons. Monk humming a harmonic convergence rainbow mantra. Wald farting in short staccato bursts. Myself emitting Tourette yelps and Xhosa tongue clicks. But the noise don't matter, long as we move in sync, which we do. Long as it invoke the Meister's Notion, which it does.

We complete the salutes, put out a collective bark and stand easy, loins ungirded. Silence, the dragon lantern steady.

"Your call slut," John thumping my shoulder, "get it over with."

I frown. Step out of line. Turn. And begin stentorian:

"The ritual at an end, brothers, and the sun well pleased, though long dead. But soft. Hold on yet a while, prithee do not disperse. Hear me out now, attend to this brief homily from the *Annals of Congenital Intelligence and Coagulate Erudition*. Topic du nuit: Freedom.

Freedom, comrades, is a term oft employed, oft heard.

FREEDOM! shout the Imperial Commissars.

FREEDOM! the sweatshop bosses.

FREEDOM! the fanged fuglemen.

FREEDOM! the ravening satraps who extract day–labor, light denied.

FREEDOM! the Vampires of the Demon Machine.

But what, compadres, what in fact and essence do *Freedom* rightly mean? What is its feel, its odour, nay, its TASTE? What, it's CONTRANMAGNIFICANDSJEWBANGTANTIALITY?

Answer:

Freedom taste like a fifth of *Dickel* on the Fourth of July. Like chopped *peppers* on fatback. Like chicken fried *steak* on grits. Like pork *rinds* soused in moonshine. Like red *tabasque* on chitlins. Like Twinkers soaked in *tequila*. Like molassers on a barbecued *rib*. Like the fabled jellybean on smokin' cheese. Like gum bears in a Louisianne *gumbo*. Like cold *spam* in Hersheloon's syrup. Like a *corndog* in chowder. And *more*. Much *much* more. Similes *abound, brothers*. My cup runneth *over* but my tongue furleth *tight*, cleaving to my palate as did

Jehozophat's in the shadow of the Cursed Marsupial and the Abominate *Gnome*. I would fain continue but I *won't*. The offense *rests*. Simon say: here endeth the lesson – "

I pause froth-lipped, my comrades staring.

"Well?" I go slapping my right tit, "WELL?"

Monk cough, grab his beard. "Message received and understood."

"Fuckin' twerp," John.

"Pork tongue gumbo," Wald, "heh heh."

I suppress an oath, turn on my heel.

"Fall in now, dong-whackers. Grotto time."

They fall in: John behind me, Monk behind John, Wald behind Monk behind John behind me (by the Transitive). Silence. A truck roaring past behind.

"Whut you waitin' for ho," hiss John, "fuckin' Halloween?"

"Low wiener," Wald, "heh heh."

I look up: red dragon in slow dance.

"Samhain," I go foot forward, towards the Gateway moving.

***

A dirt track cuts through the woods past the Gateway: pale crease through dark hair. Us on this very track single file, myself watching my sneakerdogs with head bowed, palms joined. Restless, them dogs, I can tell. It's the woods that do it: call of the wild, atavistic stirrings, bestial regression –

"On course Cornelius," I whisper, "on course Valdez."

My footsnouts quicken, trees in their sleep sighing. *Where be our spirit guides,* I wonder. *Can't be far. Cannot. For we be connected. Super-subtle cilia link us. Thick, blood-gorged umbilici join our brittle ovoid souls. Thus Stinger and John wedded. Finesse and Monk wedded. Oblongata and Wald wedded. Noodlebear and I WEDD-ed.*

The track lead on straight a while, then hit a clearing. A large circular clearing with a structure in the middle. A structure that at first sight resemble a log cabin. Also at second sight. And third. Pretty large, this here cabin. Large and solid, with a porch, a roof, a chimney.

"Switcheroo," I go cutting left, my comrades in tow. Light shows over the cabin porch: a bare bulb with a placard beside. BILLY'S GROTTO: *Drink Here, Fuck Elsewhere. Fight Here, Kill Everywhere.*

"Harf!" goes John walking up, "dig the new sign."

"New sign yes," Monk, "but the same old Ted. Trencherman Ted."

I chuckle. Ted at attention on the porch, under the bulb. Big Ted with horsehair wig, plastic monocle, walrus mustache, lantern jaw, fustian greatcoat, canvas waistcoat, no trousers, no skivvies, no schlong-sheath, no testicle-truss, no socks, no shoes. Just bare-bark legs with tubed veins snaking up to a colossal hardon.

"Ohhh yeah," John with a snicker, "Teddy and his T-bone dick."

"*Pinewood* dick," I clarify, "he's pinewood, all of him."

"Dick pine," Wald, "boner woody. Heh heh."

Monk whistle. "Well I've said it before, but I'll say it again. A stroke of genius putting Ted on guard."

I nod. "Billy figured a cigar store injun be too trite, so bought himself a ciger store prezi-dent."

"Harf," John, "sweet."

"And speaking of sweet," Monk, "I wouldn't mind a jellybean or two. Anyone have a quarter?"

I click my tongue. "You're out of luck, Monk kid. Ted got no jellybeans left to give. The dispenser went bust, so Billy quit fillin' him up."

Monk shrug. "A pity."

I nod rueful. Time was, you could stick a quarter in Ted's navel, crank his boner and watch jellybeans spill out of his asshole into a styroplex cup. Nine beans, red, white and blue, your dejected confection. But not anymore. Someone put a crimp on Ted's hardon so he quit shitting beans. Left him with a bladder full of quarters and a gut fulla sugarturds –

"HO!"

I turn. Trotjohn.

"You plannin' oane hangin' out here all night?"

I shake my head. "Headin' in now. Y'all go on around."

John bare his teeth. "We'll go when we're good'n'ready. We gon' play around with Ted some."

"Oh quite," Monk, "the Wald to fellate the Presidential Erection. John to ream the dispensing foramen. I to consume (if fortune smiles) the excreted electuary, the colours that never run."

John whoop. "Sound like a PLAN. To WORK, fellas."

"Fellate," Wald, "excrete. Heh heh."

I turn, climb the porch steps, walk up to the door. John vaulting smooth onto the porch, Wald failing in the attempt and collapsing with a shriek: much mirth.

I goof on the scene a moment, chuck-chuckle. Then I grab the knob, push, step in. Wham: nasal strike, the old Grotto hell smell. Ethylate effluvia, hillbilly halitosis, geezer gangrene, biker fungus, beefeater sweat. I shut my eyes, inhale deep. *Mmm, sweet pestilence* –

Clack: the door falling to, behind. I blink, look around. Grotto lights up and on. All of 'em. Candles at each table fixed to bits of stained porcelain (a shattered crapcan put to good use). Two drainpipe menorahs on the bartop, one at each end. A vineyard chandelier, grape-bulbs clustered purple and green.

Three plastic pigs pendant, assholes beaming red. Five dildoids in a circle, rubbers stretched over low-watt phallic bulbs. A bearded Mansonus, eyes ablaze, forehead-swastika candent. A Happy Buddha fulgent, brow and navel beaming blue. These and others I can't think of, much less name.

"Lights," I murmur nodding, "*these* lights. Ebola."

Grotto lights on this night, but not every night. Most evenings I come in, find the place all dark. In deep umbrage. Myself waiting on bended knee, biting hard on my lip till it bleed. Or lying prone, face pressed to the hardwood floor, feeding on my inmost cheek till the lights come on. Ever crouched low or curled foetal in a darkened booze shack out in the sticks? It's no picnic. Not unless you make it one. In the mullioned fastness of your death-scorched oneirium...

I smile, letting my eyes wander. Not wander, more like rove. Right to left over the ruck of ill-fashioned furniture, the horse-shoe bartop, the swan-neck beertaps. Past oakwood columns scored with yokel scimitars and rorschached with baccy spit, to the far wall pasted with pin-ups in salacious array. Thence up across knotted rafters and corrugate asbestos, pausing over Jukebox Jane (dig her tinsheet wimple and battered corset, her push-button console grinning rows of blackened teeth) before moving on to the niche opposite, Billy's pool-table set there under scrutiny of an eye-lamp, balls racked in line of sight.

This scene your daddy glomming moist-eyed, recalling the way it used to be. Billy's Grotto in the old days. Crazier back then, more weird light. Taps wired to shine when the wassail flowed. Gas jets on the walls spurting amber flame, Leyden jars full of angel-dust fireflies. Dishonorably discharged vets settling accounts with flame-throwers, suicidal pyromaniac gymnasts tumbling naked, buttocks aflame. High-volt homosex thanatopes playing cathode/anode (arc-light crackling glan to glan), pathic hillbillies goosing themselves with blowtorches. Snuff-love deathrow aficionados strapped to jerry-built kill-chairs, faces going snap-crackle-pop, peckerheads rutilant, assholes farting blue ball lightning –

I start. John guffawing outside, Monk issuing Ted-torture instructions.

I step away, move towards the bar. Past tables hacked and jagged, chairs designed to gouge and maim. Tough going as always. Like wading through a moat fulla gators, vampire barnacles, killer manatees. Across, I take a short runup, jump, land crotch-first on a barstool: mute squelch of mashed nutsack and stunned glanhead, pain lancing white-hot through my loins, brief vision blackout, stellar effects.

"HOO lawd!" I gasp, "HOO lawdie lawd!"

My voice in echo, the echo in turn echoing in echo (regressus). I sit still a moment, head bowed. John's voice drifting in faint: *you crap oane my boots boy, I'm gon' kill you dead* –

I sigh, look up. Directly ahead, my likeness in stained glass, Billy's God-of-Eyre shakin'-shamrock saloon mirror. Myself with elbows propped, palms upraised, head hammocked low between humeral cusps.

I shut my eyes, breathing deep. Darkness. My brain in vague silhouette: a shattered skyline. Firefights in that city, flash, and quake. And far above, the Meister's Notion: jewel of my pated sidereum –

I blink, sit up, bring a knuckle down on the bartop.

"Billy," I call, knocking, "friend Billy."

Echo-cho-o. Above, the grape chandelier a-tremble, shadows waltzing to the blushful hippocrene and purple-stained mouth.

"Billy. Billy Dang. Now Billy."

Echo and shadow waltz. But no Billy Dang.

I exhale through a glutted eustachian, knock once more. Twice more. Rushmore. Faces of stone, dead *wasichu*, Black Hills desecrate.

"Billy. Now Billy. Come forth now Billy – "

Pause. Then a bootscuff, thud. At left a door opening: a form shadowed there immobile. Giant.

"Billy," I go, "Billy-O. Big daddy Bill."

The giant take a step. Two steps. Aletheia: Billy Hyuck'n'Dang at full height. Another step and pause, his hands on the bartop, fingers cocked. Injun Bill with a Stetson high on his brow, hair fanning out behind. His face sharp-etched, grander than any at Rushmore.

"Damned if it ain't ragass Tom Sawyer."

His voice: the sound pitched to a rumble, distant thunder.

I nod. "Ragass Tom come to see Injun Joe."

Billy chuckle: a deep sound. Like that deep ol' sound come from *Bobby Peru*.

"Uh-huh. Friend JB first up, here to drown his marrow, wet his gristle."

His words gather, disperse. Myself looking on silent, his face polished granite, hazel eyes ashine.

"Heard you boys up to nasty business. Same as usual."

I blink. "That time of year, baby. Who told you."

"Who? A little birdie with no wings, no beak, no feet."

I nod, staring. Brine accrue in his right eye, outer canthus. A teardrop. He got a duct problem, Billy, his right eye weeping perpetual.

"So what'll it be. What'll it be this night."

I don't answer. My gaze homing on his teardrop grown gibbous, trembling scintillant on the cusp of a lash –

"Chuang Tzu call it: sitting while wandering. I call it: the barroom brainjerk. Name your poison."

I take a deep breath, shake my head.

"No wassail this night of their Lawd and Massah two thousand and rat-a-tat hoola hoop rumpelstilt-rinky-dink on page two of the Hong Kong Book of Kong Foo, First Edition."

Billy stare, eyes bright. "Damn. Must be important."

I nod. "Important yes. Important and necessary. As per our Meister's Diktat. And the Principle of Sufficient Reason – "

"Friends," Billy turning, "friends."

"Huh?"

"Look like you got some friends here."

I nod. "If you wanna call 'em that. Outside, hosing Ted."

Billy shake his head. "In here. There."

I turn, following his gaze. And see them. All four: Stinger, Finesse, Oblongata, Noodlebear. Our eidolon spirit guides, hazed in aureole.

I smile. "Yay girls. Glad y'all are back."

The eidolons titter, exchange glances. They look different, I notice. Their heads not on fire any more. Their faces etched pale, hair coiffed black.

"You boys been hangin' with the Duke I see."

I turn. "Affirmative. Four spirit guides. Procurer: Madame Duquesne."

Billy blink. His teardrop tremble, break free. In that instant a sweat-bead detaching itself from my brow, catching in the grooves of an eyelash, catapulting with a rainbow shimmer.

I bow, palms joined. "Billy Dang hath spoken. Pine Ridge will burn again."

Billy stare speechless, his hands on the bartop playing absent keys, fingers in slow ghost-dance. A fresh tear in his eye welling.

"Peltier," he husks, "Peltier, Means and Trudell spoke to me in a vision-quest dream. Black Elk and Lamedeer blessed them. They said there's a shitstorm comin'."

I nod. "Gifts of power, vision and insight. Shaman at spirit height brooding – "

Movement. Corner of my eye. Not quite the corner, but close. Click of paws on hardwood, shadow approach.

"Reefer," I go, "Reeferdog."

Reefer rear up, tail wagging furious. I tug his ears, scratch his neck. Thump his back, knead his scruff. His tongue loll, breath coming in gasps.

"Reefer," I go, "Herr Privatdozent Reef."

Reefer drop, rear up, stick his snout in my crotch.

"Not tonight hon'," I go pushing him away, "got me a headache. The other head."

Reefer back off, settle. Him staring with head cocked, eyes luminous. He's hypersapient, Reefer. Body of a mongrel, mind of a sage. A dog savant, is what.

"Reefer says don't do it. Reef says don't."

I turn: Billy staring. "Don't do what."

"Whatever it is you boys plannin' tonight."

I throw Reefer a hard look. "Ya little shit."

Reefer yawn, suppressing a grin.

I shake my head. "NOT funny. It's a Bull Run we on here, our Meister's Notion."

Reefer sneeze twice, cross his forepaws. His eyes say: *I am privy. I am one who KNOWS.*

Smart as hell, Reefer. Bright as a shoeshine spitball. Critter figures stuff no man ever could. By way of dogsnout ausculation. Like he'll sniff your butt, tell you if you're ailing. Woof for Yes, Whuff for No. Or he'll probe your crotch to see if you got a sickness unto death –

Boom. I start, turn. The front door in recoil, Trotjohn in the doorway a-grin.

"We fragged his ass!" he announce, "cigar store Ted. Hashed his boner good – "

Stepping in as he speak, Monk and Wald after. Them by the door flushed damp, pleased as putz.

"You boys look all worked up," goes Billy Dang, "way up."

John nod vigorous, brows raised. "Ohhh yeah. How now, Injun Bill. HOW."

"Boner hash," Wald, "heh heh."

Monk silent, watching.

Billy exhale with a low growl. "You boys go on round back and set easy. Your buddy here be with you directly."

Pause. John's grin faltering.

"Well FINE," John, "we'll be your BACK door boys to-NIGHT. Long as it ain't no kinda trap. Some ol' injun gizmo."

Billy blink. A tear shimmer, break free.

"Y'all go round back," he repeat, "set easy."

John scowl, turn, yank open the door, stomp out. Monk and Wald moving after, their steps in echo.

"They're gone," goes Billy in a tone of wonderment, "gone."

I frown. "Well you asked 'em to."

"Not them," Billy, "THEM."

I turn, look up. They're gone, all right. Stinger. Finesse. Oblongata. Noodlebear. Blipped out.

"They're Tathagatas," I intone, "critters that come and go, come and go. Thus."

Billy nod. "Reefer gone too. Good and gone."

I look down, around. No sign of Reefer.

"Well hell," I go, "guess I don't smell good enough. Shoulda scrubbed down good before I got here. At the carwash. Strip off and walk through with arms raised. Get a mean pit-scrub: blood, hair, soapsuds flyin'. Get your nipples shaved down, but no matter, they grow back soon enough – "

I break off, my voice in echo. Billy's eyes on me, tear fulgent.

"For you," he murmur, "for you someone somewhere weeps."

I nod. "That'd explain my booze yen. Grotto beer-thirst."

Billy blink. "Offer's still on. First one on the house."

I click my tongue, rueful. "Tempting, baby. Very temp-tingaling. But no. My brown ass be on assignment tonight. Got me a job to do."

Hard words. Hard for me, that is. Your daddy never refuse a drink, specially not at Billy's. Love that Grotto grog, best firewater this side of KL-KLL-MM. Some nights I wake up in a sweat thinking: *man I'd kill for a dram of Billy's vintage.* And I would too. Kill for Billy's swill. Because it's special, is what. Rumor has it he flavor his wassail. With powdered rawhide, carbolic acid, crushed mothballs, amniotic fluid, ash from charred plantain skins, refried bat guano, baccy juice from an outhouse spittoon. Grotto lager go down fine by itself, but really hit the spot with Billy's nosh bites. Like steamed sumac wads, gator-skin fry, cartilage kebob, rooster beak dumpling, gizzard patay on cooked crowfeet, pasted pituitary with moose-horn crisp, plover droppings in turtle-shell croustade, corpse-grown mushrooms poached in woodpulp, adrenalin, biotox effluents, swamp dreck –

"Manitou. Jungle manitou."

Looking past me, Billy Dang, eyes bright.

I swivel around, smile. There at last: apparition in the doorway.

"Rick," I go, "Scavenger Rick."

The door swing shut noiseless, the apparition in. Rick the Scavenger: ghoul, manitou, aghori, golem.

Billy step sideways, raise a fist in salute. "*Umkhonto We Sizwe* Rick. Spear of the Nation."

Rick take a step. A second step. A grin flash: glimpse of white teeth. Very white.

"*Umkhonto We Sizwe,*" he grate, "Spear Nation."

I wince. Hurt to hear that voice. Splintered vocals, laryngeal fracture, freak microtones in discord. Think rusted drill working a demon molar.

"Come on up Rick," goes Billy, "drinkie drink. Drink drinkie drink."

Rick don't move. Him spraddle-legged at the far end, arms hung loose. Image: some old clap-loused cowboy set to draw.

I swivel full circle, lean back digging him. Same as always, Rick. Dirty burlap poncho over a kilt. Not really a kilt, more a patchwork sarong: bits of rancid leather, treebark, turf, sheet-tin and plastex sutured with catgut, twine, banjo string. This here sarong reaching below his knees, the saw-tooth hem chafing his shins bloody, bluebottles clustered there feasting.

I sit up, trying to catch his feet. *Bare?* Yayup. They are, this time. But not always. Sometimes he wear moccasins fashioned from brambles, poison ivy, crushed pinecones, swatches of diseased skin. But not tonight. Both his feet bare, this night of their Lord. Lacerate and befouled, yes, but bare.

"Drink Rick," goes Billy beckoning, "slurpie drink. Slurpie slurp drink."

Rick flash a grin, look down, look up. And begin shaking: his body jerk and twitch, eyelids like wounded moths aflutter.

"Thar he blows," I go, "junkheap jactitation."

Billy slam a hand down on the bartop: gun boom.

"Rick," he go, "RICK!"

Rick freeze, tongue on the loll. Yellow bubbles erupt from his nose, stream back over his head.

"Aww baby," I go, "yeah! YEAH!"

Rick's tongue undulate in extrusion, snake downward, press up under his chin. Then it relax and rise stiffening. I notice how clean it is, his tongue. Pink and clean. About as clean as his teeth, so bright and pearl-white.

For anent the Scavenger, it is written: his flesh was a repository of untrammelled organic horror, but his tongue and teeth were beyond reproach –

"RICK," goes Billy leaning over the bar, "RICK!"

Rick mumble, crouch low, spring up, land with a heel-thud. Tremors shake his frame. Clods of desiccated muck fall from his hair: black rain. I watch ecstatic. Rick's hair a sight to behold if not adore: cascades of crudded shag down to his hips, a thousand soiled sheepscuts bunched, a hundred feculent manes bound to his prosimian skull –

"RIIIICK!"

I cringe. Billy's Lakota power-shout.

Rick stiffen, bouncing. His tongue out, rigid as a pre-dawn boner.

"Come on now Rick," Billy command, "come right up."

Rick withdraw his tongue. Shake his head. And move: his arms and legs whirring like chopper blades, him leaping from table to table, chair to chair, table to chair, chair to table. Hell of a sight. Like watching an outsize crustacean on adrenochrome. He blur across the sprawl, Rick, tumble thrice in flight, land dead even on his feet. Rabble applause, judges score 9.9879, give or take a worm.

"Slurpie slurp," he croak shaking back his hair, "drinkie slurp."

Billy straighten. "That's right Rick. Slurpie drink."

Rick pad up grinning, hop off the floor, land crotch-first on a metal-top stool. Thunk-squelch.

"Oof," Billy.

"Yowch," me.

Pain by association, transmission outside the nutsack. Me clutching my three-piece bijouterie, Billy clutching his.

"Hoooorrr!" Rick, "hooorrrRRR!"

Him still a-grin, not having registered the impact. No pain

that I can tell. And I'm thinking: *maybe he don't have nads. Or if he do, they're tucked up high and safe, like nesting sparrows.*

I've always wondered about Rick. About his origins. Legends and rumors abound. Rick legends, Scavenger rumors. Some say he's the immaculately conceived feral spawn of a backwoods geechee crone in her nineties. Others say he was whelped by USUL-4, that old time gene experiment folks keep talking about: lab geeks splicing a gila monster and a hillbilly hermaphrodite –

"What'll it be Rick," goes Billy, "what'll it be tonight."

Rick's head jerk. His tongue flicker out forked, ophidian.

"Drink," he gravel, "slurpie drink."

I nod. "Uh-huh. That narrow it down considerable."

Rick cough, turn grinning. "Boo hoo," he rasp, "boohoo hoo."

I bare my teeth, look him in the eye. He look me in mine. And then for some reason, our eyes meet.

Fucker's got weird eyes, Rick does. Like, eldritch. The kind you want to prise out with a rusted shiv and replace with phosphorescent slag. One green eye, one violet, both spangled gold. Look of a rabid lemur in a jungle photo flash. Pretty, though. Pretty eyes, even with all them sap-sucking thrips clustered in canthus. And the swamp-crud matted in his eyebrows and lashes.

We lock eyeballs, Rick and I. Me squinting, him chortling and blinking. Rick don't blink like anyone I know. Not with both eyes simultaneous like people do when they're asleep. He blink alternate: first one eye, then the other, then the one eye again, then the other again, ad nauseum. Rick's ultra-rapid alternate blinking never stop. Rain or shine, sleep or waking, it know no surcease.

But it's not the blinking per se that grab me. It's what shimmer within: the vitreous expanse beyond the portals of his retinae. Looking into Rick's eyes, I see a vast fissured plain dotted with lights. Violet, gold and green lights. This plain strewn with cooked entrails and varnished vertebrae, night sky echoing with the howls of the cannibal damned –

"Draft it is," goes Billy, "foamhead draft."

"Yeah," Rick, "foamhead."

I exhale, detach my gaze from Rick's, proceed to dig the rest of him. His brow to begin with. He got a broad brow, Rick, broad and wide. Strange for a feral cacodemonic cretin. You figure a guy like Rick come with, at most, an inch between eyebrow and hairline, give or take a foot. I mean I've seen chthonic retards, hadal half-wits with no foreheads at all. Not so here. Rick have it broad. Wide. And boiling.

Rick's brow be in tumult this night of their Lord: lesions, furuncles, bird-egg buboes swelling and bursting rapid, about once every second, give or take a minute. Them swelling with a hiss and bursting with a pop. Hiss-pop, hiss-pop: a happy sound. But it ain't just Rick's brow (no such luck). Fucker's popping all over: boils bursting on his dibbled cheeks, his quashed and snotted nose, his bruised sausage lips, his lantern jaw, his scabid neck, his gnarled hands, his duck feet, his hammer toes. Eruptions everywhere, going hiss-pop, hiss-pop, hiss-POP?

For anent the Scavenger, it is written: his leprous and rebarbative form evidenced a teeming richesse of pustule, papule, whelk, bunion, bubo, furuncle, carbuncle, blain, cyst, ulcer, running-sore, thrombus, tumor, rash, scar, wart and cicatrice –

"Here you are Rick," goes Billy, setting down a bowl, "drinkie drink."

Rick shudder, sneeze, look up. A beige strand hang from his right nostril, long and quaking: tapeworm. Rick scrunch up his nose and snort, the worm sucking in traceless.

"Drink Rick," repeats Billy, "slurpie drink."

Rick turn, prop his elbows on the bar. Before him, a clay bowl a-brim, some infernal potation Billy brewed up. Smell like venison marinated in hog-bile, slow-cooked in pulque.

"On with the show Rick," I go, "we're waiting."

Rick grunt, nod. His face stark now in profile, left lateral. Leeches at the corner of his mouth, fat from feeding. Thrips squirming in his glutted canthus. Ticks clustered in the lee of his bashed rhinus. Fleas and chinch-bugs hopscotching in his fungoid tresses. Some kinda sanious ooze trickling down the line of his jaw, dripping off his chin. Infected cerumen most likely. Gouts from a distempered eustachian.

Seconds pass. Rick propped motionless in profile, myself digging the leeches, ticks, thrips, fleas, chinchbugs, goofing on the blebbed and lacerate skin, the swollen nephritic earlobe. And the hole. There be a hole in the middle of Rick's left cheek, about the size of a silver dollar. This here hole frayed and cauterized around the rim, the teeth inside splintered or missing. Rick look to be breathing through this cheek-hole, air moving in and out with a low whistle –

Rick mutter, lean forward, cough. Black catarrh shoot out his mouth into his drink. His tongue wriggle, worm out the hole in his cheek, begin probing a nostril.

"Drink up now Rick," urge Billy, "drink up."

I throw Billy a look. Him standing back from the bar with arms folded, watchful.

Rick make a hooting sound. Lower his face into the bowl. And begin lapping. Lap lap, he goes, lap slurp, lap lap slurp. No surprise. We've seen it before, Billy and I. Seen it through through time's dream prism, past the provenance of the Age of Iron, the millennial reich of the plunderers, the people of northern ice. Rick never quaff his swill like regular folk, no. He lap it up like a hound dawg, like a beast at a waterhole: that long pink tongue darting in and out, in and out. A champeen lapper Rick, no question, but he's got other ways. Grapevine say he's become a snorter. Say he snort moonshine up his nose, up his cheekhole, up the variegated fenestrae and crenellations of his liberally trepanned skull.

Rick lap on sedulous. With bestial brio, ghoulish gusto, concupiscent verve, cunnilingal zeal, demented industry. Seem like it never end, but it does. He finish lapping, Rick. Then he straighten, tilt his head and belch explosive. The blast rock the bowl, send it brattling down the length of the bar and off the edge: crash.

"GodDAMN," I go, "now that's what I call BRISANCE."

Laughter rumble in Billy's chest, the revetments of his visage quaking. A tear break free, fall with a shimmer.

"You gonna have to pay for that there bowl Rick," he goes, "cold cash."

Rick sigh (rattle of clotted lungs), lick his chops, turn sudden.

"Zebtharkus," he grate looking me full in the face, "Zebtharkus watch."

I frown. "What now?"

Rick simper, lean in conspiratorial. A rash of pustules pop in quick succession, his brow crepitant. I flinch, gleet hitting my face in a fine spray.

"Zebtharkus see you," he croak, "Zebtharkus like."

I click my teeth. Suck spit. "Zeb like?"

Rick wink, lips working. Look like he's going to launch into one of his harangues, a heteroglossic rant perning towards a bathos of brecciate syntax and dismembered meaning, but no. He just pucker his lips in weird embouchure. And blow in my face. Whooofff: myself inhaling deep, thinking: *here it come, death by oral pestilence.* But it doesn't, thank yutz. Rick's breath don't kill. Au contraire it induce a high, a sourceless exalt. Rick's breath smell of sweet posset, of stir-fried pemmican. Balsamic it be, like the breath of spice island *Lotos Eaters*. And I'm thinking: *mysterious and surpassing strange how Rick, a plague-spawned basilisk, exude such heady redolence –*

"Zebtharkus," I go, "Zebtharkus the Drone, lord of the periclinal junkhill. You're saying he approve of our present pernoctation?"

Rick stare, lesions blooming suppurant. "Yaaah. Huh?"

I smack the side of my nose, fingers rigid.

"Oww. Well, superlative. Glad to have his blessing, his nihil obstat, his imprimatur."

Rick chortle, draw back, cock his head and spit black phlegm into the fall of his hair. His tresses teem: titian-winged roaches emerging, closing in on the spew.

"Ricky boy," goes Billy soft-voiced, "no spittin' in here kid. You know the rules."

Rick look up sheepish, look down, blow snot in a handful of hair. Fleas leap, chinches hop, roaches scuttle. It be feeding time this night in Rick's mane: his Koch spit their sustenance, his catarrh their pabulum.

"None of that either son," adds Billy frowning, "nosirreebob."

Rick look up contrite. "Ba-aad," he wheeze, "bad bad Ricky."

I snort. "Not GOOD enough, baby. You got to BLEED in apologia."

Rick turn, eyes alight. "Zebtharkus gift," he slur, lids drooping ptotic, "gift."

I cock an eyebrow. "Gift you say?"

Rick flash me a grin, draw up his left foot, prop the heel on the edge of his seat. "Gift. Zebtharkus gift – "

I look down, nod. There it is in full view: Rick's left foot. I try to spot his nads, his pecker, but can't: his rot-crotch concealed by a sheet tin pelmet on the hem of his sarong.

I study Rick's foot with interest. Mark it in close detail. This gangrenous and spatular wedge that end in eight hammertoes shaped like snakeheads. These toes conjoined and kindred, except for the hallux (big toe) which stand apart. He got a monstrous hallux, Rick: about the size of a turtle-egg peened flat by buckshot triggered hot and proximal.

Rick's heel, by contrast, show small, nugatory. A protrusion appear above the heel, a shade above the talus. A hook-shaped protrusion that resemble a horse's fetlock. But it's not a fetlock, no such luck. It's a prop that keep Rick from toppling back over his tapered and fleshless heels. It's also a pawl that keep his serrated bunghole from rotating at prohibitively high angular velocities. But above all (nec plus ultra), it's an auxiliary penis, sluicing rancid bladder-juice when the main vein choke and succumb to strangury.

Rick's left foot be, in short, a large fetlocked hammertoed triangle plentifully embossed with corns, papules, pemphigoid blisters and necrosed pocks bridging the raw fissures and bleeding fault-lines of its parched, pellagrous integument (*mocha daddy shittin' out his mouth again, Clem*).

But it's not his foot per se that stokes me, not the foot *qua* foot. It's the warts bunched on top. Rick got this cluster of smoke-green, grape-sized warts near the front of his foot, somewhere between the hallux and the middle toe. Warts that ooze sap when chewed with diligence, when masticated with aplomb. A bitter, resinous, psychotropic sap that taste like spurge milk and flare shamanic at the core of amygdala and hippocampus –

"Gift. Zebtharkus GIFFFFFT."

I blink, look up. Rick with eyes wide, candent. At left Billy motionless, tear welling.

I press together my palms. Bow. "Ready to receive, Rick. Accept and receive."

Rick grunt, reach with his right hand, begin plucking warts off his left foot. He pluck them one by one, with mantic discernment.

"Goo goo," he rasp, plucking the first wart.

"Goo goo," I echo, whispering.

"Moo moo," he croak, plucking the second wart.

"Moo moo," I echo, whining.

"Poo poo," he gurgle, plucking the third wart.

"Poo poo," I echo, groaning.

"Doo doo," he husk, plucking the fourth wart.

"D-d-doo d-doo," I echo, stuttering.

Snapshot: four moist grape-warts on a fungoid palm.

I whistle, applaud with both elbows. "Kudos, Rick. The grapes of wart. Diseased harvest."

Rick look up, mouth stretched in a lopsided grin.

"Gift," he repeat thrusting his hand up under my chin, "Zebtharkus gift."

I regard the warts a moment. Them and his blistered palps. Then I look into his eyes. Them alight with a pale fire, the kind you'd see in Pnin's skewed and proptotic orbs –

"Don't. Don't do it."

I turn. Billy looking straight at me, his visage a bronze mask lambent.

I shake my head. "Got to, dude. It's been ordained. Rick's edible periapt."

Billy blink, a tear pearling in descent.

I look away, hold out my hand palm up.

"Give over now, Rick kid. Entrust and bestow."

Rick flash me a pink-gum grin, sprue-rash under his nares showing like powdered sugar.

"That's right," I go, "commend and deliver."

Rick grunt, tilt his hand. The warts slide off his palm onto mine. They feel like real grapes, the warts, only heavier.

"Zebtharkus watch," grate Rick, "Zebtharkus SEE."

I nod, lean sideways, stick the warts in my pocket.

"Gratitude and blessing, Rick. Gratitude from me and my Run team, our Meister's blessing. Buford Aloysius Howell, *Lord Baron of Pain.*"

Rick make a high choking sound. Slide off his stool. "Meister bless," he rasp, "Zebtharkus SEE."

I shrug. "So be it. Fare thee well and god speed thy fiery extinction."

Rick flash me a grin. Shudder. Mince up to the sprawl. And start in. Some display: Rick twirling, tumbling, leaping in cabriole, table to chair, chair to table. Put me in mind of a ravaged mandrill in a high volt cage, pathic lab geeks gathered around masturbating.

He make it across the sprawl, Rick, but not in a straight line. He carouse around some, left to right, right to left over the Grotto's raddled bricolage. Clouds of yellow dandruff waft as he skip and soar, fluorescent squamae falling like Christmas snow. *Don't let it end,* I plead, supplicating my astral double, *don't.* But it do end: Rick pulling a final somersault and landing on all fours like a jungle cat.

"Gib!" squawk Rick straightening.

"Daw!" bark Billy, fist raised.

"Mac!" I shriek, knocking together my elbows, funny bones zinging.

Rick turn with a quinsied gurgle, his eyes catching lamplight: tapetal shine.

"Farewell Rick," I go, "dose of adios."

Rick don't answer. His left hand in slow ascent, travelling up his side. Past the scrofulae lumped on his chest, the strumae on his neck, on up to the hole in his cheek, myself sitting up sudden going: "Yeah! YEAH! – "

Thwumpf: Rick ramming his fist in through his cheekhole,

working two fingers up into his sinuses, forcing them out through his nose. Some sight: his forefinger poking out his right nostril, his midfinger out his left.

Rick's fingers hold a moment, working like bug feelers. Then they vanish up his nose, his fist emerging with a loud shlup: sound you hear pulling a gout leg from radioactive slag.

"Hayyyfeffefff," goes Rick, holding up his snotted fist, "hayyyfefffeff – "

"That'll DO Rick," Billy rapping the bartop, "go head and LEAVE now Rick."

Rick chuckle, his sodden hand on the move. Fingers descending with annelid alacrity: sphincterward.

"Yeah work it," I go, "WORK it – "

Rick with his left hand up his rump, routing vigorous. Slack-mouthed, like Mr. Nackybal addressing his prurit.

"Rick," goes Billy, "Rick?"

No response. Rick heavy-lidded, drool-thread in downward extension. His hand thrust way up, past his caecum by the look of it. Past his pylorus. High enough to worry a tonsil, tease the uvula, scratch the palate –

"Gnuuuu," groan Rick shuddering, "gnuuuuuu – "

"RICK," Billy slamming the bartop, "RIIIICK!"

Rick start: his eyes wide, mouth snapping shut.

"Leave, Rick," Billy pointing, "leave now."

Rick grunt. Corkscrew his hand out his bung. Thrust his arms up in chevron. And vanish out the front door in a weird display of light.

"Him," Billy, "the luminous."

I nod. "Bremsstrahlung shifting into the visible spectrum."

My gaze still on the spot vacated by Rick. Silence, my thoughts guttering. Echoes in my skull, psittacine tumult in the aviary –

I blink, frown. Sounds outside. Distant.

Billy sigh. "Fratboys comin' in."

I nod, slide off the stool. "Best get on in, before my so-called mates start to get happy."

Billy raise his hand, trace a finger across his cheek: "Them's three sorry sons you ride with."

I shrug, start for the back door. Parting glimpse of Billy impassive, staring.

"Adieu Billy," I murmur, "gratitude and adieu."

Past the pool table, past Jukebox Jane and wall pin-ups scored and torn –

Thunk: sound of the front door opening. Voices, a guffaw, feet trooping in. I don't turn, don't pause for a look. On till I hit the back door: white paint, red lettering. A caption that read: HAVE YOU HUMPED YOUR HARLEY TODAY. Above, a faded poster: some old time screen icon on a lunar scape, getting his rump sputniked by space droogs.

I push the door open with my foot, step through. Corridor. Light there, blood-dim, ceiling lamps running left to right, glass buttocks with pensile turd-bulbs. I snicker, pull the door shut, head right. Myself moving with knuckles joined, steps muffled by layers of chaff, sawdust, pumice, powdered bonemeal, flaked rooster-blood, regurgitate horse-hair, desiccated sperm, salt from the Trail of Tears. The passage run ten steps, then cut left. A door ahead, voices beyond. I walk up, grasp the knob, push.

"About fuckin' time."

"Fuck time. Heh heh."

"And they rejoiced."

I step in, elbow the door shut. They're seated around the table, Monk, John, Wald. A round table large enough to fill the room. Not a room per se ipso facto. More a closet, a cloacal recess with four walls, no windows, a door directly across. The walls plastered with old print tessellated in a merz collage.

"Slut call," warble John waving, "midnight slut call – "

I curse, take a step, pull up a chair.

"Took your time didn'tcha," John, "ay?"

I sit easy, give him a look. His features stark by lamplight: pantomime erlking murder mask.

"Watcha lookin' at, ho."

I blink, point. "The lamp."

John grin. "Cute ain't it? Made it m'self while you were out strokin' Billy."

I snort. "You couldn't make shit from shine-wax at gunpoint."

John cackle, Wald going: "Shitwax. Gunstroke. Heh heh."

I lean forward, digging the lamp. Dimestore medieval retro: some geek being burned at the stake with a book under his arm. Red glass flames with bulbs inset, the geek's head shining white, the book under his arm blue like his crotch, his clogs –

"Giordano Bruno," goes Monk, "yes?"

I turn. Monk with his capuche pulled low over his brow, face etched gaunt.

"Nope," I go, "look like Art Clark to me. Art Clark: space dweeb and netscribe. Fucker got his ass torched for porking pickaninnies on Isle Ceylon. I'd've paid to see it happen. Folks said the flames gave him a hardon that wouldn't burn. After he was dead, they boiled his skull clean and stuck that boner in his teeth: death's head chompin' dick like a cheroot. Fuckin' precious."

"Dickchomp," Wald, "boner burn. Heh heh."

I chuckle. Wald at left grinning gap-toothed, dimple cheeks roseate: the Devil's own round-eyed catamite –

Boom: John flat-palming the table. "Nuff of THIS crap. Rick. Did the fucker show."

I nod, lean left, fish the grape warts out of my pocket, slap 'em down on the table.

"Gift from Rick. By order of Zebtharkus. Imprimatur, Meister."

John bend close, peering. "Whut in HALE?"

I reach with both hands, line up the warts. "Four snotgreen nuggets off a festering foot."

John curse. "Whut you gon' use these for, plug up your bunghole?"

I flash him a freezing grin. "You WISH."

Monk cough. "Can't say I've seen glitterpills like these before. Nor bliss buttons. Nor sizzler psychotropes – "

"Grape warts," I interject, "Rick nuggets. Kickass shit. If it don't kill you, it'll make you stronger."

"Sheeat."

"Snot plug nugget. Heh heh."

I exhale sputtering, pick up a wart, place it before Monk. Pick up a second wart, place it before John. Pick up a third, place it before Wald. The fourth untouched, innocent before me.

John pinch up his wart, start kneading. "Dang. Feel like one them home-cooked hawg nipples they sell out at Hooter Bopeep's."

"Nipple home," Wald, "peeEEP! Heh heh."

I clear my throat, begin in resonant declamation.

"With these warts brothers," I go, "with these nuggets, I thee wed. Huh? No, scratch that. What I mean is: these nuggets we now consume and ingest. That's CON-SUME and IN-GEST. Why? Because the proof of the pudding is in the eating, as them oldtime folks liked to say. And the proof of the eating is in the shitting. And the proof of the shitting is in the reeking. And the proof of the reeking is in the burning – "

"Har!" John, "HARF!"

"And the proof of the burning is in the screaming," Monk, "and the proof of the screaming is in the dying – "

"And the proof of the dyin' is in the humpin'," John, "and the proof of the humpin' is in the jizzin' – "

"And the proof of the jizzing is in the flooding and drowning," me, "well spoken all, no more entries prithee."

Pause. John under his breath "harf! harf!", Wald "heef! heesh!", Monk hooded, mirthless.

I smile grim. Reach. Scoop up my grape wart. Pop it in. "Mmm," I go chewing, "mmhmmm."

John stare a moment, distrustful. Then he grunt, pop in his wart, Monk and Wald likewise.

Seconds pass, mandibles squelch and chomp, faces indicating dismay, revulsion, depthless loathing.

"Tastes like rancid compost," pronounce Monk, "rancom."

"Dawg dung on a dry puke cracker," John.

"Curdled protoplasm," me.

"Cracker compost," Wald, "hawg puke. Heh heh."

A minute pass. On hobbled phlebitic feet. Us chewing viscous and audible: a sound like farm hogs mating in slop.

"Gift from Rick you say," goes Monk sudden, "yes?"

I blink moist-eyed. "Gift, yes. Rick know of the Meister's Notion. As do his overlord Zebtharkus. Zebtharkus the Drone."

Monk lean back, nod. "Good to know we have a quasi-mythic trash-heap deity on our side. Makes it all worthwhile."

I cant my head, retrieve spit. "Heard that. But it make a body wonder: what'd happen if Meister Howell took on Zebtharkus the Drone. Like, who'd win?"

Monk swallow, wincing. "Be a titanic battle, I expect. Sort of a *gigantomachia peri tes ousias* – "

Wham: Trotjohn, hand down on the table. "Nothin's happenin'! Nothin's fuck-in' HAPPenin'!"

I look him in the eye. Both eyes. Night fire, flash storm.

"Youse got to keep chewin', son," I go heavy-lipped, "Rick's shit kick in sudden, sans preamble. This ain't like a short con catnip if that's what you're thinkin'."

John glower, jaws working. On his lip, a surf-line of buccal froth. "Whut I'm thinkin'," he goes, "whut I'm thinkin' is, if I don't trip and zoom real soon, you gon' bleed."

"Yehhh," Wald drooling, "blee-eeed. Hehhh. Hehhh."

"Mzdhqioihmf?" Monk.

I turn slow: creak of rusted hinges. "What now?"

"Rick!" gasp Monk, "did Rick stay lon-uhh-long?"

I nod sideways. Back to front. "LONG enuffffffffff."

Monk smile beatific, a weird sight. Him tooth-white, capuche fallen back, hair wisping gold. His eyes gone bright, changing colour: grey, turquoise, electric green –

"Strange fellow Rick, yesss. Quite quite strange – "

His voice metallic, distant: star child humming in sidereal dream.

Flop: my hand on the table, fingers working. Jellyfish throes. "Strange ain't the word Ethel. Is not. Isn't. Tisn't – "

My voice echoing loud: boom thrum in vacant hall.

The Wald sigh. Shut his eyes. Lean forward. And fart. He fart long and plaintive: whiff of turnip boiled in sewage.

"Brahhv-vo," I husk, "the W-wald's keestered swansong – "

A groan erupt from John's throat: "NnnNNGnahHHN!"

His mug gone slack, eyes rheumy. Mule-kick in the custard apples: agony, relinquishment, incipient delirium –

"Thar she blows," I boom, "thar she hahh! Wahhhahhh! – "

Monk make a bleating sound. "Wormmm. Isss worm gut?"

Robot voice, serpent sibilance.

I turn: crrrreak. "W-huhhh-worm?"

"Wormmmmnfpfpf," Monk starting to slobber, "worm in Rick's g-gut I mmhear. An enormous ph-prr-parasite."

I blink heavy-lidded, look down at my hands: palm-lines squirming, time out of joint.

"Tapeworm, yayyyupffmm. But the s-strongyle's BIGGER? A lot bigger."

"What?" Monk, "wha – aaa?"

"The worm in Rick's gut," my voice in machine crackle, "a strongyle. Big f-fucker. Size of a fullgrown b-boomslang. Make you wonder who the parasite is. Do the strongyle feed on Rick or R-uh-Rick on the strongllmh? Signs point to YES! NO! MAYfff! – "

Monk blink: lid-squelch. His eyes wide, swirling vibgyor.

"Prob'ly sym-ukh! Sssymbiotic. They f-feed on each other. Rick on the s-strongyle, the strongyle on RickffmM!. Someday th-they'll eat each other down to a sin-khh! sing – "

"Singularityyyy," I moan, "b-blackhole with blood-stained event h-HORizon, super-ahh! superstring and sen-hmmbrrph! sentient whoaAH! plenummm – "

I pause overcome, Monk with nares in rapid twitch, eyes brimming: "You s-speak with oracular force b-b-brother JB. Or sh-should I CALL you brother bonze ahhh! Or father P-Panchen or Gelugpapa or mmh! Nyingmama. You p-possess the hierophantic IF NOT SACERDOTAL c-clairvoyance of the doubly anointed, the th-thrice blessed – "

John groan, louder this time. Him slack on his seat, face gone to mush.

"To those who WAIT Johnny boy," I snarl, "for those who mnNHH! Wai-uhh – "

Thubwumf! I turn. Wald slumped forward, mouth in full foam.

"He suc-succumbs," I go braying laughter, "and not a mo-moment too s-soon."

"Suckh," Wald, voice sparged through spit-froth, "cum. Hehpf. Hehpf – "

Him with arms outspread, gnawing the table top.

I take a shuddering breath. Nod. Blink. Nod. A glow in my head now, a rumble in my gut. And heat building in my loins. I start to speak, break off with a loud retch, my pulse racing on crutches. On a bum leg dodging bullets –

"Strange," whispers Monk, "ssstrange."

I snuffle, flick sweat off my brow. "Nay not strange. Brrr. Brrill. Brrrrillllly. Brrrrrilliannnnnt."

Brilliant yes, Monk's eyes. Points of light streaming tears. Tears dripping off his beard in slow time, like pearls through glycerine –

The Wald shriek, rear up and topple back, taking his chair with him. Wald floored belly up, head against the wall, mouth foaming.

"Whoa-ho-ho," John, "whoa ho ho ho – "

I turn whimpering. Far gone, Trotjohn, his mouth open in a gawk. His left eye spinning clockwise, right eye counter. Different quantum numbers, Pauli Exclusion in effect –

"Whoa ho ho ho," John, "I can SEE em, maaan, I can SEE-eeee whoa ho ho – "

I look up with a sob. Smile lopsided. Stinger, Finesse, Oblongata, Noodlebear up near the ceiling. On a floating grapnel. White grapnel lotus with flukes for petals.

"Noodlebear," I moan, "THOU: Noodlebear."

Noodlebear look down, gouge her nose with a finger, punch herself in the teeth. She look different, Noodlebear. They all do. They've morphed again: our eidolon spirit guides gone sapphic, them dyked clear and unmistakable –

"Ohhh ho HOOO," John's eyeballs spinning, "ohhhhHHHHH."

I retch, mouth half-open. My lips the fissured lids of a spitball orb, my tonguetip a roving iris.

"Boo hoo," Monk, "boo hoo HOOOOO."

I turn sniffling. Monk bolt upright, teeth bared in a grin. Sobbing. Monk grin-sobbing, his tears in orbit around his head, dozens of blue pearls circling. And making music. Monk's tears make music as they orbit. Strange music. Like Erich Zann scraping a viola with a mastodon tusk. Monk's teeth respond to the music. They come loose, twitching in dentoid concert –

I start, hearing a loud gurgle. Wald still aground, feet up. A mound of foam on his chest, spit-froth hillocked on his upper moiety. Appetizing, somehow. Like spun sugar skimmed off a drool chin –

I rise, sphincters clenched. *It's turning, Ethel. Spinning. Tinnying. Spurning.* And it is. The tabletop. Spinning like a roulette wheel. Fast. Light corposant at the rim, darkness at the centre –

I groan out loud, clap a hand to my belly. Pain there, my guts writhing colubrine. *Papa peristalsis, his thunder –*

Giggle. I look up. There still, our eidolons. On the grapnel lotus. Stinger buffed, flexing her guns. Finesse akimbo, working a lat spread. Oblongata skirt-billowed, salacious. Noodlebear on one foot, knuckling her own skull. All four with teeth bared, cachinnate.

Somewhere in my head a neuron flash, flare brilliant. Visions race, searing the volutes of my cerebrum. I see hairless epicenes dismembered, scattering their limbs to the winds. Caped baboons with sapphire eyes leaping off a cliff at night. Patricians at an equine stable-rut, squirting fondue up thoroughbred recti. Decorticate razorheads leap-frogging across a copper desert. Tranny clerics suckling cloned wombats. Trepanned whalers humping a dead orca. Fluorescent rats on an exposed backbrain, nibbling at the frayed edge of memory –

I move, gut rumbling. In full spin now, the table. And the room. John, Monk, Wald, with arms outstretched, dervished around the vortex. *And so it must have been, Clem, in that first spinning place, all them gonads rolling on fields of glaze –*

I bawl gape-mouthed, lunge at the door, burst through. Corridor, my feet moving. A face loom: redmeat mug. *Outta my way fratboy,* blam, thud, my viscera now in tumult, quick now, here now, my entrails ablaze, Grotto crapper quaking into view, my body hurtling headlong and boom, raw stench slamming my snout, a cubicle with door ajar –

"NNNNNNNNnnNNGRRAAHHH! – "

And in: collapsing backward, my baggies torn down, mouth and bunghole in simultaneous erupt, magma seething up, down and out under snapshots grime-lit in lewd roil, graffiti scrawl all hunger and torment, and the Notion in my mind's eye coruscant over a sea of flame with giants fucking, rat-headed gulls keening, the Meister in extremis at cliff's adge howling under a vanished moon, crazed paraclete wild-eyed, ranting Erebus and Gehenna.

PART THREE

SACRIFICE

It's empty when I return. The alcove empty, lamp shattered on the floor, fading. John, Monk, Wald, absent, Stinger, Finesse, Oblongata, Noodlebear gone. I sidle in halt and spent, surveying the damage. The table kneecapped and canted, chairs bent and smashed, walls raked and spattered with nameless plasms. *Be hell to pay when Billy sees this. Best get out while you can –*

I pinch up my baggies, start across. Moving dainty and finical, me, in a manner befitting an ephebe of stature and virgin flesh. At the backdoor I pause, push, step out: night wind like a cool hand on a fevered brow. I look around blinking: hesitant moonlight, woods fringing a swath of grass –

"HEY!"

I turn. My comrades out by the corner: Monk, John, Wald, lounging easy, hands pocketed.

I shake my head, hitch up my baggies and move, damp grass brushing my ankles. *How nice, Ethel. How nice the feel of dew-soaked sumac on hot tendons, Ethel –*

"Rhino-farts," I go tramping up, "fuckin' hawg testicle troglodytes."

Monk sigh. "The lad has a grievance. A plaint. Yes?"

I scowl. "Grievance is right. The mess you guys left back there. Table busted, chairs – "

"YOU guys," John snarling, "that's a fuckin' laugh. YOU did

most of the damage PECKERhead. You went fuckin' berserk, weird juju primetime. That shit you pulled on them wall pics, blood and jizz all over – "

"Blood," I go, "BLOOD. Do I look like I'm BLEEDING?"

Monk whistle. "Not now you're not, but you were then. Inverse bipolar Pho Wa. Blood squirting from your priap, semen from your fontanelle, top of your head. Hugely entertaining if nothing else."

"Huge priap," Wald, "semen font. Heh heh."

Pause. Monk regarding me regarding John regarding Wald.

"Well it matters little," I go shrugging, "we all get our asses fragged when Billy finds out. Best to leave before he does."

"Quite," Monk, "best."

"Little ass," Wald, "heh heh."

John curse, shoot a spitball in Wald's right ear, turn on his heel, start walking. Monk following wordless, Wald in pursuit hopping on one foot, arms locked overhead.

"Wreckage," I mutter, my feet on the move, "flotsam."

We march around the side of the cabin to the front. I figure there be fratboys thronged there working a quickie circle jerk, blowing their rank suds into the night air, but no. None in sight. Just a lone figure by the porch digging Ted. Tall dude in a trench coat, Bhutanese mountain cap spilling dreads.

John stop short, veer right, fetch up near the porch.

"Whoa now," he goes clapping twice, "Kid Afrika."

The figure turn, raise a hand in greeting. "Well if it isn't Trotjohn, de scourge of Babylan."

The voice musical: island singsong.

John clap once, bend, touch the tips of his boots, straighten. "Whoa hey, ha ha. Well sheeat. Been a while no see, Kid. So like, watcha been doin' with yo' TIME."

The Kid clap, brush his chin with the back of his hand.

"Not all dat much, maan. Prayin for de love of Ja, waytin' for de fall of Babylan... maan."

John bark, slap his thigh. "I ain't waitin', dude. I'm gettin' out there and tearin' the fucker DOWN."

The Kid shake his dreads, chuckle. "You do dat, maan. You go do dat. Is dat you in the shadows dere JB, maan."

I blink, smack hard my right cheek, thump my sternum.

"It's me in the shadows, Kid. Me in the half-light stroking my perdition."

The Kid clap twice, shake his locks: yellow porch light caught there in lambent nimbus.

"You and Trotjohn and de two others, maan. Monk and little Wald by de look of 'em. And de Babylan prisoners weeping, maan. De Babylan prisoners weeping."

Pause in glaucous penumbra. Wind gust, foliage whispering.

"Well sheeat," goes John, "ha ha. Dang."

"Prison stroke," Wald, "heh heh."

The Kid nod. Bow deep. Turn. Climb the porch steps. Push open the door. And vanish into the Grotto.

John cough, shrug. "Well that's that. Let's get the hell out."

"Hell," Wald starting to whimper, "out."

I turn, slap his flank. "Shit, fella. You can drop 'em now."

The Wald yelp, lower his arms with a sigh.

"Move it now pecker-sluts," John, "MOVE."

I smack my thighs open-palm, start walking. John jogging up and falling in behind, Monk and Wald likewise. On wordless, towards the breach and into the woods, foliage bristling. Trees awake and angry by the sound of 'em. No surprise. *Frat-hawgs messed around on their way in. Them chewing on branches, pissing on leaves, nailing tampons to trunks, fellating pinecones, sucking sap out of gashed bark, humping arboreal crepuscules, jizzing in abandoned birdnests –*

I walk silent at first, scorning the leafy tumult. But then pity supervene and I begin singing. Me with mouth open wide, putting forth a nocturne, a Tuvanese triharmonic throat-warble. The song quickly take effect. Trees return to slumber en masse, varmints fall silent and resume foraging. Some cicadas stay angry (a coterie of embittered Jacobins) but most relent, rasping out a message of tearful reconciliation in New Morse.

My footsnouts falter halfway up the trail. Falter and stop. A shape appear ahead: large, threatful. Signs point to: bulljock, meatmug, hammer-schlong –

"Out of my way putz. NOW."

The voice matching the shape. Idiot husk.

I harrumph, raise a hand. "I am Robin of Schlockley, notorious and renowned jungle bitch. Behind me stand the heavy-bollocked Little John. Behind him a hirsute, consumptive Marion. Behind her a dissolute, cherubic Friar Tuck. So what say we skip the stick fight and you let us pass without so much as a squeak, a fart, or a murmur?"

Pause. The shape looming close: whiff of loin-mold, jocksweat. "I'm gon' count to three now girls. After that it's gon' be PAIN fuckin' PRIME time – "

I yelp: John digging an elbow in my ribs, shoving me aside.

"Tell you whut, fuckwit," John's voice silken, "let's do it MAH way. First I count to three REAL slow. Then I tear your heart out and lung-fuck you. Then I reach way down, yank your nuts out your throat and chew oane 'em some. Then I rip your leg off and whale you bloody with your own fuckin' foot. How's THAT sound. Ay?"

Pause. Night breeze. Wald giggling.

"John," goes the shape, "Trotjohn?"

I smile. Fear in that voice. Sweet.

"ONE Mississippi," John, "honey miss."

"Awww shit," the voice, "Trotjohn man, I didn't – "

"TWO Mississippi. Honey miss."

The shape step aside, melt into the woods. Leaf rustle, whipoorwill jeering.

"Well," I go, "that's – "

John turn with a curse, grab my T-shirt, pull hard. I stumble, trip over John's boot, sprawl face down, Wald "YEEH!", John "HARF!", Monk clicking his tongue rueful.

I howl profane, leap up and start marching, the triad in tow. On up the track to the end, through the Gateway into the lot. Overhead the dragon lantern wind-tossed, shadows in red skitter.

I figure the lot be about a quarter full, but it isn't. Just about a dozen vehicles in evidence. At right a parcel of fratboys, voices raised in badinage. Far above, the moon in retreat: discoloured tissue ringed with cloud-fungus –

"Nothin' you ain't seen before," John, "keep it movin'."

I move. Us heading left across the lot, the Durerro parked there at the far end. Walking with feet splayed, me, near spraddle-legged, night wind balming my heat-rashed crotch. With each step my cankered lungs breathing, breathing. *A fragrance in the air, yes. Fragrance such a rarity around these parts, Ethel, yes. Odour of chrysanthemums, cherry blossoms mantling the warrior gutted in spring snow –*

VRROOOM!

I jump. John gunning the engine, brights on. "OUT!" he yell, "we OUT!"

I run around, yank the door open. "RUT!" I shriek diving in, "RUT! RUT! RUT! – "

And VRROOOM: the Durerro churning dirt, hitting the road with a squeal, Wald agog going: "Yeeh! YEEEH! – "

We don't go back the way we came, no. Not west towards Dinglevale. We go the other way instead, Route 54 going East, branching a mile up onto the freeway headed South, this drag gone bare past midnight, twelve lane tarmac stone empty, John flooring the pedal with the roof down, windroar like a twister howl, us moiling in our seats all darkness and delirium, the Durerro in sonic overdrive with Lem, thrashland Angstführer screaming in on a distortion firestorm going:

Hellspawn, Mark of Cain
Nothin' to lose, nothin' to gain
Blood rain, demon fire
Watch the flames rise
Higher and higher
Up from the Pit
Final Conflict
Total war
What we're here for
The Beast lives
We're here still:
Burn. Fuck. Smash. Kill.
Burn. Fuck. Smash. Kill –

***

I lie flat on warm sand under a night sky, feral midgets using my gut as a trampoline. They leap high, screeching rhythmic, sharp turds shooting out my rump with each bounce. The turds soar in flaming trajectory, hit the horizon in soundless aurora – cut.

Ten grim-faced homunculi work their way up my right leg with pickaxes, nostrils gouting epoxy. Six make it to the rim of my bunghole but I blast 'em off with a fart. The other four retaliate in kind: their flatulence scorching the fine down on my right buttock. I curse wordless, in hieroglyphic cartoon bubbles – cut.

Five boarhogs in red bonnets, frill diapers and decorative brassieres sit on chaise longues in the lee of a windmill. They have cheroots stuck in their snouts, smoke rising to form a question mark. I try to speak but I can't. There's a ball gag in my mouth, my limbs riveted to grey stone, my prick aimed in silent accusation –

And awake, voice in my throat a thin squeal.

"Visioneering again. Yes?"

I sit up corralling drool, blinking through eye-gunk. Monk at left, disdainful.

"Bad juju in hypnagogue," I mumble, "boarhog inquisition."

"On a Friday night?" Monk.

"Hog juju," Wald up front, "heh heh."

I comb crud from my lashes, look around. Woods either side, the road a narrow strip climbing. The roof back up, Lem silent, canned air sibilant.

"Where we at TJ," I croak, "road don't look familiar."

"We at where we at," John.

"Anywhere near the State Park?"

"Uh-huh," John, "anywhere."

I curse, swallow. "Fucker ain't feelin' chatty."

"Sheeat."

The road rise, round a curve, hit a straight stretch. The TV tower slide into view, red points on the blink. Above, a leached moon-rind caught in cloud soot. *Where them spirit guides gotten themselves to. Wish I could see them bardo dryads by moonlight, kicking and clawing in a frenzy of Sapphic love –*

"Bitch better come through," John, "better."

I blink. "You mean Gilmer?"

"Nah," John, "yo' dong-whackin' pawdaddy."

"Daddy dong," Wald, "heh heh."

I stick a pinkie up my nose, cork out a crust, begin kneading. "Think he'll have the mayor all trussed and ready?"

John snort. "If he know whut's good for'm."

I flick the booger, lean back. "Visited ol' Gilmer down at his shack a while back. His clapboard shack at the State Park. Just one room and a chimney, no windows. Dead squirrels everywhere, no surprise. Still can't stand 'em critters, Gilmer. Squirrels nailed to the walls, hung from the ceiling. Only thing squirrel-free was his rack of boomerangs. That and his kiddie-smut snuff stash."

"Uh-huh," John, "that there stash keep mayor Bob hopped and trippin'. Gilmer been feedin' him that sheeat reglar."

"Shitfeed," Wald, "rack, hung, heh heh."

Monk sniff. "Man certainly knows how to wield a boomerang. Worth a look."

I nod. "Sure is. Gilmer work some crazy-ass mojo with a boomerang. Fucker can knock a good man's teeth out at a hundred yards. One at a time. You name the tooth, he'll knock it. Gets his practice killin' squirrels. Knock 'em straight off trees. Gilmer hate trees near as much as he hate squirrels. I asked him why once. *Ah hate 'em cuz they smart,* he said, *them squrrls is smarter'n coons, hawgs, gators. Evil too. More evil'n trees. And green taters. And cold corndawgs. And boiled sawsij –* "

"HARF!" John, "slut sound just like him."

"Cornslut," Wald, "heh heh."

The car slow, pinking. John curse, shift to meet the incline.

"Mystical though," drawls Monk, "man Gilmer."

I cock an eyebrow. "Gilmer? MYS-tical?"

Monk exhale purse-lipped. "Gilmer's boomerang to be exact. The way it swings out and back: evolution, involution, mergence: one Kalpa cycle."

I nod appreciative. "Mystical and symbolically loaded yes. Not to mention accurate. I've seen how accurate he is. That one time he pulled a William Tell on Bitch Tit standing eighty yards off. Knocked him clean out from under a cooking apple, plenty blood, worth every penny – "

"Harf!" John, "ha-HARF!"

"Tit cook," Wald, "blood load. Heh heh."

I cough, smack my right eye. "Ow. Yowww. And speakin' of blood: you oughtta see some that new kiddie-snuff Gilmer got stashed up. Cuttin' edge dreck from the Dutroux Foundation Euro-Belgique, from Father Freddy way out in the Indus. Good ol' Father Fred, gotta love'm. You want Grade-A kiddie-snuff, boy, shake down a priest. Gilmer got it all: burn'n'drown, flog'n'fuck, nail'n'drill, the gamut. You'd think Fatman have the pick, but no. Gilmer's the man: biggest kiddie-snuff cache this side of the Big Apple-achian."

John grunt, suck spit. "Gets the job done. Mayor Bob homin' in like a shark to chum."

Monk chuckle soft. "Flog'n'fuck you say? That must bring back memories, eh Wald?"

"Ohhh yeah," John, "Wald's had his fair share you bet. Poondawg say some of it's on film. Say he caught this snuffhouse clip down in West Tex, little Wald baby pink at year eight or nine catchin' hell in a trailer, some Semper Fi razorhead workin' him over real savage. Gotta get mah hands on THAT scene, boy."

I sit up, peep around the headrest. Wald slumped speechless, staring. Ahead, the road running level, an object in shadowed accrual –

"Rice," I go, "doghead."

"Huh?" John, "wha?"

"There. Up ahead."

"Ahead mah – SHEEAT!" John sitting up, "DAWG?"

"A canine skull to be exact," Monk.

The Durerro approach, brights zeroing in: a bowl, middle of the road. Red clay bowl heaped with white rice, a doghead perched atop. Head with eyeless sockets, teeth bared, tongue lolling.

"Slow up some kid," I suggest leaning forward, "could be dangerous."

John turn, spit on my left cheek. "That a real dawghayd?"

"Plenty real," I go wiping off on upholstery, "recent. Look like the pitbull jumped us back on the Route."

"Well I'll be humped bloody with m'daddy's dong," John, "that's the one awright."

"Ye-ess," Monk stroking his beard, "ye-esss – "

"FIVE!" I bark, "FOUR! THREE! TWO! – "

Thud-squish-crunch: the car in brief shudder, backward glimpse of soiled rice and shattered clay, one doghead on the roll, John slapping the dash: "HARF! HAHAAARFF!", Monk well pleased, mouthing snippets from the Lankavatara.

But Wald, whither Wald? Surprise: him slouched wordless in erstwhile sorrow, the road ahead an illuminate seam through the dark I behold, my thoughts gone atomic, circling a stillpoint void with hard clarity setting in along the edge of a bright knife, Ernst Junger looking on lidless, steel-girt anarch on a floe of dirty ice under a Prussian moon.

***

He slow a mile up, John. Slow and cut left over a dirt patch onto a road paved, winding.

"Well hell," I go, "I know where we at now."

John snort. "Let's break out the fuckin' wassail."

A signboard drift past luminous: MONTE GUANO STATE

PARK. My pulse quicken. I swallow and my left ear pops: whine. Voices waft in murmurous, voices filtered through Our Lady's Morphogenetic Aureole, across the Sambhogakaya Spectrum.

The car slow some more, branches clawing the roof. John curse, wrench the wheel: the car cutting right, screeching to a stop before a painted barrier. A kiosk at left in silhouette.

John honk, flash the brights. Nothing at first. Then a shadow emerging from the kiosk, light in hand.

"Well whaddya know," John, "our own parkville retard."

"Fuckbreak wassail," Wald, "heh heh."

"Ah," Monk, "the Wald back from hell's bourne."

The shadow hobble up, torchbeam wavering. John slide down his window, spit.

"Who we got," rasp the shadow, "who we got."

John thump the side of the car. "It's ME fuck-knuckle. Now get that flashlight outta my face and let us in fore I build a fire under your nuts."

I lean left, wave. "How now, Gilmer."

"Nut fire," Wald, "heh heh."

Gilmer wheeze, turn, hobble back to the kiosk. Can't see his face clear, but that's all right. I know what he look like. Cropped bullet-head, absent brow, hang-dawg eyes stuck in a grey ooze –

"UP, PECKERHEAD!" John, "HOICK IT UP!"

The barrier rise with a groan: John gunning the engine, surging on through.

"Didn't see his boomerang," I go, "did not."

"He's got it," John screeching to a halt, "wedged up where the sun don't shine."

"In rectal gloom," Monk, "with malignant stool."

"Took the words right outta my butt," me.

"Malignant butt," Wald, "heh heh."

John curse, kill the engine and jump out, us right after. A paved road show ahead bedarked, woods densed in gauntlet. At left, a dirt track moonpale.

"Where you at ho," goes John turning to the kiosk.

Him posed in profile, his führershine in corona.

"Jes closin' up," Gilmer's voice floating in, "be there faster'n yew c'n say whoa Gilmer – "

Sound of the kiosk door grating shut, John cursing under his breath. Gilmer appear a moment later, approach with a spavined hobble, light in hand.

"That's right," John, "take all the fuckin' time you want. We got all night."

Gilmer grunt, his hobble turning urgent. But it's not good enough. John spit, stride up impatient, snatch the flash from Gilmer's hand, train it on his bashed grey mug.

"Now Gilmer," John, all honey and dulcet, "you know whut I'm gon' ask you now, don't ya?"

Gilmer grimace, eye-flaps twitching over marbled orbs, lipless mouth in weird rictus. That's when I notice: John's boot in extension grinding Gilmer's left foot. This here foot clad as always in a raddled moccasin.

"Ah guess," rasp Gilmer, teeth grit.

"You GUESS?"

"Ah... ah mean ah know whut you gon' ast."

John grin, his visage ghouled stark in penumbra.

"The question, Gilmer, is this: do you have mayor Bob all trussed up and ready."

Gilmer nod vigorous, still grimacing. "Ah sure do. Up 'ere in mah shack."

John step back a-grin, beam still trained on Gilmer's pan.

"Mah man. That's whut I like to hear. Bob have his muscle boys with him?"

Gilmer blink, his face slackening. "He sure did. Not anymore though."

"Not anymore?"

Gilmer shake his head. "Ah had to... ah killed 'em dayd jes like you ast."

John's grin widen, shaping a clownish death mask.

"You killed the mayor's muscle boys. BOTH of 'em."

Gilmer blink rapid, shuffling in place, his pongid mug ashen.

"Ats whut ah did... jes like you ast. Ah whupped thur hayds awf with mah sickle aydge boomerayne."

John titter, teeth bared white. "You did WHUT?"

"He decapitated the mayor's sentinels," offer Monk, "took their heads off with his sickle-edge boomerang."

Him shadowed at left, arms folded nonchalant.

John titter once more, longer and louder this time.

"Bet they wudn't expectin' THAT. Ay?"

Gilmer shake his head. "Naw ah guess they wudn't. Them boys wuz settin' easy watchin' mayor Bob stick a cornpone to Eveline."

"Ah," Monk, "element of surprise. A plot twist."

John's grin fade, eyes narrowing.

"Eveline," he goes, "who the ever-lovin' FUCK is Eveline."

Gilmer's mug congeal in strange topology: panic in those faded orbs. "Ev... Eveline's a kid girl ah keep oane hand – "

"KID girl," John, "you let mayor fuckin' Bob stick a cornpone to some kid girl? In your SHACK?"

Gilmer's mouth gape and shut, gape and shut in piscine alternation. Ripples run down the flank of his mug: clonus.

"Ats whut happen," he rasp, "whut happen ever' time the mayor show up. Ain't no other way..."

I don't see it coming, but I'm not surprised when it does: John taking a step, slamming his boot in Gilmer's crotch. Gilmer doubling over with a gasp, knees hitting the ground.

"Timber," I sigh, "tim-fuckin'-ber – "

"You best go get the mayor now, Gilmer," goes John casual, "no tellin' whut I do to you if we stick around yakkin' – "

He train the beam on the soiled nest of Gilmer's hair: him crouched on his knees gasping and sobbing, hands groined fruitless.

John toss the beam, turn on his heel and step away.

"We'll be waitin' oane you in the lot now, Gilmer. You go get the mayor... and them two heads. Say you whupped the heads off'n his muscle boys, two of 'em? Well I want them heads in a sack, hear me? Mayor Bob and them two heads – "

He stalk up to the car John, yank the door open, duck in and hit the ignition. Vrrrrooooom.

"Bitches be gettin' in quick," he call, "I ain't hangin' around all night – "

Us hastening sans demurral, back into the car, brights coming on and vrrrrrooom: up the road into the nighted fastness of the state park.

***

"I suppose they'll be there," goes Monk, "the lot of them."

"Who," I go, "Thrillboys?"

"None other."

"They'll be there awright," John tapping the brakes, "if they don't want their peckers bit off."

I nod sage. "World of pain if they don't show. World of PAIN – "

John curse, veer right: the car screeching through a narrow wooded isthmus into a parking lot.

"Well lookee," John slowing, "lookee lookee."

I blink, spot them. Boonside Thrillkillers posed motionless, edge of the lot. Thrillboys in shitkick boots, baggies, padded bomber jackets. Behind them, high-grip choppers in array, a black van hulked beside.

John cruise up, ease to a stop with his brights still on: Thrillboys spotlit.

"Check 'em out," John with a snicker, "fuckin' cherryass cuntlicks. Make you want to take a hatchet to the bunch of 'em."

"Then begin negotiations with a view to establishing a just peace," Monk.

"Harf!" John, "HARF!"

"Cherry peace cuntview," Wald, "heh heh."

John spit on his palm, wipe off on his crotch.

"Look like they showed up anyhow. Most of 'em."

"They're all there," me, "every last gash-whelped, tit-spurned one of 'em."

And they are all right. In clear evidence. Beast there at left. Bitch Tit. Hammerhead. Poondog. Peckertrash. Jizzpony. Booger Dumpling. Dung Nugget. Gutterputz. Slutmush. Pussywuss. Fartmart. Hogball. Ratsandwich. Snatch Weasel. Kill Kraut. Stain. Dingus. Shagpie. Cap'n Gangrene. Muttfuck. Leper Luke. All present save Aladdin, dead and eaten. And the four killed yesteryear in a freeway blood-feud: Mudguts, Kundalini, Toe Cutter, Bubba Zanetti –

"Fuckers cold look like slaughter meat," John, "ay?"

"Look like they just got yanked outta bed," me, "after smokin' some bad shit on a catnip. And gettin' cornholed by hillfolk on a brimstone crusade."

"HARF!" John, "yowp."

"Catsmoke shithill," Wald, "heh heh."

Monk cough. "Moments pass. Precious moments."

John mutter, wrench the wheel: the car surging left, jolting into the kerb.

"Ow," me, "yeow. Harder next time, hon."

John cut the lights, kill the engine, kick open his door. "Last man out sucks hawg dick."

"That'd be me," I go climbing out last, "dang! Night air gettin' nippy."

John stand by the car a moment, yawning expansive. Then he stroll across and pause, arms folded. Thrillboys silent ahead. Above, the moon cysted yellow in the eye of night.

"Well now," John scratching his belly, "whut we got."

Silence. Thrillboys in lunar tableau.

John snicker, turn. "Yo Poondawg!" he bark, "Poondawg!"

A shadow detach itself from the pack, step up. Something in one hand: a sack. Can't see the face but I know the form: bull-necked, pyknic. Prognathic jaw, bare piltdown skull: Poondog.

John scratch his beard audible: sound of a talon scraping frosted glass.

"Whut you got there boy. Whut we got."

Poondog grunt, hold up the sack. "Stuff. For the barbecue."

John hawk, spit. "Whut stuff."

"Coon," Poondog lowering the sack, "boar. Possum. Gator. Armadiller. Grandpaw."

Pause. "GRANDPAW?"

Poondog run a hand over his pate. "Bitch Tit's grandpaw. Ol' diddlebone got whacked cheatin' at poker. We found him, sliced him up, brought him along."

John finger his medallion: flash of moon-gold.

"Well fine. Like the Good Book say: finders eaters, losers shitters."

"Yeh," Poondog, "finders."

"Shitters," Wald sotto voce, "heh heh."

"Eat 'em all," John, "let your gut sort 'em out."

"Yeh," Poondog, "gut."

"The best absorbed en route," I mutter, "the worst expelled with passionate intensity."

"For the centre cannot hold," Monk.

John lean sideways, press a thumb to his nose and blow. Snot shoot out phosphorescent, hit the ground with a sizzle.

"Well you did awright," he allow, "now get the fuck outta my face."

Poondog step back, merge.

"Now where," goes John turning, "has that fuckin' ape gotten himself to?"

I squint. "There. That's got to be him."

A light appear, bobbing in the dark. Faint clink of metal.

"HAUL ASS PISSANT!" bawls John, "WE AIN'T GOT ALL NIGHT!"

The light draw near, wavering, sound of a chain clinking rhythmic. Gilmer hobbles into view, pant and wheeze, a shadow shambling beside. Can't make out the shadow, but no prizes for guessing who: mayor Bob.

John step up as they draw near, click on his flashlight. Some sight: Gilmer in stained overalls, a miner's helmet shafting a yellow beam. In his left hand a burlap sack. In his right, mayor Bob. The mayor in a pale pinstripe shirt torn asunder, black bowtie askew. His legs worm-white under grey briefs, feet blue-socked. Mayor Bob bald, corpulent and bug-eyed: mouth sealed with duct tape, wrists cuffed, ankles chained.

"Hot-DAMN," John, "that there is one sadsack simple-son bitchass trussed up fuckin' TURKEY."

Mirth: Thrillboys hyuck yuck. Mayor Bob blinking into the light, throat-apple working spasmodic.

John cock his head, mock-solicitous. "Whut's that you say, Bob? You want in oane our late night shindig?"

The mayor's eyes go wide with recognition. And outrage. He advance convulsive, foot-shackles dragging, a growl sounding in his throat. Trotjohn seem to sigh: his elbow rising to meet the mayor's arched beak. There's a dull crunch: gore blossoming bright on the mayor's mug, him toppling with a mute squawk. Thud-clink: Bob landing heavy on cold tarmac, balls up in chains. The mayor of Churchtown supine, cough and retch, torchbeam trained on his sodden pan.

"Now Bob," John stepping up casual, jamming a boot heel in the mayor's neck, "I'm gon' say this but once, so listen up. Next time around, it won't just be your nose. It's gon' be your nuts gettin' ripped out and barbecued for mountain oysters. Dig?"

"Aahhhkh!" Bob turning cherry red, "aaaaakhhh!"

John chuckle, step away, turn the beam on Gilmer.

"That's fine work there, Gil. But you sure took your time comin' over. Whut'd you do, stop for a shit sandwich?"

More mirth: Thrillboys yuckety yuck.

"Naw," rasp Gilmer, "ah jes – "

"Don't need to answer that'n Gil, cuz I don't rightly give a fiddler's fuck. Pull one them heads out that sack now, would ya? For mah boys t'have a looksee."

Gilmer blink. "Yew want ah shud – "

"Don't make me say it again now, Gil. Do not fuckin' make me say it again."

Gilmer nod rapid, brow beam quaking. His right hand dip into his burlap sack and emerge, holding a head by the shorthairs. One of the mayor's muscle boys: the face rigored in bloodless amaze, lips parted, blue eyes sightless. A pale bone-stump show at the base, gore clotted around shorn throat-flesh.

"Now THAT," John with a grin, "THAT there's whut I'm talkin' about. Whut y'all think. Ay?"

Boot shuffle: Thrillboys milling around yip and whoop.

John move up a step, stick his flashlight in Gilmer's cheek.

"Now Gilmer, this here's something I shoulda asked you before: you got one them boomerangs oane you, don't ya boy?"

"Ah sure do," Gilmer, cheek glowing crimson, "ah allus keep one oane me right close – "

"Uh-huh. You wouldn't be shittin' me now, would ya?"

Gilmer start to reply, his words drowned out by a medley of whoops: Thrillboys playing catch with the head seized from Gilmer's grasp. Mayor Bob gorgonized aground in mute scream.

John turn cackling, track the head with his beam.

"Yo Jayb," he go, "think we got time for a touch of meatskull football?"

"I think not," I go, "best get a move on now, friar. We startin' to run late."

John roll his eyes, curse inaudible. Then he turn, torchbeam wavering:

"Poondawg! Toss them goodies over now, boy."

Poondog step back from the game of catch, swing his arm. The sack in his hand sail across torch-lit, land open-mouthed: a boarsnout spilling into view, a geezer's foot lodged within.

John whip the beam around to Gilmer's mug.

"That's TWO sacks you got to carry now, Gilmer. But first, get mayor Bob up off'n his sorry ass and let's get a move oane double fuckin' quick – "

"Third sack," I cut in, "there's a third sack need to be carried. Remember?"

John turn, his scowl ogred in backshine. "NOW you fuckin' tell me. NOW."

I shrug. "Now's the time, massah boss. Car's right there."

John curse, tear his keys from his pocket, toss them at Gilmer's feet.

"There's a goody sack in the trunk of m'car, Gil. Go get it, hand me m'keys, and let's get this fucktruck oane the goddamn road – "

He step away, put out a piercing whistle.

"HAWG PARADE!" he bawl, "Y'ALL START MARCHIN'.".

We fall in moments later: Gilmer leading the way with the mayor chainganged beside, John, Monk and Wald in tow with the Thrillkillers thronged after. Across moon-silvered grass into the woods, down a trail leading white: Gilmer laboring in drayage, mayor Bob whimpering, John a-chortle masturbating his flashlight, trees in dark REM sighing. Myself cabosed in grim remove, as ever and anon, with head bowed, mendicant, my footsnouts pulling eager, ravening in blind augury of a bloodkill.

**

The trail rise to a knap, start to descend. At left a shimmer: glimpse of Nipponese fire ants on a tree trunk disposed in linear ascent, each with a grain of argentum. *They march in lapidary tribute bearing gifts for the Holy Sumo Triumvirate of Antilles Muus. Silver for the acolytes, silver for the Yokozuna Primus –*

I frown. A hoarse whine up front: Gilmer humming toneless. John with curse skipping up, planting a boot in Gilmer's rump.

"None of THAT now, Gil. You gon' be singin' loud enough when we through with ya."

Minutes pass: Gilmer hobbling on silent, the mayor lurching abreast, groan and whimper. Then it happen: John without preamble cutting loose in raucous canticle, bawling an oldtime bluegrass ditty: *MAMA DON'T LET YOUR COWBOYS GROW UP TO BE CUNTHOLES –*

Laughter from out back: Thrillboys in high mirth, Wald yip gibber.

John sing on, myself with ears plugged thinking: *this shit never gonna end, never ever going to end –*

But it does, thank putz. The song end, and with it the trail, myself stepping aside, yanking my fists out my ears: loud schlup, knuckles dripping cerumen.

Gilmer shamble on a few feet, fetch up at the mouth of a clearing, drop his three-sack load. The mayor hunched beside, tottering.

"Awwh!" Gilmer swinging his arms, "that there wuz gettin' a mite heavy, awwwhhh."

John don't stop instanter, don't break stride. He walk on past Gilmer, pause, turn.

"Did I," he goes, spotlighting Gilmer's mug, "did I say you could STOP?"

Gilmer blink, lick his chops. "Naw. Naw yew didn't – "

"COURSE not. And did I say you could set them there sacks DOWN?"

Gilmer's nares twitch, eyeballs aquiver.

"Naw," he repeat, "naw yew didn't."

John shake his head. Look down. Look up.

"And did I say you could YEEEP-WOOOPRRRUP-RRUFFF-WOOOP?"

Loud merriment from out back: Thrillkillers cachinnate.

Creases appear on Gilmer's brow. In his eyes, dull panic cut with confusion.

"Wayell," he begin, "wayell ah reckon – "

John bark, raise his right leg, stick his boot square in Gilmer's gut and shove: Gilmer flying back with a squawk, crashing into foliage.

"Y'ALL COME BACK!" John, "Y'HEAR?"

"WAHHH!" Thrillboys, "WAAAHHAAARRRAAHHH!"

The clearing in dark echo.

Monk step up tight-lipped, Wald a-giggle.

"Gilmer exeunt. Alarums. Yes?"

I don't answer. Myself looking for Gilmer to emerge. No dice.

Him occluded by vegetation.

John's beam whip around sudden, catch the mayor in flagrante: him attempting to sidle off in vain hope of escape. John striding up with a cackle, kicking the mayor's feet out from under him. Thud reprise: Bob supine once more, nose blotched rutilant, gasping and sobbing.

"Ain't no place you can run, Bob," John grinning down at the mayor, "you gon' fuckin' DIE next time you try, hear? You best stay down there till I call for you. Half a chance you live... but you gon' have to be good boy. A REAL good boy – "

John step away, beam sweeping the clearing. The light reveal a grassy ellipse, a pair of rusted barbecue grills at the foci. Between these, a stack of briquettes and a pile of tinder.

"Well ol' Gilmer did awright," John, "we all set."

"Set," grunt Poondog, Thrillboys murmuring in echo: "set, set – "

John's beam jerk left, skewer Poondog: Thrillboys falling silent.

"Whut y'all oane about. Ay?"

Poondog blink, shake his head.

John snicker. "You feel like bein' a champeen honeybunch, Poondawg? Daddy's little swee'pea slut?"

A smile touch Poondog's scarred lip. He nod.

"Well awright then. Go Dickel that wood."

Poondog nod, turn, shuffle out into the clearing.

"Dig that hump," John, "cornfed boarhawg with HAM'rhoids."

Hyuck yuck, Thrillboys, hyuckity yuck.

Poondog shuffle up to the tinder heap and stand motionless, beam on rump.

"WHUT YOU WAITIN' OANE HO," John, "YO' PAPA'S PANTYWAIST PECKERBUNNY?"

Thrillboy rumble, Wald going: "Peckerwaist bunnyho. Heh heh."

Poondog's hand vanish into his pocket, emerge. Glass glint: fifth of Dickel.

"GO TO IT HAWGHUMP!" John.

Snickers. Wald squatting aground, spitting on his crotch, kneading it with a chortle.

"Sick puppy," husks a Thrillkiller voice: Booger Dumpling.

"Peepee sick," Wald, "heh heh."

Poondog uncap the bottle of Dickel, hold it at arms length and tilt: whiskey pouring golden over dry wood.

"YEAH! NOW SPARK IT!"

A match flare, fall. Whup: tinder bursting aflame.

"YEEEE," John, "HAWWWWW!"

Thrillboys in applause, offering paean and panegyric.

John turn, teeth grin-white. "Y'all gather round now. Uncle Remus got hisself some country meat he aim to beat."

The Thrillboys fan out, stand equidistant around the fire. They walk funny, I note anew, feet in ursine clodhop. And I figure why. They got bags of buckshot codpieced in their crotches: something Trotjohn insist on, one of his rules. Go a long way to explaining Poondog's bung-racked shuffle –

"Not you Wald," Monk putting out a restraining hand, "we stand here and watch."

"Stand and watch," Wald, marching in place, "hand on crotch. Heh heh."

Mayor Bob still sobbing muffled at right, belly up in lambent fireglow.

Silence fall: like dust on a lunar scape. Silence and firecrackle, Monk and I with arms folded, digging the scene. Thrillboys spraddle-legged around the clearing, John in middle, flame-girt. Trees wealded ashen at the rim, the moon lesioned pale on mottled nightskin.

A minute pass. Two minutes. John motionless, black-orbed, his medallion flame-gold –

"ASSWIPES!" he yawp sudden, "dickbrains! Peckerheads! Jackoffs! Hawgpimps! Ratfucks! Dongchompers! Numbnuts! – "

His arms rise, spread messianic. His teeth flash, spit lancing four-ways into the fire. Laughter tinkle around the circle. Laughter hard and bright. Thrillboys up and ready.

John's gaze sweep the enclosure, scowl lines etched dark.

"Now y'all are most likely wonderin' whut in hell y'all are here for. Ya'll stickin' thumbs up your bungholes, jigglin' them hard, nasty little turds thinkin': *whut this all about? Whut am I doin' here with m'filthy roach-humpin' piddle stick this time o' night?*"

Sniggers and yips, Wald going: "Turd-hump piddlestick. Heh heh."

John sneer. "Well I'll TELL ya. You wanna know, I'll TELL ya. You here cuz I fuckin' SAID so. You here cuz I fuckin' WANT you here... so DROP EM!"

Pause: John's voice in echo, Thrillboys unmoved, staring.

John spit, shake his head. "One more time. One more time for re-fuckin'-tards. I said: DROP EM!"

The Thrillkillers respond: buckles coming undone, zippers rasping, baggies in swift cascade, codpieces dropping in succession.

"Well sheeat," John, "bitches got THAT right."

"Not you Wald," Monk, "just them."

The Wald slapping his bare pecker with a giggle, pulling up his shorts.

I glance around, hoping to catch some freakshow skivvies: maybe sackcloth boxers, horsehair jocks, rustmetal groin cups, a spiked testicle truss or some such but no, not much to see this night. Just bare asses pale and pocked, scalped glanheads on the nod.

John grin, fangs winking. "Uh-huh. We catchin' oane. We gettin' there. Only problem is: WE GOT A MAN MISSIN'!"

Pause. Thrillboys murmuring in echo: "Man missing, man missing – "

John cough, cock his head. "Giiiilmer!" he call mellifluent, "oh Giiiilmer!"

Silence: sigh of wind-soothed foliage. Somewhere afar, a lovelorn whipoorwill.

John's grin vanish. He cup a hand to his mouth, give voice once more:

"Don't make me come oane out there and yank your nuts off now, son. Don't you make me do THAT."

Foliage stir directly across: Gilmer's wax mug showing grey and timorous, miner's helmet gone.

John grin. "Come oane up, Gilmerdawg. We been waitin' oane you."

Gilmer emerge halt, reticent. Him hobbling past Bitch Tit, past Peckertrash, on up to the fire. He's got his hands full, Gilmer. In his right, a wide, raven-winged boomerang. In his left, something dead.

"Whut you got there Gilmerdawg. Ay?"

Gilmer stop, hold up his hand. No surprise: pair of dead squirrels.

"Well sheeat," John, "you kill 'em this time o' night?"

"Aw yeh," Gilmer, "ah did. They cain't git away. They kin run, but they cain't hide. Ah kin see 'em in the dark, yew bet. See 'em movin' evil, lookin' at me evil – "

"More meat for the barbecue. You did awright Gil. Now go git the mayor, stand him up here and yank his skivvies down."

Pause. Gilmer stock still. "Whut's that yew say now?"

John sigh, shake his head. "Whore got a hearin' problem. I'm gon' say it a SECOND time cuz you done good so far. Make me go THIRDS, I'm gon' choke you dead with your own suckpole sausage, hear me?"

Thrillkiller chuckles, Gilmer's head quaking affirmative.

John clear his throat, hawk vigorous and spew: a spitball sailing across, landing on Gilmer's moccasinned foot.

"Whut I said was: go git the fuckin' mayor, stand him up here and pull his dadgum skivvies down. I know you got dawgshit in that skull o' yourn, but it ain't that fuckin' HARD."

Gilmer snuffle, squint around the clearing, spot the mayor.

Then he drop his squirrels, shamble over to the mouth of the clearing, reach down and haul the mayor to his feet. Mayor Bob trying to pull away, his mug streaked with gore, snot and brine.

"That's right," John, "now bring him oane over and do whut I asked you to."

Gilmer grab Bob by his handcuffs and start across: Gilmer undeviate, the mayor in durance vile.

"Here," John pointing, "stand him up here."

Gilmer tramp up claudicate, position the mayor and step back, boomerang still in hand. Mayor Bob swaying in place, his flesh in tumult.

"Forgot somethin' didn't ya Gil?"

John's visage aglow, eyes obsidian.

Gilmer blink, start to speak. Then he break off, step up, jam his boomerang between his teeth, bend and pull the mayor's briefs down with both hands.

"That's m'boy. Good thing you remembered, Gil. You'd've been chokin' oane your own dawgpecker right about now, you hadn't."

A murmur around the circle: Thrillkillers titillate.

Gilmer step back, wedge the boomerang in his armpit. The mayor now in stark profile: buttocks swagged hepatic, nuts petrified in recoil, pecker drooping like a failed proboscis.

John bare his teeth, exhale with a long hiss. "Well I think we just about ready to get this ol' hootenanny hummin'. Wouldn't ya say Gil?"

Gilmer scratch his head, shuffle his feet. "Wayell, ah guess we ready if yew – "

"We gon' do it like we planned, Gilmerdawg," John softvoiced, "just like we planned a couple nights back. Remember?"

Gilmer's head cants peculiar, brow furrowing in recollect.

"I ain't gon' say it now, Gilmer. Ain't gon' remind you. You just gon' DO it when I tell you to."

Gilmer's brow clears, a grin smudging his pan.

"I'm gon work it nasty," he husk, "just like yew sayd... whuf whuf whuf – "

Gilmer chortling tubercular, an eldritch sound. Far above, the moon brindled askew thinking: *oho, the old earth planet sure be frolicsome tonight –*

"Well now," sneer John, gaze spanned lightless, "Gilmer know whut it's about, but you fuckers DON'T, so I'm gon TELL y'all whut gives. Y'all are gon' paddle your popsicles is whut. Y'all are gon' give yourselves a bone-hard, hammer-pulse blue fuckin' Buddha that talk the HOT HOLY LANGUAGE O' JIZM."

There's a pause, an instant of dead silence. Then the Thrillboys erupt in bestial holler going: "CIRCLE JERK! CIRCLE JERK! – "

Wald leaping like a toad on a hotplate, Gilmer grin-gashed in risible quake, mayor Bob looking on stricken.

"DOWN PUTZFUCKS!" John, "DOWN!"

The Thrillboys corral their mirth, settle. Them graven in formation, dongs gone stiff. Wald on all fours, shadow-humping.

John sweep a death-glare around the circle, his form girdled aflame.

"Y'all listen up, now. Listen good, cuz I ain't sayin' it again. I'm gon' count to three real slow. Oane the count of three y'all gon' start beatin' your meat, beatin' it good. BUT: you don't BLOW till I SAY so. And when you do, you don't let it fall. Y'all gon' HOLD oane to that puddin' like your LIFE depend oane it, cuz it fuckin' DO, y'hear me?"

Murmurs of assent, Thrillboys nodding. Gilmer still agrin going whuff, whuff, rousting his nuts, working a flap in his overalls.

"And that goes for YOU too, Gilmer. You drop your nad chicle, start spurtin' suds all round, it's gon' be PAIN fuckin' PRIMETIME, hear?"

"Aww yeh," Gilmer jittering, "whuff whuff – "

Thrillboys bestirred, chuck-chuckle, the mayor a ravaged sentinel trembling in cynosure.

"Gorbellied chuffs," mutter Monk disdainful, "little rumpfed ronyons – "

"Nadspurt," Wald rising, "painfuck. Heh heh."

Silence fall, a breeze nuzzling my cheek. Ahead, Trotjohn in flame-wrought apotheosis, hand rising.

"ONE!" he bark, tensing.

"One!" echo the Thrillboys.

"TWO!"

"Two! – "

Pause. John smirking in caesura, Thrillboys like gunslingers waiting to draw –

"THREE!"

John's hand flashing down, Thrillboys falling to in unison, Gilmer galvanized an instant later, going to work.

"NOT YOU PECKERHEAD!" yell John, catching sight of Wald. Him standing pigeon-toe, whacking spasmodic.

The Wald pause, giggle, resume whacking.

242

John bend with a curse. Straighten. Make like a pitcher. And let fly: a rock swinging in like a curve ball, catching Wald square on the brow. Kathud: Wald keeling back, yelping like an injured poodle.

John flash me a grin, jerk a thumb at the assemblage.

"Dig 'em," he goes, "DIG 'em."

I dig. Thrillboys hard at work lambasting their lollies, fists working like jackhammers. Gilmer hunched in slow drool, pumping sedulous.

"YEAH, WORK IT!" I yell, "WOICK!"

John turn with a cackle, take a step, lean over and spit on Gilmer's dick. Gilmer flinch, but keep pounding.

"Spit-lube!" John, "no extra charge!"

"Lube," Wald struggling up, "jerk. Heh heh."

Him with boner unvanquished, a bloody knot on his forehead.

"Observe," goes Monk pointing, "their tumescence."

I nod. "Embryonic slug to foetal dugong."

Monk chuckle. "Quite."

We watch. Gilmer shafted bluesteel, smoking his slickpole. Juddering palsied as he work the crotch harmonic.

My eyes cross, zero in on his glanhead. Flashvision in lurid sequence: Gilmer strapped to a Texas hotseat, dead squirrels stapled to his tits. A thousand volts of deathjuice searing his flesh, his mouth gaped in Bacon scream. His eyeballs oozing glutinous, teeth spraying like bullets, tongue in bloated extrusion: a charred penis. A boomerang lopping off his pate, his brains boiling forth, schlong bursting through his britches spurting ichor. Painted prison punks ogling the scene, shattered ribs gouting marrow. A priest with wang in the warden's mouth, granting absolution, sacramental jizz spritzing out the supplicant's ear. Gladiator guards running riot, flogging inmates with spine cords, entrails and umbilici. Dickie Dachau the deathrow mascot presiding in a pigsuit, snout smeared with dung, an ulcerate crooner in chains singing: *see my sow do the coprophage snorkel –*

"OANE THE COUNT OF THREE!" John, "ONE!"

The Thrillboys quicken, wanking furious.

"TWO!"

Their hands a blur.

"THREE!"

A tremor pass around the circle: grunts, a collective moan, jizm blooming dense in Thrillkiller crotches. Gilmer venting a howl of anguished triumph, in my mind's eye a white whale impaled, bursting up in red orison from the roiling waters –

"YEAH!" John, "YEAH! HOLD OANE NOW! HOLD OANE TO THAT HOT HAPPY HUMUS – "

I look up, hearing laughter. Our spirit guides manifest once more. Stinger, Finesse, Oblongata, Noodlebear with frizz coiffs, dog collars, g-strings, tit pasties, mugs painted garish. Them perched on an airborne wolftrap, shining.

I click my tongue rueful. "Aww girls, y'all look like boon trash harlots down on their luck."

The eidolons guffaw raucous: black gums, filed silver teeth, studded tongues.

"*Et tu* Noodlebear?" I go querulous, "*et tu?*"

Noodlebear snarl, smack herself in the head, spit a pair of black bugs. The bugs hit the ground, scuttle divergent. I watch them in exeunt thinking: *they must ascend to a higher light: Tarn-Omnium, the perigeal insect kingdom –*

"END CIRCLE JERK!" John, hand slicing down, "HOLD 'em UP!"

The Thrillboys whoop, raise their hands like hussars toasting death by orgasm: jizm oystered in the crooks of their fists.

"Yeah!" John surveying his harvest, "THAT's whut I'm talkin' about."

Thrillboys bellow, whistle.

"Uh-huh," John a-grin, "look like Beast and Booger Dumplin' cooked up some mean red crotch-caviar. You boys want to hold off oane them cattle-slash bloodsucks."

Booger Dumpling whinny, twitch spastic. Beast pop a drool bubble, shake his barrel head.

John turn, smirking. "Now Gilmerdawg, do tell: whut you got fo' daddy."

Gilmer look up slow, real slow, as from a dream.

"Knock knock," John, "Johnny Jizz callin'. Knock knock."

Gilmer hold out his right hand palm up: spunk dolloped bright orange.

"Well sheeat," John cackling, "you ask the man to blow his wad, he fry a fuckin' egg, sunny side up."

"Hawwhhaarf!", Thrillboys, "yeehawwrrf! – ."

Wald routing his nads going: "Blow. Eggfuck. Heh heh – "

John scowl, raise a hand: Thrillboys falling silent. Them gone limp, fists crowned with nut-glue.

"Ya lousy shit-eatin' humps," pronounce John, "I'd kill y'all in a heartbeat if y'all wudn't dead awready."

Silence. Thrillboys limned motionless.

John bare his teeth, spit lancing triune into the fire.

"I ain't done with y'all yet, nosirreebob. You got to PAY for yo' dinner. Like m'pawdaddy's ol' kitchen-bitch used to say: puddin' before supper. Got to eat your puddin' before you get your supper – "

A murmur pass around the circle: "Puddin' before supper, puddin' before supper – "

"Triple count again," John, "count of three, you boys chow down oane your puddin'. You chow down GOOD, not a smidgin left a-wastin'. Like the ol' grub gash used to say: *there's critters starvin' in Outer Bungholia –* "

Laughter echo mirthless around the clearing. Wald worrying his left nut going: "Bunghole puddin' bitch. Heh heh – "

"And that goes DOUBLE for YOU, Gilmerdawg. Count of three you scarf up your nad yolk in a hurry, dig?"

Gilmer nod simpering, lips peeled perverse.

John cough, raise his hand in führer-salute. "ONE!"

"One," Thrillboys in toneless echo.

"TWO!"

"Two" Thrillboys.

"THREE!" John, hand slicing down.

Thrillboys with heads thrown back howling simultaneous. Flashvision: mayor Bob in purple glan-throb, goring a rope-trussed kid girl under a brace of skinned rodents –

"SCARF!" John with a double fist-pump, "SCARF!"

The Thrillboys scarf: mouth over fist, glomming jizz.

"Gourmands and gormandizers," Monk nodding appreciative.

"Epicured alimentarians," me.

"Nad scarf," Wald, "heh heh."

Booger Dumpling finish first, hold up his fist.

"DONE!" he yawp, "DONE!"

"DITTO!" Poondog, fist aspirant.

"DUN!" Beast likewise.

"ARF!" Peckertrash.

"YOOP!" Bitch Tit.

"MMMM!" Slutmush.

Thrillboys in triumph, fists porrect, lips glazed. But John isn't looking. Him posed rigid, gaze fixed baleful on Gilmer's mug. Gilmer unmoved, spunk jellied orange on his palm.

A hush settle on the clearing. Thrillboys intent, John in

lambent chiaroscuro with hand raised, fingers skyward. Click: his wristblade shafting out fire-bright.

"You got two seconds Gilmerdawg," John, "one."

Gilmer twitch, raise his hand to his lips, tip the glob into his mouth. In thought a rot-gum cracker sampling a tainted clam.

John stare. "Did you swallow, Gilmerdawg. Did you suck that fucker down like it was kiddie juice."

Gilmer nod, mouth gawped witless.

John lean forward, head cocked sympathetic. There's a steel-glint blur: his wristblade flashing. Gilmer scream, the sound near human. His hand up, cupping his chin.

"YEEEHAWWRRRHH!" Thrillboys, "YAWWHAWWRRR!"

Wald hopping on one foot, keening lunatic. The mayor hunched violate as before: eyes twinned in nightmare reflect.

John straighten, his blade vanishing in retract.

"Man got to keep his dawg honest. Got to."

Gilmer don't move. His chin cupped, gore showing dark between his fingers.

"And don't you go feelin' sorry for yourself now. You lucky I didn't slash you stone fuckin' dead."

Gilmer let his hand drop. On his chin, a smeared blood-smile.

"Yeh," he croak, mouth working, "lucky ah ain't dayd."

John reach back, wiggle his own braid. "We almost done here, Gil. Just one thing left. Just like we planned. Remember?"

Pause: Gilmer stock still, face scrunched obtuse.

John shake his head, roust his jodhpur nuts, hawk a mean loogie and spit. The wad flare out his mouth like ball lightning, circle the fire twice, burst with a hail mary and a hosannah in excelsis.

"Oooohhh!" Thrillboys, "ooooooohhh!"

"HeeEEPF!" Wald, "heh heh."

John smack his lips. "Give you a hint, Gil. Whut you got stuck there in yo' filthy stinkin' armpit."

Gilmer lower his head, looking askance. Then he look up: his visage clearing lucent.

"Boomerang," he husk in idiot afflatus, "ah do rightly ruh-cawll – "

"Well fine," John, "glad it came back to ya. Woulda had to cut you up some more, it hadn't. It's all about completin' the circle Gil. You completed one circle when you chugged down your own chowder. Now it's time to complete the other."

"Ah," Monk, "our sachem waxes arcane. Rare moment of profundity."

"Jizzwax," Wald, "heh heh – "

Thrillboys applauding polite, like haute monde ofays digging the philharmonic.

"Now or never Gil," goes John, "now or never."

Gilmer stand slouched a moment, as though in doubt. Then he inhale deep, yank the boomerang out his armpit, transfer it to his right hand, bend low in partial twist and whip up sudden: his hand slicing arcwise, the boomerang in flight.

"OOOOH!" Beast, Bitch Tit, Peckertrash, Shag Pie, Hogball, Gutterputz.

"AAAAAH!" Hammerhead, Poondog, Slutmush, Skum Nugget, Stain, Dingus, Cap'n Gangrene, Pussywuss.

"MMMMM!" Jizzpony, Booger Dumpling, Fartmart, Rat Sandwich, Snatch Weasel, Killkraut, Leper Luke, Muttfuck.

Silence in interregnum: the boomerang soaring blackwinged out the clearing, blotting indistinct on the warp of night, against the skydark.

"Well it's gone," I sigh, "and it ain't comin' back."

But it does, thank yutz: the boomerang morphing sudden above the trees, wings angled in descent.

"What goes around," Monk, "etcetera."

John cackle, spit sidelong.

"Well Bob," he goes, "it don't matter how much pelf you got stocked up, don't matter how important you are, don't matter how many kid girls you stuck a cornpone to. Somethin', somewhere's always aimin' for you, JUST for you – "

But mayor Bob isn't listening. Him staring up aghast, in voiceless catalept. The boomerang in meniscal plummet, closing in like a demon bird beaked ravenous, talons drawn, eyes firelit –

"Awww yeh," rasps Gilmer grinning up at his pet, "awwwwww – "

Thwack: the boomerang striking the mayor's brow dead-centre, blood in floral erupt, him keeling back soundless, Thrillboys putting out a long collective howl.

"Timber," John, fist up, "tim-fuckin'-ber."

"And so it comes to pass," Monk.

The Wald in a squat, knees conjoined, farting thunderous. "Come. Timberfuck. Heh heh."

I raise myself on tiptoe, squinting. The mayor stretched out supine, the boomerang beside him triumphant.

John step up, prod him with a boot. He seem to stir, moaning liminal.

"You did good Gilmerdawg," goes John looking up, "you gon' eat barbecue with m'boys here, maybe cornhole the mayor for dee-zert."

Gilmer's eyes torch concupiscent, mug split in a grin.

"Aww yeh," he husk, "I'd be proud to, bawss. A barbecue hoedown... roundeye cornpone for dee-zert – "

"Bob ain't out cold," goes John giving me a look, "but he out enough. Come do your thang son. And bring that there sack o' heads with you."

I take a step, snatch up the goody sack with my left hand, Gilmer's sack with my right. Then I stroll into the clearing, past

Poondog diddling his half hard, past Cap'n Gangrene sucking on a finger-nub. On up to the fire.

"You want I should do it?" ask John as I approach.

"You know it's got to be me," I go, tossing him Gilmer's sack.

John curse, pull open Gilmer's sack and tip it over: a pair of heads rolling out unceremonious.

"No games while I'm doing my thing Teej," I go, "the meister's not gonna – "

"Ain't gon' be no GAMES, bitch," John, "I want these two fuckers lookin' up at you while you work – "

He grab the two heads by the ears, stalk up and plant them down by the mayor's noggin, one on either side. Now the mayor flanked face up, in cephalic trinity.

I reach into the goody sack, pull out a bag of sealed syntheplast and hold it up to firelight.

"Look like it's all there," I go, "spike, syringe, plunger, three vials red, white and blue."

John run his tongue around his mouth. "Sheeat. Ain't no surprise."

I unseal the bag, fish out the syringe, push the plunger all the way down. Then I uncap the needle and step up to the mayor. Him shackled inert, briefs around his ankles, pecker corpsed on sodden pubes.

"Painless if done right," I go, "almost."

John click his tongue. "Too fuckin' bad. Was kinda hopin' to hear one last scream."

I chuckle. "Well you just might hear it yet. Just might – "

I kneel, lever up the mayor's head with my left hand and prop it high on my right foot. In my right hand the needle bristling long and bright.

"Hurt just to look at it, don't it?" John.

"Yayup. Hurt a lot more if you stick it in your eyeball."

"Uh-huh. Or in your nutsack squattin' over a gasoline fire, pecker caught in a beartrap, blowtorch in yo' mouth, a midget hammerin' your skull open, your hands in a pail of nitric."

I blink. "Man after my own heart."

John bare his teeth, canines flame-tipped.

"Get to it, ho."

I shake my head, aim the needle at the mayor's fontanelle and push down into the crown of his skull. I figure maybe the needle bend or break but no. It go clean through: the mayor unmoved, his mug slacked pale.

"Boom," I go, "chalk one up for the gipper."

John snort. "Sheeat. I could do better BLIND."

"Blind," Thrillboys murmurous, "blind – "

I grin, hold the syringe with my left hand, pull up on the plunger with my right. The plunger suck back slow, the syringe filling with a clear plasm tinctured red: brain fluid. I draw out an ounce, look up.

John nod. "That oughtta do it."

"That oughtta do it!" I mimic with a tranny lilt.

John scowl, strum an absent boner. "Bitch beggin' for a prick whip."

"Prick whip," Thrillboys in rumbled chant, "prick whip – "

"Blind bitch prick," Wald off at right, "heh heh."

I hold the stem of the syringe and pull: the needle emerging slow, bloody, the mayor still insensate, eyes shut.

"Red one first," goes John, "red blood, red boner."

I nod, reach into the bag, scoop out the red vial.

"Easy now," John, "easy – "

I hold up the vial, push the needle through the seal and squeeze: the vial filling slow with brain fluid.

"Mmm," John, "turn me OANE."

"Turn oane," Thrillboys, "turn oane – "

I mutter a prayer, draw out the spike, hold up the vial. "Yayup. We got us a winner."

John grunt, step up, lean over. Splotch: a spitwad hitting the mayor's sullied brow.

"One minute you're porkin' a girly in a state park shack. Next, you're butt nakkid with a needle in your skull. Funny how THAT works. Ay?"

I nod. "It is kinda funny. Somewhere."

John step back, click his tongue. "Fucker didn't make a sound though. I figured that there needle-stab get him squealin' like a stuck hawg."

I cap the needle, bag the syringe and vial.

"Like I said: no pain if done right."

"Well sheeat."

I rise, stick the bag back in the goody sack.

"End Act One. Bring on Act Two."

John stare, eyes stygian. "Act One ain't over yet, baby."

I curl my lip, spit out the side of my mouth. "The hell it ain't."

John mutter, stalk up and stand astride the mayor.

I shake my head. "Well shit. Shoulda known."

John cackle, bend, turn the mayor over, grab his hips with both hands and hoist up his rump. The mayor groan soft: face down, butt steepled dirt-yellow.

"ALL YOURS COMPADRES," John announce, "IT'S SUGARDADDY TIME!"

"Daddy time," echo the Thrillboys, "daddy time – "

Poondog shuffling up, wang in full throb pointing north. Gilmer still agrin, jiggling his junk. Mayor Bob starting to come around, groaning indistinct, rump-meat bestirred., .

John smack his lips, give me a wink and smile. I turn to our spirit guides, flash them a wink and smile. The guides give

Monk a wink and smile. Monk wink at Wald and smile. Wald slap his boner and smile. And in the dream labyrinths of his glanhead fastness Tio Mate smiles, the Chief smiles, Old Sarge smiles, The Wild Boys smile.

***

"Fucker probably lowered it before coming in," I go, "we gonna have to get it up ourselves."

"Get it up," Wald, "heh heh."

We approach the park exit, brights flaring.

"No sweat," John, "it's still up."

And it is, the barrier: the car cruising under, past Gilmer's kiosk, cutting left on Guano. In that instant, the scene rising to my mind's eye: mayor Bob face down, howling, bung fulla Thrilljizz.

"We shoulda maybe stayed for the BBQ," I go, "gotten a bite of Bitch Tit's grandpaw."

John shift gear, hit the pedal. The car surge, whooshing downhill.

"You know we cain't eat till it's all over. And besides, m'boys won't be done with Bob for a while yet. They know a good cornhole when they see one. They gon' fuck him dead fore the night's out."

"Dead corn fuck," Wald, "heh heh."

The car slow some, screeching around a curve. Trees whisper past in gauntlet. Far distant, the TV tower winking.

"Speaking of cornholes," I go, "how we doin' on time."

"Huh?" John, "wha?"

"We're on schedule by the feel of it," offers Monk.

I turn: Monk in back crosslegged, fingers locked over his belly. Wald slouched beside, pawing his pecker-mouse.

"Feel," I go, "feel of what."

Monk shut his right eye, exhale blue dust.

"My left nipple. Delays induce a tumescence of the left nipple. I felt it in my front yard earlier tonight, awaiting three horse-tupped whoresons. But I don't feel it now. Hence, on schedule."

John make a choking sound, scowl up in rearview.

"Man if I wudn't drivin' I'd stop and make you shit out your own skull, ribs and all."

I nod. "That makes sense. In another language."

"Whoreshit nipple," Wald, "heh heh."

"Speaking of time," I go, "there was this kid I knew, vandalized a country churchfane: smashed the stainglass windows and ate the pieces. Then he swallowed a moon-dial watch. For a week after, you could see lunar sacerdotal time kaleidoscoped in full colour: if you squinted up his rump at midnight."

"Haarf!" John.

"Heesh!" Wald.

"Rebarbative," Monk.

The car zoom up an incline, top the crest, sail free an instant, land bouncing.

"Yowsh," me, "that shook some turds loose."

"Turd shake," Wald, "heh heh."

John tap the brake, steady the wheel. "I had Bitch Tit play an hourglass once. Turned him oane his head till his tongue showed all fat and bloody. Then turned him back oane his feet till he got a blue steel boner. Then back oane his head, back oane his feet and oane till he passed out in a mess o' blood and jizz. Wudn't pretty but a good man got to know TIME – "

The road rise, dip. I wince. "Track's a bitch, boy. Like humpin' one them caged babooners on a coaster."

"Vide Nat G Funhouse," Monk.

John curse under his breath. Him slaloming down Guano fast and hard, the road cresting, dipping. I shut my eyes queasy, thinking of Pater Jed. The look on his face when we hit. *It ain't Christmas Pater, but we got you a little something –*

"Huh?" John, jerking the wheel, "say WHA?"

I look up: a snouted shape bounding across.

"Brujo," Monk, "shape-shifter."

"Eep!" Wald, "yibble."

I shake my head. "None of the above. That there was Elmer the East Yazoo Wolfman on a pre-Samhain all night sack race."

John shoot me a scowl. "Who he racin'."

"Who? Why, rookie wolfmen from deep Appalachia of course. Possum-fucking lycanthropic greenhorns tryin' to earn their stripes."

"HaHAARF!" John, "yowp."

"Heesh!" Wald, "yeesh!"

"Abou Ben *Loup Garou*," Monk, "may his tribe increase."

The road hit a final hump, ease off in descent. A light shows ahead, pulsing yellow. John grunt, floor the pedal: vrrooom, the car glomming the gradient in overdrive, me thinking: *demon mouth Heaven Papa's celestial noodle –*

The car balk approaching the light, veer right, hit the main drag.

"Hillview!" John yelp, flashing me a grin.

I frown. "Bad move. We coulda hit somethin'. Like a weaponized combine harvester with metal alloy tusks, a steel hull, a six-ton sodomizer piston – "

Thwack: a two-finger whiplash across the jaw, courtesy Trotjohn. My vision swim, voices in my head bursting into song. Crud shake loose from my right ear, gout forth steaming. Somewhere onstage, a corpulent diva buckle and fall, crushing the billionaire octogenarian seated below.

"Well shit," I croak, "another bad move."

John cackle, steadying the wheel. "That'll teach ya."

I stick a thumb in my omphallic navel, squeeze my right nut. My vision clear, thoughts settling around the jawbone of an ass. Trees show at left, bare rock at right. Ahead, Hillview in descent, winding.

"Third light down's Mason," I remind, massaging my jaw.

John snort, give me a look: in his eyes, red microbes ravening.

A church loom ahead at left: neon cross alight. Fronting it a signboard I haven't seen before: FATHER GOD, NOT MOTHER EARTH.

John snicker. "Papa Schlong, not Mama Snatch."

"Bubba Roundeye," me, "not Missy Gash."

"Larry Lingam," Monk, "not Yolanda Yoni."

"Hot sausage," Wald with a giggle, "not tuna melt."

John glance back grinning. "Well HALE. Waldo got his mind WORKIN' again."

"Mind?" Monk, "you exaggerate."

"Doggie beef," Wald, "not pussy fish. Heh heh – "

I raise a hand in admonition. "Not to get too scabrous now, brothers. There's work to be done. The LORD'S work."

"Harf!" John, "yowp."

Monk sniff. "Three ineluctable modalities: the seen, the unseen, the obscene. We opt for the third."

"Hear hear," me, "llnngnnooth."

The car round a curve, tyres in faint caterwaul. A light show ahead, flashing yellow. I watch it approach: flash-flash, flash-flash. Illuminate pulse. Demon heartbeat. Killer in darkened hallway –

The light zip past overhead. I pat my crotch, humming a ditty: *safe for thee, my three-piece bijouterie –*

"Vista," announce Monk, "bird's eye view."

I turn: the hillside gone at left, Churchtown spread otiose on the valley floor. Darkness at the centre, lights winking concentric at the rim.

"Orb," I go, "black iris in a scintillant sclera."

"Apocalypsis Revelata," Monk.

Yellow light flickers past overhead: two down.

"Next one's Mason," I announce.

The car judders around a bend. Ahead, yellow light flashing in redux.

"Mason," I go, "Mason."

John tap the brakes, slow a mite. Churchtown obscured at left, woods rising serried like Dunsinane. The car slow some more, drift right.

"Yee," John leaning on the wheel, "haw."

The car veer, cut a tight curve under the light. A roadsign glimmers past: Mason.

"Been a while," John shifting down, "ay?"

I nod. "It has, boy. Sure has."

John drum the wheel, cruising. Mason stretched out ahead, dead level. I look around gimlet-eyed: the old neighborhood familiar, yet strange. Fences, walls, flowerbeds, gazebos, pools, lawns all in shadow. Groves, greenhouses, mansions in deeper shadow. These scenes passing dim and glaucous, like some old fever dream.

"Hard to believe," goes John, "ay?"

I turn. "Huh?"

"Hard to believe you wuz raised in this neck."

Monk sniff. "Not raised, lowered. Into the gutter."

"Hard gutter," Wald, "heh heh."

"Well one thing's different," I go, "no Pigs in sight. No fatsnout Pigmobiles on the prowl. Back then, I'd catch no less than three, most nights."

John stroke the gearshift, wag his braid. "Not tonight, baby.

Not tonight."

I sit back, rub my eyes. "There'd be plenty Pigs around, weren't for that jailbreak, Delroy County. Gracias Klan Clems. Gracias Gomer Gestapo. Gracias Bubba Brownshirts – "

I pause, hand on my shoulder.

"Shut the fuck up," John, "or I'm gon 'have to hurt ya."

I stick out my tongue, bite down hard.

"Nnngn," me, tasting blood, "nnngnn."

The road dip, hit a mean gradient. The car slow, pinking.

"Well fuck," John shifting down, "slope's worse'n ever."

I chuckle. "Bad as it ever was. Pater Jed always had trouble on this stretch. He'd stall, roll back downhill. Piss him off no end. Come home all hot and bothered, ornery and cantankerous. Then I'd have to smooth him out, rubbin' scented oil on his dick, suckin' sweet milk off his tits."

"Arf!" John, "HARF!"

"Eep!" Wald, "heesh!"

"My friend, the things that do attain," Monk.

John shift down once more, the car climbing.

"Helluva way to unwind, boy: dick oil, tit milk. Most geezers get their kicks off the SAT tube."

"Thus has he heard," Monk.

"Dick kick," Wald, "heh heh."

The car top the gradient, gather speed. The road level once more, dead straight.

"Not too fast now," I caution, "we gettin' close."

John grunt, the car cruising. Pickets whisper past, chalk white. Porchlights and mailboxes. Above, the moon jaundiced on black cloud-grime.

I read the names off the boxes: all familiar. Stunkard. Boopneth. Chook. Irigaray. Zaigkrupp. Menthe. Quadruss. Tehsil. Fobwitch. Schlumpf.

"Wish I had me a swing bat," I go, "slam them boxes to kingdom come."

"Come box," Wald, "heh heh."

The road narrow, hit a curve: the beams catching painted kerb markers. I study the markers, ignite them with a dry optic flame. The numbers grow hot, link up via flesh-coloured operators to form a stochastic lattice, a transnumeric web of infinitely variable meaning –

"I'm guessin' you had to dongsuck Jed most nights. Ay?"

I shrug. "Had to nibble his nub to get to his library, read the shit I wanted. Scarf caviar off his nuts some nights."

"Haarf!" John, "waahaaarf!"

"Heep!" Wald, "wheep!"

"Quid pro fellatio," Monk.

I give John a look. "Course I had me a PICnic compared to what YOU got. Coffins and cages, spikes and branding irons – "

"Sob sob," John mock-tearful, "sob fuckin' sob."

"And Wald," I go, "snuffhouse razorhead goin' at him flog and fuck, truckers jizzing on his steel-braced skull – "

"WaaHAARF!" John, "sheeat."

Wald speechless, gurgling.

Monk smack his lips. "I suppose I had it well enough. Apart from being born Saxon."

John scowl up in rearview. "WELL mah ASS. Yo' mama banged midget ponies with a red bulb strap-on. Mastiffs lapped lunchmeat off her clit same time she blew a fuckin' BURRO. She made you take pictures. Then she ran off and left you holdin' yo' pappy's cheese dick in both hands."

"Waaah!" me, "waaaHHAAAH!"

"CheeEEESE!" Wald, "heh heh."

Monk cough, suppressing a chuckle. "Oh quite. Harsh but succinct, sad but true – "

"That's the one," I go pointing, "on the right."

John snort, tap the brakes. "Not like I didn't KNOW."

The car slow, drift right, ease to a stop. The beams catch the mailbox just ahead: BENTHAM.

John cut the lights, kill the engine. "We here, girls."

No one move. Silence, yellow gloom.

"Porchlight's off," goes John, "don't look like he's in."

I smile. "Oh he's in, all right. Under the sheets, gettin' his foreskin furled with a toothpick."

"HaHAARF!" John.

"Hmmph!" Wald.

"Whiff of alpha-dweeb pore-musk," Monk, "geriatric gamma halitosis. Hence in."

I nod. "Roger that'n."

John turn, thump open his door, surge out.

"Showtime, girls."

"Showtime," I echo ducking out, Monk and Wald after.

John walk around back, crank open the car trunk.

"Santy come a-visitin'," he hum, "Santy take a ride – "

I inhale deep, step up on the sidewalk. Ahead, Pater Jed's two-storey squire cottage unchanged: same old picket fence, thatch roof, oak door –

"You ready honeybunch?"

I turn. John spraddle-legged, goody sack slung over his shoulder. Monk and Wald behind.

I grin. "Ready, willin' and illin'."

John bare his teeth. His fangs flash, aura flaring spectral. His führerblaze, his überkampf shine.

I turn, start away. "Please to follow, children."

I walk over to the gate, work it open, start up the cobbled dogtrot. Monk's voice sounds behind: "No time to soil that hydrant Wald, not now."

"Doggie poo," Wald a-giggle, "doggie poo poo – "

Thud. I gasp: John's boot hard on my rump.

"Hurry it up, slut. We ain't got all night."

I curse, lope up to the arched awning and pause panting. Before me the door hard and white. *Now as then, then as now, only worse –*

Thwack: John slapping my shoulder as he shove past.

"Bitch workin' the wrong job."

He move left, John, stand flanking the door. Monk and Wald stepping up seconds later, taking a stand at right.

"You could maybe set the sack down," I murmur, "take a load off."

John stare a moment. Then he let it drop: the goody sack sliding off his shoulder, hitting the porch with a thud.

"Anything ELSE 'fore we get it OANE, hon?"

I chuckle, step up, aim a finger at the doorbell, push. Dingalingding, dingdingaling: echoes fading to silence. More silence. Still more silence.

"Bet the fucker's dead," John, "dead and rotten."

"Deadrot fuckload," Wald, "heh heh."

I sidle up close, run a finger around the peephole, caress the doorbell with my thumb and push.

Dingalingding, the chimes muffled, dingdingaling.

I listen, ear to the door. Moan of nightwind. Old Glory flapping overhead.

"Fuck it," John, "I'm – "

I thrust up a hand, palm out. Sound behind the door: creak, creak. Steps in hesitant approach and click: porchlight coming on white. I step back, look up squinting.

"JB?" the voice, "that you JB?"

Petulant whine edged with suspicion: Pater Jed.

I take a deep breath. Put on the old sloe-eyed, pout-lip kiddie booboo face.

"Yes it's me, Pater. Young JB back from the dead as it were, so to speak. Bad timing indeed, Pater, sorry as hell to get you UP this time of night, no pun intended, and true, it's been a while, a long while since we last GMBRLF! but I've got to see, MUST see you now Pater, because it's, like, IMP-ortant?"

My voice pitched high, like Oliver asking for more: the old cocksucker coax, plaintive catamite plea –

"You've got some nerve showing up at my doorstep," Pater, voice rising, "some nerve after what you hrrgnnkh! after all you hnngrrkh! ringing my BELL this time of night, NO PUN INTENDED. You're not getting a red cent out of me JB, not one solitary penny, so I suggest you – "

"Pater!" I exclaim, eyes wide, shaking my pickaninny skull, "Pater, you shock and disillusion. I crave neither cents nor pennies, red, solitary or otherwise. My purpose be not pecuniary Pater, no, perish the presupposition. This here visit pertain not to pelf, lucre or prosaic emoluments, nor to treasures hoarded on earth or in heaven. I am come, rather, by leave of a higher power, in deference to a Notion, a matter of overarching if not overweening importance, Pater, a concern most pressing and of the utmost moment – "

I pause slobbering, nares flared, eyes moist. John at left, smothering a cackle.

"I haven't the time JB," the Pater in derisive singsong, "NO TIME hnngrrakh! for your games this night. I'm afraid it won't hnngrrnkh! wash. You better leave before I – "

I put out a yelp, press up against the door, raise myself on tiptoe. And run my tongue over the peephole.

"Worth your while Pater," I croon, "worth your while, sure. Tits and ass, milk and caviar. Snake tongue bung rim, foreskin peckerchomp. Yum yum slurpie slurp, yum yum slurp – "

I break off froth-lipped, humping the door. Monk at right,

easy, arms folded. Wald hashing his crotch, eyes like marbles –

"If you think hnngrrannkh! If you think I'm going to – "

"Thy scented prepuce, Pater, thy milch cow dugs. Thy anointed dungbung no less and plenty more, yum yum slurpie slurp, slurpie yum yum – "

I step back, face motile with bogus lust. Counting two, three, four, five, six and clink: sound of the chain coming off, bolts sliding:

"This better be good JB," Pater's voice gone to a husk, "really better be – "

The door ajar, Pater Jed in evidence at last: his mug scowling in the breach, hair tousled, eyes crudded, sunken mouth twitching. Face I see in nightmares –

"Well?" Pater, "what – "

"Thrash," I go smiling, "thrash – "

John's boot in coiled spring release: whipping up and in, steeltip roundhouse slamming into the door. Thud-blam-squawk: Pater's face gone, the door humming.

"Timber," John hoisting the goody sack, "tim-fuckin'-ber."

I step up, Wald a-giggle, push, step in: light in the foyer, the old limegreen wallpaper, checkered floor tiles. The living room dark at right. And just ahead, the Pater on his back, gasping.

I move aside, John, Monk, Wald, filing in. Boom: John kicking the door shut.

"Yeh!" Wald, "heh heh."

Monk shake back his hair, smooth his robe. "Do you suppose the neighbors saw any of that?"

I shake my head. "Doubt it. Wouldn't matter if they did. No love lost in THIS 'hood."

John cackle. "Check him out. Fucker look like a beached bass at high noon."

"Beach fuck," Wald, "heh heh."

"Bloodless crustacean gone belly up," Monk.

"Asian blood belly," Wald, "heh heh."

We stand and watch, digging the scene. Pater sprawled shuteye, mouth agape, his monogrammed bathrobe open at the chest. Behind him the stairway leading up.

"Dig that sound he make breathin'," John, "rattler in a fuckin' snotbucket."

"Phlegm bowl hookah," Monk.

"Hooker phlegm snotfuck," Wald, "heh heh."

John hawk, spit on a tile: fire-green loogie shaped like a rat claw. "If there's one thing I cain't stand, boy, it's some old geezer's bony chest workin'."

"Seconded," Monk.

"Old boner chest fuck," Wald, "heh heh."

I chuckle, walk over, prop an elbow on the balustrade. "Hnnngrrkh!" Pater, lashes fluttering, "hnngh!"

I nod. "Yayup. Look like he's coming to."

"Like to come," Wald, "heh heh."

I move up a step, bend peering.

"Touch of lipstick, I see. Rouge, mascara, eyeshadow. Look like Pater been naughty this night."

John walk up, shake his head. "Dadgum palookafuck."

"Naughty fuckstick," Wald, "heh heh."

Monk approach, step over the Pater, start up the stairs.

John scowl. "Where you goin' bitch."

"Won't be long, Mabel," Monk, "keep tugging."

I watch Monk ascend, robe in soft billow. Then I turn, squat on my haunches, tap the Pater's brow with a forefinger.

"Have you returned Pater," I go resonant, "have you returned from beyond the pale."

The Pater moan, eyes struggling open. "JB," he croak, "JB?"

John snort, kick the old man's slippered foot.

"Ass up fartknocker. It's bleedin' time."

The Pater turn slow, blink. "What," he croak, "who – "

John cackle. "We your bitches, hon. We your jive ass fucker-punks oane a night visit."

"Fuck jive punk fart," Wald, "heh heh."

The Pater make a throttled sound, eyes going wide.

"Get out!" he gasp trying to sit up, "all of you! Get – "

John put out a soft-palate warble, roll his tongue: plop. Spitwad landing square on the old man's brow.

"AwwWWWNNGG!" Pater struggling up, "out! OUT! – "

John drop the goody sack, sink to his haunches: crack. Backhand whiplash, Pater with a head-jerk thudding back in collapse.

I chuckle. "Easy there, Teej. No man must croak before his time. Meister's rules."

John rise, sniff. "Sheeat. That wudn't but a pussy paw teaser."

"Pussy tease," Wald agog, "heh! Heh heh! – "

Pater on his back "nnngahk! nngrrakh!", blood welling at his nose like new hope.

John squat once more, hold up his right hand. Click: wristblade shafting up bright. "See this Jed? You don't behave, I'm gon' stick you deep and go exPLORIN'."

"Hnngrraakh!" Pater, hand on nose, "hnngaakh! – "

Creak. I look up: Monk on the stairs descending.

"Naughty indeed," he goes, "there's a boy manacled to the bed upstairs. Naked, comatose, oriental. Shortbread lodged in his rectum, a fried roll around his penis, oyster sauce on his nipples – "

"HARF!" John, "sheeat."

"Penis sauce nipple roll," Wald, "heh heh."

I rise, step back. "Guess the Pater got creative. With me it was just caviar and sweetmilk. *Crème fraîche* glanhead. Bunghole *brulée*. Fizz-tit beaujolais on religious holidays – "

"HAHHARF!" John, "yowp."

"Bungfizz," Wald, "heh heh."

Pater cough, blink red-eyed, let his hand drop: blood smeared dark around his nose.

"Take what you want and leave," he quaver, "TAKE WHAT YOU WANT AND LEAVE – "

John's wristblade flash: a shriek issuing from Pater's maw. A two-inch nick show on his brow, gore welted there like inspiration.

"Some folks just don't learn QUICK enough," John rising, "like m'dear ol' pappy used to say."

Pater with both hands on his brow, sobbing.

"Dig that sound," I go, "last time I heard it, he had his dick up my dungbung."

"Sheeat," John, "just a LITTLE more than I needed to know."

"Dickie dung," Wald, "heh heh."

Monk on the stairs, smiling grim.

"Well," I go, "best get on with it. Can't piss around – "

"Hold up" John, "one last piece o' bidness."

I frown. "Business?"

John grin, raise his right foot, plant it square on Pater's chest.

"Say now Jed," he goes, quizzical, "I'm kinda curious 'bout yo' little coon ass punk bitch JB. I'm wonderin how OLD he was yearwise, when you first had him SUCK YOU OFF. Ay?"

"YeEEH!" Wald hopping in place, "SUCKyeeEEEH! – "

Pater wild-eyed, twisting convulsive, grabbing John's ankle: "Nngaarkh! Nngrrarrkh! – "

"How. Old." John pumping Pater's chest with his boot heel, "How. Old. Was. He. When. You. First – "

"Five!" Pater's face a blur of blood and brine, "FIVE!"

I raise a cautionary finger. "Easy now, Teej. You don't want to stomp him right through – "

"SECOND question," John ignoring counsel, "I KNOW you bought him off some fuckin' whore NUN, Island Maurice. Question is: how MUCH you buy him for?"

Pater groan out loud, retching with eyes screwed shut.

"Please! I don't know what you're – "

John bear down hard, grinding his boot heel: a wail bursting from the Pater's gape mouth: "AAaaaaAAAIIIEEEEHHH! – "

Wald leaping in foam-lipped echo, "AAaaaAAAAIIIE-EEHHH! – "

"THREE STRIKES YOU OUT!" John murderous, "HOW. MUCH – "

"THOUSAAAAND!" Pater shrieking agonized, "A THOU-nngrrAAKH! THOUUUSAAAND! – "

John turn, grinning lunatic. "Slut, you been a geezer-bitch since you wuz FIVE. And yo' brown ass be worth ONE LARGE. WAYYY too muthafuckin' MUCH for what YOU got."

I curl my lip, spit through my teeth. "Your peewee pimp dick ain't worth much either."

"OOooOOOHHH!" John hashing his crotch, "little Mowgli gettin' UPPITY."

"Ass," Wald suddenly calm, "Bitchpimp dickhard. Heh heh – "

John put out a whoop, step back with a smirk.

"SAY now, Jed," he goes, patting his own crotch, "your little PICKaninny here won't put OUT. You got someplace else I can hide all this GOOOOD MEAT?"

"Nnngnyahhhh!" Pater tear-streaked, "nnngnnaahhh! – "

I turn with a chuckle, step into the living room, reach for the switch: click. Sunlamps come on above, filtered white. I'm expecting the old décor, neo-Victorian dreck I grew up on, but no. Pater's got a Martian slave-plantation sun paradise theme going: wicker chairs, loungers, a Mission Mars parasol, fake palms with toy simians, red sand beach strip with midget golliwogs serving pastel brew, stuffed macaws perched on a tank of iridescent fish under a Martian sky, wallspreads showing Martian waterways, arcologies, plantation biospheres with cloned darkies bent joyous to the task. A picture hang incongruous at left: framed photo of master race rocketboys at Mittelwerk, blue eyes dreaming a reich-birthed Martian imperium –

"Gangway!" John, "steppin' through."

I step aside, turn. John trooping in a-grin, goody sack in one hand, Pater's ankle in the other.

"Shit," I go, "man can walk."

"Quicker this way," John, Pater on his back clawing the floor, "hnnrrackh! aakh!", Wald toddling in cachinnate, Monk right after.

John drag the Pater to the middle of the room, pause and let go. Thud: Pater's heel hitting the floor, him now spreadeagled, retch and sob, bathrobe bunched around his torso.

"Hotdamn!" John peering, "check out the foreskin on this hump. Big enough to wrap around on a cold night."

I cackle. "Told ya, didn't I?"

Monk steps up, Wald abreast.

"Quite a prepuce, yes," Monk, "best kept furled. Or stapled to the inner thigh. Or pinned secure to the scrotum. Or glued in folds to the perineum – "

"Harf!" John, "HARF!"

"Scrotum glue," Wald, "heh heh – ."

"A lid on the badinage now sons," I go, hand raised, "on with the show, time being of the essence."

John shoot me a scowl, pull up a deckchair.

"This oughtta do, ay?"

I nod. "Oughtta."

John bend, grab the Pater's robe, hoist him clean off the floor and slam him ass down on the chair. The chair teeters, rights itself.

"Our sachem's ideology of domination," Monk, "his critique of instrumental reason."

The Pater groan, lidded. Him slumped near naked, in steady bleed.

John snicker. "Sad lookin' turd, ain't he?"

"Mission Mars seignior in excelsis," Monk.

"Turd mission," Wald, "heh heh."

I give John a look. "Strap him in now, friar. If you would."

John grunt, reach into the goody sack, pull out a roll of duct tape.

"Arms and legs both," I go.

"Sheeat."

John strip off a length of tape, strap down Pater's left wrist. Strip off another length, strap down the right. Then stripping twice more, he strap Pater's ankles to the deckchair.

"Done," he go rising, "that oughtta hold him."

I nod. "Good work, daddy-o."

The Pater stir, cough and look up slow, very slow, like waking to a nightmare manifest. His eyes wander a moment, then focus quivering.

"JB," he croak, "take what you want and leave. Leave now and I won't – "

He break off with a grimace, eyes squeezing shut.

John cackle. "Sheeat."

"The prospect of imminent extinction makes him maudlin," Monk, "ah the travails of the moribund."

I laugh. "Pater," I go, "Pater dear."

The Pater open his eyes, blink.

"We're not thieves, Pater dear. NOT. We're acolytes. Acolytes enacting a Notion, our Meister's sovereign will. Taint not our efforts, therefore, with aspersions foul, motives ulterior, impulses base. Dig?"

A crease appear on the Pater's brow, a scowl distorting his mug.

"You're not fooling me!" he rasp, "you're not fooling me with your high-falutin nnghrrnnkh! your repugnant, despicable – "

John reach with both hands: blade flashing out and up, blood spritzing in a long, graceful arc. Pater going wide-eyed, a gasping inhalation, scream.

"Shut him up," I go, "SHUT HIM UP!"

John grin, hold up his left hand: Pater's bloody earlobe between thumb and forefinger. Pater shuddering beside, mouth gaped in Munch-scream.

"SHUT HIM UP!" me "SHUT HIM – "

Movement: the Wald bounding up silent, grabbing a fistful of the Pater's hair, clapping a hand over his mouth.

"Mmph!" Pater struggling, "mmph!"

I exhale with a sigh. Smile. "Kudos Wald. Timely action."

"Yeh," Wald shaking the Pater's skull, "heh heh – "

I turn, give John a look. "Overkill, muthafucka."

John cackle. "Bitch, whut you worried about? Nobody listenin'. And if they are, they don't give a good goddamn. And if they do, there ain't no one to call."

I scowl. "Pig reserve, remember? Stand-in Bunko Squad."

John shrug. "Fuck 'em. Ain't no pain."

"You DID fuck one earlier tonight," Monk, "yes?"

"Pain fuck," Wald, "heh heh."

John turn, flick the pater's earlobe into the fish tank: piscine swirl.

I take a step, hold out my hand. "The stuff please, Teej. Best get this over with quick."

John kiss the gore off his fingers, reach into the goody sack and fish out the bag.

"Knock yourself out," he goes, tossing it over.

I catch the bag two-handed, unseal it, prise out the syringe and white vial. "Hold on, now Wald. We gonna finish this quick."

"Quickie," Wald butting the Pater's occiput, "heh heh."

I fold the bag, stick it in my pocket. Then I hold up the syringe, push the plunger and uncap the needle. "Now Pater, give ear (hyuck hyuck). With this needle I thee... uh, no. What I mean is: I'm gonna ram this here needle through the crown of your hoary skull and draw a vial's worth of brain-juice. No cause for concern, no pain if done right. But first, the ritual of completion. John?"

John blink. "Huh?"

"Your move, fool."

John mutter, raise his hand: wristblade in extension.

"Now Jed, this is gon' HURT, but it ain't nothin' your rabbi wouldna done if you'da been a jewbird."

"That makes sense," Monk, "if you've had a concussion."

The Pater quake woozy-eyed, gore starting to clot around his missing lobe.

"Look like he's passing out," I go, "just as well."

"Passing beyond," Monk, "bodhi svaha."

John curse, kneel, shove apart the Pater's thighs, pinch up a portion of his prepuce and slice it off clean.

"Mmmmmmmmphh!"   Pater   in   slow   thrash, "mmmmmmmmmmphhhh!"

"Peckersnip," Wald licking Pater's brow, "heh heh."

John rise, blade withdrawn, foreskin in hand.

"Step back now, Wald. Bossman takin' over."

Wald roll his eyes, shake his head. "Noooo! Heh heh."

John sigh, raise his right foot, stick it in Wald's gut: the Wald reeling back with a grunt, hitting the floor in a heap of wicker.

Monk click his tongue rueful. "At this rate, he'll bust a Keaton."

"Sheeat," John, "man don't listen when you ask nice, he DESERVE nasty."

Pater groan as though in agreement, head on the loll. Red drool hang viscous off his chin, a gore-spot on his shrunken glanhead.

John spit, slap the Pater's head upright, grab his jaw pincer-like, force his mouth open.

"Awwnnnnggkh!" Pater in goldfish gawp, "awwhnnggkh! – "

John cackle, drop the severed foreskin in the Pater's maw, scoop up the roll of duct tape with one foot, strip off a length and seal the Pater's mouth with a flourish.

"Thus the circle complete," I intone, "goddamn Teej, you are one smooth criminal."

John look up with a smirk. "Your move, ho."

"Smooth ho," Wald in back rising, "heh heh – "

I step around, position myself behind the chair.

"Hold him now, John. Hold him up."

John reach, shove back the Pater's head.

"Nngh!" Pater skew-eyed, "nnnnghmmmph!"

Monk at left with arms folded, observing with interest.

I turn the syringe over, hold it like a knife, take aim and jab the needle down hard through the crown of Pater's skull. A high thin scream erupt from his throat, spread up over his scalp in blue thrombosed ripples. I feel the vibe in my carpal tunnel, dig it with a shudder.

John snort. "I guess practice DON'T make perfect."

"Don't make!" Wald shuffling up, "heh heh – "

I hold the syringe with my left hand, pull the plunger with

my right. A gore-flecked lotus blooms within, Pater's brow writhing.

"Think that's enough?" I ask looking at Monk.

Monk shrug. "Looks enough."

I nod, brace my left hand against the Pater's skull, pull on the syringe with my right. The needle emerge slow, reluctant, blood incruent at the point of entry.

"Mmmbaby," John, "oooomama."

"Titillating," Monk.

"Tit," Wald, "heh heh."

I hold up the needle, aim it at the white vial, push through the seal, squeeze.

"Second vial full," I go pulling out, "that's strike two. Angels rejoice."

The Wald yelp, raise a leg, vent a fartburst.

"Whoof!" John stepping back, "sheeat."

"Wrong angel," Monk.

I snort, cap the needle, stick the syringe in the bag with the vial.

"Now Johnny boy," I snarl, tossing him the bag, "Johnny boy do tell: are you in a KILLIN' mood."

"Goddamn RIGHT I am," John, "sheeat."

"Well then, that's just fine. Cuz the FACT of the matter is, if RIGHTEOUS truth be RIGHTLY told: IT'S KILLIN' TIME!"

"YEEAAARRHH!" John executing a heel kick, foot whipping an inch above the Pater's skull.

"EEeeeEEEP!" Wald pounding his crotch, "eeEEEEP!"

Monk nodding sage, going: "The old earth certainly IS frolicsome tonight."

I snicker, point to the goody sack. "Bring out the beast now, good son John. Diddle dumpling, my son John."

John bark, reach into the sack, rummage around.

"Titties and peckermen!" he lilt, "tonight we present: KEVORK'S KOSHER KILL KIT! – "

Whirling as he speak, John, the contraption flying across, landing by the chair in a heap.

"YEEEH!" Wald, prick wagging in extrusion, "KILL!"

"Revelation," me.

"It lives," Monk.

John step up, grinning fiendish. "Look like hawg innards, don't it?"

"Yayup," me, "it's meant to."

"Ship your crotch-oar would you, Wald," Monk, "time enough for such when the time comes."

"Come time," Wald trying to sheathe his boner, "heh heh."

We gather around, digging the kit. The Quadruple-K on the floor inert: a flesh-pink entrail tube with a needle at one end, a puckered bunghole at the other, an automated pump bag in middle. This here bag resembling a rufose hog heart.

Seconds pass: the Pater groaning sub-audible.

"Well," I go, "enough of that. Hook the man up now John good son, hook him up good."

"Good hooker," Wald, "heh heh."

John bend, pick up one end of the tube, needle first.

"Duct tape, please nurse, ya little jive ho."

Monk shrug, grab the roll of tape, hand it to John.

John give me a look. "Whut we gon' drain him into, slut."

"Easy," I go, "fishtank over yander."

John nod. "Works for me."

Pater moan, raise his head. His eyes struggle open, lids in slow quake. "Mmmgn! Mmmgmmph!"

John cackle, hold up the tube needle. "See this, Jed? We gon' stick it into ya, bleed you dry and white. That way folks know whut you really are: a bone-ass dead geezer."

"Indeed," Monk nodding grave, "truth must out, Jed. Authenticity as being-towards-death."

"Dead boner," Wald, "heh heh."

The Pater turn, eyes swimming. "Mmmb! Mmmbnnf! – "

I raise a hand in reassurance. "It's all right, Pater. Not to worry. Death ain't as bad as it's made out to be. First you hit the Chickhai Bardo, see the Clear Light. Then you hit the Chonyid Bardo, see visions. Then the Lord of Death stick a boot up your butt and you hit the Sidpa Bardo at high velocity. There, you see couples fucking and you choose the palest, ugliest pair. Then you're reborn and mammy stick you squallin' in the closet while she spit-lube pappy's pecker-pole – "

I pause, John and Pater staring, Wald a-giggle, Monk regarding me with dispassionate interest.

"Duuude," John hush-toned, "I DIG that sce-NARIO."

"Chronicle of a death foretold," Monk.

"Spitlube chronicle," Wald, "heh heh."

I smile droop-eyed, oozing dolor. "Hook him up now John, prithee. Hook him up, pray."

John nod, turn. I figure maybe Pater thrash and screech again, but he don't. He give me a last look: accusatory, despairing. Then he lower his head and shut his eyes.

"Awww," John, "you quittin' oane us Jed?"

No response. The Pater with head bowed, rib-rack working.

John smirk, grab the Pater's left forearm, mark out a vein. Then he point the tube needle and stick it in. The Pater grimace, but make no sound.

"Think the exit tube reach the fishtank?" ask John turning.

I nod. "Likely."

John step away, scoop up the exit tube, walk over to the fishtank, drop the bunghole in. The fish quicken in colourful morass.

"Ahhh," me, "lovely."

"Oh quite," Monk, "if at all."

John hawk, spit in the tank, walk back, stand by the heartshaped pump bag. "Turn it oane?"

I nod. "On."

John reach with his foot, flip a switch. The Kill Kit start up with a whine, hog-heart pumping.

I point to the fishtank. "Dig it now, fellas. Dig."

A moment pass. Another moment. Then the exit tube twitch, bunghole in sudden gout, blood blossoming like an aquatic rose.

"Awww mama!" John, "bay-BEE."

"Corpuscular colloid," Monk, "the fish approve."

"Pus call," Wald, "heh heh."

I jerk a thumb at the Pater. "That's him in the corner, him in the hotseat losing his pabulum."

John snicker. "You ever see a Kill Kit hit before, Jayb?"

I nod. "Saw this juice-head catch one in a flophouse basement, through a whoreshack rut mirror. Man didn't know what was comin'. *The look in his eyes when it hit, kid it was TASTY.*"

We stand quiet a moment, watching. Pater with head bowed, the Quadruple-K in steady throb. The fish swarming in gorefroth.

"Make a pretty picture," John, "don't he?"

I shrug. "I guess. But he coulda looked prettier. Other shit we could've done. Like shave his pits with a scalpel washed in sacramental wine. Or tape a grass and dung poultice to his right eye. Or pin three black dahlias to his pudendum. Or scrawl a seppuku death sonnet on a plantain leaf and paste the leaf to his skull – "

I break off, hearing a hoarse cackle. Our eidolon spirit guides again. Stinger, Finesse, Oblongata, Noodlebear, lashed to a sheet metal Mobius Strip, an inch from the ceiling. Them decked out like hadal termagants: partlets and pointy hats, pale bludgeoned mugs wart-ridden, teeth bared in rotgum grins.

I groan, smack my crotch in dismay. "Awww, GIRLS. Y'all look like SHIT. Shittier'n EVER."

"Huh?" John "wha?"

I point. "Them up there. Our spirit guides."

John look up, turn slit-eyed. "Bitch you losin' it again. We outta here. NOW."

I scowl. "Listen, ya shit-eatin' – "

"OUT!" John turning on his heel, "OUT! – "

Stalking out the room, John: Monk and Wald starting after.

"Awww fellas," I go, "don't leave now fellas, don't – "

I wince: Noodlebear shrieking a harlot's curse, myself looking up to see ichor spewing from her mouth, a dark flaming projectile that land in the fishtank, the water all hiss and steam, the fish leaping like piranha, a carnivorous rainbow.

I gasp, back away, eidolons above, laughing raucous. In the foyer I pause, click off the light switch. Last glimpse of Pater slumped in silhouette, the Mobius Strip angling down, fish ravening out their tank in multi-hued fulgor: *I will miss him, Ethel, yes. The way a dry nutsack miss fresh jizm –*

***

A light approach, zip overhead flashing yellow. Trees rush past, the city showing between. Darkness, lights in faint speckle. *The rabble indoors mingling humors, Clem. Dishwater jizz erupting loveless, washing silent across the valley –*

I sigh, look over my shoulder. Monk in half-lotus, chin tucked in the hollow of his throat. Wald with feet up, whispering. At left, John with eyes shut, steering with his knees.

277

I reach, stick a finger in his ear. "You keep that up, son, you're gonna shit us out the dentured bunghole of tellurian time."

John curse, whack my hand aside. "You pull shit like THAT, you ain't gon' HAVE a bunghole to talk out of."

"Bung pull," Wald, "heh heh."

The road dip, level out. Lights show at right: the A9 station still lousy with neon. I watch with interest, love, squalor. No rigs in sight, no vehicular aspirants gasless, snoozing. Just a trio of masked attendants working a Noh scene for absent Kabuki enthusiasts: the first on a monocycle with no wheel, no seat, the second twirling a hoop of iced milk around his ankle, the third balanced on an elbow, face down on a trundle board in perpetual motion.

"Fuckin' circus," goes John, "I've heard tell they got a bear back there. A city-bred grizzly."

I nod. "I've seen it. Wears green camouflage, blue shades, a beaverskin busby. Armed with a Colt and a shotgun."

Monk sniff. "Right to bear arms, right to arm bears."

"Woof," me.

"Sheeat," John.

Wald whispering.

The car cruise on, run a red light, cut through a four-way Stop into Zone North. Ahead, Westwood Avenue flaring out, ten lanes.

"You shoulda taken the Beltway," I go, "the exit, back the way we came."

John shake his head. "More fun this way."

"Way we CAME," Wald, "heh heh."

I slump, stretch my legs. Not much to see on this drag. Westwood dead quiet this time of night: all the freaks, juiceheads, smack-pappies out in Zone East, Carnivale Beast'n'Midget. Visored storefronts drift past at left, plex-glass displays secured alight –

I yawn, look away. A prowler glimmer past, ersatz Pig wedged behind the wheel.

John snort. "Fat muthafuck. Them Pigboys get shittier lookin' by the week."

I chuckle. "Reserves, remember?"

"Sheeat," John speeding up, "same difference."

"Shitty Pigfat," Wald, "heh heh."

We zip on a while, speechless, vented air in steady hiss. Somewhere we cross an invisible barrier and the road start to lose lanes, boutiques and brasseries yielding to pawn and porn, grog dives, *Liquor'n'Kimchee.*

"Ohhh yeah," John tapping out a rhythm on the wheel, "here's MAH scene baby, here's MAH scene – "

Segueing into a blugrass yodel, going: "*I'm back where I belong, honey, the butthole end o' town – "*

The car crest an incline, a light coming into view ahead. A red bejeezus cross in neon, a scut church there for skidrow revenants, street trash huddled outside.

John point. "I've seen Bartlett down there lookin' to make an impression. Him with his pecker out pissin' all over them bums yellin': YOU'RE BAPTIZED!"

"Waah!" me, "wahhhaaah!"

"His mobile baptismal font," Monk.

"Pissbum bapjizm," Wald, "heh heh."

The car slow, veer left into an alley. Brick walls loom either side, open trashcans in gauntlet. John speed up, flashing his brights: glimpse of a mutant roach riding a gutter rat. And ahead, hairless alley-cats feeding on a vagrant, sozzled or dead.

"Whoa," John sitting up, "WHOA!"

I shake my head. "Same shit, different drag."

The car surge, Wald's voice in crescendo. Close, closer, the car a four-wheel torpedo, the cats freezing an instant, blood-mouthed, eyes like diamonds, then exploding in wild scatter, the vagrant spotlit for an instant and boom, the car in brief lurch, John putting forth his jungle bwana victory cry, Wald in back gibbering glossolalial, the car barrelling on to alley's end and out, John turning with a snarl going: "Shut him up, someone SHUT THE FUCKER UP – "

But no one does, not till John stop the car, dive in back and force Wald's face into the upholstery, muffled hog-squeals fading to silence.

"Think he'll be ready for Bartlett?" I ask a minute later, the car moving.

John snort. "Fucker ain't DEAD. Just restin' a spell."

"Quite," Monk.

Silence. The car threading through Zone South, Arrondissements Six, Seven and Eight, John with both hands on the wheel skirting potholes, squelching nescient juiceheads, toxic ordure, fresh roadkill. A ripe death-stench fill the car, my thoughts quickening. Flash-image in sharp outline: T. Carter Bartlett in a sewer tunnel preaching to a pack of feral rodents, his ribcage open like a cupboard, a wreath around his neck aflame, his prick stretched and driven into the floor with a tent peg –

" – home?"

I blink, turn. "What now?"

John curse. "I said: you think there's a chance he WON'T be home?"

"Who, Bartlett?"

"No, your churchpaw's fuckin' four-leg prison-bitch."

I cackle. "This time of night, sure. Don't see why not."

"This time of night," John, "is when the fucker like to go walkabout, baptizing bums with peckerjuice."

"Wahhaaah!" me, "yayup."

"Not tonight though," offers Monk, "Friday night's sabbath night, Church of Ancients. He'll be home mumbo-ing his jumbo."

"Cornponing his little freak gook," John.

I nod. "More likely than not."

A jive coiff shack show ahead at left, alight. Three mamas in the doorway, glass slippers and spangled gowns, green fluorescent lipgloss, beehive naps strung with bead bulbs aglow.

"STOP!" bellow John, cruising past, "IN THE NAME O' LUUVE!"

I wince. "Don't think they will. Not with the windows up."

"No indeed," Monk, "but they'll live on, nonetheless, their image inscribed for all time in the Akashic Record."

"Sheeat," John, "fuckin' ragass gooroo."

Wald in back silent, still out.

"But speakin' of Bartlett," I go, "I got some dope on him last month, courtesy Fatman. Fucker was in Nam: The Tenth Sequel, policing the action."

"Who," John, "the Fatman?"

I frown. "No, fool, Bartlett. Fucker volunteered."

"Ah," Monk, " A chaplain among Hessian killtroopers."

I shake my head. "Wrong. He was no chaplain. Fucker piloted a gunship, strafing paddies and hamlets. Had a good time of it, gunning gooks. No surprise. Man come from a long line of boondock, coon-killin' lynch-pappies. Man dug it so deep he wrote a poem in ode: *Ghostfuckers in the Sky*. Fatman's got a copy, weird shit. So one day, he's up spittin' death out that groovy Nam blue, when all of a sudden he see the Light of God through a slew of paddy water and mangled limb, manna and revelation like Papa Moses after buttcheek and burnin' bush. Next thing you know, Bartlett's this neo-napalm holy roller preachin' the spiel, yammering in tongues like he got Dad, the Kid and the Spook revving his ragass three-in-one. He become a stone menace, a hazard. One evening he try to baptize a trooper with a white-phos squirt-gun and two baby scorpions. That get him a dump discharge and a *Semper Fi* brand on his swingin' dick. So Bartlett head home and build the Church of Ancients. Fucker's had it goin' for a while now, got himself a goodsize flock, mostly skidrow swills and boon trash hawg-humps. Also some folks higher up: DC patricians, killtroop generals, mercantile mandarins. Hard to tell what doctrine Bartlett preach, no one seem to know for sure. Some kinda goofball Manicheanism, far as I can tell. Idea being, you got to create Hell on earth to bring down Heaven. Then God and Satan stalemate each other and Earth become this blankass voidoid limbo where anything goes and no one comes – "

"CUM! heh heh."

I frown, turn. Wald smash-mouthed, rising.

"Where you been Wald," I go, "walkin' on the sun?"

"Blank hawghump," Wald in a tremulous croak, "heh heh – "

The wheels screech, the car hanging a sharp right. On under the overpass and there: the Old Mall at left, the lot dark as a croupe-hole in costive eclipse.

"Out there, Monk," I go pointing, "out there he lie, dead Pig reserve with a crawfulla Johnny-jizz."

"Harf!" John, "damn right."

"Dead craw Pig jizz," Wald, "heh heh."

Monk whistle. "The throat-shagged corpse: think it's been found and taken?"

I snort. "HELL no. There he stay till the light of day, hip hip hooray."

"Hell shag," Wald, "heh heh."

We watch it go past: the lot bedarked, the Mall in vague

outline, the golden bird frozen lightless. Soon the lamps appear ahead, yellow streetlamps of Brooke, John tapping the brakes as he draw near and cutting left. Now the car as before, zooming up Brooke, trees blurring past. I watch for the sidewalk geezer and spot him: old tramp supine on his bench, his dog crouched above, dejecting.

John cackle, the scene greasing past. "Nothin' funnier'n a dawg droppin' a turd on some old lush."

"Oh there is," I go, "a diarrhoeal street hound shittin' fire on grandpaw's shoe, him blowin' his ticker, keeling over dead."

"HARF!" John, "yowp."

"Shit blow," Wald, "heh heh."

"Saw something similar once," muses Monk, "a pet shoat pissing in a bowl of eggnog, Santaclaus night. Good thing too. Tasted better that way."

"What," me, "the eggnog?"

"No," John, "the shoat."

"Ixnay," Monk, "Santa."

I nod. "Aged whitemeat in shoat-piss eggnog. Delectable."

"Quite," Monk.

"You eat the shoat too?" John.

"Needless to say," Monk.

"Whose shoat was it?" me.

"Mine," Monk, "rescued it from its mother sow, the kind that eats its farrow."

"Uh-huh," John, "nothin' like eatin' your own pet. Got that special flavor."

"Yayup," me, "explain why Wald keep chewin' on his little pecker."

John chortle. "TRYIN' to chew oane it. He want a big bite offa THAT bratwurst, only he cain't bend enough to reach it. His hawg-belly keep comin' in the way."

"Pecker bite belly come," Wald, "heh heh."

John tap the brake and shift down, the gateway showing ahead: PLANTATION SOUTH. On under the arched sign, past the bronze lions couchant, the road in slow wind going narrow. Matchbox domiciles lightless on either side, occupants in sorrowful sleep post-coitum, dreaming the same dream: assault, dismemberment, necrophilic copulation under blazing Klieg lights on a bloodswept prairie –

John curse. "Fuckin' lost my way again. Where you live, Wald bitch."

I shake my head. "Don't ask him. Just cut right while turning left, keep both feet on the wheel and hum an idiot nocturne. We'll get there."

And we do, sure enough. Block D showing minutes after John get done driving around in circles, rhomboids, figures eight, transdim swastikas and other post-euclidean oddities discovered by lamplight.

"Thar she blows," I go pointing, "right thar."

"You don't SAY," John spitting gnashed teeth, bits of tongue.

"Blow you right she say," Wald, "heh heh."

John hit the brakes, swerve, pull in beside Wald's car, a kerb lamp directly ahead. Bartlett's wagon still in place, off at left.

"He's in," I go, "thank spit."

John grunt, cut the lights, kill the engine.

"Well, time we got – "

I put out a yelp, raise a pinkie. "Hold. One last thing before we hit. Bartlett's got bodyguards: pair of iron-pumped Hmong twins he smuggled back from Nam: The Tenth Sequel. Twins named Phuc and Thuc."

John turn, smiling tight-lipped. Grab my hand. And squeeze. I cry out like a wounded bird, pain up my arm slivering blue-white.

"YeeEEH!" Wald, "mmMMBRR!"

John bare his teeth, loosen his grip. "Shit I coulda been told BEFORE we got here."

I retrieve my hand whimpering. "Awww honey, that was SWEET. Got me all weak-kneed and teared up – "

John lean left, push open his door. "Bitches out. Now."

I nurse my hand a moment, licking knuckle and thumb. Then I push, climb out. They're up on the sidewalk, Monk and Wald, John around back, corking open the trunk.

"Need any help with that hon?" I ask lilting.

John slam down the trunk lid, hoick up the goody sack, start walking. "Bitches follow."

We follow. Wald behind Monk behind John, myself bringing up the rear. Yellowheads glow either side in humid nimbus, crickets in seven-beat cycles creaking. On up the walkway, up the porch steps into the foyer, John with a grunt hitting the stairs three at a time.

We catch up with him on the landing, him squatting ceremonial there in the gloom. The bucket still in the corner, eggshell and toenail.

"Your move, ho," he goes, looking up at Wald.

"Ho move," Wald panting, "heh heh – "

John spit, jerk a thumb. "Get to it 'fore I slap your nuts off."

Wald turn giggling, sidle into the hallway.

"Nutslap. Heh heh. Heh heh – "

John rise, step back. "Bitches in that corner."

I frown, back up three steps. Monk following suit an instant later. Now Monk and I in one corner of the landing, John stationed opposite.

Seconds pass, recede in echo. John immobile, staring.

"Where's he at," he mutter, "Wald."

I blink. "Huh?"

"He ready to roll?"

I scowl, peep around the corner. Wald in front of Bartlett's door waiting.

"Ready," I go, "on your cue."

John don't answer. Him with head bowed in what look like prayer. I'm about to rouse him with a yelp when he look up, nod. I nod in return, hold out my hand with fingers splayed, thumb in slow wiggle. Wald catch the cue, step up, push Bartlett's doorbell.

A strange sound issue from within: skincrawl glissando. Put me in mind of a limbless castrate wailing mournful, a soused ape nodding over a theremin. Silence. Wald waiting with arm raised, one leg crossing the other: a boykid asking to go peepee.

I hold out my hand once more: fingers splayed at impossible angles, thumb in agonized twitch. Wald giggle, take aim, push. Again the horripilate yowl, followed by silence. And more silence.

John make a snarling sound, take a step. "Fuck this sh – "

I hold up a hand. Light under Bartlett's door: a thin bar of red.

"I seeeEEE you!" comes the voice, sudden, "cuckOOOooo, I seeeEEE you!"

Voice from behind the door: reedy, adenoidal. T. Carter Bartlett.

Wald look up, clasp his hands to his chest and begin talking. Him mimicking my catamite spiel going:

"Please sir!" mouth in moue, "please sir it's me, Waldron Baines from across. Grant entry if you would please sir, a matter of great importance, Reverend sir – "

"HAH!" the voice, "COOOkoo! HAH! – "

"Succor please sir, suck! Succor. The touch of your hand, of your MMNGH! Reverend sir. My last refuge youse, this dark suck! This dark night – "

Pause. Me shaking my head thinking: *weird to hear the Wald talk normal. Normal to hear him talk weird* –

"Mr Baines," the voice suddenly businesslike, "what is it you want now, Mr – "

"Waldron to you sir!" Wald, eager beaver, "Baines to them that care less. Waldron to you, Reverend sir, your own: Wal-DRUNNNNN! – "

A cough sound from within. Cough and a harrumph.

"Yayuss. Mmhmm. So what was it you wanted now, Mr WALLLL-dron. I'm a BUSY! maaan? you KNOW Mr – "

"ConFESSION sir!" Wald tearful, "must conFESS in the bosom of your mmNNG! Heavy laden me, Reverend sir. In travail and likely to proceed drastic if you don't nnNNKH! The slashed wrist in soapwater for example, sir. Blood in egress, soapscum tainted sanguine, squire sir – "

"BLOOD," the voice, "BLOOD and SOAPscum you say, Faugh A BALLAGH! HMMMMMMMMMMM – "

"Please sir!" Wald, quavering lachrymose, "PLEEEHEEEZ! – "

Pause. Wald in rigid entreaty, lone supplicant with face turned heavenward. Us poised aside, watchful.

"Confession, you say," the voice, "con-FAYYYHHH! Yayuss. A man of the cloth must OWL! must ASSIST, yayuss, must YAYYH! – "

Rattle: chain coming off the door, bolt sliding –

"Well now, young Mr Wal-khooOO! Our fine young neigh-kh! MMMhmmmMMMM KH! – "

The door ajar: wedge of red. Glimpse of a black top hat, green shades, beard, coat-tail: T. Carter Bartlett, Pastor, Church of Ancients.

The Wald move. His arms rising birdlike, his foot swinging up vicious: toe-kick to the sanctified nad, Bartlett doubling over with a grunt, his mug smashing square into Wald's upraised knee, thwupf, stagger, thud: out of sight.

"Timber," goes John stepping out the shadows, "tim-fuckin'-ber."

Wald turn, giggle. "Nadcrush. Honkermush. Heh heh."

John walk up grinning, sack in hand. "You did good, baby Wald. GOOOOD."

Wald gurgle, beaming ecstatic. John ruffle his hair, pat his cheek, step through the doorway. Wald follow, Monk right after. I wait outside a moment, scoping ambient. Then I enter, push the door shut and wham: rhinal assault, the reek hitting me plumb. Shit and blood in sweet cocktail, pain and death, shaken, not stirred.

I turn, pulse quickening. Bartlett's front room: hell of a sight. A blend of *mal du siècle* torture funk, damnation chic retro. Dung all over the parquet floor, shitpiles coppled fresh and desiccate, goat turds arranged to spell the word REALM.

At left, pictures in gore-streaked collage: deathcamp dragoons pissing on emaciate corpses, jackbooters buggering shackled starvelings. A Dahmer Club circle jerk in full colour, dusk-light jizz and smoking entrail. Frame stills of a slash'n'lash kiddie gangbang, prepube snuff from Dutroux Belgique. An old plantation fresco featuring a slavedrive bullwhip, chained cotton-pickers knouted bloody.

At right a Goyaesque canvas: ravaged squaw with infant in arms, conquistador bashing its head open with a mallet, robed Jesuit standing by, crucifix raised in benison. Beside the canvas, a lifesize gloss: lab monkey in clinical torment, its skull uncapped, brainmush pierced with wires, eyes burned out, arms nailed to a backboard, charred feet strapped to a hotplate.

Miscellaneous objects fill the room in pathic bricolage. A wolfhead mounted on a post, fangs bared, sockets fitted with red bulbs. Outsize roaches in a dibbled plex cage, blackwinged splice mutants teeming in clusterfuck. A street feline impaled on a wrought iron spike, flesh mangled livid. Bloodshot eyeballs hung on fish hooks, mongrel orbs in array. A six-foot totem pole with foetuses riveted top down, its surface smeared placental. A bouquet of snakeheads wedged in the maw of a prolapsed rectum, fork tongues braided erect. Gilded infant skulls conjoined in a ring of baboon fangs, a mandala in floral ossature –

I frown, turn: John tearful, groaning ecstatic.

"Awww maaama! DIG this FREAKY sheeat, DIG this FREAKY – "

I tune out, look up: mildewed ceiling peppered with molluscs. No, not molluscs. Haemorrhoids. Fuchsia haemorrhoids excised off screaming Saxons, transported subzero, warmed in purple glue and shot ceilingward with blowpipes. A constellation of distended sphincters out to room's end, an eight-foot bejeezus cross erected there. On this cross, a dead goat gutted and crucified, its horns sheened golden. At the foot of the cross, a rusted gurney that serve as an altar, a brass chalice placed atop. This here chalice brimming with what look like clotted ichor, its base ringed by a fat turd fresh out the crapper –

"Hmmmnnng! Awwhhmmnnngh!"

I sigh, dab my eyes, look down. Bartlett curled on his side, one hand to his nose, the other in his crotch.

"Awww Cart Bart," I go maudlin, "you big, big BARTlett you."

Bartlett stir, groan. Fucker cut a sorry picture, but I dig what he's wearing: a black fustian coat with tails, a grass skirt, red hooker-pumps on both feet, his top hat and shades floored beside.

I shake my head, turn. "Well. Guess we best get on with it, hey?"

Silence. John, Monk, Wald, wide-eyed in mesmerville.

"John," I go waving, "ground control to Major JOHN!!!?"

John start, turn groovy-eyed. "Huh?"

I point. "Bartlett. Remember?"

He blink, a grin spreading across his mug.

"Well HALE, Cart Bart!" he go, "you got yourself a whole BUTT load of SWEET honey SHEEAT in here, boy!"

"Quite," Monk soft-voiced, "art of Abaddon. Demon décor."

"Demonshit honeybutt," Wald, "heh heh."

Bartlett groan, turn on his back, sit up grimacing. I smile, digging the raven-black hairline, the knotted brow, the hooded eyes, the crow beak, the fleshless cheeks, the blue stringbean lips, the forked beard, the discoloured tawn of his teeth –

Crack: John's boot-tip on Bart's chin, head-jerk, thud. Bart back on the floor belly up, ribs bared.

"Not just yet, Cart Bart," John, "you stay down till I tell you different."

Bartlett's eyes wander, lungs rattling. Then they jerk into sharp focus, blue mouth stretching in a grin.

"Horsemen," he gurgle, "here at las-kh! Horsemen."

John scowl. "Say what?"

"Pay no heed," Monk, "we figure in his eschatology. The chiliast saw us coming."

"Huh?" John, "chili WHO?"

Bart's grin widen, button eyes agleam. "Yayyyuusss! Onward, horsemen. For thine is the gnn-kh! Kingdom."

John step up with a curse, plant a boot on Bart's chest and lean over: plop, a spitwad fizzing grey on Bart's brow.

"You gon' see my KINGdom soon enough, bitch. And I ain't HORSIN' around."

Bartlett's grin shade to a grimace. "I yield, horseman! I ffp-kh! yield!"

John give me a look. "Corny little putz, ain't he?"

"Little horse putz," Wald, "heh heh."

John step back, hold up his hand: his wristblade shafting out agleam. "See this, Bart? You don't behave, I'm gon' rip your ragass to ribbons."

"True," Monk nodding vigorous, "he's deadliest when he alliterates. Resistance is futile."

Bartlett blink, blood blotching his nose and chin. A weird look in his eyes: not fear. More like relish. Look of a lone vulture at a desert hecatomb –

John mutter, turn, start walking. "Showtime, girls. Got a stage to set."

I grunt, give Monk a look. "You want to give him a hand, Monk son?"

Monk nod, take a step, pause. "No, I'm afraid I don't. Not really."

I shrug. "Whatever."

John stride on to room's end, pause at the gurney altar and shove it aside with his foot. Crash: gurney hitting the wall, chalice toppling over. Old ichor on new turd.

"YeeEEH!" Wald, "ooOOP!"

Monk with hand raised, going: "Idiot children, desist. Musn't rouse the neighbors."

John spit, step up to the cross, tear the dead goat off its perch and fling it across the room.

"Flying satyr!" yips Monk, the corpse in degenerate trajectory landing heavy on Bartlett's mug. Bart flinching spasmodic, his cry muffled by the critter's bloody flank.

"DON'T YOU MOVE NOW, CART BART!" bawl John from room's end, "DON'T LET ME SEE YOU MOVE."

Pause, the room in echo. Bartlett motionless, arms outspread, face obscured by goat-flesh.

"Bartlegoat the Snoutsucker," I go laughing, Wald hopping cachinnate, John "Harf! Harf!", Monk's smile rimed with frost.

John turn cackling, grab the stem of the cross, pull one of its arms over his shoulder and start walking. The foot of the cross drag along the floor, catching rhythmic on tile seams, John squishing turds in approach, squelching dung like old Abner Snopes. Us watching appreciative, Wald yelping each time John step in crap, Monk humming a countrified Saxon hymn:

When I survey the fulvous cross,
That bleedin' hebe, that sad ol' hoss,
My richest gain I count but loss,
When I kiss the ass of Massah Boss –

He drag his wood to room's centre, John. Then he position himself and drop the load. Thud-squelch: the cross landing lengthwise on floorslop, its head pointing north, foot south, one arm east, the other west.

"Bravo," Monk applauding, "neatly done."

"Radical," me, "copacetic."

John look up, brow mottled. "Zip it and hand me that sack."

I blink. "You mean this here goody sack?"

"No, yo' little puppy chow nutsack."

"Nut chow," Wald, "zip sack. Heh heh."

I mutter, grab the sack, drag it over panting.

"You gonna, oof! You gonna do him now?"

John spit. "Nope. I'm gon' wait till fuckin' Santyclaus show up nakkid."

"Santyfuck," Wald, "heh heh."

I let go the sack, straighten wincing. Bartlett by the door immobile, goat on face.

"Say now, Cart Bart," I go, "you ready to get it OANE?"

"Mmph!" Bart, fingers wagging, "mmmph!"

292

John snort, walk over, kick the goat off Bart's mug. "Trippin' time beeyatch. Saddle up."

"Yeh!" Wald, "trip. TRIP – "

John bend, grab Bart's beard, straighten, start walking.

"Waah!" me, "wahhaaah! – "

"Yeeh!" Wald, "yeeHEEH! – "

Bart's mug in red contort, heels dragging, John like a squire taking his shag-dawg for a country stroll.

He haul Bart over, position him over the cross and let go. Ka-thump: Bartlett supine once more, in pantomime crucifixion.

I nod approving. "Good work, friar. We all set."

"Sheeat," John, "no fuckin' thanks to YOU."

I smile pollyannish, turn. "Come on up now, fellas. Dig the hatchetman's handiwork."

We gather around, goofing on Bart. Him with his coat pulled asunder, chalk chest ribbed in intaglio. His belly caved, spine-stuck.

John cackle. "This gon' be a first for you, Bart. You gon' LOVE what's comin' up."

Bart's head turn, orbs unblinking. "I yield," he croak, "I yield to the kl-kh! horsemen."

John scowl. "Slut, you best quit with that horse – "

"Whoa," me, "whoa HO!"

"Huh?" John, "wha – "

I point. "Dig it. Bart got himself a boner."

John blink, break out in a grin. Bart's grass skirt breached, an engorged glanhead poking up through the fronds.

"Well SHEEAT!" John, "preacherman runnin' up his FLAGpole!"

"Yeh!" Wald, "BONER FLAG! Heh heh."

"Ohhh that sweet pine woody," me, "that old time priapus."

"My very words," Monk.

Bart slack-mouthed, unblinking.

Minutes pass. Us like garden-keeps digging a new sprout.

"It's curved," goes John, "fuckin' sickle."

"Nope," me, "this sickle don't fuck. It slice and cut."

"A heliotropic phallus," Monk, "it bends sunward."

"Sick fuck," Wald, "heh heh."

"Dig that glanhead," I go, "discoloured pyramid with an eye at the apex."

"Glan dig," Wald, "heh heh."

John mutter, reach with his right foot, tap the curved shaft of Bart's dong. Bart grunt, blow his wad: curdled jizm erupting from his toadstool in three spurts. Spurt One hit Monk's eyelens, Spurt Two his beard, Spurt Three in failed ascent landing on John's boot.

Silence: Monk impassive, beard and lens a-drip, Wald shuddering ecstatic, John studying his boot, preacher-spunk globbed yellow on black.

"Well," sighs Monk, stepping back, "another day, another dollop."

"Heeesh!" Wald flailing tarantistic, "yeeheeeesh! – "

"An offering, horsemen!" gurgle Bart, eyes lidded, "an offerrr-kh!-KH! – "

John make an animal sound, extend his sullied boot, wipe off on Bart's thigh. Then with a banzai warrior-shout he leap high, land hard on Bart's crotch: iron heel on limp bizkit.

Bartlett sit up with a long rasping inhalation. For a second he stay that way, graven in voiceless scream. Then he convulse, torque out from under John's boot and begin scurrying on all fours, yapping and pissing, Wald with a yawp leaping astride going: "HOSSIE GIDDYAP! HOSSIE GIDDYAP! – "

John stand by a moment, nonplussed. Then he skip up, slam a boot in Bartlett's flank. Bart yelping out loud, shooting a sharp turd through the fronds of his skirt and collapsing in a heap, Wald rolling off nimble, leaping upright.

"Well goddamn," I go, "sprightly move there, Wald."

Wald grin, point. "Turd. Heh heh."

I look up, spot it: Bartlett's turd up on the ceiling, stuck in the eye of a haemorrhoid.

"Well sheeat," John mystified, "how'd it get up THERE."

I shake my head. "Wonders abound, brothers. Wonders abound."

"Strange ascension," Monk.

Him still with jizz-sullied lens, beard clotted.

"Monk son," I go, "you gonna wipe off that colostrum?"

Monk look at me cryptic, take off his glasses, wipe off on his robe. I watch, awaiting the next move, but no. He make no attempt to get the jizz off his beard. Nor even to spread it around, work it in. *Why,* I wonder, *why. The novelty of it mayhap? No, can't be. He's had nad-aspic trapped in his beard before. In his lashes, nosehairs, pit-tufts. And way down where the sun don't ever shine, not unless you bend over and spread 'em with a spud wrench at high noon –*

"You'll never know, I'm afraid."

I frown. "Huh?"

"The answer," Monk, "you'll never ever know."

I make a sputtering sound, move. "The pox on THAT. You boys get the preacherman ready. I'm gonna go check out the joint."

"Sheeat," John, grabbing Bart's beard, "figures."

I walk past the roach box to a passage leading in. Grope for the switch, click: some sight. The floor lousy with raw chitlins, turkey necks, duck bills, ox-tongues, snakeheads, toad legs, crow beaks, bloody rooster wings, sheep scuts, regurgitate goose liver, masticated corn, mounds of caseated kidney mush piled knee high, spilling into the kitchen at left.

I trudge forward three steps, reach, flip the kitchen switch. More of the same, only worse. Piles of sodden offal on the floor, the walls slathered with nameless colloids and micturate plasms. In one corner, an object that resemble a jerrybuilt cello: a polished pachyderm ribcage with mooseguts stretched end to end, a humeral bow resting atop. Flash vision: Stradivarius eating his dead heart out.

I turn off the kitchen light, wade on five steps and pause: the crapper door ajar. I shove the door open, hit the switch. Fresh vista: severed dog-ears piled ankle high, smashed land-crabs, the sink clogged with green vomit. In the tub, a bloated hog mired in concrete, a red ribbon around its neck, the words UNCLEAN BEAST scrawled on its flank. Grunt, goes the hog trying to move, grunt. I bend, scoop up a handful of chitlins, toss it in the tub and move on.

A door stands ajar at corridor's end, light showing dim within. I tramp up, push, step in and pause. A cauldron sit in the middle of the room, a cast iron vat brimming with jungle boar hogballs and rocky mountain bull testicles. Above, a taxidermal skunk hangs snout down, forepaws extended like it mean to dive in and scarf up them gonads.

I turn squinting. Biolab snuffshots show on the flanking wall: pustular ectomorphs with stub hardons roasting, slashing, skewering, drowning critters with bright torture-tech gizmos. Biblical phrases phosphoresce on the wall opposite, lines scrawled in commination (Hank 2:4, Bubba 3:2, Dalmatians 7:9, Ingrid 6:8). But it's not the Word I'm interested in, nawsuh. It's them dudes beneath: Phuc and Thuc sixty-nined on a soiled mat, Phuc with Thuc's hallux (big toe) in his mouth, Thuc with Phuc's hallux in his. Them laid shut-eye, naked in uroboric stupor –

"Gnnyaarr! Gnnyaaarrkh!"

I turn, blinking. A bamboo cage stand in the near corner, a

figure crouched within. *Anthropoid?* No, sapien. Female. Bart's gook slave.

I eyeball the cage a moment, hackles rising. Then I move up a few steps, wave: "How now, mama kid."

"GnnnyaaAARH!"

I make a shushing sound, move closer. "Easy now, kid. No hurt. Looksee is all."

"GnnaaaRRH!" the kid retreating, "gnnyaaakh!"

I sit on my haunches, smile reassuring. The kid look pubescent, but it's hard to tell. The cage hasn't been hosed out in a while, her skin caked with blood crud.

"You ok in there, toots?" I go, "hey?"

The kid cower, eyes swirling lucent. Her pupils injected with gasoline by the look of 'em, her lids scorched. Half her head raked bald (the scalp embossed with bits of stained glass), the other half sprouting yak hair matted and clumped. Her nose scarred and battered, her tongue drawn out askew and stapled to bruised lips. One side of her mouth sewn shut with twine, the other side sliced wide, teeth missing. Chancres and running sores on her arms and legs, strips of beef jerky thatched over her crotch. Nasty, sure, but not all bad: her cage don't have a lock, just a bolt.

I rise, reach, slide back the bolt. The cage door swing open soundless, the kid leaping out with a shriek, ripping my nuts off with her teeth: CUT and REWIND. The cage door creak half-open, the kid shrinking back with a hiss.

"Easy now hon," I go, "no hurt. Come forth, Lazarus the Younger (distaff)."

The kid cringe, eyes glossed in rondure.

I step back and wait, counting. *One-hockaloogee, two-hockaloogee, three-hockaloogee...* nothing. No movement. Don't look like the kid's going anywhere this night.

I shrug, smile. "It's all right, toots. You come out when you're good and ready. No fear. We're takin' goooood care of Massah Bart."

The kid blink, emit a low growl.

I nod, snap a salute, start for the door: thunk. My foot striking something: elk antlers fastened to a pair of pink stucco menhirs, procured from the Ordo Templi Orientis. I castigate the menhirs, chastise the antlers and move on, pausing an instant at the door. Last backward glance: Phuc and Thuc still in Urobor, kid in her cage staring.

Back through the passageway to the front room, John on his knees looking up as I enter: "Well lookee. Bitch go walkabout, come back filthy and stinkin'."

"Bitch stink," Wald, playing idiot punchinello, "filthy cum. Heh heh."

I chuckle, walk past the roach box, pause. Bartlett belly up on the cross, arms outspread and taped down. His ankles taped left over right, foot-perch pushed up against the right heel. Bart's boner in evidence once more, puce glans pulsing obscene. His lips parted wet, eyes alive with a mad shine –

"Look what I found, Gunga Din."

I turn. Monk at room's end, holding up a buckled tome.

I smile, walk up nodding. "I know what THAT is. The Omega Bible: breviary, Church of Ancients. Its spine fashioned from infant vertebrae, each page a flayed visage marked with a warlock quill scratching glyphs and ciphers abstracted from reverberate hell-screams, the many-keyed excruciata of the multiply damned. YES?"

Monk blink, exhale tussive. "Not quite. Just a dowser's guide to the Pacific Rim."

"Ex-screw-shitter," Wald, "heh heh – "

Rustle. I turn. The roaches done with their clusterfuck,

arrayed now along the walls of their box. Big critters, five inches on average, an ochre exclamation mark on each thorax, tiny fire-lit fanions on the tips of their feelers –

"Your call, slut. We waitin'."

I blink. John still on his knees, deep scowl.

I shrug, walk around to the foot of the cross. A square, white display cloth laid out there, objects placed atop in neat dispose. Sacrificial desiderata agleam, ready for use: one heavy duty nailgun, one hard glass cruet full of blue treacle, one wash-leather fob bulging with leeches, one pair of latex gloves, one pair of ridge-tooth pliers, one pair of tweezers, one large staple-gun, one dead goldfish, one pair of syntheplast sunflowers, one black-tulip corsage.

"All there," I go straightening, "let's rock."

"Yeh!" Wald slapping his nuts, "ROCK!"

John shoot a spitball over his shoulder, reach for the nailgun.

"Hold," I go, "you forgot the Manoeuvre."

John pause, look up with a snarl. "The hell with THAT. Let the fucker scream."

I shake my head. "Too risky. And besides, the Meister's Notion call for the Manoeuvre."

John mutter, rise. "Now Cart Bart," he go, "this here Manoeuvre 's gon' HURT like the muthafuckin' dicksuckens. But think of it this way: it be a fuckin' PICNIC compared to what's comin' next."

"Hurt fuck," Wald, "come picnic. Heh heh."

Bartlett raise his head, frown quizzical. "Manoo-ver?"

I smile indulgent. "Yayup. The Maeterlinck Manoeuvre, devised by Modred Maeterlinck: Teutonic hermaphrodite smut icon and netscape idoru. The Manoeuvre mutes screams down to a hoarse exhalation."

"Whore's exhalation," Wald, "heh heh."

Bartlett smile, let his head drop. "Kingdom!" he croak, "exile and kingdom! – "

My breath catch. Flashvision: Bart's chest a galley, his ribs oars, his belly a heaving sea, his schlong a defeated leviathan in red spume –

"HEY!"

I wince. "Yeah. Go ahead."

John curse, step up, bear down on Bart's chest with one knee. "Awwhh!" Bart, "awwkh!"

Wald with a squeal breaking into a jig.

John reach, grab Bart's throat-apple pincer-like, yank it up hard, twist it like a knob, push down hard. His movements forceful, precise, Bartlett's mouth in agonized rictus, blood and catarrh sparging.

I applaud mute. "Good work there, friar. Been a while since the last time, but baby you still got the TOUCH."

"Sheeat," John rising, "like humpin' a hamster in a chicken coop. Kinda dreck you don't forget."

"Oh quite," Monk strolling up, "with similes like that, who needs metaphors."

"Meta-hump," Wald, "heh heh."

John suck spit, bend, scoop the nailgun off the display cloth. "Nailgun crucifixion now, Bart. New-fangled sheeat, but a man got to keep up with the times. You still be a saviour, but danged if I know whut it is you be savin' – "

He take a stride, John, step on Bart's right wrist, aim the gun at Bart's palm and pull the trigger: kathunk, kathunk, kathunk, three nails through, Bart with mouth agape screaming soundless.

"Well hell," I go, "that ol' Manoeuvre sure workin' good."

John snort, straighten, step sideways over Bart's mug, press a boot to his left wrist and repeat the procedure: kathunk,

kathunk, kathunk, three nails through the left palm, Bart putting out a faint throat-whistle, bug eyes brimming.

"Ain't smilin' NOW, are ya," John, "AY?"

"He is," Monk six paces off, "from the wrong end."

John cackle, step back. "Keep them feet together now, Cart Bart. I know you taped up and all, but you still got to be a good boy."

"YEH!" Wald, hashing crotch-meat, "goooOOOD! Heh heh – "

John squat, align Bart's toes over the foot-perch, take aim, fire: kathunk, kathunk, kathunk, two preacher-feet nailed to one oakwood perch, Bart's mouth narrowing to an 'O', eyes in crazed nystagmus streaming tears.

"Not to worry now Bart," John rising, "it get worse before it get better. Only, better's worse'n worse, so we're talkin' one NASTY little hoedown."

"That makes sense," Monk, "post mortem."

"Nasty little ho," Wald frothing buccal, "heh heh."

I click my tongue. "Speed it up now friar, sirrah. Sands of time, and such."

John give me a look. "Mah own muthafuckin' SWEET TIME or not at all. Dig?"

I slap my right cheek hard, stick a knuckle in my left eye. "Dig GOOD, massah boss, dig GOOOOOD."

John chuckle, step sideways, replace the nailgun.

"Doctor TJ," he announce, pulling on the latex gloves, "Doctor TJ go to WORK."

"Oh yeah!" me applauding, "YEAH!"

Wald breathless, quaking rapid, Monk impassive.

He grab the pliers with his left hand, John, hold up his right. Click: wristblade shafting up hungry. Bart with teeth bared, eyes shut, blood pooling around his hands and feet.

John step up, pliers in hand, straddle Bart's chest, lever his mouth open with the wristblade. Then he reach in with the pliers, pull out Bart's fungoid tongue and slice it off clean at the root. Bartlett in deep tremor, gurgling red.

I nod approving. "Sharp work there champ, but dig it: Bart's boner ain't dead yet."

John look over his shoulder, look away. "Fine. Make it easier to cut."

"Mmmnnngff!" Wald in orgasmic tumult, "mmnnnffffrr! – "

John rise, tongue in hand, move back a step, squat, slide his hand under Bart's rump, locate the anal aperture and work the tongue in with thumb and forefinger.

Bart twitch, gurgle.

"Bet THAT'S a first," John rising a-grin, "first time he have his tongue up his own tripe-hole."

I shrug. "You never know with preacherboys. No tellin' what they get up to, tongue-wise."

John cackle, spit: loogie at my feet green and steaming.

"Capital work," me, "onward."

John grunt, toss the pliers back on the sheet. He hold still a moment, clenched and glowering. Then he whip around sudden, grab Bartlett's boner with a bloody glove and whack it clean off with a blade-stroke. A red geyser burst up from Bart's crotch and arc across, Wald with a strangled cry leaping sideways, intercepting the arc with his hand. Bart white-eyed, a loud sputter sounding under his croupe.

I shake my head. "Oh well, that tongue didn't stay in long. Sound like Bart shit himself good."

"Aahglllmnn!" Wald on tiptoe, stemming gore, "nnglllmn!"

John curse, grab the staple gun, move up, cram the severed schlong in Bart's gape mouth. Then he push up on Bart's jaw, pinch together his painted lips and staple his mouth shut:

kerchunk, kerchunk, kerchunk, kerchunk. Bart now quaking livid, lashes aflutter.

"Circle complete," goes John rising, "Bart chompin' pecker chow, preacher style."

I tilt my head indulgent. "Aww hon, the things you say, the things you DO."

"Quite," Monk, "he resurrects the Albigensian heresy."

"And intimates a new Defenestration," me.

Wald on his knees, gore-drenched, Bart's geyser diminished to a gout.

John step back, drop the staple gun, turn.

"You know whut else we oughtta do? We oughtta cork out Bart's eyeballs and pluck off his nuts. Then stick them nuts in place of his eyeballs and them eyeballs in place of his nuts. Then slice off them little preacher nipples and stick 'em in his ears."

Pause. Silence and slow time. Us motionless, staring.

At length, Monk hush-voiced, going: "Well, colour me impressed. And more. Brother John overwhelms with his inventiveness, his PANACHE. A testicle-orb exchange. Nipple earplugs. I second the motion without reserve. By all means, more sacerdotal mutilation. Imprimatur and nihil obstat."

"Nut cork," Wald in a whisper, "testicle plug. Heh heh."

I take a deep breath, shake my head rueful.

"Sorry fellas. Bart's already had his motion, by the look and smell of it. No further motions AT THIS JUNCTURE, I'm sad to say. Friar, your suggestion have much merit, it tempt and titillate. And normally I'd PAY BIG to see the fucker's nuts in his eye-sockets, his eyeballs nestled warm in his nutsack. But not here, not now. The Notion make no provision for it. And chances are, the Meister wouldn't approve. So let's just finish up. The trimmings as planned."

John frown, look at Monk, look back. "You sure?"

I nod rueful. "Sure. Sorry to say."

"Warm trim," Wald, "heh heh."

John shrug, bend, pick up the nailgun, the dead goldfish, the syntheplast sunflowers, the black tulip corsage. Then he step up, stand astride Bart's chest, bend, nailgun the goldfish dead centre between Bart's eyebrows: kathunk. Bart flinching with eyes closed, a throaty groan.

I chuckle. "Sound like that dickhead startin' to push up against his tonsils."

"Uh-huh," John, "deep-throatin' his own meat."

"Deep tonsil dick," Wald, "heh heh."

John move back some, position the corsage between Bart's tits, nailgun it to his sternum: kathunk. Bart flinch, no sound, eyes shut. Yielding to nescience by the look of him. Destination: Erebus.

"And flowers for the preacherman," goes John, sticking the sunflowers up Bart's nose stem-first, "reeeeal PURTY."

"Accolades, friar," I go, "clinical execution of procedure."

"Grace and precision," Monk.

"Execution," Wald rising, "fry. Heh heh – "

He shuffle up bedraggled, Wald, scoop up a palmful of Bart-gore, slap it over his own crotch.

I applaud with one hand, both elbows. "Good move there, Wald. No sense lettin' that spill go to waste."

"Yeh!" Wald unzipped, greasing his dong, "spill. Heh heh."

John mutter, step back: squelch.

"Well sheeat," him looking down, "preacherman bleedin' up the joint somethin' FIERCE."

I nod. "Pretty soon be a blood-dimmed tide washing our ragasses out and away."

John chuckle, drop the nailgun on the tainted display cloth, grab the wash-leather fob and the tweezers.

"Well," he go grinning, "like mah ol' pappy used to say most every night: it's SUCK TIME!"

"Waahhhaaahh!" me, "yayup."

"PAPPY SUCK!" Wald blood-crotched, "heh heh."

"The crucified one shall be leeched pre-mortem," Monk solemn, "so it is written."

John frown, work open the fob, stick in the tweezers, draw out a leech.

"Hm," Monk, "rather large for an unfed leech, yes?"

I nod. "Yayup. But these ain't the usual kind. These boys be splice mutants rejiggered for fun and profit. They suck long and hard, swell to the size of South Texas shoats, burst with a deep basso organ note. Worth waitin' around to see and hear, but we can't. The Meister beckons."

John step up, place the first leech on Bart's left palm. Step sideways, place the second leech on his right palm. Move back, place the third and fourth leech on his brow, flanking the goldfish. Move back some more, place the fifth and sixth leech on his needle-point tits. Then taking a big backward step, he place the seventh leech on Bart's crotch, right over his missing dick.

"Superlative," Monk, nodding.

"In excelsis," me, not nodding.

"Sexcelsis," Wald, sheathing his daubed wang, "heh heh."

John move a step, drop the fob and tweezer, reach into his pocket, bring out the sealed syringe bag.

"Time to play doctor again, bitch."

I scowl. "Play. PLAY?"

"Ketch," John, "whore."

I catch the bag two-handed, shoot spit through bared teeth, walk around and stand by the head of the cross. Bart's leech and goldfish brow directly below, his eyes shut. Far gone, by the look of him, pain a seething excrescence in catacombed nerve-depths.

I kneel, humming a bardo prayer, unseal the bag, fish out the syringe and the blue vial. Then I uncap the needle, push down the plunger, wedge a foot under Bart's skull, take aim and stab down hard through the crown. The needle go in easy enough, but the thrust seem to trigger something: a faint banshee squeal erupt from Bart's throat (cry of a rooster castrate), his torment gathering in his belly and squeezing out of his navel. Torment sarxed in the shape of a tarantula.

"HotDAMN!" John, "a frickin' SPIDER!"

"Alimentary arachnid," Monk, "immaculately conceived."

"Not an arachnid per se," me, "an arachno-crustacean birthed in an amniotic blood-swill – "

"HhhhhnnnrrraaAAAGRRNNKH!"

I start, turn: Bart's feral hump-slave crouched in the passageway, hip-deep in filth.

"YeeEEP!" Wald bolting aside, "wooOOP!"

"Ah," Monk nodding, "quite."

"Well I will be PECKER-whacked at a wiener PARADE," John, "I will be – "

"NNNnNNRRAACKH!" goes the kid, gasoline eyes fixed on Bart's gut-whelped critter-bug.

I clap, punch the air. "Go for it, kid. GO!"

The spider-crab hold still a moment. Then it crawl off Bart's belly, hit the floor with a click and head straight for the passage. The kid watch it approach, swirl-eyed. Three feet from the roach-box, the critter pause, change direction. Too late. The kid pounce on it with a shriek, crush it with both hands, cram it sideways in her mouth and shuttle back into the passage.

"Awww MAAAMA!" John ecstatic, "wish I'da had me a HANDY cam!"

"Candy, yes," Monk, "ham."

Wald wide-eyed, whispering.

"Well," I sigh, "that's that. Over and out."

John turn, grin shading to a scowl. "You ain't done yet."

I look down, hold the syringe with my left hand, pull on the plunger with my right. Brain-fluid sucks up slow, blue, cloudless.

"Mmmm," John, "juice me."

"Indeed," Monk, "delectable in its way."

Wald still in shock, whispering.

I brace a foot against Bart's skull, hold the syringe with both hands and pull. The needle emerge smooth, but Cart Bart grimace, put out a subsonic throat-squeal.

"Huh?" John mock-solicitous, "that you Bart? That YOU?"

Bart's eyes open wide an instant then shut fast, candent fire ants squeezing from his canthi. I rise with a yelp, step back. Some sight: ants streaming out the corners of his eyes, fanning around his head in fulgent aureole.

"Well, I will be humped and hashed by a corn-fed cracker," John, "it just keep OANE gettin' better."

"Oh rather," Monk, "somewhere."

"Corn crack shit hump," Wald in a whisper, "heh heh."

We watch: ants around Bart's head in a spreading halo. Myself goofing on the scene with head bowed, knees half-bent, John gnawing on a hangnail, Wald putting out a series of well-timed yips.

At length Monk with a cough, going: "A thing of duty is a ploy forever. But on with the TASK. YES?"

I blink, straighten, hold up the blue vial, push the needle through the seal and squeeze.

"Mmm," John, "make it hurt."

"Humors capsuled for posterity," Monk.

"Posterity pudding," Wald, "heh heh."

I chuckle, pull out, hold up the vial.

"Well," Monk, "there you have it."

"Uh-huh," John, "that about wrap it up."

"UP," Wald, "heh heh."

I nod, cap the needle, bag the vial and syringe, look up with a grin.

"Brothers, I am DONE for the night."

"Donne?" Monk, "I would've said Baudelaire. Poe. Byron. Rimbaud. Even Suckling or Lovelace."

"Lovesuck. Heh heh."

I turn. Wald on his knees, eyes bloodshot. Before him a dwindling cuesta of spit-froth.

I raise a hand to my lips, blow him a kiss.

"Terminus, Wald. We through for the night."

Monk make a trilling sound. "Not quite. Bellyburn."

I frown. "How could I forget."

"I could show ya how," John, "but it'd hurt. REAL bad."

I wink, toss him the bag. "Tempting, toots, but we got to get on."

John put away the bag, step over to the display cloth, grab the cruet of blue treacle.

"You'll dig this'n Jayb," he goes, "it's a new one."

I bite down on my tongue, slap my left tit.

"Don't doubt it for a minute."

He uncork the cruet, John, step up, lean over Bart's torso and pour a blue ounce in the hollow of his navel.

"Death be not proud," Monk.

"Extinction omphalos," me.

"Dead phallus," Wald, "heh heh."

John straighten, cork the cruet, drop it on the display cloth. Then he draw up the four cloth-ends, tie a fat granny knot, pull open the mouth of the goody sack and shove the bundle in.

"Capital," Monk, "swoop most foul."

"John, thy name be something other than decorum," me.

"Dick-in-rum," Wald, "heh heh."

John hold the sack by the neck, hoist it over his shoulder.

"You ready, Monk?"

Monk nod, step up, stand facing John. Bart crucified between.

"On the count of three," John, "one. Two – "

They begin at three, Monk and John, their lips pursed, nares flared: a whistle toneless, high-pitched, unwavering.

"Nngnnaa!" Wald, hands clapped over his ears, "nngnnaaa – "

Myself with a grimace thinking: *music of Erich Zann. Etheric barriers shattered. Amorph and polymorph demons pour through. Usher in Armageddon and apocalypse –*

"Phhweeee – " Monk and John, "phweeeee – "

On and on, the roaches in their keep frenzied, Wald on one foot ataxial, the treacle on Bart's gut starting to smoke, sparkle –

Whup: the treacle bursting aflame, a blue votive shimmer there on Bart's navel.

They whistle on for a bit, Monk and John, then stop simultaneous. Silence. Roaches capsizing moribund, Wald working an elbow out of his ear. Silence and blue fire-crackle.

"Ohhh," I sigh, "oooOOHHHH."

"Ahhh," Monk nodding, "aaaAAHHHH – ."

"The pox oane THAT," John turning with a scowl, "fucker don't look like he's breathin'. Look like he's DEAD."

"Dead pox fuck," Wald still on one foot, "heh heh – "

"KLLLKHRRRFF!"

I start, look up. Spirit guide redux. Stinger, Finesse, Oblongata, Noodlebear, on a crown of thorns zipping about at great speed, inches from the ceiling.

I watch, eyes brimming. Bright tear-pearls squeeze out of my fossilized brine-ducts, merge at the tip of my nose, fall in trans-audible coronach.

"Awwww girls," I whimper, shaking my fool skull, "y'all started out cute as buttons, but here y'all are, hag-sluts gone bestial. Y'all with simian mugs, eagle beaks, fur on chin and chest, sabre teeth. Not to mention pointed lynx ears and non-reflective compound orbs, nictitating membranes included on a strictly need-to-blink basis – "

"HEY!"

I cringe: John glaring.

"Whut you oane about, ay?"

I sniff. "Nothing you'd understand or apperceive – "

"Oblongata!" exclaim Wald, "oooooh!"

Him looking up gape-mouthed.

He SEES them Ethel, the neonate SEES –

Boot-thud: John brushing past. "Time. Bitches OUT."

"But wait!" I go plaintive, "wait – "

No use. Monk heedless moving doorward, Wald still gape-mouthed, following automatic.

I watch them step out, turn for a last look. The Right Reverend T. Carter Bartlett martyred supine. Cart Bart ritually mutilated, leeched, ornamented and sanctified –

I throw back my head, vent a loud idiot yodel. Nothing. Bart immobile, the fire on his gut burning blue.

I shrug, hop back thrice, pause by the door.

"Exeunt now, Cart Bart. Exeunt and alarums. Destination armadillo. Withhold laudanum? – "

"NNNNnnnnNNNGRRAAARRKHH!"

Bart's hump-slave bounding out the passage (glimmer of coloured scalp-glass) and falling to, scarfing fire ants by the handful (*entrée*: bugs, *plat*: Bart), Noodlebear above, thorn-fleshed, clawing a ceiling haemorrhoid, myself recoiling in crash satori, lunging for the door, *bash mah dawg-meat Ethel, BASH IT:* out.

***

Ruffled shoreline, sea foaming white. Dusky nymphs in slow dance, swaying palm fronds, myself a morphologically challenged midget conductor waving balsa batons, monsoon clouds in dark orchestra, liminal music of mama rain: cut.

Myself naked on a roach-wing raft, blue rapids. Steering with a pair of pliers, my pecker a six-barrel nailgun shooting leeches, tweezers, staples, black tulips, goldfish. Bwooph: the rapids bursting aflame, the sky a mirrored pate raining ants through a hoop of fuchsia haemorrhoids –

I start, blink. *Where?* Here. Purr of engine, hiss of vented air. John at left silent, Wald in back yip and mumble, Monk working a denouement mantra in fierce whisper.

I sit up, rub my eyes. Signs on either side, bright neon. Signs in dog-Latin, hoch-Yoruba, Basque-Hopi patois. Signs I recognize: East Zone, Ching Hwa Mbogo Stein Avenue.

"Makin' good time Teej," I slur, "look like we're well on schedule."

John snort. "No thanks to YOU, suckin' sleep-dick."

I chuckle, scrape gunk off my teeth. "I'll pretend I didn't hear that."

The car gather speed, crunching glass. Ching Hwa Mbogo Stein alight but silent, not a soul in sight. A post-riot calm: cars bellied, storefronts smashed, hydrants a-gush, sidewalks lousy with trash and cullet. No glam whores with rainbow-mesh coiffs, no Beast'n'Midget streetside acts, no boon country bottom-feeders trawling slumspice, no gangland proles rumbling with chain and knife –

"The news got around, it would appear," Monk, "yes?"

"Huh?" John, "news?"

"Prisonbreak news," Monk, "Pigs out of town."

John grunt. "Hard to keep dope like that under wraps."

"Hard under," Wald, "heh heh."

Ching's open air market drift past at right, redolent: pluvial reek of fishrot and glandular incense, food odours in olfactory conflict: shit and balsam. Ahead at left, a battered Pigmobile on the sidewalk.

"Dig it," John slowing, "harf!"

I dig. Dead Pig reserve cross-legged on the hood of his car, a lamp shade screwed into the top of his skull, red bulb in his mouth alight.

"A work of art, no less," pronounce Monk, "East Zone avant-garde."

I nod, watching it recede. "Sure enough. But what I'm wondering is: how in hell that bulb stay on?"

John snort. "Easy. You stick the bulb in his mouth, yank the cord out his ass and hook it up to the car cell. Old trick, done it before."

"Oh no doubt," Monk, "couldn't be otherwise."

"Old hooker bulb ass," Wald, "heh heh."

The car slow some more, nose right, ease to a stop. Just ahead, the mouth of an alley.

"Well girls," John killing the engine, "been a while, but we here again."

I slap the side of my head, take a deep breath.

"I'm startin' to get the jitters, boy."

"As well you should," Monk, "the Meister soon to judge our offerings."

"Sheeat," John shoving his door open, "ain't gon' be a problem."

We emerge, secure the car, start walking. Past an open gutter, a sign that read *Seahorse Sushi, Bear Gland Soda*, on into the alley, a glam pimp sprawled there, face down in his own sick. Scrawny little putz with a fur cape, peacock headress, shock-pink slacks pulled back to reveal bloody shin-stumps. His boots sitting by, with both feet in.

The alley take a turn ten yards down, dead-end at a door. WOLFMEAT read the sign above, *For Madmen Only*.

We walk up, push through. A bar room: wan light, fauvist décor, wharf grunts at box tables nodding out over grog steins, lamps nimbused phlegm-yellow. In the corner a stripper dais, sign above that reads VINCENT VAN GO GO. Above, a domed ceiling black, with vortices of sidereal light, a severed ear hung from each vortex –

"Sheeat," John, "dig it."

I turn, squinting. Mickey Coltrane hunched asleep by the bar, tribal scars fluorescent. A row of bright alloy grafts spiked across his bald pate, front to back.

"Yo Mickey," goes John, "ya hear me, Mick?"

No response. Mickey stupored immobile, soundless.

John curse, stomp the floor. "MICK! Your MUSCLE-bitch need to give us a bungwash, HEAR?"

Mickey start, look up bleary-eyed.

"Hey there fellas," he mumble, "what gives."

"Same dreck that give this time o' year Mick," John, "the ol' gut-wash, Big Mama Grace."

Mickey sigh. "Go on in. She's waitin'."

John shake his head, step away. "Fuckin' freak," he mutter, striding into the vestibule, us following indian file. A light show ahead, a small lounge coming into view.

"Mama Grace!" bark John stomping in, "sheeat, where she at."

I step in, glance around. "She'll be in. Best sit and wait."

"Why THANKye," John, "I'd've plumb PISSED m'self if ya hadn't TOLD me."

"Piss-plum," Wald, "heh heh."

I sink in an armchair, John and Wald slumping opposite, Monk folding himself in full lotus. Silence. The lounge refracted through the gauze of my lashes, smell of musk and old leather, the walls pasted with muscle droogs in deep flex, blood-gorged beef in vascular writhe.

Minutes pass, purling. Mind-echo, my thoughts adrift, fatigue washing up like dark water. In hypnopomp a vision spreading like a scroll. A tattoo drill-pic on muscled flesh: Red Riding Hood banging Big Bad Wolf with a corkscrew strap-on, grandma perched with prurient handycam, tittering –

"You boys ready for a CLEANOUT?"

I start. Grace at the door, grey eyes sardonic under a cropped red mohawk. Her thick, ungulate form sheathed in leopardskin leggings, chamois brogans and a blue compression crewtop that cling like sealskin. Muscles bunch and roll under the crewtop, tattoos flaring up her bison neck to the ridge of her jawline.

"Sheeat," John, "danged if it ain't the dagger dyke of Diddleville."

Grace's lips peel back from a rampart of metal teeth.

"You better be nice, hotshot. It's gonna be your ass in a minute."

"Sheeat. I had me a pain in the ass way before YOU showed."

"Hot pain ass shot," Wald, "heh heh."

Grace wink and flex: cannonballs rolling subdermal.

"Mean on the outside," she declare, "clean on the inside."

"Ah," Monk, "her aphorisms."

"Apho-jizms," Wald, "heh heh."

Grace clap: leathered palms in strike. "So which one of you cheese dicks gonna be first."

I shrug. "The medic gets washed first: part of the Meister's Notion. I was the medic this time, the one who worked the syringe."

Grace jerk her head. "You first then. Come on DOWN."

"Sheeat," John strumming his crotch, "next time you want yo' butt cleaned out, you come talk to Doc Peckerwang."

"Peckertime," Wald, "heh heh."

I rise, move to the door, wave a gladhand, step out. On through a passageway, Grace in lead. Watching her glutes ripple, arms swing wide over pulsing lats. Glaring down at my sneakerdogs going: "En garde Cornelius, attention, Valdez."

It look the same as ever, her clinic. Little square atrium cluttered, windowless. The walls lined with stool samples, pocket-size squirt pistols, suppositor spud guns. One large gloss showing a naked trucker hooked up to his fuel tank at midnight. With a caption that read:

My big rig colonic keeps me feelin' swell
Way out on the road, my shit don't smell

"Strip and sit," comes Grace's voice, "I'll be right with you."

I turn. "You want me to STRIP?"

Grace frown. "Not like you haven't done this before."

I shrug. "True. Can I keep the bandanna?"

She snort. "We're flushin' out your gut, not your head."

"Yayup. More's the pity."

"Set yourself up," she goes stepping away.

I sigh, start stripping. My eyes now on the Flusher, middle of the room. A mean-looking contraption: part womb-scrape unit, part neo-medieval torture gizmo. A cushioned perch with an inclined back, raised legrests in wide chevron. A metal culvert leading down to a heart-shaped floor drain, a tank above with a bung-tube pendant.

I finish stripping, pad over to the Flusher, plant my bare rump on the perch, spread my legs high and wide, pull down the greased bung tube and work it up where microbes feed darkling. The Flusher come on automatic, a whirr and a hum, fluid reaching into me like a cool finger.

I sit back, lulled by the hum. A strange scent fill the air: shit and Flusher Fluid. This here fluid being a melange of wassail, yak milk, fennel, fenugreek, blue nitric, powdered pitchblende, gator bile, fermented boar spit –

I start, turn. Grace looming up, grabbing the bung tube, yanking it out my ass.

"OW!" I go, "what in – "

"No more of this PUSSY shit. Time to get DOWN and DIRTY."

I stare. Big Grace now in green fatigues, hair pulled back. In her arms a Model-'T' Suppositor Spud Gun: GI Jane on dung detail.

"Awww SHIT," I go trying to sit up, "you're not – "

"SHIT is RIGHT! – "

Her boot on my bare chest, Spud barrel ramming cold up my croupe and thwumpf! thwumpf! thwumpf! thwumpf! four Suppositor missiles seething up my gut, myself yielding with an anguished croak, counting *one-hockaloogie, four hockaloogie, eight hockaloogie,* a rumble now in slow wax, rolling thunder in descent, a series of alimentary Richter-quakes and BOOM: Grace side-stepping with a flourish as a huge, horned bull-turd burst from my bung, seethe across like a torpedo and smash a stool-sample beakered opposite.

Pause in echo. Flusher hum. Grace turning wide-eyed:

"Jee-EEZ. That was MAJOR."

I groan, manage a smile. "Sure look like it. My spice-laved bowels pure, HELL-elujah. You gonna keep that there turd?"

Grace snort, lower her gun. "Damn right I am. Gonna pickle the sumbitch on the display case, replace the one you busted.

Hell, that's the biggest one I've killed yet."

"Glad I could help. But it ain't right, you killin' my first-born and KEEPIN' it – "

Grace step up, jam her hands under my armpits, hoist me off the Flusher. "No time for bare butt bellyaches, kid. You boys got an offerin' to make, remember?"

I rub my eyes, turn. My threads heaped by the wall.

"Offering, yeah. Thought we'd head down through the waiting lounge. That ok with you?"

Grace stare, shrug. "Figured you'd take the old Warehouse route, but this'n's fine with me."

"Yeah well," I go stepping weak-kneed, "I figured the same thing, but it was HIS call. What the Meister want, he GET."

"Uh-huh," Grace, "you need help gettin' dressed?"

I snort. "You WISH."

Grace grin: metal flash. "Go tell the hotshot I'm waitin'. Man owes me a whole mess o' NASTY and a buttload of pain."

I nod, finish dressing, snap her a scout salute, step out. Back through the passage into the waiting lounge, John looking up as I enter.

"Well now. Look like Mowgli got hisself flushed out GOOD."

"Yeh," Wald, "good flush. Heh heh."

I shake my head, shuffle across, lower myself in an armchair.

"Laugh it up while you can, fuckers," I go, "dish out the giggles. Because the FACT of the matter is, if RIGHTEOUS truth be RIGHTLY told: YOU'RE NEXT."

***

I, a bolus lodged in a rancher's gut. Directly below, the Elder Boli gathered in sederunt, pining for the Porcelain Celestium. *No such realm exist!* I squeak, *we are gut-bound, doomed to decay and compaction!*

Young whippersnapper! croak an Elder, *thou of little faith! Our Bible promise it! Our Prophets rant of it! The dark tortuous passage! The terminal light! The blue cooling waters! The White Porcelain Kingdom! –*

"Hmml?" me, "hmMMPH? – "

Struggling awake.

"Ass up slut. We done."

My vision swirl, clear. John with his boot on my crotch, scowling. Monk and Wald slack-faced beside.

I shove aside John's foot, cackle dry-mouthed.

"Look like you boys got worked over good."

John snarl, spit: colloid on my crotch sizzling green.

I grit my teeth, rise with a curse. "Where's Grace."

"Suckin' oane her dry milk jugs," John, "we ain't got time to kill."

"Jug time," Wald, "killsuck. Heh heh."

I stand in place a moment, muttering. Then I turn, move to the corner of the lounge. "Let's get to it."

"Yeah," John coming after, "git."

There's a camel-skin rug in the corner, pulled flat between two armchairs. I shove the chairs apart, kick aside the rug. A manhole cover shows beneath: smooth, two handles. I reach, grab both handles, lift the cover an inch, haul it aside.

"We-ell," John, "mean muscle mojo. For a bitch."

"Muscle mo-bitch," Wald, "heh heh."

I kneel, peer down the manhole: rungs leading down, light below. I grunt, turn on all fours, look up with a smirk.

"Last man down's a smack whore."

"As always," Monk.

"Sheeat."

"Whoresmack. Heh heh."

I descend easy, one rung at a time. Ten rungs down I pause, let go: thud, landing on both feet.

318

"Through," I go, "y'all come on down."

John appear a moment later, landing cat-footed. Monk next, robe billowing. Wald last, dropping clumsy, sprawling with a squawk. Brief spasm of mirth.

It's a catacomb we find ourselves in: the Meister's Warren. Limestone tunnels worming off in three directions, translucent cressets riveted to the walls. These here cressets full of burning creosote: spectral shine.

"Well," goes John looking around, "same as I remember it."

His voice in echo-cho-o.

I raise a hand, counselling silence. Then I turn, head into the tunnel at right. John and Monk fall in behind, Wald keestered, whimpering. Fast, faster, gathering speed as we march, ten steps duckfoot, ten pigeon-toe, switching one t'other as is our wont. Strange scenes drift past, visions through smoked glass: acolytes bound naked, blood scourge and slow death, privation and exquisite torment.

On tireless, my footsnouts a sullied blur, marching perfervid till it show ahead: tunnel's end, a door we've seen before. White door with blue glyphs in fractal mandala. Glyphs that at zero hour in a breathless void read: *res extensa, res cogitans, religare connubium.*

I slow in approach, pause, sink, scamper up on all fours, push: the door yields silent, myself lunging through, my comrades scuttling in after.

"The Chamber of Chthonus," announces Monk, "the Meister's third sanctum."

"Yessss," me in grave sibilance, "third among many."

We rise and stand by the door, gazing. The Chamber of Chthonus: a vast circular enclosure carpeted blue, steel walls in rainbow shimmer. Above, a mother-of-pearl canopy shaped like a monkey paw cupping the adamantine culet of eternity.

Directly across, a high-backed chair damascened blue-green: a Peacock Throne sans cock and pea.

John hawk, sniff. "Smell good, don't it?"

I nod, inhaling: blended fragrance of camphor, pasteurized ox-blood, the sweetbread scent of oven-dried sperm. Minutes pass penitent, on barked knee. Us motionless, exhaling blue aspirant wisps in double-helix –

"Huh?" John, "say who?"

I turn: a wall panel sliding aside at left, a figure stepping out of the breach. A dwarfed figure in slow approach, pitch and yaw.

"Artie," I go, "Artie Mangus."

"Indeed," Monk, "none other."

"Sheeat," John, "it's him all right."

"ArrrTEEEE!" Wald, "heh heh."

I cup my hands around my mouth, speak in megaphone.

"HEARD YOU'D REPLACED HUNTER TEXAS THERE, ART. GOOD MOVE."

Artie hobble up, stop. Him with knees half-bent, hands in dystrophic quake, mouth working sonant:

"*That name. Not to be mentioned. Here. That name ana-thema. Here.*"

The words issued in a voicebox drone: scratched, halting.

John cackle. "GodDAMN Art. Whut you been DOIN' to yourself boy."

"He means we shouldn't mention Hunter Texas," Monk, "that name excruciate verboten."

Artie blink, speak in reprise:

"*That nammmme. Ana-themmm. Uhhmmgm –* "

I chuckle, look him over. Artie in white clogs stuffed with ground glass, gore from his feet lapping at his ankles. His shins scraped and splintered, tricolour pegs nailed there in parallel. At his loins a hyaloid pouch teeming with wasps, his crotch-meat discoloured, swollen. On his gut, a varnished plaque hung from bleeding nipples, a calligraphed verse etched there in red:

Now the sneaking serpent walks
in mild humility
And the just man rages in the wilds
where lions roam.

"Billy Blake," I go, nodding in approval, "*Marriage of Heaven and Hell*".

Artie's had his mug flayed by the look of it, a bone-shard driven through his nose. His lower lip sliced transverse and stretched around a muddy horseshoe. His head scalped and trepanned, a sheaf of quills stuck in his sinciput. His throat-apple sheared and capped with nettles, a barbed dog-collar fixed beneath. A red monocle covers his left eye, the rim soldered to the orbit. Fine, bright pins extend inward, piercing the eyeball around the iris.

"Well I'll be skewered and skullfucked out to tarnation," pronounce John, genuinely awed, "I will be – "

Artie make a rasping sound, point to the chair-throne far across.

"*If the Meister,*" he crackle, horse-shoe lip wagging, "*if the Meister appear in red, your sacrifice is accept. If he appear in blue, your sacrifice is reject. If he appear in white you are excommunicate. Place now your offering on the throne and wait – "*

"Excom?" John taking a step, "EXCOM? – "

I put out a restraining hand. "Easy there kid. He's only the factotum."

John curse, Artie turning and retracing his steps, sloshing foot-gore. Him shuffling up to the breach and stepping through, wall panel sliding shut –

Thwud: John's boot on my rump. "Get on with it, ho. We ain't got time to burn."

I turn with a snarl. John with hand raised, the syringe bag held between thumb and forefinger. I snatch the bag, fish out the three vials red, white, blue and start walking. I move with speed, with care: on my toes bow-legged, arms straight up, fists bunched.

I sink obeisant as I draw near, waddling on shorn kneecaps. The throne looms, colours in lapidary swirl. I shut my eyes, advancing in abortive genuflect till I feel it: my knees fetching up against something cold, adamantine. I inhale deep, blink. I'm at the foot of the throne, the seat directly ahead, the back towering immense.

I mutter in orison, my pulse racing fibrillate, my vision homing in on the panel. The panel outlined on the seat: a small square inset with bits of jade. I regard it a moment, moist-eyed. Then I reach with my right hand. And begin.

"Vial red," I intone, placing the red vial on the panel.

Red-ed-d: my voice in echo.

"Vial white," I lilt, placing the white vial on the panel.

White-hite-ite.

"Vial blue," I yodel, placing the blue vial on the panel.

Blue-lue-ue.

Silence. The three brain-juice vials now arrayed, myself with bated breath waiting, waiting, waiting –

There's a whirring sound, the panel with a twitch giving way, the vials vanishing down the chute below. Then another whirr: the panel rising, locking in place.

I watch the bare panel a moment, knuckles joined. Then I yelp, smack the sides of my face open palm.

"Thy will be done," I whisper, backing away on my knees, my ankles in violent clash.

About five yards off, I leap up dramatic, whirl around and break into a run, the tails of my bandanna flying.

"WHOA," John, hand raised, "HOSSIE WHOA!"

But I don't whoa. I buckle instead, segue into a series of bruising somersaults.

"YOWF!" me leaping up, "DONE!"

Pause. Monk impassive, John with a scowl, Wald sniggering. Myself dizzy, anhelate, tottering like a woodland critter newly whelped.

"It's all right!" I gasp, "they went down."

"Go down," Wald, strumming his left tit, "heh heh."

"The panel gave," I go, "the vials – "

But they're not listening. Monk and John looking past me, eyes gone wide. Wald soundless, grabbing his crotch.

I frown, turn, choke off a cry. The Meister imaged enormous on the throne, seated in hologram red.

"Meister!" I exclaim, dropping to my knees.

"Meister!" John dropping to his.

"Meister!" Monk following suit.

"MEISS!" Wald leaping high, landing in an adipose heap.

I sink back: my buttocks bearing down on my heels, toes interlocked, bones snapping in hallelujah.

"Hologram red!" I whisper, "our sacrifice accept!"

"Accept!" Monk, John and Wald, "accept!"

Seconds pass. The Meister's image soundless. Immobile. *Is he aware of us at all,* I wonder. *Aware in any sense of us, his abject and grovelling minions. Doth he with his inner eye behold? Doth he hear, feel, smell? Doth he extract day labor light denied? –*

"Extremis," murmur Monk tearful, "Meister in extremis, nec plus ultra. Meister Howell ganz andere in extremis, mysterium tremendum in extremis, apocalypsis revelata in extremis – "

I nod, eyes brimming. Extremis indeed. Far gone, Meister, by the look of Him. Far, far, gone. Some impossibly remote empyrium of torment, a depth not to be plumbed by mortals (mere) or critters of cognate ilk. His torso burned, crushed and hacked with every known implement. His skull pierced with a halo of candent wires. His eyes churned bloody with corkscrew drills. His ears ravaged by needles lancing deep. His nose plugged with electrodes plunging rhythmic. His mouth crammed with a Masher Unit working cyclical: gum-slash, tooth-shatter, cheek-shred, palate-roast, tongue-grind and lip-dice. His limbs gnawed to the bone by steel-tooth rodents, hypertrophic chiggers clustered thick. Thus our Meister resplendent, transfigured in optic holocaust, Buford Aloysius Howell, *Lord Baron of Pain* –

I blink. Movement in the corner of my eye. Trotjohn rising prayerful, Monk and Wald beside. Them now shoulder to shoulder in voiceless orison.

I watch them a moment, ducts quickening. Then I shudder, stick a thumb in my eye and leap up, kicking my nuts double-heeled. My comrades shouting aloud then, hammering their skulls two-fisted, biting down on extruded tongues, the Meister's hologram vanishing with a flicker, myself turning brine-eyed with a cry, arms outspread: us four, we four gathered in embrace, limned there for none to see, cenobites triumphant in their Meister's sanctum, spilling tears.

***

A grey mist fringes the sky as we head out: dawn heralded in ombre. Moving silent through silent streets, the car languid in gasoline dream. My thoughts in echo, visions wafting like smoke: scenes sunlit, birds in flight, corpse in dew grass, a blood-spotted flower. Engine hum, sunglow in cetacean depths, time drifting –

"Wh. Nn. Ay. Ing?"

I twitch, blink. "Mmmf?"

"I said whut time," John, "whut TIME he say he was comin'."

I turn, eyes leaden. "Who?"

"Yo' daddy's big dick tranny queen. Who 'dja think."

I cover my eyes, sit up with a groan. "Twelve. Twelve on the nipple. Always on time to collect, Rotgut."

"Come rot," Wald, "heh heh."

The car turn once, turn once more. I uncover my eyes, look up. We're in the parking lot of my dung hutch, John pulling in beside Polly Pukemobile.

"Dig it," John killing the engine, "JB's puke pig."

"Porcine behemoth," Monk.

"Pork puke," Wald, "heh heh."

I mutter profane, push, stumble out. Cool air, the lot about half-full, dawn light washing pale.

"This is the day," I croak, stretching, "this is the day that the Meister hath made – "

Slam. I turn. John by the trunk, sack in hand: "Still need the ol' goody sack. Cain't do it without THAT."

I nod, hit the kerb, start walking. "Step lively now, girls, step lively."

They fall in behind: us marching brisk around the side, in through the door, starting up the hallway –

"This where he at?"

I falter, stop, turn. John profiled dim, staring at a door, Monk and Wald beside.

"Huh?" me, "wha?"

"We heard 'em oane our way out," John, "dude fuckin' his kid girl up against this here door, oane the inside."

"Fuck way out," Wald in a murmur, "heh heh."

"That's the door all right," I go, "you want to take a good look at it."

John snort. "I ain't gon' take a LOOK at it. I'm gon' bust oane in and PLAY, like I said I would – "

"That door's set apart from the others," I go, "and it's a different colour. A special kinda door for a special kinda pad."

John turn, face-lines gnarling. "Whut in the name of MUTHAfuck you tryin' to SAY, bitch – "

"It's where the MAN live Teej," I go, "the man who OWN this spread. Mister Rent Boss himself, close and personal."

There's a pause. John and Monk staring, Wald giggling soft going: "Bitch name rentfuck. Heh heh – "

"You SHITTIN' me," John, "that wuz ROTgut in there?"

"You better believe it," me, "Jimmy Rotgut stickin' a cornpone to his kid girl. He's got three of 'em, the oldest a twelve-year prepube. He porks 'em all, one every night."

John scratch his beard, grinning tooth-white there in the hallway.

"Well HALE," he goes, "our little hootenanny's gon' be more fun than I thought."

"A saturnale to end all saturnales," Monk.

"Hooter fun," Wald.

I nod. "No need to bust in there. He's gonna come to us all spry and chuffed."

"Well sheeat."

"Indeed," I go turning, "onward now, brothers. On and up – "

I start forward, my compadres falling in behind as before. On to hallway's end and up the stairs to the landing, my door showing pale at left.

"You boys brace yourself," goes John stepping up, "JB's got it REAL sweet in there." ·

I chuckle, fish out the key. "Yayup. Think biker bung."

"Sweet bung," Wald, "heh heh."

I stick in the key, turn, push: darkness.

"Still got your prison-punk scent in here Teej," I go stepping in, "Rotgut gonna think I rent my rump out for a livin'."

"You oughtta," John right behind, "use that cred to hose out this shithole."

"Hose hole," Wald, "heh heh."

I grope my way to the gooseneck: click. Ratpad flotsam showing stark by lamplight.

John sniff, spit: green wad in trajectory.

Monk whistle. "Work of art here JB. Trash pastiche."

"Work o' fart," Wald, "heh heh."

I turn with a grin and start kicking crud, clearing a space in the middle.

"Wheee!" goes Wald joining in, John circling around and punting deliberate, Monk with arms folded, playing spectator.

"You boys keep at it," I go backing off, "I'll go get the floor-spread."

"YEH!" Wald gettin' jiggy, "YEEH!", John slamming cartons against the window.

They're standing easy when I emerge, floor-spread in hand. John, Monk, Wald, around a clearing at the room's centre, bottles, cartons and food gunk leveed around. I nod approving, walk up, roll out the floor-spread. A Yin/Yang appears in padded syntheplast, a circle black and white.

"Lovely," Monk, "a perfect fit."

"Uh-huh," John, "if you're a fruit at a fairy camp."

"Your perfect fruit," Wald, "heh heh."

John yawn, stretch: bonecreak medley. "Coulda used a drink before shuteye."

I nod. "Me too. Snoozeville shake at the Korova Milk Bar, *Alex and his droogs peeting their moloko with knives in it, spoiling for a bit of the old ultraviolence.*"

"Sheeat," John, "buncha boyscout pussies."

"Pussy scout," Wald, "heh heh."

Pause: John working a hamstring bend, Wald hustling his nuts, Monk combing his beard.

"Well," I sigh, "best get to it."

"Quite," Monk, "best."

We gather silent around the spread, standing equidistant. John and I face to face, Monk and Wald lip to tit.

I jerk up my hands, palms out. "Ten hut!"

"Hut!" they echo, jerking up their hands likewise.

"Down!" I go, "hut!"

We fall: us keeling forward simultaneous, palms hitting the spread with a thud. Now John and I face down, heads touching. Monk and Wald likewise, skulls kissing. Wald breathing heavy, a fart escaping him in quantized bursts.

"Well?" John, voice muffled, "whut now."

"The light," I go, "what else."

John grunt, give command. "Lights out! Hut!"

"Hut!" I echo, my foot swinging up and out, knocking over the gooseneck: thump, darkness. Us stretched prone in axial crisscross, sinking Lethewards.

Seconds pass in mazy drift. Minutes. In my mind's eye, an idiot cuckoo on its perch putting out a warble in melodic refrain: *pooteewee teepoowoo woowootee teepootoo* and on, bird echo lullaby en route to winken, blinken and nod.

***

A room with green walls, tub in the middle. Black marble tub shaped like an eye, sloshing milk and blue ink. Three old geezers in there bathing: rouged cheeks, purple eye-shadow, lashes caked black. Them soaping each other with loofah mitts, slapping each others' tits. Toothless grins, cooked flesh sliding off brittle bone. A proboscis monkey perched nearby on a raised pedestal, turning a prayer wheel. Monkey with a wine-red bonnet, black brassiere, yellow polka dot knickers. I watch from an adjoining room, crucified to the roof of a limousine. At my feet skinned rats eat from a bowl of spiced venison, darting phosphorescent –

Light: gauze rainbow. My left side numb, my hand wedged under my hip. I mumble, turn over, push myself up. Sunlight filters in through the curtains, my comrades floored asleep. Silence punctuated by yelps and farts (Wald), tooth-grinds (John), sacerdotal muttering (Monk).

I rub my eyes, glance at the clock. Fine. Thirty minutes and counting. *Breath be not loud –*

I straighten, rise wincing, slouch into the bedroom, on into the crapper. In, I ablute sans ado, whelp a dugong in haste and emerge, belching barbarous.

"Sheeat," John's voice, "which end THAT come from."

I chuckle, walk in. Monk up, over by the window with arms folded. John on the couch yawning. Wald with butt steepled, face down in drool.

"Crapper's free and stinkin'," I go, "y'all take advantage."

John curse, scoop a crust out his eye. "Place look worse by day. Like that's possible."

I grin, proud. "That's sorta the idea."

Monk walks past, heading for the crapper, John stepping over to the mantelpiece. Pictures displayed there, gilt-edged.

"Whoa now," John, "haven't seen these before. Harris and Klebold from way back when."

I nod. "Yayup. Them framed in gold for the feast, watch doom become real."

"Yeast feast," Wald on all fours, "heh heh."

I turn, smile benevolent, blow him a kiss, head into the kitchen. No change, everything as I left it. Two-gallon saucepan ready on the range. Chopped onions, spice bottles arrayed beside.

"Ok in there?" ask John outside.

"Oui chéri," I go, "all set."

I step up, shove the chopped onions into the pan, slop on a hillock of hog-lard and turn the flame on high. Sizzle, go the onions, sizzle.

I wait till the onions brown, then toss in the spices: salt, black pepper, cayenne, cloves, cinnamon, garlic, ginger, cumin, coriander, chili, curry and pube dandruff, stirring the mixture with a broom handle, a prosthetic leg, a craphole plunger, a dipstick, a crowbar and a shotgun barrel. A powerful fragrance fills the kitchen, wafts out in molecular calm. I stir on till the mixture achieve the consistency of catarrh, warm glue, cerumen and grave wax. Then with a peckerwood, shitkick, grubfucker's prayer, I turn off the flame, cover the pan with a flush-tank lid and step out.

"A fine spice redolence," avers Monk, turning away from the window.

John snort. "ANYTHING to choke out the reek."

"Fine reek," Wald, "heh heh."

John give me look. "Boy, you cryin' awready?"

I shake my head, blinking lachrymose. "It's them onions. Strong shit."

"What they all say before their eyes fall out," Monk.

I chuckle, turn squinting. The minute hand and hour hand joined in supplication: almost.

"One minute and counting," I go, "minute and counting."

Silence. Myself with eyes glued to the clock, counting down. Four, three, two, one and there, right on schedule, boots in ascent, someone coming up the stairs, footfalls unmistakable: Jimmy Rotgut. A bootscuff on the landing, a grunt, brief pause, doorbell. DING DONG!

John snort, shake his head. "Man, that is one predictable little putz."

"Dick table," Wald in a whisper, "Heh heh."

DING DONG!

I start for the door, John right behind.

DING DONG! DING DONG! –

My hand on the knob, twist, open: no surprise. Jimmy Rotgut at high noon, Shitsville rent boss come to collect. Him with pig eyes bloodshot, jowls aquiver: swag-gut cowpoke in a white frill shirt, bolo tie, denims, boots, white Stetson, blue gatorskin belt. Rotgut packing heat this day of his Lord: a classic ivory-grip Colt jammed in the lee of his belt.

"How now pilgrim!" I go, flashing him a grin, "you stayin' over a while or just passin' through?"

Pause: his lipless mouth working, hog peepers nested cold.

"Mah money," he grunt, "ah want mah money NOW or yew gon' find your coon butt out oane the sidewalk."

"Oh he's got your money awright," John over my shoulder, "not to worry."

Rotgut blink, reach for his revolver. "Ah wudn't tawkin' to YEW, hotshot. Ah'm waitin' oane your little spook to cough up – "

John move. Fast. Him shoving me aside, smacking the Colt from Rotgut's hand, hooking two fingers up his nose, yanking him in like Moe do Shemp, kicking the door shut. Rotgut reeling in with a strangled shout, sprawling halfway into the living room, John with a leap bearing down and clamping his mouth shut, wristblade out, Rotgut starting to thrash, screams muffled.

"Quit hollerin' now, you'll live," John, "quit thrashin' now, you'll live."

Rotgut struggle on a few seconds, go limp. Him gasping belly up, mug flushed crimson.

"Man cotton oane quick," John with a grin, "ay?"

"Cotton, yes," Monk, "quick."

Rotgut huff, panic in one eye, rage in the other.

John cackle. "I'm gon' take my hand off yo mouth now, Rotgut. You start hollerin' again, I'm gon' slice you dead in a heartbeat. Dig?"

Rotgut blink, his Stetson pillowed under his depilated skull.

John take off his hand, rise. "Ass up now, Rotgut. You got WORK to do."

Rotgut rise slow, breathing hard, hand over nose.

"Yew c'n keep the money," he husk nasal, "your buddy's rent cred. Yew keep it, ah walk out, this never happened."

John grin, brows cusped like arrowheads.

"Well now. We got us a THINKIN' landlord here Jayb, a thinkin', stinkin' slophawg. Reeeeeal SMART... for someone who FUCK his younguns."

Rotgut flinch like he's been struck, blood draining from his mug.

"Thaaaat's right Jimbo," John grinning feral, "we HEARD you down there stickin' a cornpone to yo' kid girl. SWEEeeeeeet – "

"Whut's that yew say?" Rotgut, bristling indignant, "whut's that now?"

"Cornstink hawgfuck," Wald on the couch, "heh heh."

John reach with a snarl, put a pinch-hold on Rotgut's cheek.

"Here's how it's gon' work now, Jimbo. You play this little GAME of ours for a bit, then you walk out a free man. MINUS the rent cred. Your money for your life. That awright with ya?"

Rotgut blink, panic yielding to guile. "Ah c'n live with that."

"Bet you can fatboy," John letting go, "now drop 'em."

Rotgut frown, uncomprehending. "Hunh?"

John curse, hold up his blade. "Your dry goods, Rotgut. Your cowpoke threads. I want 'em off. Now. And I'm talkin' BUCK fuckin' NAKKED."

Rotgut stare, eyes gone to slits. Then he begin to undress, his nose-bleed going drip drip. Boots, denims, shirt, skivvies on the floor. Rotgut bared in rank albus, just his socks on.

John shake his head, lip curling in disgust.

"Boy you are one SORRY lookin' stack o' HAWG sheeat."

"YEH!" Wald, "shitstack. Heh heh."

Rotgut with shoulders slumped, face mottled, his fuck-tackle crimped pale.

John spit, step over to the goody sack, reach in, pull out a mouldering jockstrap and brassiere.

"Get these oane first," he go, tossing 'em over.

Rotgut hesitate a moment, face tightening. Then he bend, pull on the jockstrap, straighten, strap the brassiere over his sag tits.

"Well HALE," John, "look like you done this BEFORE, Jimmy boy!"

Rotgut motionless, eyes bright with hate.

John reach into the sack once more, pull out a stripper's stiletto and a logger's boot.

"Cooze heel on your left foot, boot on your right," he goes tossing 'em over.

Rotgut obey: silence as he slip on the stiletto, pull on the boot.

John cackle, reach again into the sack, pull out a burlesque wig, a workman's glove, a kid girl's mitt and a tightly wadded roll of dollar bills with a wick at one end.

"C-spot dynamite," he go, tossing me the roll, "hold oane to it."

Rotgut make a choking sound. Him posed awry, preposterous.

"Time out," he husk, fists clenched, "ah don't know whut this here's about and ah don't care. All ah'm sayin' is – "

John put out a bark, toss the wig, the glove, the mitt.

"GET these oane NOW, WHORE. Get 'em oane and you'll live. Stand there and YAK, I'll come over and BLEED ya dead, DIG?"

"Live whore," Wald, "bleeding yak. Heh heh."

Rotgut stare, fists bunched, breathing heavy. Then he bend, jam the wig over his head, straighten, work the mitt and the glove over his hands.

"Well awwwright!" John, "hit it the SECOND time."

"Impressive," Monk, "a study in contrasts."

Rotgut stand rigid a moment: garish, risible. Then he turn, give me a look: animal hate, gore at his nose clotted dark.

I grin. "Don't sweat it now, Jimbo. You lookin' prettier'n ever."

John cackle. "Got THAT right."

"Pinnacle of porcine pulchritude," Monk.

"Pretty pork," Wald, "heh heh."

John clap, point. "See that floor-spread over yander?"

Rotgut don't answer. Him staring fixed, face gone sweat-pale.

"DO. YOU. SEE. IT." John's blade rising, his face twisted.

Rotgut turn, lick his lips, nod.

"Well then," John taking a step, "I want you to get OANE it, GET DOWN on all fours like a GOOD DAWG."

His hand up, face obscured by blade-shine.

Rotgut look down a moment, nares flared. Then he turn, limp over and descend in slow swag, gasp and grunt. Now Rotgut on all fours, middle of the floor-spread.

"Goooood dawg," John moving, "now you – "

He pause, John, eyes fixed on Rotgut's rump.

"Well SHIT oane me with a bleedin' HAWG head. That a HAEMORRHOID up ayre?"

I step up, bend close: a smokeblue donut ringing Rotgut's bunghole, donut bisected by his strap thong.

"Well godDAMN," I go, "it's WAY bigger'n I imagined. I'd heard it was big, but this here's a fuckin' FLOTATION device."

"Harf!" John, "HARF! – "

"ME SEE!" Wald leaping off the couch, "ME SEE! – "

Monk walking around casual.

"Never seen anythin' like it," goes John, hands on his knees, "look like he shittin' out a burned bagel face first."

"Quite," Monk, "some sort of aneurystic prolapse by the look of it."

Wald toddle up chortling, bend close, blow soft on Rotgut's bung-swell. Rotgut flinch, his head lousy with matted wig-hair.

"Don't you lay a fart on us now, Rotgut," I go, "that haemorrhoid come blowin' out, knock your daddy dead."

"HARF!" John, eyebrows raised, "WAHHARRF!"

Monk sniff. "No fear of THAT. The strap would impede, if not restrain."

Pause. John disappointed, going: "Well sheeat, didn't think of that."

I shrug. "Not a problem. Snip the thong, the rest stays on."

John turn, brightening. "Why HALE. Bitch got a BRAIN oane him."

"Hell bitch," Wald, "heh heh."

He step up, Trotjohn. Bend. Pull the thong strap off Rotgut's bung. Snip it with his blade. Rotgut on all fours, tense, motionless.

"NOW," John straightening, "maybe NOW we see that bagel FLY."

I nod. "Tomorrow's SAT tube lead story: flyin haemorrhoid kill North Zone ephebe."

"Haarf!" John, "wahHAAARF! – "

I frown, hold up a hand. Rotgut's voice. From under his harlot wig.

"Rotgut?" I go stepping around, "you talkin' to me Rotgut?"

Cough, grunt. "Ah make yew a deal," Rotgut in his best salesman's voice, "just yew 'n' me. Yew tell your friend here to let me go, yew c'n live here lawng as yew want. Rent-free."

Pause. Monk smiling frosty. "Hope springs eternal, what?"

I nod, take a deep breath and slam my left foot hard in Rotgut's flank: Cornelius rising.

Rotgut gasp, roll over on his side.

"Ohhhh!" Trotjohn, "papa SAN!"

I snarl, cock my right foot, slam it in Rotgut's plexus: Valdez rising.

"NnnNNGH!" Rotgut curling foetal, "ukhh! Uhh! – "

John and Wald in high mirth, Monk observing with interest.

I kneel, bend close. "That's RIGHT, Jimbo. THAT's the sound I wanna hear. The sound old lady Grable made when you and the Pigs dragged her out last winter."

"Ah," Monk, "the plot thickens."

"Winter pig plot," Wald, "heh heh."

Rotgut still curled, gasp and croak.

I rise, step back. "I'm gonna count to three now, Rotgut. You don't make like a bitch-dawg in heat, I'm gonna sic my hellhound on you. ONE."

John step up, grinning homicidal.

"TWO."

Rotgut put out a sob, roll over: back on all fours coughing, retching.

"Sheeat," John with a scowl, "had m'boner all hot'n'ready."

Monk shaking his head going: "Bah. Foiled again."

"Let's get to it," I go, giving John a look, "can the goof."

John nod, reach into the goody sack, draw it out slow and tender: a burnished Billy Tell, metal alloy crossbow with an arrow muzzled in the groove.

"Dig it," John unmuzzling the arrow, "stone fuckin' savage."
I smile. "Hotdamn."

"Purity," Monk, "sun and steel."

Wald panting wide-eyed, hand on crotch.

"You got that roll ready Jayb?" ask John turning.

I hold it up: dollar bills rolled tight, a wick at one end. "Ready when you are."

John nod, reach into his pocket, toss me a lighter. Then he spit, grasp the bow firm, start ratcheting. Creak. Creak. Creak. Rotgut agitated, trying to look over his shoulder.

"Not to worry Rotgut," I go, "game's almost over. Co-operate and you walk out a free man."

John grin, saunter around, stand with his back to the window. The crossbow in his hands tensed murderous, his death's head medallion gleaming golden. Rotgut at his feet crouched in kowtow, sobbing muffled.

"Here dawg," goes John soft-voiced, "here dawg."

Rotgut cough, look up. And for an instant I flash to what he see: gold shine and bright steel, death angel haloed in sunlight.

"Whut," croaks Rotgut, "whut're yew – "

I put out a yelp, thumb the lighter, torch the wick on the dollar roll. Then I lunge down and ram the roll up Rotgut's bagel, him putting out a shriek and BOOM, the dollar roll blasting concussive, spraying green confetti and violet bung chunks, Rotgut rearing up, arms outspread, mute twang of John's crossbow, arrow-flash and kathunk: Rotgut jerking astonished, kneeling an instant in mute hallelujah before toppling back over his heels, the arrow half buried in his brow, third eye blind, him shuddering with lashes aflutter, mouth agape.

"Timber," John lowering the crossbow, "tim-fuckin'-ber."

Pause. Rotgut going quiet, throes in permanent surcease. His corpse belly up, legs folded under. His skank wig still on, tit cups aimed at the ceiling.

"Well," sighs Monk at last, "*Mistah Kurtz, he dead. A penny for the old Guy.*"

I grunt: wiping gore, bung-spatter and cash confetti off my mug. John with a curse stepping up, dropping a spitwad on Rot's gut. Snotgreen bellybutton sizzle.

"Ssffooth!" Wald, "heh heh."

I turn, walk into the bedroom, return with my steel: a Tibetan Phurba blade turned carving knife.

"Saucepan," I go, "get that saucepan out if you would, please Teej."

John mutter, walk around, stick the crossbow in the sack. Then he head into the kitchen and emerge moments later, saucepan in both hands.

"Awwright," me, "bring it on up."

John stride up, set the pan down. Myself kneeling by the corpse, knife in hand.

"Hurry it up, slut," goes John hitting the couch, "this boy's gettin' HUNGRY."

I bow obsequious, lick the knife blade and start in: cutting through Rotgut's dead flesh, carving out choice morsels, dropping them in the pan. I work swift, clean: slicing off jowl, tit, upper arm, thigh, testicle and dick before turning the carcass over for a cut of croupemeat, carving the upper back and tossing in a handful of scorched bung chunks for good measure –

John drool-mouthed, going: "Mmmm, cain't wait. You get his dead dick in your bowl, you're a prince. You get his dick and a nut, you're king. You get his dick and BOTH nuts, you're the fuckin' emperor – "

Myself straightening with a laugh, tossing the knife aside, going: "You wanna take the saucepan back in?"

John with frown sitting up going: "You done already?"

I rise, exhale theatric. "You betcha. More meat'n we can handle."

"Well awwWWRIGHT!" John jumping up, "it's COOKin' time!"

I watch him head into the kitchen, pan held aloft. Then I turn, point to the corpse. "Monk, Wald, roll him up in the floor-spread if you would and bring my wagon wheel out the bedroom – "

"SSKRIKIKEEK!"

I start, look up. Back again: Stinger, Finesse, Oblongata, Noodlebear, buzzing around in a circle. Them part beast, part insect (mostly insect) with dragonfly wings, black scorpion tails, compound eye Brundle-heads, horned boar-snouts and slug torsos with hairy roach legs.

"On second thought," I go, "move the fucker aside and leave him uncovered."

Monk blink, touch his beard. "Uncovered. And why, pray?"

I slap the side of my neck, grimace cryptic.

"Eidolons, baby. Our spirit guides shall feast on his consecrate flesh, as shall WE."

Monk stare, shrug. "His visions numinous. To the task, Wald."

"Flesh feast spirit fuck," Wald grasping one end of the floor-spread, "heh heh."

I watch them work a moment. Then I turn, head into the kitchen. John by the range intent, flame on high.

"Stand back son," I go, "master chef to work."

John grunt, step aside: myself grabbing the broom handle, plunging it into the smoking spice-meat.

"Anything else I can do?" ask John restless.

"Yayup," me stirring violent, "set the bowls out on my wagon wheel. And the spoons, the cups, the ladle, that bag of wafer bread, that bottle of burgundy."

John bark, salute, get to work humming a ditty. I stir on vigorous, adding water, two-year old cream and sulphur salt to the mixture.

"Wafer bread," goes John holding up the bag, "where'd you get this from."

"Communion wafers," I go, "mail-ordered from New Vatican. Taste like shit, but you feel all pure and pollyannish afterwards. Like the good folk used to, when they got done lynchin' niggers, shootin' injuns."

John cackle, stick the bowls, the spoons, the cups, the wafers, the burgundy into a garbage sack. Then he hoist the sack over his shoulder and walk out front. Twelve minutes later I put out the call: "TEN HUT! SPICED ROTGUT COMIN' UP!"

"YeeEEH!" Wald out front, "eeEEP!"

John walk in, tongue on the drip. "Mmm baby, that smell GOOOD."

I step aside with a flourish. "All yours, friar."

John wink, step up, grab the pan handles, lift.

"Easy there," I go, "don't spill."

John flash his incisors, turn, walk out. I step out after and smile: the old wagon wheel tabled and ready, four discoloured and shapeless cushions around the rim. At left, Rotgut on a trash mound, ravaged, uncovered. At right, the SAT tube pulled in close.

I frown. "We gonna watch the tube while we eat?"

John set the saucepan down on the wheel, turn with a grin.

"A vid disc, honeybunch. Funhouse snuff pastiche. Latest from Bluto's."

I chuckle. "Well shit. You bought THAT?"

"You betcha!" John clicking his heels, Monk bending over the pan going: "Curry climax, yes?" Wald sticking his finger in, pulling back with a yelp.

John step over to the goody sack, reach in, pull out an Ono Sendai vid biscuit with the disc slotted in.

"You gon' LUV this," he goes striding over.

"Hold up," I go stepping over to the table, "don't start it yet."

"Wudn't goin' to," John hooking up the biscuit, "y'all grab yourselves a seat."

We grab. Myself settling on the cushion at left, Monk taking the seat to my right, Wald slumping down beside Monk, John coming around with the remote, smacking Wald's skull and sinking beside.

"Y'all ready?" John aiming the remote, "GOOD and ready?"

"Fire away, ombudsman," I go, "with extreme prejudice."

Snow hiss, darkness. Then the screen coming alive, scenes in livid throb: capuchin monkey fellating a quadriplegic grunt. Moray eel worming up the ass of a marine lab geek. Coroners in a candle-lit morgue fucking a dead dowager. Rogue sasquatch in harness ravishing an eviscerate woodsman. Dome-head reticulans in a ship hold, probing a mutilated rancher. Trapeze boys humping aerial, cum-threads in lucent arabesque. Saxon mountaineer on a summit, buggering a frozen sherpa. Fag Sumos deathmasked, coupling in a tank of piranha. Camouflaged razorheads cornholing a campesino, sucking up his brains through a coloured straw. Pathic midgets crapping on a chained cleric, goosing him with a candent crucifix. Blond tourists in a psychadelic flophouse masturbating a decapitate tiger. Starved lepers on display, working a jungle fuck for robed evangelists. Cannibal Teutons marinading a Turk in spiced jizm. Caged whore pissing gruel in a ward for the criminally insane. Bearded carny wench blowing a boarhog in a city laundromat. Ricket-legged Klanboys in the sticks, playing catch with spook testicles. Obese cretin naked in a barn, porking a boiled rooster. Junkbond icon in fetish gear, reaming a limbless hobo. Mutant yokels fornicating in tubs of lard, bonemeal and offal. Ofay incest orgy with grandad, dad, son, grandson and dog next door. Bull dyke snatch riot on a floodlit gridiron. Doc Clarke on Island Ceylon, stroking brown kiddie buttocks on white sand. In Siam, tonguing a new trade route on silken flanks. In Nouveau Chine, diddling the epicanthic fold. In Nippon, getting the geisha rubdown on tatami mats. In Samoa, lapping wind-girt wahines. In the flesh-dens of Maroc, wolfing hot harlot meat –

"STOP!" I bark, slamming a fist down on the table, "SSSTAWWWP!"

Pause in echo, John turning a-grin, remote in hand. The screen frozen at a bucher-knife cumshot.

"Whut gives now Jayb," he taunt, "this stuff gettin' too much for ya?"

I shake my head, turn. "Apostle Monk. By your leave now, apostle Monk."

Monk nod, bow votive, breathe in deep and vent an ear-splitting Zen shout.

"KAAAATZ!" Monk, beard wagging fierce, "KAAAAAAATZZZZ! – "

In the echo of which, we fall to, slopping meat in our bowls, wine in our cups, grabbing wafers by the handful, slurp, chomp, crunch and "SKRRIKIKIK!", our eidolons diving headlong to feed on the corpse, Rotgut in the corner carved sanguine, slurp, chomp, crunch and the SAT tube once more in lurid flicker, montage slaughterporn, my tongue curry-burned, Rotgut's dick in my craw, his nuts in my bowl, slurp, chomp, crunch and my vision in imperial retreat, drifting out the back of my head, through the curtains on up, way up, boundless azure gone dark at the core, void at the heart of a glacial sun.